HEARTTHEFT

COVENANT

RUKIS

HeartTheft Book 1: Covenant

Published by FurPlanet Productions
Dallas, Texas
www.FurPlanet.com

eBook ISBN 978-1-61450-622-5
Paperback ISBN 978-1-61450-621-8

First Edition Trade Paperback 2024

This is a work of fiction. All characters and events portrayed within are fictitious.

CONTENTS

A FOREWORD FROM THE AUTHOR

HeartTheft is part of a collection of novels in the *Red Lantern* universe, a Historical Fiction setting that is not intended to be analogous for the real world, at any set point in time. The characters, places, events, religious practices, and cultures in this world are also not intended to be compared to reality, either past or present. It is a fictional setting, and the opinions and thoughts of its charactesrs are similarly fictional. These animal people are not role models. They are flawed and messy, as is their world.

While my writing is inspired heavily by history, my own lived experience, and the lived experiences of others, I did not create *Red Lantern* as an analogy for our human world. *Red Lantern* is meant first and foremost as entertainment and to inspire creativity, open-mindedness, and empathy for those around you.

This book contains themes some may find uncomfortable or hard to read, including:

Violence, Sexual Content, Religious and Familial Abuse, Self Harm, Substance Abuse, and Suicide.

A FOREWORD FROM THE AUTHOR

If you or anyone you know or love is considering suicide, or would like emotional support, the 988 Lifeline network is available 24/7 across the United States.

PROLOGUE

Good Friend, allow me to tell you a parable, a tale God desires we learn from. It is the story of the First Canine. A man named Ciraberos.

Ciraberos was the first creation of the Lord capable of truly understanding the Kingdom He had made, the first to perceive his place as not simply alive, but as *being*. And this set him apart from the Ferals, the lesser beasts, who lived only to satisfy the needs of their life moment to moment. Ciraberos could understand the passing of time, could come to have expectations for the future, not simply days but years ahead. He could plan for that future. He could look back retrospectively on the time that had passed and regret.

To this end the Creator, the one we now know as God, gave Ciraberos three heads. He felt that had he but one, his thoughts would be consumed by lamentation and regret for the past, trepidation and fear for the future. For even in the good world our Creator had given him, in the paradise of all the earth, there was pain. The perfect, flawless, unmarred world He had made was despoiled by the want and choices of his creations from the moment they set foot upon it.

But Ciraberos was His chosen creation, as close to his own likeness as the Creator had ever made. He was merciful and thus wished for Ciraberos to know a good life, a content life. As painless a life as possible.

And so, Ciraberos was endowed with these three heads. One could perceive the past and watch his tail. One always looked ahead to the horizon and to the future. And one stayed firmly rooted in the present to focus on the tasks at hand and the joy that was to be had in the moment. Each head had a different perspective to see the world from, each an assigned role.

But Ciraberos came to resent his God's mercy. For in creating him thusly, free to claim this Kingdom under his own will, free to want, to hunger, to yearn for more, the Creator had unavoidably created in him the sin of desire. Ciraberos desired not just what he had been given already, but *more*. He believed himself the equal of God because he resembled Him so and was able to know all, to perceive the world as God Himself did. But he was not its master. Forever on, this desire burned in him, an unquenchable flame… and it began to drive him mad.

Ciraberos was immortal, immune to the ravages of time but not death itself, and the more time he lived, the more he desired to change in the past. The more he desired to lay claim to in the future. His central head, grounded to the present, remained the voice of reason. Focused, as ever, on what could be done, what could be accomplished, *then*. Moment to moment.

But in time the other two became too loud. Too consumed by this sin of desire, for which there was no remedy. Within him arose a conflict so great, no resolution could be found, no middle-ground met.

Ciraberos became wrathful, gluttonous, depressive, greedy, and most of all, ruled by his *sin*. And in his sinful state, he consumed and destroyed much of the Kingdom he'd been meant to shepherd. His armies of feral dyre overtook, devoured, and conquered all they could reach. They burned, and killed, and raped, until their Kingdom was desolate and all the innocent had fled, leaving only the ravenous.

In the end it was Ciraberos's own dyre soldiers who slew him. While his flesh could not age, it was no more immune to violence than the feral dyre. In their ravenous hunger, they piled upon him like logs heaped on a pyre. They tore him apart. And with him, the First World died.

For time untold, there was nothing more. The Creator mourned what Ciraberos had done to the Kingdom he had gifted him, and held his soul in Judgment—the first world he had created, abandoned long ago, for it was imperfect, fractured and poisonous. When darkness overtakes the moon, the Throne of the Creator, we have a glimpse briefly through a doorway into this place. This realm is where He banished his failures to, and it became Ciraberos's new Kingdom. A place he would know only regret, only pain, only loss. We common folk now call this place Hell.

Long following Ciraberos's fall, our Creator at last perfected His work. And this we know is when He brought life to Canus. The first, most perfect Canine. Our Patriarch.

Canus had but one head, but was still capable of retrospection, of looking ahead, and of living in the moment. He would need to learn to balance these perspectives in one mind, and his struggle continues on in us to this day. Of course, with this understanding of the world, came with it again the sin of desire. So, to temper this, the Creator reduced his time. No longer would his flesh be immortal, but bound to the same laws of entropy, the cycle of life and death, that the dyre and the ferals, that all of the lesser entities, flora and fauna alike, were bound to. Only his soul would remain immortal.

In this he was unlike the Creator. But while Ciraberos squandered eternity, Canus would treasure his shorter time. He would live each life more firmly rooted in the present, in the tasks laid out before him that need be done, and in the joy of each passing moment. He would learn from the past and desire to better his future, but when one short lifetime ended... he would forget. And he would begin anew, again.

The cycle of death and rebirth. The greatest gift He ever gave us is a punishment for our ancestors' transgressions. This in and of itself is a lesson, Good Friend. Punishment—and moreover, death—can be a gift.

The Creator made many of these Patriarchs and Mothers. Canus was merely the first. In time he was given a wife and many followers. These early canines were the First Wolves. The first souls that began the cycle. Like the moon waxes and wanes, so do our lives, brightening and dimming, and throughout them we know regret and hope. But now, we must turn to look to the past. We must lift our heads to look to the future. And for either we can only imagine, remember. Our eyes can only see the present. The sky above, the dirt at our feet. The Kingdom He has given us.

Our memory is imperfect. Time wears it away. And *no* man can recall their previous lives. This is His plan. This is meant to protect us from the sin that knowing so much can bring. It is a mercy.

But the Sin of desire is still within us. One can liken it to a poisonous seed which can take root at any time. To want is natural. To desire is dangerous and less easy to temper. It drives men to take leave of their senses, of their morality and rationality. Left unchecked, even in the short lifespans we now live, it can lead us to burn down the world. To echo the mistakes of Ciraberos.

The souls who commit such foul acts are claimed for Judgment. They are marked and removed from God's good plan, from the cycle of life and death, and sent to the Kingdom of Ciraberos. The inky face of the moon. Hell is a dark and fractured place, Good Friends, Hell is a barren land of pain and regret and little else.

But in the place of light, the Throne of the Creator, God's own place of vigil, there is everlasting peace. There is final and complete understanding, every answer one has ever sought, the resting place for all enlightened souls. It is rapture, it is the end of death, rebirth, of darkness and pain. Only those souls closest to Him will know its rest, and it is upon the lowly—the rest of us in the world—to uplift them so that they may purify themselves and our world in the radiance of their lives, before they leave us forever. They are our Saints, our Martyrs, our Knights and Kings. The Pedigree. The first most close to God, on the very last leg of their journey through countless lifetimes. If we live well, and die well, we will be reborn as they are, some day. And we will have the chance to succeed or fail in achieving enlightenment and final, peaceful rest, as they do.

Until then, we serve. We work. We are obedient and faithful, and like the phases of the moon, we accept that while we may exist in dark times now, we will rise again and again, lit by God's love. More and more. Until we are with Him.

We must live these short lives, thankful for whatever little we are given, and fight against this desire for more. For it will destroy us if we let it fester. It will consume us, as it did Ciraberos.

Look, Good Friend, at the earth beneath your feet. At the sky above your head. Even if all you can see of it is through the bars of a cell. Even if the land is barren and yields nothing for you to eat. This is the Kingdom we have been given, and we must make the most of what we have and be grateful for it.

Because Hell awaits. Judgment awaits. And no quenching of desire is worth forsaking the good world He gave us. No sin in this one short life is worth suffering for eternity.

God help us if we stumble.

1

FIRST MEETING, THE HUDSON ESTATE

I consider myself a man possessing of diligent politeness, social tact, and careful consideration of propriety in most circumstances. So, it was a point of shame that on this day, in my harried and panicked state, I forgot myself.

I had little trouble shouldering through the throngs of tailored shoulders, cravats, laced necklines, and all manner of finery adorning the unsuspecting and innocent partygoers in the Hudson's Great Hall. The Hudsons were a family of stout, fine-cheek-boned Bull Terriers, exquisite in their Pedigree, but far smaller in stature than I. And though they had many a guest at this gathering, I had a head and shoulders on most, regardless. I was born to the Akita line, a marginally-recognized northeastern bloodline of canines here in Amuresca, but my breeding was long since diluted from any of the very few Pedigree Akita lines of note. I was common stock. Accepted just barely above a wolf, or wolf mix. I was acutely aware of my fortune in birth despite my lower station amongst my kin- I was still a son of Canus, after all. And blessed with the size and strength of the more robust lines. Which made it far too easy to push past and through the intimate crowd in my rush to the Solarium.

I heard no one call out for me, save proclamations of offense, and not a soul followed when I burst through the Solarium door, the glass rattling in its ornate iron binding behind me. That my sudden departure from the party was not worrisome to them was hardly surprising—I was in no one's confidence in this estate. I hadn't even been on the guest list. I was a late appointment, an interloper, signed off on by the Hudson family's personal attending Templar. And he wasn't even present; he was in Absolution with Father Helstrom during the whole duration of my weeklong stay on these grounds. The Hudson family felt that only one Templar on the grounds was what was proper.

It seems to me that no righteous man who is secure in his place in God's heart should object to the presence of a holy minder. And what difference could two make as opposed to one? But, as my Bishop had reminded me upon taking up this task, Pedigree Lords can cling stubbornly to mortal tradition, regardless of whether we feel it serves God's ends. So long as they maintain the holy doctrine in their lives, it is not our place to question any bureaucratic quibbles. The Priests and Bishops handle that.

I wished—as I stumbled out into mottled sunlight, blinking against the glare filtering down through the small citrus trees in this stiflingly hot glass cage—that Templar Olvar was here. While he wasn't from my Parish and had taken a different path in his clerical studies to attain his ordination, he *did* know of my troubles. He had been a frequent visitor at our Solstice Mass in Auldfuster, and I knew he'd been present at least once when the subject of my dietary weakness came up in conversation.

He would be able to do little, of course. But it would have been comforting to have an elder Brother at my side in my time of suffering.

The thickening, choking sensation in my throat was growing in intensity with each passing moment. I knew what came next. I came to a stop in the center of the Solarium, an intricate, multicolored brick spiral in the shape of a waxing moon, held in the clutch of a bed of fragrant hibiscus bushes and lemon trees. I looked frantically for anywhere that I might rest my body… and came away with nothing. The Lady of the house may have had a liking for citrus and the luxury to take her morning walks in a warm, sunlit, miniature forest, but she clearly did not prefer to take her leisure here. There were no stone benches; no chairs of any kind.

I could lie on the ground out here, and I probably wouldn't be seen by the elites inside. The thought lingered in my desperate mind for longer than it should have as the first labored gasps left my panting muzzle.

Ridiculous. The indecency of it, the *weakness* it would portray! I had only received my investiture as an Acolyte of the Templar Order last spring. This was but my third posting at a Pedigree house, although the first had only been shadowing Senior Templar for a few days when I was younger, so they weren't official assignments. I was not seeking a permanent appointment, given the nature of my ordination, but that hardly mattered. We represented the whole of the Order when we formally took up a position in a Manor home, or any posting. I was not going to embarrass my Parish. I *was not.*

So then, where could I lay myself down for a time? Wait for this to pass….

My rasping breaths filled my skull, joined now by the high-pitched whistle that signaled that very soon, I would start choking. I'd only had a bite of the little fried cake; I hadn't eaten enough that my life might be in danger.

Lord help me, when would I learn? Especially in gathers like this, when pungent alcohol was flowing, when all the Ladies and Gentlemen in attendance were perfumed and powdered, when there was so much fatty meat and savory desserts spread out in the serving hall. I had to smell my food before I ate it! If I'd taken even a cursory sniff of the little fried cakes on that platter, I would have smelled the crab in them.

I'd realized it the second I'd swallowed a bite. Shellfish had been my bane since childhood, but that didn't mean I hadn't enough experiences to know the taste by now. And so began my flight from the hall.

If I'd been calm and reasoned about this, I would have headed for a parlor. A spare bedroom. Anywhere I might find privacy that wasn't a cobblestone-inlaid Solarium with no places of rest in sight.

God, where could I go? How did I weather this without bringing disgrace to His name and my Parish?

I had not heard the Solarium door open again behind me, but I was deep into the grove of miniature trees and thoroughly distracted enough that it was no surprise. All the same, I nearly leapt out of my spats when a gentle, quiet voice spoke from behind me, along the pathway back to the Great Hall.

"Are you alright, Lord?"

I spun on my right footpad to discover who had caught me in my moment of struggle. The sight that greeted me was not any soul I would have expected, nor anyone I had taken note of in the manor prior to this. He was feline, black-furred, far shorter than me, save for the prominent ears that adorned his forehead and added to his height. He was clearly not gentry, which almost went without saying in the heart of Amuresca—he was, as I said, feline after all.

He wore a simple but clean white servant's blouse, well-worn but also well-tailored britches, cotton spats, and a leather-braced men's corset. That last accented his already lean figure and added to his diminutive-ness. But he looked like some of the felines I'd seen that worked at the grounds' bakery, and if you were going to be lifting sacks of flour all day, back support was all but essential, I suppose.

Lord, how my mind wandered when I was deprived of air.

What was important here wasn't the man's corset or how he wore it, but that I'd had the good fortune to be found not by one of the Pedigree Lords, but by a worker who would know the grounds and could help me. And if I embarrassed myself with the help, it was far less injurious than it would have been to lose face with the family here.

I gagged on my own saliva and swallowed as well as I could a few times, trying to get the words, "Not… a Lord," out. I don't know if I really succeeded.

"Ah, yes. You're the House Templar, right?" he asked in that respectful, but vaguely guarded tone most servants used when conversing with me. As a matter of course, anyone in a household I was overseeing would be wary of my presence.

I could answer that easily enough with a nod, so I did. He inclined his muzzle up and I think he may have tried to give a polite smile, but it was lost in all the worry. "You probably should have saved your breath, there. Your station matters less than your health, after all. How can I… I wish to help…"

I blinked through a narrowing field of vision. My eyelids had grown heavy and swollen. If I didn't find somewhere to tough this out soon enough, I'd lose the ability to navigate the grounds altogether.

I opened my muzzle to ask him where I could go, and instead gave a wracking cough. His already oversized green-gold eyes widened and he took a tentative step towards me, reaching out a hand while keeping a respectable distance. "Are you choking?" he asked.

I shook my head in between a few wheezing coughs, sucking as much breath into my deprived lungs as I could, before saying with a weak, thready voice, "Not… choking. Need… somewhere… to lie down…"

"I understand," he said with a confidence and immediacy of action that you didn't usually see in a servant. He took one of my hands in his and began to lead me down one fork of the Solarium path.

For some reason as he led me along—perhaps because my mind got fuzzy around the edges and tended to wander when my breath was being stolen from me—I found myself fixated on his slender, dark fingers clasping my own thick, clumsy hand. Our furs were opposing colors, so it was very easy to pick out the margins. His paws were soft, softer than a servant's had any right to be. Perhaps he didn't work in the bakery after all.

He may have noticed the missing finger on my right hand-my smallest. He paused briefly when he'd taken hold of it, but was polite enough not to say anything.

They weren't extended then, but I could also tell his claws were very clean and unstained, from what little I could see of the tips protruding. Like a Pedigree Lady or a dandy. Some Lords preferred it as a sign of their domesticity, and some workers' professions required it. Especially in high society. I wondered what his position was here.

My own claws were as thick and cumbersome as the rest of me. And dirty... oh, Lord, how humiliating. I'd forgotten to scrub them after training this morning. Father Helstrom would have had my head if he knew.

He pushed open a glass door ahead of us, much like the one I had come through, but this one led outside to the courtyard abutting the deer park. We were at the back of the manor; I knew at least that much from my brief time here.

"Where...?" I choked out.

"The Dovecote," he explained, hurrying us across the grounds towards a corner of the courtyard I'd not had much occasion to traverse. It was less planted than the areas closer to the house, save the ever-present rose bushes and the occasional well-manicured tree.

I had no ability to question his logic, but internally, I had to assume I'd been misunderstood. The Dovecote at this estate was very large, but it was still an oversized stone birdhouse, essentially. There was unlikely to be anywhere inside to sit, let alone lie down, and if I did, I would be covered in bird excrement.

I soon discovered his plan when we rounded the rose bushes, though. Outside the Dovecote, tucked back amongst the cherry trees and a fresh down blanket of fallen blossoms from the early spring we'd been treated to, was an elegant and very wide stone bench. Somewhere even a man of my bulk would be able to rest his body.

By now I was nearly gagging on my tongue, so the feline lad had to help me sit down. I could do little other than disentangle our fingers and give his hand a soft pat to show my gratitude.

He sat down gingerly beside me, looking on like he wanted to do more. But I knew—although I could not explain to him as much—that there was little more anyone could do to help me at this point. I simply had to wait for it to pass.

I felt his eyes on mine as I slowly stretched my body out, denying myself the useless gesture of scratching or pawing at my throat. It wouldn't help. I knitted my fingers over my chest to keep myself from doing it.

"Some kind of affliction of your body?" he guessed softly.

Again, I nodded. I could do that much, at least.

He was silent a spell, before murmuring, "How unfortunate. I'm sorry. It will pass?"

I nodded.

"Not quickly, though."

This time, I shook my head.

I felt him fidget from beside me, just a slight tensing, and a flick of his small tail. I could sense his discomfort, and of course wished I was not burdening others. Even someone as lowly as house staff.

My head was close to where he was sat, my legs propped up on the arm of the right-hand side of the bench. I had my neck craned back, trying to find a position of comfort that kept my throat as open as possible. But when I turned my head to the side, I found my nose inches away from where his hand paw was clutching at his thin knee. And I noticed something I had not before.

I didn't know what variety of feline he was, nor did it matter. Huudari species were common enough in our Empire, especially amongst the worker classes. But whatever his kin, there were the subtlest hints of spotted patterns beneath the black of his fur. An equatorial cat, then. Someone from closer to the tropics. The black variation in his fur was a deviation from God's plan for his people, and an unfortunate one, at that. Not only would it avail him poorly in a hotter climate, it was a dreadfully common coloration for a species whose limited assets usually included their exotic beauty.

My target in this investigation, the whole reason I was here, was thusly blessed. She'd yet to show herself, either on these grounds or in the surrounding township, but if she did, she'd be hard to miss. She was a feline of renowned beauty, with a golden, intricately-patterned foreign coat. Her charm had availed her thus-far, seducing and fooling many a dull-witted, lascivious gentleman. She'd have no such power over me.

The beauty of this place of respite worked on me as I lay there considering my unfortunate situation, as well as the misfortune of the kind fellow beside me. My vision as I looked upwards was of a blue, midday sky, patchy with wisps of clouds, and the fluttering hints of pink from the remaining blooms caught in the cherry tree's branches. I could feel that I was lying on a thin bed of the fallen blossoms; no one had cleaned this bench in some time. The distant fluttering and cooing of the denizens of the Dovecote was the only sound save the mild wind, and the overwhelming floral scent drowned out any unpleasant odors I may have smelled from the birds otherwise.

It was almost romantic. Not in an amorous sense, but in the way poets and writers might characterize the word. I could all but hear my Amurescan instructor, exasperated—'there are many definitions of the word, it merely suggests a view of reality that is idealized'. I had asked him about it once when he had patiently explained to me that not all 'romantic' poets were writing of mortal love, but rather of a dramatized view of the world. It was one of those memories that had formed so clearly in my mind, I would think on it at the oddest moments.

With my state of rest, and not least of all the admittedly quiet beauty of this place, came a relaxation in my chest. Slowly, I was able to steady my shallow breaths, fight back the panic, and fall into my meditations. I would weather this. I always had.

"You seem to be improving," the fellow beside me noted after a time. "Are you out of the woods? I am not certain how long the danger in this lasts for you. But I would rather not leave you if this could yet take a turn for the worse."

"No," I croaked. "Not... out of danger... yet."

I didn't want to ask him to stay, but there really was a chance this could still get worse before it got better. And I had no one else.

"Then I'll stay at your side," he said calmly. I felt him shift, and then a slim shadow as he leaned over me. His eyes briefly looked down into my own before moving over my chest. "Shouldn't we take the—that's some kind of a weapon harness, right? Shouldn't we take that off? Isn't it restricting your chest?"

He was right. I felt like a fool for not realizing it earlier. It's the first thing I should have done.

I gave a tight nod and shifted up, grimacing around a short gasp. Before I could prop myself up further on my elbow, I felt his thigh and knee slide under my back, holding me up just enough. He reached around and beneath my cloak with deft hands and began navigating the straps to undo my chest harness. It was, as he'd said, a weapon belt. But it was also something of a badge of office. The family here found it far too intimidating for me to be armed inside the house. I had no blades on my person right now, so there was no issue with a civilian handling it.

I couldn't tell him how to remove the thing and it could be complicated if you didn't wear one yourself regularly, but he managed it after a few moments of figuring out the strap and buckle and slid one end 'round my back to the other side of my chest, before tugging it free of my torso. He draped it over the side of the bench, I think, then set to un-bunching my cloak from where I'd lain down atop it, smoothing it out down my sides to my belt line, clearly intending to make me more comfortable. He showed not a single sign of discomfort or awkwardness while doing so, either. Probably a tailor, then. I suppose that made sense.

He stood afterwards, smiling down at me in a way that was almost so delicate as to be un-masculine. I felt a lightness in my chest that was unbefitting the allergic reaction I was suffering and wondered at myself for a moment.

"Better?" he asked.

I nodded, clearing my throat as well as I could. "Much," I agreed. And it was. I'd ingested very little of what was causing my plight, but the panic and the harness may have exacerbated my reaction. I was beginning to calm, some of the pressure was off my chest. And someone here had seen fit to show me kindness.

I would thank God in my evening prayers, but for now, I sent my praise heavenward through my thoughts. This could have been far worse.

"Rest here," the servant said, settling a hand once more on mine for a moment, giving it just the slightest squeeze, before slipping away. "If you're going to be alright now, I must return to my duties."

I was feeling better, so I nodded. And I tried to smile, to assure him. I knew from experience my features were puffy and ugly though, so I'm certain I was a fright.

He took it in stride, giving me one last, quiet, "Take care, young Templar," before turning and heading back towards the manor the way we had come.

I'm not sure how long I lay there. It may have been an hour. I'm certain at least it was not two. I watched the cherry blossoms fall, listened to the doves sing, and I thanked the Lord for every blessing that lightened these moments of pain. Truly, I had been given the gift of grace this day. And I'd not soon forget it.

Strangely, it wasn't the feline servant who came to check on me again. It was a woman, a spotted pig whom I'd seen serving in the Great Hall earlier. She came with fresh, cold water from the well for me, treating me like I were one of her piglets. She helped me to my feet after insisting I drink the whole of the pewter cup she'd brought out to me, and upon the fifth or sixth time I assured her I could find my way back to my quarters on my own, she fearlessly batted me on the arm and said, "You young lads! All of you, a-feared to admit when you're under the weather. On your way, then. I'll have oatmeal and plain bread sent up for your dinner, later."

She, at least, knew of my dietary failings. The whole kitchen staff did. But it wasn't their fault that I'd eaten a crab cake without knowing it. The food at the party wasn't catered for me, after all. And I'd been careless.

"Oh, ma'am," I said, clutching at my throat even though I shouldn't have been. It was so hard to avoid. I spoke slowly, between breaths. "The... feline fellow... who told you... where to find me. Where does... he work? Want to... thank him."

She twisted up her snout oddly, lifting a brow. "One of the

serving lasses brought word from the Main Hall you was out here in need of tendin'. I don't know who told her. Feline? We have no felines on staff, none that are male, anyway. And I'd know." She leaned in, like what she was about to say was conspiratorial. "The lady of the house thinks they *reek,* man-cats. And I don't entirely disagree."

I didn't know what to make of what she'd said. "Then... he works the grounds, maybe?"

The pig shook her head. "No, lad. None I know of. Not on the whole of the Estate."

Something, I don't know what, perhaps a flash of insight from above, made me remember the gentle touch as his hands smoothed down my cloak. Under my back, along my torso... my belt....

My hand shot down to my metal belt hook, where I kept my—

Nothing.

I was in no condition to run. I was in *no condition to run,* but I did, leaving the pig aghast and yelling her outrage at my foolishness to my back. I rushed in through the gardener's entrance, navigating my way into the servant's hallways, headed for the one staircase that connected these hidden corridors—the places in this house I'd memorized ahead of this *so* carefully, because I'd been so very certain the thief would need to use these to pilfer the artifact—to the second story.

My lungs and my throat nearly instantly closed to a clench again, and everything was burning and spinning, my field of vision shrinking and sporadically bursting in black dots as I tore down the hallway.

Not to the Lord's quarters. To the humbler rooms that were in the west wing. The Templar's Residence. My room, while I stayed here.

The room I had insisted we keep the Artifact hidden away in. Because I had changed the locks, because the thief would never expect it was here, because *I would know* when a feline fitting that description made an appearance and *we needed to catch her in the act—*

My door was open.

I came to a halt, falling to my knees, barely able to draw breath. And I checked my belt again, to be sure. I don't know why. I had closed and locked my door when I'd left this morning.

My door was open.

And my keys were gone.

Stumbling to my feet, clutching at the doorknob, I staggered just inside the room, knowing what I'd see. Namely, the open chest in the corner.

And so it was.

What I hadn't expected was the small, folded letter on my desk.

2

A LETTER FROM A THIEF

That night, as I had every night since I'd left the Hudson's Estate, I dreamt of her.

I had always been a man subject to vibrant and very convincingly real dreams. Father Helstrom said it was proof positive that I was amongst the listless, the wanderers. Those who could not find satisfaction in the mundanity of average life. Owing perhaps to my birth, to the father who had walked out on our family and left my mother with four pups and no coin to raise them, chasing perhaps after one of his own dreams. Or, my whimsical mind could be due to the inevitable injury in a young man's heart that comes from knowing he has been willfully orphaned. A resentment for both mother and father, and thus a weaker understanding of social good and the importance of my responsibility to society.

I liked to think I had been diligent in pursuing instruction in understanding social good, in being a benefit to society as a whole and not a continuing burden upon it. But I did not—could not—deny that I had inherited my father's moral deficiencies. I was half his, after all, and had always been prone to my mind wandering, to imagination when I should have been focusing on the tasks at hand. I *was* unmoored in that way.

I had been working at bringing order to my mind and to my life since the Ebon Gables Abbey had taken me in as a child. Lord knows I hadn't made enough progress, but I was trying. My disposition was truly one to be deplored. I found myself fighting against my corrupt nature every single day, in some way.

But such was the curse of man. Every one of us grappled with different demons. I had to remember my struggles were not special. They were not unique.

For all that I could self-correct in the waking world though, taming my mind while at rest seemed impossible. And oh, how it tortured me then.

The dream was similar, but always just slightly different, each night I had it. It nearly always made sense in the moment, but afterwards when I woke, the pieces didn't fit together quite so neatly.

I was in the narthex of my Abbey—or at least it seemed that way at first—the wood older, mossy around the edges, the clay tiles above the small patio cracked and broken, several having slid off and lying like garden stone around the entranceway. Daffodils grew between the shattered shards and other pebbles that may have at one point formed a walkway. The door was missing entirely, welcoming me into the sunlit nave.

I stepped inside, into a kaleidoscope of color and dusty warmth. The portraits adorning the stained glass windows on either side of me shifted in every dream, sometimes Saint August looking upon me with a benevolent smile, a pup held in each of his burly arms. Sometimes it was the Holy Vestal Abyssinia, squash, pumpkins, and gourds gathered at her feet, blooms rising in a pathway behind her. It was always one of the heroes of the scriptures that I'd loved reading about growing up, and still loved. Always one of the Saints or Holy figures I'd hoped were looking down on me, guiding me. Never Saint Kristoff or Pious Charles, who *actually* adorned the nave in Ebon Gables.

But then, this place wasn't Ebon Gables. It *was*. But not quite. Enough about the choir was similar, the podium was adorned with my very own Holy Tome. Open to what passage, I knew not. But so much else was… different. This place was older. Less cared-for, almost derelict. And somehow, brighter? Perhaps because in some versions of the dream, the windows were broken-in. Perhaps because it was a dream, after all. And in the waking world, the Ebon Gables I knew was not always a place of light.

It was a reformatory, after all. A place the unwanted were taken in, and our worse natures and inherited failings were restructured. Shaped. Molded. And change like that was hard.

Change like that could be painful.

Ebon Gables had not always been a sanctuary for me. But then, expecting my adopted home would always feel safe was foolish, arrogant. No man, save the Pedigree Lords and God Almighty Himself, was Master of his home.

But in this place, in the dream, I felt… safe. Utterly. That, more than anything, was the feeling I was wrapped in when first I woke. I felt at one with it, this place unlike the home I knew, but near enough and warmer, welcoming, that I'd begun to look forward to returning there. I would have seen the dream as a treasure, as a gift, then… if not for whom I shared it with.

She was always there. In the moment, in the dream, I don't think I entirely knew what to make of her presence. Despite having had it many times, it was always a surprise to find her standing there, always at the end of the dream, always at the altar.

I would walk between the pews, hear the creak of the old

wood, smell the damp in the beams and the pollen from the daffodils outside, wafting in through the broken windows. Saint August's colors would fall upon my cloak in relief, and I was overwhelmed by the sensation that his arms were around me. Despite my misgivings and many painful memories reminding me that I was loved here. That he was watching over me, as he did all orphaned children. Vestal Abyssinia's eyes seemed to crinkle, as she smiled upon me. Promising me bounty in life, fertility, and plenty. I almost felt as though they were watching over me like the loving parents I'd never had, as I went to receive communion with Canus. Or ascended the altar, to accept my bride, or to be Ordained.

But I was no Priest. I was an orphan, so I could never receive Communion with Canus. And the woman waiting there for me at the altar was no bride.

I knew by the shape of her figure, despite the dress she now wore—the squared shoulders, the slight curve to her spine, the flare of her lean hips, and her long legs—who she was. If the large, butter dish ears hadn't given her away already, the rest of her would have. She was burned into my mind. I had, admittedly, begun to obsess in silence over the many details of her appearance. Details I *should* have caught, realizations I *should* have had.

The effeminate quality to her voice was so very obvious in retrospect. How gentle she'd been. The patterns beneath the black dye or ink in her fur, indicating her true pelt coloration beneath. How soft her hands had been, despite ostensibly being a laborer.

Of course, I knew now… she was no man. Sometimes she'd be in a long, simple gown. Too fine for a lady's maid. But modest, pastel-hued, or shifting with the array of colors coming in through the stained-glass windows.

Sometimes she'd be wearing the very same outfit she'd worn

when we'd met. The way it was so well-tailored to her while still not giving away her sex, even when she turned to greet me—

She always turned towards me. In those final moments of the dream, she always looked at me. And I stood there, frozen on the spot, like a hare pinned down by the predator destined to consume them whole.

Her eyes were honey yellow and clover green all at once, sometimes shifting between the two. My mind filled in whatever tint the dream took in that moment.

Her ears curled forward. Her whiskers twitched. She blinked slowly at me. The corners of her feline features turned up ever-so-slightly in a fond smile.

And then I woke.

A patched gray ceiling greeted me. Lime plaster, caked thick in repairs and multiple coats of fading paint, the same color as the clay we brought in buckets from the riverbed nearby. A particular spot in the corner, several feet above my left foot, marked where some careless fool (the very one telling you this story) had put a broom pole through the low ceiling while horsing around with his fellows during cleaning duty. I'd gotten a good and just strapping for that one, if memory served.

That patch job was mine. The others here belonged to brothers both from recent memory and long before us. This Abbey had stood for nearly two centuries, growing in size and expanding in function after Reformation, when the Templar Order had decided to make use of it as an arm of the Grooming and Training division.

This was the dorter—the west wing of the dormitory reserved for laymen and boys, and all lay brothers when they came to visit. Those of us who'd either chosen to live more secular lives while maintaining our service to the church, or like myself, whose breeding was too lowly to take on fully monastic vows and commit ourselves to God wholly in body and spirit.

I'd spent the entirety of my life since five years of age here.

When my mother, a poor woman from a nearby village (I knew little more about her life after she'd given me up, and that was for the best), had turned me over to the Order. Given that she'd been unable to care for me, I bore her no ill will. She'd committed no sin; I'd just been too hard a burden for her to bear. A particular weakness of constitution I'd been born with meant I could not be fed on common fare. Most of the poor canines who lived along the river ate shellfish as their main meat since game was scarce and hunting was outlawed in most forests on Pedigree land besides. She couldn't very well be expected to buy red meat and poultry to keep one pup alive.

I could eat fish, but it disagreed with me. Perhaps the taste reminded me of too many attacks, I'm not sure. It nearly always came back up. I was a frail, starved little thing when I first arrived here. When I spent my first night in this room, I remembered lying in one of these very bunks, staring at this very ceiling, wondering if the severe men here would allow me to starve.

It wasn't but an hour after I'd drifted off that one of them—Father Helstrom himself, younger then—had sat down beside me and spoon fed me chicken stock and soaked bread.

This Abbey may not have been the sunlit, warm façade of welcomeness that I'd just walked the halls of in my dreams, but it was real, and it had been my salvation.

And *she* wasn't here. Tormenting me with my foolishness.

I scrubbed a paw over my face, nosing at the spot where my bone ended abruptly, where a pinky once was. Every morning, I felt the need to toy with the spot. Confirm it was really gone. It was a habit I'd never quite shaken.

The wooden frame of the bunk shuddered with a heavy rap from below, and I gripped the edge of it, peering down to ground level, where the bright russet eyes of a familiar mutt greeted me. Brother Nicholas was already dressed and harnessed, unarmed of course, and looking fondly if impatiently at me.

"Isi," he rapped on my top bunk again, unnecessarily because I was *obviously* already awake. "Gotten into a very *comfortable* routine during those Pedigree assignments, have you? Dawn was an hour ago."

"I'm sorry Nick," I murmured groggily, still shaking off the dream. The rosy glint of the early morning sun scattered down over the floor below was dancing with soft flickers of honey and green from the leaves filtering the sunlight outside.

I saw her eyes in it for just a moment.

An irritated noise rose in the back of my throat, and I reached down to shuck the worn blanket down my body, while Nick continued to speak up at me from where he stood below, hands on his hips, a chiding and thoroughly amused lilt to his voice.

"You can probably get by on the excuse of arriving so late last night. Father Helstrom won't accept it." He very nearly chuckled when he said that, giving me a knowing look. "But the other lay monks and the neutren will, and that oughta keep him reserved at least until he gets you alone."

He paused, seeming to catch on to my frozen state. Nicholas was normally… 'slow-witted' was a kind way to say it. He was sharper than I might have preferred in this moment, though. He'd caught the brief flash of panic I'd tried to hide.

"Isi?" he tipped his head, reaching up for the edge of the bunk frame. "You're awake, right? Not another'f your walking dreams?"

"Stop slurring," I said around a suddenly dry tongue. "We're not field workers anymore. If your Pedigree Family hears you talk like that while in service, your Parish will hear about it."

"Alright, you're awake," he sighed. "Well, report to the Infirmary for a weigh and measure before you break your fast in the refectory—"

"I was already measured at the beginning of the month," I insisted, a tense hitch blooming in my chest at the mere mention.

"You were on assignment, were you not?" he parried back. "You *know* how rigid Father Helstrom is about temperance. He ordered the Physician look you over this very morning. If you don't report in *before* you eat, he'll have you do so after. I thought I'd give you a heads-up. Better before than after, no?"

"I did not imbibe any drink but tea and water during my stay there," I insisted quietly.

"I don't doubt it," he snuffed. "You're a bore, Isi. But it doesn't matter. Go now or go later. I was just trying to warn you."

"I do appreciate it," I assured him.

He banged on my bunk again with two leather-gloved paws, his features brightening. "Then let's go already! C'mon, I'll help you groom, get the road off your fur. You're gonna miss out on bread if you take much longer."

"'Going to,'" I corrected him, clearing my throat. "And I'm sorry Nick, but I'd prefer privacy this morning."

"Good luck with that," he laughed, "the pups'll be in and out until their lessons start. They've already had their time of prayer."

"All the same," I insisted.

He gave me a confused look, his expression falling slightly. For a moment I felt a pang of guilt. Nicholas was two years my junior and still in training. He had yet to be ordained, let alone assigned, and I think he'd missed me. We were the only two senior Brothers in the house this season, and while I'd been away it had just been him with a pack of the young pups. Which meant much more dedicated time from Father Helstrom on his training and studies, but that wasn't always so pleasant.

"I'll weigh and measure with you if you want," he offered, hopefully.

I couldn't turn him down. Not when he was making that face at me. Not when he'd been the first to greet me in the dead of the night and the first to greet me this morning.

He didn't understand it was *worse* if I was being compared.

"Fine," I agreed softly. "But I'd still like to groom and dress alone."

"Suit yourself," he shrugged, turning on his heel. "I'll wait for you in the cloister."

I watched him leave, sorry I'd had to dismiss him. Especially given *why*. But it could hardly be helped. Nicholas was a young man, he'd understand. But the shame would absolutely eat through me, all the same.

I finally drew back the blanket entirely, making sure none of the pups were dashing in through the open doorway for something in their own bunk. The hall was quiet. They were probably all eating in the refectory. I honestly could have used Nick's help to groom and dress in time this morning. There'd be no bread left at the table by the time I got there, I was certain of that.

My smallclothes were less distended than they *had* been. A prolonged conversation and I daresay, my own panic, had seen to that. But the receding bulge there was dotted with a small wet spot, evidence of my sin as clear as day. There would have been no hiding it.

I knew, of course, that this was a common enough trouble for young men. The Priests did not talk about it, the Scriptures did not talk about it, but other young men did. And while my raising here had been in the cradle of grace, we were hardly cloistered, we brothers. Most of us had been raised lowly, we made trips into town often to sell wine or get provisions for the Abbey at market.

You heard things. You *saw* things. While we Brothers were being groomed and prepared for life amongst the elite, we were between worlds, moving throughout civil *and* lowly society. You learned what to disregard, what kinds of living and pleasures were poisonous for your soul. It was good preparation for life lived alongside the Pedigree, whose souls were already so perfect, so close to His grace, they were permitted the indulgences that the poor would be too intemperate to handle.

Indulgences *I* was not fit for, either.

Although my breeding was less muddy than most born poor (my parents knew well enough at least to marry and procreate within their kind, which could not be said of poor Nicholas) my soul was hardly close to grace. That's why I struggled with these lowly problems, with these urges and untoward physical manifestations of sin. The Pedigree had no such struggles.

No, it was not the tumescence in my loins that disturbed me. That had, regrettably, happened readily enough since I was thirteen. Especially in the mornings...

What unnerved me was when it followed these dreams. It was hard to deny the connection.

"The viper may wind herself 'twixt his thighs," I growled, throwing off the blanket, "but nobler is the man that denies her at risk of her venom, than allows her sanctuary in his bed!"

"What?" a sleepy voice, half yawned-out, called from the doorway.

Startled, I hopped down out of bed, turning my back to the doorway and the tousled young mouse standing in it. "Nothing, Wesley! Just... morning prayers."

My stomach was growling. I'd elected to miss breaking my fast entirely after the weigh-in and measure. Would do me some good to miss a meal every now and then. And besides, all that would be left by now was watery oatmeal.

I knew it was folly to waste His time on prayers of so little importance, so instead I just... hoped... Father Helstrom didn't hear it. The jarring squeak of the legs of his chair pushing back from his desk announced he was done looking over the report there, and soon the aging bloodhound was bracing his palms on the desk and standing, reaching for his steel-tipped cane. He forced himself to stand at a proper posture, even now in his sixty-eighth year. And his eyes were as sharp as they'd ever been, even beneath the bags and pink drooping eyelids that inevitably came with time for those of his breed. He walked around his desk, the tap of his cane a third foot in his gate, and then stopped before us. I braced for it.

The cane rapped at Nicholas's side when it came, though. Correcting his slouch, which I could have told him to fix myself, if not for the fact that Father Helstrom was already in the room when we arrived. The library was quiet at this hour, the lay monks, the cloistered monks, and the neutren deep in their morning contemplations.

"Back straight," Father grumbled, then twisted his grip on the cane expertly as one might the hilt of a blade, snapping the inside of both of Nicholas's calves. He had his spats on, but I heard him hiss through his breath all the same, then obediently close his legs more firmly together.

"There," Father sighed, giving him a long-suffering look. "How many more times must we go over this, Nicholas? You are months from being ordained as a Templar, and you still slouch and stand about like the son of a harlot you used to be."

"I'm sorry, Father," Nicholas said with a barely-suppressed, amused smile.

"You find that entertaining, do you?" the old bloodhound queried, not missing a beat.

"No, Father."

"Does it delight you to have your shameful parentage brought up or assumed in every conversation?"

"Certainly not, Father."

"Then don't louse about like a whore's son," he said pointedly. "Your Pedigree Lords will deduce you are unrespectable and unsuitable for their home soon enough, if you cannot muster the decorum to portray our Order with the dignity God expects of us. And moreover, your Lords will come to believe you are a young man of low virtue, and that your silence or compliance can be *bought*. These men will walk upon your back over a puddle in the rain if you let them, and we are not their servants. We are their *minders*. We must be above reproach, virtuous in all ways they are not. And staunch in our defiance of sin, whether it be by nature, or sin that is *offered*."

Father Helstrom had been pacing the room and now turned with a crisp tap of his cane upon the weathered floorboards at that, the sound echoing off the stacks. The shelves of books in this place had been my stalwart companions most of my life. More so than Nicholas, if I was being honest. Despite having spent nearly a decade together now and only separated by a few years, he hadn't really grown close to me until the rest of the elder Brothers had aged out, and we were all that remained in ordination training.

"Do you understand what I mean by that, Nicholas?" he pressed.

Nick clearly hadn't been expecting that he'd have to give a thought-through answer and fell back on his usual. "Err," he stammered, "yes? Yes."

The bloodhound sighed and crossed the room to him again, lifting and prodding his cane forward, and tapping it square on Nicholas's forehead. The young lad's brows furrowed, the two brown dots adorning his eyebrows tipping inwards into a few rolls of black fur. Nick was the unfortunate result of an affair between a Dane family and a woman of low repute who must have been some mix that favored rottweiler. Unfortunate breeding aside, he was tall, trim, and strong, with no illnesses or weaknesses of constitution. He certainly didn't fear the weigh-ins the way I did, which I shouldn't have resented him for. But I was a fallible man.

Despite his physical gifts, he'd never been good at giving Father Helstrom the answers he wanted and seemed to lack the aptitude for most academic studies. He was a good lad, and he'd make a fine Templar. I just hoped he was assigned to a Godly family that didn't test his investigative skills too much.

And that, I suppose, was Father's point.

Father Helstrom had this way of seeing through you. It was like he'd heard my inner thoughts. "Brother Isidor here understands me. Do you not?"

"Yes, Father," I agreed.

"Explain it to your younger Brother, then."

I looked to Nick, who was flushed in his ears, grimacing a bit in my direction. But smiling, even through it. He looked so cowed. He didn't mind being talked down to by his elders. Earnestly, I think he wanted the explanation. But that was part of the problem.

And this was a rare chance for me to show my aptitude for instruction and recitation. As a young Brother, I would not have many of those.

"You need not just to *act* more certain of yourself," I explained to him patiently, "but to *become* more certain of yourself. Posture, temper, and your way of speaking are your face for the world and your eventual assigned Pedigree family. You are not only representing the Order, but also most crucially, yourself."

I vaguely saw Father Helstrom nod out of the corner of my eye, so I continued, emphatically. "You must not waver. You must not even *appear* to waver when you are in fact in crisis or in doubt. No man is a fortress, but remember—as Templar, it is our job within a noble family not only to be role models in our grace and deference to God and scripture, but to be *minders* for their behavior. To be the eyes of the Church within the halls of the elite and the powerful. And to be vigilant for—and ultimately curtail—any Ungodly behavior or fall to sin within said family. To protect them from the dangers that may threaten their house from the world at large... and from themselves, if need be."

Nicholas listened patiently. He knew most of this, but it bore repeating. I let out a breath and continued, "That is why Father corrects you so often. Because we—all of us Brothers—are brought up from the lowest reaches of society and redeemed through our training, our diligence, and our service to God and to the Order. But there are those who are accustomed to power, who will see that low breeding in you as a crack they can chip away at. As a weakness they can prey upon. And you mustn't let them. What their souls can be washed clean of, ours cannot. We haven't the strength of character or means to absolve ourselves of the sins they dabble in. And even in their case, there is a limit. That's what you are there to remind them of. You are their caretaker. You are there to assure they ascend when they die. To show them the way, all through life. To keep them from stumbling."

I put a hand on his shoulder, giving it a soft squeeze. "And they will not listen to you, or rather they will see no *reason* to listen to you, if they do not respect you."

"Very good," Father Helstrom nodded. "As you were."

I assumed my stance again, and Father Helstrom began to speak once more. But, much to my horror, Nicholas cut him off.

"I guess I still don't understand," Nicholas said.

"What don't you understand?" Father asked curtly. I dared not look Nick's way, keeping my arms folded neatly in front of me. I tightened my jaw though, fearing his answer.

"Well, just," Nick made a noise with his mouth, a 'tch'. "They'll respect me because we represent the Church, because we're the arm of the Church in their home. And because that'd be enough to scare most people. They already *know* none of us were born high. Even if they think ill of me, they'll behave s'long as I'm there. Because that's what most people do when they know they're being watched."

"You're on clay drudging for the day," Father Helstrom said sharply, his tone brooking no argument.

Nicholas opened his mouth as if to protest, but he ultimately said nothing. Only looked briefly to me, then stomped one foot back down into a proper stance and growled through gritted teeth. "Yes, Father."

"Get that growl out of your tone, boy," Father Helstrom warned. "Now go."

Nicholas stalked off, and I felt his eyes on me as he left, as if pleading for help. But what could I do?

Foolish, foolish lad.

I was as likely to be sent to the river today as Nicholas had been. If not worse. I shouldn't judge.

Father Helstrom's green eyes were on mine. I didn't dare look away.

"You were over your range on your weigh-in *and* your measure today," he started out with.

"It's winter, Father," I reminded him quietly. "My undercoat has grown in."

"You're already given an extra allowance for that," he shook his head. "And don't make the petulant excuses anymore; you're a grown man now. Your range is adjusted for your height and breed, you've been topping out above an acceptable weight since you were fifteen. This is about temperance, boy. And self-control. You may be diligent in your studies, and I do not doubt your adherence to faith and prayer, but we are *house guards* in addition to our other duties. You won't impress an air of authority over any class of person, Lord or no, if you grow soft."

I knitted my brow, staring at the floor. "I try to be diligent in my diet," I insisted quietly, doing everything in my power to keep the vulnerability, the hurt out of my voice. Father Helstrom would pick it out for what it was—weakness. He reserved his mercy for those in dire need of it. And my feelings of shame for my body and my seeming inability to keep weight off it were hardly requiring of his compassion. They would have to serve as motivation.

Father Helstrom's features softened a moment, and he approached me, placing a hand on my shoulder. An accepted gesture amongst Brothers and Fathers. It was very nearly the only contact allowed once you reached ten years of age. I couldn't feel his palm through the layers of my garb. The Library was no more heated than most of the rest of the Abbey, so what we wore inside and out didn't differ.

All the same, the gesture was comforting.

"I know it's hard for you," he said, "because of your restrictions."

"Yes," I breathed out. "I'm not imbibing wines, or beer, or liquor… Father, I swear to you—"

He waved a hand, dismissing anything further I'd say. "I know my boys," he scoffed. "You are not given to vice, Isidor."

I winced at that, but he hadn't seemed to catch it.

"-but you *can* be given to sloth and indulgence in fatty meat and sugar, *bread*," he said that last bit pointedly. He knew me.

"I have extended my morning and evening drills both by an hour," I said, pushing down the inkling of pride I felt when telling him that. I'd always put in the requisite hours in physical training, so increasing them thusly had been a strain. I ached all day and night the first few weeks, and even since, it could be hard to find comfort at night. The cold air burned my lungs when I ran in the winter, and some part of me feared I was walking a delicate line between honing and exercising my body, and weakening it.

The measure wasn't just belt line, there were ranges for our arms, thighs, inseam. Perhaps it was folly to think my fur was why I'd fail a measure-in, but… it just seemed that no matter how much I trained, I could not fit the standards the Order required of me. I'd skip all but one meal a day for weeks, and somehow, I'd be bigger. I was only nineteen, so maybe I was still growing, but…

It's not as though I was an enormous man. Men of the Akita type were naturally thicker of body and coat, and I'd certainly met Pedigree larger than I. But they were Pedigree… Templar were not permitted the appearance of indulging in excess.

"I know you do not laze about all day," Father Helstrom said with a click of his teeth. "But I've caught you losing time in the library, and I know the Hudsons had a good collection of their own. Their passions are not ours. And those are *worldly* books, besides that, Isidor." He gripped my arm tighter, tight enough that I felt it through my clothing, and leaned in.

"I sent a list of titles," I said, even though he knew that. "I only read the ones approved by the Parish house."

"Which?" he asked. And were he any other man, it might have seemed an innocent question borne of mere curiosity. But it was not just anyone. It was Germain Helstrom, High Templar and a man who had once led an entire investigative wing of the Inquisitors. The man's nose was as famous for sniffing out corruption in the ranks of the elite as it was at smelling pilfered wine on the breath of troublemaking young Brothers.

"All of them," I eventually admitted.

He leaned back, looking mildly impressed. "There were at least twenty books on that list that weren't crossed off. I supervised your reading list myself. You were only there a few weeks. And you say you increased your training hours? How?"

"Once the artifact was secured, there wasn't actually very much for me to attend to in the manor," I said. "The Hudsons are a very Godly family, and there are but three members of the house remaining on the grounds. The eldest sons are married; the daughter is pious, quiet, and needs little instruction in her studies or prayers. The couple attend Church nearly every morning, and their Priest has naught but good to say of them.

Their connections and friends are few, but all good society. And they seemed to want for very little, save a guard for the relic—the incense burner from the Old Kingdom."

"A task which you failed at," he reminded me.

"I had an attack—"

"-and it happened during a busy party, during which the house was quite suddenly full of guests and their servants, dozens of unknown people moving in and out, with too little time for you to screen them all," he continued for me. "The artifact was hidden in a lockbox in your quarters, rather than in use in the main parlor where they preferred to keep it..." he recited almost directly from my report, "...which you'd moved into the day before, in a wing of the house few should have known the location of. You were doing your duty to the best of your abilities, when an unexpected situation arose and divorced you from your vigil for just long enough that this thief was able to seize her moment, abscond with the keys from your person, find said room, pen a *letter* for you, and steal said artifact."

"Yes," I said, my fangs digging into my lower muzzle.

"I've read your report, Brother Isidor," he said. "Knowing the whole of it does not make explaining it to the Bishop any easier. You fought for this appointment, specifically. *Because* we had reason to believe the incense burner would be a likely target for the Heart Thief. I warned you it would be difficult, especially for your first assignment as an Investigator. You could have taken on an easy posting with a family like the Hudsons and done very well as a House Templar. I would not worry nearly so much over you, in that case. You've a passionate disposition, but you're firm in your faith and stricter in your adherence to doctrine than a boy like Nicholas. But that wasn't enough for you. *This* is what you wanted."

"It's not that being a House Templar wasn't enough for me, Father," I insisted. "I just..."

"Don't stammer," he chastised.

"I want to serve God as you have," I said as solidly as I could. "You have always inspired me. With your stories. The many people you've met, the places you've been. I want to follow in your footsteps."

The words had the intended warming effect. But I meant them, so it wasn't as though I was willfully manipulating the man. Not that I ever could have.

He sighed. "Earnestly, boy," he said, "I didn't expect you would catch the Heart Thief on your first mission. The Church has had seasoned Inquisitors trying to sniff her out for over a *year* now, to no avail. I was hopeful the Hudsons wouldn't even become a target, and you'd just waste a season there. It may have bored you, but it would be good service to have under your belt. Still." He gripped my arm again, led me over to his desk and gestured to a chair he'd pulled up in front of it. He rounded the desk to sit back down, wincing as he did. "This isn't the worst outcome."

I blinked. "It isn't?"

"You're safe, are you not?" He gestured at the whole of me. "Alive. Do not discount the ferocity of women, least of all foreign women. They are not gifted with the gentility and civility of canine women. This feline is more than a thief; she is dangerous. She has hurt people before to get at what she wanted. Killed, even."

I looked down at the papers on his desk. At one in particular. Its folds and creases were familiar, worn by my very own trembling claws. "Yes," I said softly, "I know."

"I'm honestly concerned you encountered her so quickly," he said bitterly. "I'd been hoping you wouldn't get this close on your first mission. Let alone *meet* the damned succubus. You're fortunate she had no reason to disable you any further than you already were."

Something was jarring about the reality of what he was saying and my actual memory of her. The soft way she led me to the bench and helped settle me down. Her thigh beneath my shoulders as she undid the straps of my harness. The way she'd *sat* there with me for… I knew not. Whittling away at the time she had to act. Why?

Why?

The honeyed softness in her voice as it echoed in my memories curdled in my gut like bad food. I'd been seduced by her kindness. I'd never thought myself capable of that. I hadn't even wondered when I'd seen the pattern beneath the dye in her fur. Hadn't thought to question her sex, even though *every* indication had *been* there that something was off…

"I didn't think she'd be dressing and acting as a man," I said bitterly. "I don't know why that thought had never occurred to me. I was not at my best, but still."

"The witch is capable of far more than that," he assured me. "But take heart. You're not the first to encounter her in one of her disguises, nor the first to be fooled by her. Accept the humiliation and grow from it. The Order has new information thanks to you. We've never seen her use dye in her fur before. That's invaluable. And you remembered her eye color."

"Green-gold," I said automatically.

"She can't change that," he narrowed his eyes. "Your investigation in this case was a failure, Isidor. But we can learn from failure. And then there's the letter…"

I looked again at the solitary piece of paper nervously. "I take it you've read it?"

"Of course I have," he scoffed. "It's the first thing I did this morning. And this evening, a courier is coming to bring it up the ranks. *This*, son? This will hang her." He tapped his claws on the folded letter, the hollow tap ringing out in the empty library far too loudly. I felt the words like a blow to the chest, but quickly self-corrected. It was instinct to flinch at the idea of any woman being put to death.

But this was no normal woman.

"This is proof positive of her crimes in her own hand writing," he explained. "Once we've caught her, they'll use someone—an agent of some sort—in her prison to pass letters to or ferry notes for her. They'll use those in court as comparison, and damning proof of her crimes. That will secure us a judge's order for execution. We will need that to coax the location of the Heart of Faith out of her, I've no doubt."

"That's how we recover it," I said, jaw trembling. "The Heart."

"Yes," he nodded, "that's how we recover it. But, obviously," he sighed, "we must catch her, first. It's only a matter of time, really. She'll slip up eventually. All thieves do. And she's gotten *especially* bold, of late."

"I want to be the one to catch her," I said before I could think about it.

He smiled a little. "I'm sure you do. Is that your pride I hear, Isidor?"

"Perhaps," I conceded between my teeth. "But it is all to glorify Him, not myself. I swear."

He did not look as though he entirely believed me. But he reached down and opened the letter, rather than press the matter. "It's short. I suppose she hadn't much time to pen it. Strange that she took the time at all, and I cannot make much sense of it. Can you explain any context I may be missing?"

"No," I shook my head, leaning forward and turning the letter right side up in my direction. "I'm afraid not."

He took the letter away and folded it up again, opening one of his desk drawers and setting it inside, before closing the drawer, pulling his keys from his belt, and locking it.

"Isidor," he said, his voice gravely serious. My Father was rarely not serious, but I'd detected a shift. He had his pulpit voice on.

A lesson. I was about to receive some of his wisdom.

"You have no formal Inquisition training, as of yet," he said. "You're only serving as an Investigator, until you have your patents. Do not forget that while you pursue this criminal. You are permitted to follow leads, even affect an arrest if you get close enough to do so. Although I pray you'll have the sense to seek the aid of your fellows, if you think you've discerned where they are."

"If I have the time," I nodded.

He sighed. "That is precisely the attitude that worries me."

"Father?"

"I can hardly train you in the ways of an Inquisitor in one afternoon," he said. "Nor would I wish to. I have no desire to inure my own son to the ravages of this kind of work. You'll be trained by many... *very* hard-nosed men, when you're ready. But," and here he held my gaze. Intensely.

"I won't send you off knowing you may come to be involved in an Inquisition, even tangentially, without at least some preparation for how to speak their language."

"Father?" I repeated, dumbfounded. I wasn't certain what he meant.

"There are three core principles of any Inquisition," he said. "Memorize this. Each and every word."

I took him seriously, and began to form a quill and a blank page in my mind. It was a device he'd taught me to use to aid in eidetic memorization. As he spoke, I inscribed the words in my mind.

"First," he began. "Discomfort them, force them to take a submissive posture."

He gave the words space to breathe. When I nodded, he continued. "Second: Use their name. Use it as an *accusation*."

I swallowed a bit of air, trying to understand what that meant. I assumed I would know in time.

"Last resort," he said, narrowing his eyes. "Use your body to speak louder than your words can. But remember that you can damage resolve far before it becomes necessary to damage flesh."

"Do you mean hurt them?" I questioned to be certain.

"Never assumed you'll be in control of an Inquisition, son," he said, like he pitied me. "This education is for your own protection as well as to aid you in your investigation. We are the stewards of a great many secrets and can easily find ourselves on the wrong end of a blade because of them. Keep your wits about you. Trust only family, and God."

His words still felt somewhat unclear to me, but I dared not disagree. Like many things my Father told me, I knew I'd see their wisdom in time.

"That's enough for now, then," he said. "You should begin your exercises. Unless you've need of confession?"

Lord, help me.

"I... do," I admitted in a strained voice.

He only nodded. "You were gone nearly a month. A transgression or two is disappointing, as ever, but expected. Give me your hands, son."

I reached out across the table and placed my palms in his. This was the only other form of contact allowed. And at least for this, I could feel the warmth of his hands.

It's unfortunate I had no good memories associated with these moments.

He put his thumbs on my pulse points and held my wrists, reciting the Relief of Burdens.

"God, hear through mine ears the willing testimony of sin from this, your son. Relieve him of the burden of bearing it alone and show him the way to redemption."

I waited, gave time for our prayers to be heard, and then spoke.

"I've woken the last four mornings to unsanctified and lustful reactions of my body, to thoughts of..." and here I paused, "... women. Whom I am in no agreements of courtship, nor am I joined by marriage to."

Father Helstrom did not seem surprised or nearly so aghast as I was at myself. He only nodded. "Continue."

I had little else, or at least little else I could bear to tell Father Helstrom. Which was blasphemy in and of itself. So instead of saying which woman I suspected had inspired my lust, I blurted out, "I… there was… sometimes I stain my smallclothes. God, forgive me… I cannot contain my seed—"

Father cut me off, at that, with a huff. "God… understands, Isidor," he cleared his throat. "You can be cleansed of this sin… by…"

I already knew.

"… joining brother Nicholas in the river and gathering clay."

I nodded tightly. I'd been right. God wanted that new cask house built, after all.

He released my hands, we said our final prayers, and then he stood, guiding me to do the same.

"Oh, and Isidor?" Father Helstrom said as I made to leave. "Strip down to your smallclothes today while you dig for clay."

I nearly tripped. "I… Father. It's—it's nearly winter."

"Your inner fire has always burned," he chose his words carefully, "hotter than most. Your passions need cooling. Besides. Best to put all that fur to use, no? It will be a lesson you will not soon forget. I want you to remember that chill whenever you think of this woman."

His eyes bore into mine on those last words.

He knew.

Oh God, he knew.

As I walked the cloisters, preparing myself for a long, cold day digging clay in near frozen water, the words in the letter tormented me. I didn't need to see it again to remember it. Perfectly. They were etched into my mind.

Young Templar,

I apologize to have taken advantage of your condition thusly, but I hope you are well now when you read this. I do not understand your Organization as well as I would like to, but you are no domestic House Templar, are you? You are some kind of Investigator. If that is so, please do your job properly and look inwards. Your Church has a history of theft that puts my paltry crimes to shame in comparison. I suspect your holy relic is not missing at all. It is precisely where they intend it to be.

- *Darcy*

3

WHERE DO YOU HIDE

The water was as cold as I'd known it would be, the current unforgiving and fattened by a sudden melt the week prior. My arms burned from the strain of the sifter and buckets, but my extremities were still fearfully bitten by the icy water. I may not have had the gall to complain as Nicholas did—loudly and for the entire duration—but my body was certainly lamenting the punishment it was enduring because of my transgressions.

But my soul felt cleansed, as it always did following the completion of repentance. I walked back down the staggered shadows of the Cloisters, outpacing Nicholas, who'd spent more time hunkered by the brazier than I.

And I considered my prayers for the day.

The Cloisters themselves had always felt more holy to me than the pews, even when I was listening to a sermon. Some might call that heresy, I suppose, but Father Helstrom once assured me it was not. We all worship and feel God in different ways, and I felt closer to God here, beneath these stone archways, than I did listening to recitations of scripture. After all, the Tome of The Faith was not God's word direct, but a mortal retelling. Only Canus himself and some of the Saints and Martyrs had ever heard God's voice directly. And I did not personally believe any mortal, no matter how pious and perfect, no matter how close to divinity, could be anything other than an echo for God. Distorted by our failings and sins.

That was, after all, the essence of being a Templar. Respecting and being subservient to the Order of the World—to the Pedigree, King, and Country, and the Church itself—while still understanding each and every single one of us, no matter our station, were broken and vulnerable to sin. Even Canus knew sin. And we all had to be accountable and willing to call it out within ourselves and in others.

That's why I didn't resent Father Helstrom's punishments, even when like today, they taxed my body so. I knew he would expect no less from himself, and I knew it was borne of love. He was the shepherd for my soul.

The icy water in my fur, what remained after my short rest at the brazier, had sunk so deep into my undercoat I knew there'd be no easy way to dry it. Very few areas of the Monastery were heated, so I decided that at least for the latter half of the afternoon I would remain in the Cloisters, since it tended to stay sunnier and warmer here during this time of day.

I found a bench and a position of comfort where I might begin my afternoon prayers and closed my eyes, listening to the pups and other young children playing in the garden. They were in between studies and chores, and there wasn't much to be done in the garden this time of year, so they were playing hide and seek, I think. I remembered many a winter afternoon spent this way in my youth. I was never very good at it.

I was hardly immersed in prayer for a minute or two before the chortling of children came perilously close, followed by the more distinctive patter of paws on cobblestone, and I was forced to open my eyes to greet the inquisitive face standing at the edge of the pathway nearest to me. I knew from her energetic gait and a brief but distinctive peal of laughter who it was, so I smiled despite the interruption.

The tan-furred, bright golden-eyed canine girl's features softened from her natural smile to one more demure when she realized I'd seen her. She dropped her voice to an almost-whisper, apologizing immediately. "I'm sorry, Big Brother. Have I interrupted your prayers?"

"You have indeed," I snuffed out through my nose, "but I can return to them momentarily. How fare you, Mabel?"

The girl's muzzle broke out into a happy grin, far more suitable to her. There was hardly a memory in my mind of the young lady where she wasn't wearing that exact same smile. She was an unflappable dandelion of sunny disposition, always finding reason for joy since she'd come to our doorstep seven years ago. A fact which was no small feat, given the life she'd led before that.

Mabel was an amputee, a street girl of mixed breeding with no known kin, and an orphan as far back as she could remember. Father Helstrom had brought her back with him after one of his trips to the coast, from which city, I knew not. If there were any more to the girl's backstory than that, I did not know it. And if she remembered more, she chose not to share it with any of us. But then for most of the children here, where we come from is not what need define us. It could be worth knowing of it, like in my case or Nick's, so that we could learn from the mistakes of our fathers.

But whatever had happened to Mabel to lead her here, it could not possibly be her sin to bear. She was a very young pup, then. Regardless what other men of the Faith might say, I could not imagine any reason God would punish a child. Her suffering was at the hands of men, no fault of her own. And she was certainly not letting what had happened to her limit her happiness or the light she brought into the world.

I was one of the eldest here for a time after my senior Brothers moved on to their postings or to further their studies elsewhere, so it was a normal part of my duties to look after and supervise the young ones for many years in between my own training and study. But my bond with Mabel was undeniably special. She'd been more quiet and reserved for her first year with us, still all smiles… but more nervous, clutching at the hem of Father Helstrom, unable or unwilling to speak to most anyone else. She was as skittish as a lamb, wagging her tail anxiously despite her fearfulness. Wherever she had come from, she had gotten by on those charms.

It had been my missing finger, of all things, that had ultimately piqued her curiosity and emboldened her enough to speak to me the first time. And since I'd told her the tale of how I'd lost it, Father Helstrom had not been the only one whose robe she clung to. She sat with me in the pews, would walk with her remaining hand in mine when we went to take our meals, and since I'd eventually outgrown the children's studies, she'd found every excuse she could to come visit me. It wasn't hard. We both lived in Ebon Gables, after all.

I couldn't remember the siblings I'd had growing up, but I liked to believe she was the sister God had sent to me. We had found one another in this place and filled that gap in our lives.

Mabel was thirteen now, and it gave me a lift in my chest that somehow warmed me despite the cold, seeing my little sister grow into a young woman. Literally, as well as figuratively, since I think she'd grown since I'd last been here.

"You're getting tall," I remarked with a light grin, remaining seated so she could be more at eye-level with me as she stepped up before me. Not even a year ago, she might have leapt into my arms after I'd been gone this long. But she'd begun etiquette training of late, and it had obviously had an effect.

"Not much," she insisted with an eye roll, tugging at the sleeve neatly folded just above the elbow of her amputated arm. She'd tied a bow at the folded closure, matching the one that adorned her neck. And I know she'd done it herself, so I made sure to point it out.

"Hey now," I said, pointing at it, "that's the ribbon I got you the last time I was posted, isn't it? I'm glad to see you're using it. Looks smart with that dress."

"I made the dress!" she exclaimed suddenly and proudly, pawing at the hem with her hand and showing off the... embroidery? Is that what it was called?

My eyes widened. "The whole of it? That's incredible."

"Well, Sister Clara showed me how to make the pattern and measure," she hurried her words along, "but I did all the work myself. I messed up a few things, but..."

I shook my head. "I couldn't have picked out a one. Looks perfect to me."

"Well, you're a man!" she giggled, like I'd said something outlandish. "You wouldn't know what to look for."

I gave a mock-offended whuff. "Are you saying I don't know how to dress?"

"*No,*" she insisted, far too quickly. She held in a laugh for about a second, before letting it out with a puff.

"I think that's exactly what you're saying," I said wryly. "How uncharitable. What a critical young lady you've become, Sister Mabel, mocking your poor, unfashionable Brother so."

"Did you wear *anything* other than the things Father Helstrom picked out for you on your posting?" she asked—nay, demanded—of me between laughter.

I had to think about that. At length, regretfully, I admitted, "No."

That got another bout of delighted laughter out of her, and despite the remaining chill and ache in my bones and the reminder that came with it of my recent failure, I felt lighter suddenly.

The Cloisters always brought me closer to grace. If not God,

I would frequently find my sister here. How could I ever yearn for more when I dreamed? *This* was my place of peace.

Her bubbly voice brought me back. "Your spats are tied backwards."

I glanced down my legs at where I'd hastily put my cloth coverings back on after we'd tried to dry ourselves at the brazier. Father Helstrom had been insistent that I work clad-down to my smallclothes in the freezing water, so I'd dressed myself in a simple robe lent by a monk and cloth spats, at least until I was dry enough to don my vestments again. I hadn't taken much care with any of my outfit, truth be told.

"You've caught me out." I cleared my throat. "I may not be fashion savvy, but I can usually manage at least a basic level of propriety. Apologies, Sister, that you are cursed to bear witness to my fat calf."

I leaned down to undo the lacings on my spats, when a familiar voice came from over my shoulder in the shadows under the awning to our left. My knuckle throbbed, and I stilled before completing my task.

"Re-lace them for him, Sister Mabel."

"Brother Dolus," I said, standing immediately despite the protestations of my sore muscles and the fact that I'd already begun to unlace one of my spats. I felt Mabel straighten and go still at my side as well, greeting the man properly.

The aged monk was the senior Clergyman here at Ebon Gables, pre-dating even Father Helstrom's appointment. He was a monastic monk, truly and completely having given himself over to the cloth and had been in service most of his life as far as any of us knew. Although in order to be a Clergyman and not merely a Templar, he must have had Pedigree lineage. He'd always looked to me to be a Lurcher—someone born of sighthound Pedigree and another unknown bloodline, although with a steely blue coat.

He was rumored to be younger than Father Helstrom,

although the specifics of his age were not mine to know. He'd been here the whole of my life though, and I'd long since learned to show deference to him in all ways.

But in this case, I didn't understand...

"I can manage, Brother," I assured him.

"No," he said insistently, approaching us so that he could incline his head to look over my shoulder and down at the young girl. "Young Sister, this is an excellent chance for you to practice what you've been learning from Missus Raleigh. Yes?"

"Oh!" she said, suddenly brightening. "Yes, Brother."

I arched an eyebrow, glancing down as Mabel fell to one knee and scooted forward a pace on the paving stone, so she was kneeling before my shins. I had to fight off the instinct to steady her with a grip on her shoulder, concerned she was getting her dress dirty despite the well-swept stone walkway.

"I don't..." I trailed off, noting a pleased smile from Brother Dolus. I was about to object to this exercise again, but he seemed to approve of what she was doing, so I let it go. "Missus Raleigh has been teaching the young girls?" I asked instead of what I was going to say. That had seemed odd to me from the moment he'd said it.

'Missus Raleigh' was a previous Sister here, closer to my age, named Mildred. She'd been here about five years with the other girls, until she'd married a man last year. He was a widower who owned a nearby mill the Monastery did business with. A good fit all things considered, even if he *was* nearly two decades her senior. He had children still in the home who could use a mother, and Mildred had always been a good caretaker with the children younger than she.

Mildred was, to my understanding, not very pretty. I was a poor judge, myself. I'd not ruminated much on the subject of beauty, at least not outside of natural splendor. But for whatever reason, she had not had many suitors from the time she'd come of age. I was glad for her that she'd settled somewhere comfortably. Everyone seemed happy for her.

"Missus Raleigh had been instructing the young girls—those unlikely to marry into homes with servants—in the art of housekeeping," Brother Dolus explained, "and the many other duties of married life."

I felt my spat laces loosen, and tried not to jerk away, my gaze again dropping to where my young sister was untying them one-handed, to set them right for me. It was but a paltry fabric shin-covering. Hardly improper, especially on a man. But something...

I could not articulate, not even in my own mind, why this unsettled me so. But it did.

"Laundering, organizing, and aiding her husband in his garb will be a matter of course for her and all of the girls here," Brother Dolus said, watching her work intently. I should have been too, I suppose. But I was having trouble with it.

"It will be harder for her, given her limitations," the old monk sighed, but continued looking on her fondly. "But see how she excels, despite it all? God had truly given you a servant's heart, Sister Mabel. You will be as useful a help-mate to your husband as any young woman, some day. Mark my words."

"Thank you, Brother," she said, flushing in her ears, as she began on my second spat.

White-hot guilt bit at my insides. I should have been happy to be of help to my younger sister while she practiced what she'd been studying. The same as I would be to spar with Nicholas or to study in the library alongside Father Helstrom. But something inside of me was curdling, an anxiety I could not seem to dismiss growing each time I looked down on her.

Brother Dolus eventually turned his attention back to me. "You returned from your posting last night Brother Isidor, yet you did not visit us in the choir yet today. I'm wounded."

I blanched and began to stutter out an apology before he gave a full-throated laugh at me. "Calm, calm," he assured me, "'twas but a jest. I know you arrived terribly late, and we've been in meditation most of the day, besides."

"Is something wrong?" I asked, suddenly worried.

"Brother Rolf is ill again," he said, almost dismissively. "It is nothing you need fret over."

"Ah," I replied quietly. I made a note to add Brother Rolf to my prayers, but the man's passing illnesses had more to do with the wine he peddled for the Monastery in town than any truly worrying condition of his health. He was a lay monk, though… so there was little that could be done to curtail his excesses, and no other was as skilled as he at bringing in buyers.

"I did hear you met the fabled 'Heart Thief,'" Brother Dolus said with a smile rounded at the edges with amusement. I briefly felt slighted by his somewhat mocking demeanor, then reminded myself that was just Brother Dolus's way. The other Brothers called him the 'merry monk', both in earnest and occasionally as a point of dark humor. "My young Isidor, the most pious and righteous of my flock of Templar boys," he clucked his tongue, "in his moment of weakness at the mercy of the femme fatale herself. That you returned to us unharmed and pious still, I daresay is a small miracle in and of itself."

"Done!" Mabel announced happily, brushing off her knee under her dress and standing, being careful to smooth the garment out as she did so. She looked very pleased at her work, so I tried to force a smile out for her.

"Thank you, Sister. Better than I could have ever managed," I looked back to Brother Dolus, lowering my voice. "What did you call her, Brother? That foreign phrase?"

"Ah, 'femme fatale,' not foreign but part of the old tongue from the southern countryside," he explained. "An attractive, dangerous woman, who brings disaster and even death upon the men in her life."

I thought of the woman in question, and again, as I had with Father Helstrom, could not put these disparate pieces together. But I nodded, all the same. She *had* been attractive at least, I supposed. Odd to think so of any woman wearing men's clothing, but I could not deny her physical composure and how she carried herself at least had been part of why I'd trusted her so.

"Our interaction was brief," I said with a sigh. "But I would agree that she got the better of me. I am heartily ashamed, but... undeterred. At the very least, I found her once. I will find her again."

"You sound quite certain," he noted, that smile still there. He looked once more to Mabel, giving her a nod and a pat on the head. "Well done, young Sister. Take care of your Brother here during his stay, yes? Keep practicing. I'm sure he'll be happy to be of use."

His eyes flitted back to me briefly once more before he turned to leave. "See me after we've taken supper, in the library, Brother Isidor. I have a new posting for you."

"So soon?" I found myself asking, then cut myself off before I said anything else impertinent. Brother Dolus was not merely the Senior Monk here, he was a Knight Templar himself. A monk sworn into the Brotherhood of our organization was rare, but it happened. It was a lifestyle for the truly devoted—those that eschewed the secular world entirely. No marriage, family, private property, or military titles, not even the title of Father within our own ministry. The only vow Brother Dolus had not undertaken was that of the Neutren, but Neutren could not be Templar, as the effects on the body were considered too diminishing for our line of work.

I knew little of his service or the role he fulfilled within our chapter, but even Father Helstrom crooked a respectful knee to him, and when orders came down from the Upper Ministry, they came first to Brother Dolus. His humble ascetic lifestyle here at the Abbey served him and the organization in some way, I was certain. I'd long been curious, but...

The inner machinations were not mine to know. All that was required of me was to respect the hierarchy.

The tall monk had spent the few moments following my uncalled-for questioning simply staring at me calmly, his expression as-ever hard to read, but seemingly patient, waiting for me to realize my mistake.

"I'm sorry, Brother," I corrected myself. "Of course."

"Very good then." He gave a brief smile. "Dry off, won't you? Father Helstrom's disciplinary tactics continue to perplex me. It does this order very little good to render our young, fit, painstakingly-molded agents ill with colds, coughs, or worse."

"It was repentance," I attempted to explain.

"He is too harsh," he declared, boldly but with absolute certainty. He waved a hand. "I know my boys, Isidor. You are no sinner. No more so than any young man and indeed less than most. Father Helstrom's strictness does him no credit... the man is... out of touch. There is no practicality in holding teenage boys to the impossible standards he holds himself to. And in any case, there's no need for repentance to involve such arduous physical punishment. Not at the risk of your health. We don't need clay *that* badly."

His words were a balm I felt I didn't deserve. He didn't know the reason for my confession. Or at least...

"Does," I tried not to stammer. It was wise not to stammer around Brother Dolus. "Did he make you aware of the nature of my confession?"

"Of course not," he nearly bellowed out a laugh, clapping me on the shoulder. "Your confessions to the Father are private, lad. I may know most everything that happens around here, but those are between you, the Father, and God. That being said..." He crooked an eyebrow. "You are nineteen. I could guess."

I felt my ears tremble, and I hadn't the strength to maintain eye contact with him. Just the possibility that I'd been caught out was bad enough, but the slight smirk he was wearing made my ears burn.

"Oh, no need for such humiliation," he sighed, patting my shoulder once more before turning again to go. "You'll marry soon enough, Isidor. Until then, a bit of *anticipation* is a very normal part of being a young man. There is no risk to your soul. Just hold to your vows, give confession when you feel you need to, and spend a little extra time in the yard when you feel the fires burning. Works wonders for me."

"Yes, Brother," I nodded vigorously.

"But not today," he called back over his shoulder. "Bloody hell, get yourself inside, lest you find yourself a-fevered. You get colds so easily..."

I watched him go. Brother Dolus often said things that contradicted, usually bending towards the 'practical'. The man was more learned in the scriptures than I, so I had to assume his years of study and education had given him different perspectives I hadn't the insight to understand, but sometimes his attitude was slipshod and out of sync with doctrine in ways that confounded me.

I wanted to listen to him in this case, obviously. Because it would make me feel better to do so.

But for many reasons, I had doubts.

The Library was no warmer than any other interior space in the Abbey, but the books insulated it some and the windows were closed to keep the damp out except in the dryer days of summer. There was a reading area at the far east corner with a few tables and lanterns, and some years ago, the monks had installed a cast iron stove. It did little to heat such a large space, but it provided just enough warmth in the corner that one could study in relative comfort, warm their feet, and even put a kettle on if they desired.

Truth be told, I had no stomach for the harsh black tea Father Helstrom allowed us to keep here, and I'd spoiled myself enough on good tea with cream and sugar at my last posting. In the fall we had cider, and spiced with cinnamon and dried orange peel, it was just about my favorite thing to drink in the world. But the idea of any food at all, let alone something so excessive, curdled my stomach today. With it came the bite of guilt, the knowledge of my failed weigh-in and a heaviness I could feel all-over, exhausting and dragging me down.

Or that could be from the hours I'd spent in the cold, digging clay.

God finds gentle ways to remind us of our failings, and it does us good to listen to them. I was not bitter at the order or Father Helstrom over the weigh-in and measure, however frustrated I was. It reminded me to keep myself in check, even if it *was* difficult for me. The burden of my dietary restrictions was a test and not a particularly harsh one in comparison with the trials many of the other orphans here had faced. It was important to keep perspective.

My stomach complained, rumbling angrily for about the fourth time since I had sat down. But I'd decided upon a day of fasting this morning, and I wasn't about to go back on that now. I sipped on some water I'd warmed at the stove and sighed as I set aside the field guide I'd been looking through, glancing to my left to a stack of unusual, slim, unbound reading material.

They were magazines from a locked closet in the Sacristy where Brother Dolus stored reading materials that were forbidden to the children, lay monks, and all but we Templar, really. I hadn't been permitted access to worldly reading until I'd been ordained, and even now I needed special permission to remove anything from those stacks. Thankfully the lay monk on duty today had hand-waved me through, assuming I suppose that he'd save us both the trip and the inconvenience of bothering Brother Dolus for something so inoffensive if… obscure.

I reached for one, sliding it across the table gingerly, the inexpensive, lightweight paper it was printed on yellowed and wavy, despite not being even remotely as old as most of the rest of our library. But these were not the well-bound, laboriously-crafted books our Abbey was famous for, or even something industrially-produced from one of the cities. These were cheap, common, tri-folded magazines meant to be lost and forgotten months after their printing.

The ink was browning at the edges and the few images on the first page were bled-through and rough, a poor printing from a small-town press, most likely. It had likely been crisper when new, but the stacks in the Sacristy were less protected from the damp. Along the top edge read 'Odeon's Lady's Book and Magazine – Amur Waistline Cinching and Pillow Embroidery in this Issue, From the Lower Leifolk Counties'.

I didn't bother unfolding that one, pushing it gently aside before beginning the laborious task of sifting through the stack. There were nearly thirty such magazines in total that I'd been able to find, all of them women's or fashion magazines and leaflets or books of patterns. They were popular in most small towns, sold at general stores or sometimes in parlors and boutiques, purchased generally by the lower Pedigree who were in trade. Often by Lady's Maids or seamstresses, which we'd long suspected the Heart Thief may have been in a previous life. She seemed to have a knowledge for etiquette that could only have come from time spent in service in a Pedigree household or a close personal relationship with someone else who had.

"This temptress has a knack for disguise," the gravelly voice of Father Helstrom came from the corner of the stacks behind me. He didn't surprise me. The man was a retired Inquisitor, he certainly could spy on me if he chose to, but he'd been polite enough not to do so. I'd heard him open the door, pace the center aisle, and heard the tap of his cane long before he drew close.

"Brother Robert told you what reading materials I obtained?" I guessed. I set the one I had in hand down and made to stand, to greet the man properly.

"You may remain seated, Isidor," the bloodhound assured me, approaching from behind and pulling out the chair to my left, settling down with a grunt of initial discomfort.

I gave him a sympathetic look. "Your back, Father?"

"Never you mind," he grumbled, settling his cane down between our chairs and reaching for one of the magazines himself, looking the bodice on the cover over with a barely-disguised frown. "The manservant routine she pulled on you wasn't the first time she's shown up somewhere in intricately tailored clothing that concealed her true identity so expertly."

"She wore it so smartly, too," I said, distracted, "as though she knew how to fit into the household. It suited her station."

"Disguises worn by less savvy thieves tend to be garish, ill-fitted, or cheaply-made," he rumbled in agreement.

"Hers was perfect, suitable to her role and obviously made for her," I blew out a breath, gesturing to the pile of magazines. "She either outfitted herself, or she had someone else working *with* her who did. Either way, it was distinctive, and garments like that tend to be regional. These have men's and women's patterns in them, for housewives and seamstresses. I'm hoping..."

"These are your free hours, so it is not my place to question how you occupy yourself," he said, "provided your studies concern only acceptable materials."

"I am permitted access to worldly reading material provided it concerns a case."

"Mnh," he grunted noncommittally. "You've always had an inquisitive mind, son. Which may serve you well as—"

"An Inquisitor," I said with a timid smile.

He gave me a very rare, wry stare. "Yes," he agreed, "only take care, Isidor. Leave the long hours of study to the monks. Over-education can turn you arrogant, lead you away from that which you already know to be true. Knowledge—or what purports to represent itself as 'fact'—is often the word of Academics or 'learned men' who've distanced themselves so far from the true Word, they cannot hear it any more. Being overly curious can lead one to question that which ought not be questioned by someone as pure as you. And *that* can lead to some of the very darkest corners of the world. Places I'd rather you never know."

"I am not afraid, Father," I assured him solemnly. "I'm prepared to do the good work, no matter its challenges."

He looked at me in silence for far too long following that. The bloodhound's wrinkled, aged face was always stern, his dark eyes always hard. But unlike Brother Dolus, he was no unknowable monument. I could tell he was worried.

"I know this is the path you've committed yourself to," he at last said with a sigh, "but I wish you'd consider a House posting, Isidor. There is no shame in being a House Templar. It is good work that must be done. Stable. Safe. You could marry, raise your family on your Lord's allotment."

"I am in no rush to marry," I assured him. This was the second time today my seniors had brought that up. I was only nineteen. If I were a woman, it might have made sense. But in my case, it spoke more to their concern that I'd stray from my chastity, and I didn't think a few dreams and one confession of impure thoughts warranted that.

"Besides," I continued, since Father Helstrom seemed to have no more to say on the matter. I reached for another of the magazines, sliding it over and unfolding a few pages until I got to the patterns section. "I want to see our great country and all of its counties. I want to meet many Lords and Ladies and many of the lower people before I settle on a posting. I think I'd even like to go south with the missionaries, if I've a chance at it. God has called me to this task, and He has given me the vigor and the opportunity to pursue it. As you did."

I glanced sidelong at him, hoping I'd not gotten too big for my britches there. "I speak too much of want," I said softly. "Perhaps I should rephrase..."

"No," he shook his head. "I don't think you're in the wrong to express your desire to serve God, Isidor. And I would agree; you've the right mind and the fervor necessary for the job. It does seem to be what you were put on this world to do. For my own part," he leaned back in his chair with a slight wince, "I think with time, experience, and dedication, you may indeed become a fine Inquisitor."

I smiled, flipping another page. My claws stilled over a roughly printed outline for a pattern beside an illustration of the finished garment.

"Which," Father Helstrom continued, "is what I told Brother Dolus just this hour ago."

I nearly missed the importance of what he'd been saying, absorbed as I was in staring at the illustration. I whipped my head around when the gears clicked in place though. "Brother Dolus? He was supposed to see me here—"

"He will not be ordering you to a new posting," the bloodhound shook his head. "He had intended to, but we had a chat. He has re-thought it."

"I... did think it odd that he had a new posting for me so quickly," I confessed. "It's unlikely she'll strike at another household so soon after a successful robbery; most of the previous thefts were months apart."

"The incense burner was hardly a good get for her," he tapped his claws on the table, "but you're not wrong. She's more careful than that. No, Isidor. Brother Dolus's intention was to send you back to the Hudsons. Permanently."

"Wh—" Now I did stammer. I turned in my chair. "The Heart Thief has never struck the same house twice, that would be lunacy. What would be the point?"

"The point," he said evenly, "was to assign you a permanent House Templar position. And considering your failure to protect their artifact, I'd say that means you made a particularly good impression on the family, son. Templar Olvar is unwell and has been for some time. He has a failing liver."

"I'll pray for him," I said automatically, but my words came out tight. Not because I wasn't earnestly concerned for Templar Olvar. He was a nice man, had been sympathetic to my condition in the past in fact, and we had several good conversations about the family. He had never mentioned his troubles.

But I was concerned with where this was going.

"The Hudsons need us to assign a House Templar to replace him," he said, confirming my fears. "They liked you."

"I failed their family," I said, hanging my head.

"They liked you nonetheless," he said, tipping my face back up so that I was looking him in the eyes. "The Mistress of the house was impressed by your manners, the young Lady felt safe with you, and the Lord felt you showed proper respect the whole of your time there. And there is some argument to be made that your decision to keep the relic in your quarters may have protected any other valuables it would have otherwise been stored with. Your presence there may have dissuaded the Heart Thief from violence, as well. Templar Olvar is in no condition to guard a house and hasn't been for some time. As robberies go, the damage to the family and the household was minimal."

His gaze sharpened. "They may also feel your failure gives them leverage, Isidor. A debt, if not a written or legal one, but a debt of shame. A boon they may hang over the head of their House Templar."

My chest clenched at that, and my stomach soon followed.

"That suspicion, more than anything," he said evenly, "is why I denied Brother Dolus. He may determine postings from this Abbey, but you boys are still *my* wards. The Hudsons are not a good fit for you. Both for the aforementioned reasons," he tipped his muzzle to make sure my shameful gaze was firmly rooted back on his, "and because I know it is not what you want."

I felt my muzzle twitch upwards a bit at that, despite how disappointed I was. Brother Dolus had tried to reassign me. Not just from one posting, but from pursuing the investigation into the Heart Thief entirely. That would have essentially derailed my whole career before it had even begun and relegated me to the life of a House Templar. For good.

"When you expressed an interest to sign on to this particular investigation," Father Helstrom said, long-sufferingly, "I objected to the idea on its face. You have *no* experience outside the Abbey save the few temporary house postings you'd taken to fill in for... weeks at most, at a stretch—"

"I learned more across four counties than I would have had I been stationed at only one," I said pointedly. "You traveled extensively when you were young."

"Yes, Isidor," he clipped back, "but I was not pursuing an elusive thief and *murderer* when I was barely twenty. I was unearthing paltry indecencies—affairs, mostly."

"You went to war when you were twenty-one," I said quietly. "Across the world, even."

"And I thank God every day my boys do not need to endure such a horror," he said with a quiet growl in his voice. "You live in more peaceful times, Isidor. That is a *blessing*."

"I found her!" I said, louder than I should have. Not a shout, but close enough that one glare from Father Helstrom immediately quieted me to a whisper again. "I found her," I repeated.

"By chance."

"No, sir," I said insistently, tapping one of the magazines. "Because I studied the relics in the previous cases, I think I've established a profile for the sorts of art and artifacts she is likely to target. The incense burner was in an exhibit some months ago and recently moved back to the Hudson Estate, so it seemed possible she'd been made aware of its existence; we knew she was last seen in the Eastern area of the country, and she tends to hit country estates and Pedigree families that move within the same social circles as the Equestrian Show Circuit."

"There were about three guesses in there."

"But she *did* come after the incense burner," I said, trying to keep the tremble out of my voice. "She *did*. This is the closest anyone's gotten in over a year, and I got physical details, I was *inches* from her, you said yourself—"

"Yes," he said, curling his nose, "you found her. And you lost her, Isidor."

"I could find her again," I insisted vehemently.

"Someone is going to capture her in time," he said. "The information you brought in will help assure that. I'd be willing to write your letter of recommendation for training *now*, on just that, and I think you'd even have a good chance of acceptance on that alone." He gave me a steady look. "But that won't satiate you, will it, lad? You've been enthralled by this case since you were seventeen. This isn't just about field experience for you. Is it?"

I held up the magazine. I couldn't see his expression past it, not until he curled a clawed finger around one corner and took it from me, his long ears brushing over it as he held it closer to his face to read the small text and diagrams. "What is this?" he asked.

"It's a pattern," I said, "for a leather-braced men's corset. Common amongst tradesmen who stoop for a living. You see where it supports the back?"

"Hnh," he grunted. "I don't think I could pull it off, unfortunately."

I almost snorted through a cut-off laugh, a reflex with Father Helstrom. Although in this case, I think he'd actually, truly been *joking*. And if not, that was somehow funnier.

I liked that in the moments we spent just the two of us, my Father let his guard down somewhat like this and would speak to me more as a fellow than my better. It was rare and required no audience, but it felt as though he'd begun to see me more of late as an adult and was treating me as one.

"No," I managed to guffaw out, "it's not… it's what *she* was wearing. When I met her. I got a *very* close look."

"Son, with all due respect," he looked back up at me, handing the magazine back, "you are not a *fashionable* man. I did not raise my boys to concern themselves with such things. How can you tell one corset from another? Save the fact that it's cut for a man, which—odd though it may be—is not as uncommon as you might think. There are far too many overfed gentlemen in the world who desire to suck their guts in through any means."

"The Heart Thief's corset had one shoulder strap," I said definitively. "Look."

Father Helstrom narrowed his eyes and leaned down to stare at the pattern again. After a spell, he lifted his muzzle back up, looking directly at me. "That *is* an unusual cut."

"I took little note of it at the time," I said, "but it stood out in my memory, afterwards. It's a style particular to one county. In fact, to one town. The ball where it was popularized is in the margins there."

"Alconavale," the bloodhound said, tone gone contemplative. "The lakes. Town by the name of Whyslein? You think she has some connection to this town."

It wasn't a question. In fact, he sounded certain, too.

"These magazines never circulate far," I said, "and in the Lake Country, a woman like that would stand out. All those small townships. If anyone has seen her, it won't be hard to catch her scent."

"What makes you so certain she'd return there just because she had some connection there previously?" he asked.

"I'm not certain of anything," I admitted. "But she just got something she was after, and she knows a Templar got a close look at her. She knows we'll be on the hunt. Alconavale is a good place to go to ground. Especially if she's got roots there."

"You could be wasting months chasing ghosts," he warned me. "And I can't give you any more than your usual travel allowance. You won't be on a posting either, so you won't be earning income. At some point, you need to begin to plan for your future family, Isidor."

"This woman *stole* the Heart of Faith," I said emphatically, careful to keep from raising my voice again, but *Lord*, it was hard. My passions rose every time I spoke on the theft of our holy relic. The entire reason our Order had become involved in this case, and my own personal awakening to her existence, was because of that heretical offense. The very reason she'd earned her signature name and rose from the ranks of petty burglary to inflaming the hearts of the entire Templar Order.

"There is no greater calling for me," I said softly, but passionately, "than this investigation. This is what I am meant to be doing with my life right now, Father. The Parish agreed, clearly. They have given me leave. Brother Dolus at the very least permits it. And now, more than ever, I must make penance for my past failings. Please. Father."

The aged bloodhound looked to the ceiling for a few moments, closing his eyes.

"Please," I reiterated. "I can find her again, Father. And this time, I will not fail."

"Failure is not the worst outcome here," he reminded me, gravely. "She has killed Templar before, Isidor. Never forget that."

"I know," I nodded. "'I shall never boast such arrogance as to claim I am fearless, but stand firm despite my innate weaknesses, for I am but flesh, but that flesh is the bearer of His blade.' "

"Your skill with a blade may not be your most important asset in a hunt like this," Father Helstrom said, his gaze softening for an instant. "Your finest weapon is your cunning. Moreso than I think most would assume, given your temperament."

I tried not to puff up, but compliments from Father Helstrom were a rare gift.

"Keep your wits about you, listen to your instincts—they will avail you most of all—and rely on your tenacity," he finished, still sounding unsettled, but leaning back in his chair, he looked resolved.

He wasn't going to deny me this chance. I had his leave.

"Inquisition work is dark, dirty, and thankless," he said in a low, far-off voice. Despite that, when his eyes fell on mine again, they were sharp as ever. "I wouldn't have chosen it for any of you. But you clearly feel a calling, and it is not my place to question what God has put you here to do."

4

THE HEART THIEF

I was seventeen when I first heard of her. The Heart Thief.

I was in the Choir, assisting Brother Dillard and Brother Adam in the twice-yearly painstaking task of scrubbing the grout. It was a job my diligence was well-suited to, and the other lay monks were happy to have the help each year. I found it a relaxing task, unlike most. Satisfying. Making pure and pristine what had previously been dirtied and sullied.

If only life were so simple.

Back then, we didn't realize the thief was a woman. The series of burglaries, some of which had reportedly ended violently, even up to and including the death of a housekeeper, and eventually two from our very own Order, had led to the obvious assumption that the thief would be male. And indeed, when I heard the Brothers speaking on the subject of the theft, they knew little more. A feline man. Foreign, most likely, although we'd since learned—and I could confirm this personally now—that they were either born and raised in Amuresca or had voice-trained to have no hint of any foreign accent. So, someone of foreign ancestry who'd been born here, most likely. Or a young transplant.

The Templar Order had very little information on the feline thief until they'd come for one of our own relics. Investigating burglaries, even from estates and private collections, was hardly our mission, after all. Unless the items stolen had been taken out from under a Templar's own nose, which had happened in a few of the cases but was hardly the norm, we were unlikely to even hear of it, let alone concern ourselves with it. Our priority was the health of our Pedigree and our Nation's souls and the protection and sanctity of the bond between the Church and the powerful elites who ruled the Country. Our people were stronger when both arms of Amuresca were linked hand in hand, thusly.

Meddling unnecessarily in one another's affairs could tip that balance, foster resentment, and make it harder for both of us to fulfill our roles within society. So, for some time, the Heart Thief's crimes went beneath our notice. Local law in the many different regions she'd struck in may have known of her, or at least known a skilled thief had made a target of them, and Pedigree families had begun to gossip about the bold thefts and trade stories of the man they imagined would be responsible... but all of this may have remained as it was, in disconnected accounts, if not for the crime she eventually committed.

The Heart of Faith was one of the most well-known relics of our Church and had been the final stop in a holy pilgrimage that had spanned over a thousand years, culminating each cycle on the solstice. In all that time, it had never been moved from the humble Abbey on Mount D'Amur, a mountain that was in truth little more than a large hill in Amurfolk. The grounds surrounding it and most of the adjoining townships were Holy Land. The First Parish. We'd gone once as children. I was young at the time, but I remembered walking through the ancient hanging gardens with Nicholas. We weren't permitted to enter the Sacristy to pray before the Heart, but Father Helstrom and Brother Dolus had been.

I'd hoped to pray in that Sacristy once I was ordained. But by then, it was gone.

The Heart of Faith was an iron tablet, circular and hardly larger than most dinner plates, cast from the melted remains of the head of the spear that killed Canus himself, wielded by a pagan warrior in the First Holy War. After his death, the spear had passed between the tribes of the savage Kadrush, a proud testament to their viciousness and revulsion for the True Faith. Even to this day, they had not grown closer to God, by their own design. They remained a country of barbarians, faithful only to their false pagan gods and feral spirits.

Our Church had reclaimed the spear one thousand and thirty-one years ago (the history of the relic had become a subject of fascination and study for me since its theft) and in an attempt to cleanse the weapon of its sin and remake it into an object of worship that would bring hope, instead of anger and war, it was melted down and re-forged into the Heart of Faith.

The inscribed iron tablet was written in Ancient Amuraic, in a cuneiform alphabet very few monks were literate in, in this age. But the illustrations and etchings I had of it included a translation: a short Psalm written by the monk who'd inscribed it, and the Seven Edicts of The Faith.

I would often recite the Seven Edicts to myself in Ancient Amuraic when it suited me or when it was particularly appropriate to remind myself of them. I may not have been able to read the ancient cuneiform, but I knew some of the old tongue, especially prayers I'd committed to my heart.

Now was one such time.

The Fifth Edict of the Faith was 'Presa lacriste bona maedal verducrisolum'. 'The wolf shall not covet what is beyond his due'. The meaning was simple—'the wolf' referred to in every Edict was an ancient pronoun, a series of symbols in contention amongst scholars, in that it was likely meant to refer to all subjects of The Faith, not merely canines, let alone only wolves.

But the Ancients of a thousand years ago had less ways to refer to peoples aside from canines, at least in writing. So, all persons were 'wolves' in the Seven Edicts. At least, that is how I chose to interpret it and also how most other learned men did. To do otherwise excluded all other races from the Edicts, and that was counter-productive.

The meaning, as with most of the Edicts, could vary by interpretation. And that, too, was by design. The Edicts were meant to be called-upon in many stages of life, by many peoples, in more situations than merely the most obvious. To 'covet what is beyond his due' could mean not to desire that which one has not earned, or not been blessed with. Wealth, privilege, beauty, fame, etcetera. It was not forbidden to want and aspire for more within the Faith. Aspiration had inspired betterment and ingenuity in men since time untold. But to want beyond your due, to say… resent the wealthy, the status of the Pedigree, or the God-gifted talent of another, was a destructive impulse that was injurious to the fabric of society, instilled no value for hard work and diligence, and often led to violent or covetous actions.

For instance, theft.

And it would avail me little in my own trials, as well. Such as wishing for a more equitable situation than the discomfort I was currently experiencing, traveling in a slow-moving, lurching, reeking stagecoach. Whispering holy scripture to myself, especially that which was relevant to my particular state of distress, was a means of keeping my mind centered.

It probably gave no comfort to the six other passengers traveling in the coach with me, overhearing a large, imposing, armed man mumbling in repetition to himself in Ancient Amuraic. But—and I know this was uncharitable of me—some of their consideration for my own well-being had been lacking, as well. So, I gave myself that minimal allowance.

A heavyset, large terrier—a traveling salesman by the look of his briefcase—had been puffing on his pipe near feverishly the entire trip. Honestly, I wasn't sure how he hadn't made himself sick on the amount of tobacco he'd been forcing all of us to inhale for the last ten hours. It had most likely contributed to the troubles of the other small mouse fellow beside him, who had to beg a sudden stop three times already today to be sick on the side of the road.

And a fourth time, when he had not quite made it.

Across from the three of us sat a family of four. Mixed-breed retrievers, I think, but it hardly mattered. The wife was frail and thin with a noticeable baby paunch still, trying in vain to keep her youngest, a newborn pup by the look of the both of them, from shrilly whining on *every* bump. God Bless her other child, a little girl barely three or four by the look of her, for helping her mother to try to keep the newborn calm. The father was of *no* help, hissing and snapping at the poor woman as though there was anything more she could do to control her baby. They looked to be a family in trade who had fallen on hard times. They had two chests loaded in the back, likely all they owned. I couldn't say what troubles had befallen them, but I knew I'd be praying for them later that evening.

Most of them, anyway.

I had an excellent seat on a horse and would infinitely prefer traveling in saddle over coach travel, regardless of the coming winter. Unfortunately, it just wasn't feasible for me to afford feeding a horse or pony on the small stipend I received from the Order while I pursued this investigation. I was fortunate enough to have been given the honor of this assignment at *all*, and I knew that was on no merit of my own, but because I was in the intermittent period between my Ordination and the rigorous training I'd undergo once I was accepted by the Ministry of Inquisition, and the Order currently had little other use for me. Father Helstrom seemed to think I'd be accepted by the Ministry if I applied now. I was less certain.

This was a rare time of free study in my career within my

Order, and I intended to spend it pursuing the case that had lit the fire inside me to become an Inquisitor in the first place, whether my investigation bore fruit or not. There were, of course, many other more Senior Templar pursuing the Heart Thief across Amuresca, or so Brother Dolus had told me. And I hardly thought myself above them.

But I had a *lead*.

A lead I had repeated up the chain numerous times now over the last month to no avail. I'd taken to the lake country after barely a few days home in the Abbey and had been following sightings ever since. The last town I'd stayed in had been a place called Gloury and was little more than a carriage house, a Church, and a few farmsteads. But there were *five* sightings of her there that I'd been able to confirm from all the staff at the carriage house. She—or someone who bore a startling resemblance to her—had stayed the night. She'd been wearing her male disguise in order to travel alone, but I knew better than to let that deter me. I'd even asked to stay in the same room to see if I could catch her scent remaining there.

No luck, there. They had already cleaned the linens, and while the room still had the inklings of a feline that tickled at the back of my nose, she'd either masked her scent, changed her scent enough to be unrecognizable, or I was on the trail of the wrong feline.

But that couldn't be it. I was more certain now than I'd ever been. The Equestrian Show circuit was some kind of key in how she moved through the lake country, I was sure of it. There was too much overlap to be otherwise. Between the accounts of her I'd found by paws-on-the-ground canvasing, to a string of suspicious carriage lockbox thefts, culminating in a burglary at a private art showing at a Pedigree's country estate, it all seemed to orbit around the Show Circuit. Young Lords had little else to do in the lake country in late autumn than show off their Dressage skills, after all.

It made sense. The sport competitions meant small gatherings of elites in relatively rural locations, where house guards would be minimal. A guaranteed route to follow if one were in the market to rob the idle rich and slip into their confidence at gathers where hangers-on that were unknown previously to the estate would not raise eyebrows. The Heart Thief could conceal themselves as a lady's maid, a coachman, even a groom for the horses.

And so, upon traveling said circuit, I had eventually caught her trail. Or so it seemed. A slender cat with tall ears, black-furred or spotted intermittently, although I had to attest the greater number of spotted sightings to the obvious—such a pelt being more likely to stick out in peoples' memory. Smartly-dressed or at least neat and tidy when she deigned to pretend at being poor. A low profile, but quiet and polite to the few who remembered sharing a conversation with her. She was not overly gregarious, never brazen or rude, but always went leaving a decent impression of herself in the minds of those who'd seen her.

She was a dove. Commonplace, easy to ignore, but pleasing to take note of. Even one of the Pedigree ladies whose trunk had been burglarized remembered her fondly, never the wiser that it was the demure feline at market whom they'd bought apples from who had pilfered their purse and key. I don't think she'd put the pieces together even after I'd spoken to her. She only mentioned remembering the feline because I'd asked, and then wondered aloud if she may be someone to question... someone who may have seen the ruffian who'd pick-pocketed her. She was convinced it was one of a group of young rat lads she seemed to remember as suspicious.

I did not want to believe that I'd fooled myself, that I was, as Father Helstrom warned against, chasing ghosts. My every suspicion confirmed I was on the right path, and while I would never be so bold as to claim He was directly guiding me, I felt an affirmation in my soul every time I heard a new account of her. It made something in my chest lift like my body was tumbling, my breath coming shorter, faster… I just *knew* I was growing closer in this chase… could all but feel my quarry, the distance between us shortening…

If no one else in the Order thought what I'd found was compelling, so be it. I would do this alone. Father Helstrom's concerned and obviously irritated letters were coming rapid-fire these days, attempting to recall me home. He was nearly my only contact with the Order that was consistent though, other than my check-ins with a few Parish Priests and one House Templar at the country estate that had been burglarized. And he seemed dubious that the criminal had been who I claimed she was.

A sudden yelp snapped me out of my reverie, and I thought at first it had been the pup, but it sounded too mature for that. I flicked my eyes open and glanced up from where my rosary was clutched in my left paw.

The wife was shying away from her husband, and I didn't miss the way his hand was extended briefly before retreating back into the folds of his coat. I hadn't seen whatever had happened, but the body language was clear.

The terrier blew out another long puff from his pipe, and the mouse continued to look sick. Neither remarked on whatever had occurred between the married couple.

Neither did I. But I stopped praying and started counting the miles instead. By the road markers, we were close to our destination. A sizeable town called Wrenwarren.

I was unsettled. Uncomfortable. Frustrated. And wound too tightly from the weeks of being on the chase. I'd also been having trouble sleeping on the road, in unfamiliar spaces and around a constantly-shifting daily schedule. As well as… other persistent nighttime troubles.

But that was no excuse.

It felt like we'd slowed down to a crawl for that last stretch, but at length, finally, salvation. The coach came to a clattering, jerking stop—and then another start—and then another, final, stop. It was dusk light outside, the flickering lanterns adorning the front of the hectic-sounding carriage house we'd pulled into casting a smeared glare across the windows. I had gotten nothing but a blurred look at the town when the doors finally swung open and fresh air, light, and freedom beckoned me out.

Fresh-ish, anyway. The first overwhelming scent was fresh... manure, charred cooking, and the ever-present undercurrent of soot from chimneys. And the wind that buffeted the door to nearly clatter closed again was bitterly cold, far more so than I remembered any night prior on this trip so far. Winter was making an early arrival this year.

Tucking my cloak to the side, I let the mouse hurry past me, nearly stumbling over my legs in his haste to get outside. I wasn't certain if he was just eager to be out, or about to be sick again and I wasn't keen on finding out.

"Little vermin didn't make this trip any more pleasant for the rest of us, now did he?" the terrier huffed from behind me, his bulk making the seat creak as he stowed his pipe, finally.

I gave him a look that I'm certain did not conceal my incredulity, before murmuring a quiet but audible, "Thy sins are a projection, as stained-glass colors the face of the scapegoat."

"More bloody choir nonsense. What are you on about?" the man asked distractedly as he struggled into his outer coat. "Move then, would you? You simple?"

I turned and shouldered through the door, finding my footing on the step-down and ignoring any more grumblings from the man. The coachman and his auxiliary driver were already unstrapping luggage from the back of the box, so after a quick moment spent soaking in the luxury of being able to stretch my legs, I moved in that direction to collect my few belongings.

The one travel bag I carried was a leather saddle bag with versatile straps that could be let in, adjusted, and converted to a traveler's pack. The shoulder straps hooked directly into the Templar harness, which was something of a mark of office for us. We all wore variations of it, most carried a weapon or two on it as well, but primarily, it was for this. We were outfitted to travel at a moment's notice if need-be, and our vestments were a testament to practicality, honed by centuries of missionary work back when that was the norm, before the idea of House Templar had been formalized.

Templar were Crusaders, now and for all time. We were meant to travel and bring the Word.

Of course, Templar of old would have done so on horseback. Not a box coach.

Adjusting the pack took a matter of minutes; I'd been doing it since I was ten, so I was rather proficient at it now. Still, it delayed me long enough that I unfortunately witnessed what happened next.

The tradesman's family had two large, and by the look of them *heavy* trunks, slicked with cold rain from hours ago and stacked beside one another on the back of the box. Once they were unstrapped, the auxiliary coachman left, leaving the exhausted couple to unload the trunks themselves.

The husband managed with some obvious strain to heft the one, his shoulder sagging with the weight, but the wife seemed more hesitant. I watched her shift her swaddled pup carefully against her chest and shoulder with one hand, while she began to ease the trunk by the handle towards the edge of the platform to pull it down.

That was about all I could take.

Concern overriding my reason, I strode forward and extended a hand to the woman to gesture at the trunk, raising my voice over the background din from the busy evening street to say, "Pray, let me help you with that—"

I must have startled her, and with good reason. I had spoken too loudly and too suddenly, and from behind her no less. Her shoulders tensed up, she sucked in a shrill breath and stumbled back a pace, surprise or panic compelling her to shy away from me as she had from her husband earlier.

In the process, she let go of her grip on the trunk, and unbalanced… it fell.

Thankfully it didn't fall on her feet, or anyone else's. But it thudded down onto the wet, muddy street and tumbled onto its back, whatever was inside it no doubt being tossed around. I didn't hear any noise that suggested it held anything fragile, but it *could* have. And the mud puddle was certainly doing the trunk no favors.

The latches had stayed clasped, at least. Which was the first thing the canine woman checked. She knelt down to place her free, trembling hand—trembling from the cold, I hoped, and not from the accidental fright I'd given her—over the closure to make sure it was safe.

I began to bumble out an apology, but anything I could have said was cut off when the woman's husband turned from where he had been setting the other trunk down on the drier area of cobblestone and snarled a furious, "Hell's *teeth*, you test me today. *Worthless!*" He stormed forward, reeled back a palm—

And he hit her so hard her legs came out from under her.

I was not wanting for propriety, but for God's sake, she was holding a newborn pup. I acted before I could even consider otherwise, easily catching and steadying the woman by the shoulder and arm, bending to a crouch. She was still reeling, snuffing out in obviously pained shock through her battered nose, her pup shrieking in fear where it was still clutched to her shoulder. I tipped my muzzle down for just a moment to make sure the babe was safe—he was, she had a tight hold on him—before turning my attention back to the man.

He had stalked over us, and while before he'd seemed angry,

now he was virtually boiling over, the accumulated infuriation of the day roiling out of him when he spoke.

"Take your hands off of my wife!"

The baffling lack of self-awareness in his words wouldn't occur to me until much later. Although by the law, he could handle the disciplining of his family in the manner of his choosing, there were *limits*.

"Leo, please," the woman begged, tugging away from me and scrambling to stand again. I, of course, released her. "The trunk is fine, it's just a bit of mud—

"I'm not talking to you, slag!" the small man snarled past his fangs. He went to shove her and roar something else in my face, but the woman tried to grab at his arm to pull him away, and he easily shook her off. This time, I had no chance to catch her.

The pup was still held steadfast in her one arm, but she lost her balance. She fell, mostly on her hip, splayed to her side in the mud now beside the trunk. The man was shouting something again, but there was too much blood pounding in my ears. My body was hot, my extremities absolutely lit up with the desire to *move them*.

If there is a way to contain these fires when they rage in me, I have not yet found it.

I moved in front of her as he stepped towards her. He may have simply been wanting to pull her to her feet; I'd never know. He found his path blocked, he stomped forward despite it, and swung out an arm. I think he had been trying to shove me aside as he had his wife.

It was enough.

I was no skinny young woman clutching an infant to my breast. I raised my own arm concisely in between his bicep and chest, tipped him off-balance with a slight press, and swung my other fist up in an arc to belt him in the muzzle.

I had meant to stun him, but I was less than precise, and I probably put more into it than I should have. The day had frayed me around the edges, and it would be dishonest not to admit some part of me wanted to hurt this man.

At least three people audibly gasped or shouted in alarm on the street beside us, and I swear I could feel the eyes of people watching us from their second-story vantage point above in the carriage house.

The man crumbled to the ground clutching at his muzzle, a splatter of spittle and blood beside him on the paving stone. I flexed my fingers and huffed out a puff of steam into the frigid air, trying to calm myself. I held back from doing any more and didn't bother with words for the man. I would not have been eloquent had I tried.

His wife moaned worriedly and went to her knees beside him, hunkering close and turning towards me with unshed tears in her eyes. "Just leave us *be, please*!"

I blinked at her, stunned and finding myself gesturing uselessly at the man. "He—"

"*He* is my husband!" she cried—truly cried, she was sobbing now—at me. "My children's father!"

"I'm sorry, ma'am," I found myself saying, licking at my cold, dry muzzle. "Are you—"

"I asked you to leave us be!" she said again vehemently, petting back her husband's ears. He was coming to; he hadn't been unconscious only stunned, and while he didn't look gravely injured, he wasn't handling the blow to the nose as well as his wife had.

Well. She likely had more experience.

"We want nothing from the Church," she said, trembling. "What good are you?"

I gathered my cloak around myself, willing my body to move through the rigidity of my suddenly cooling blood. "Blessings on you and your family," I murmured out quickly.

"What good are your blessings?!" she demanded of my back as I retreated.

Shutters clattered overhead, signaling even the onlookers had beaten a hasty retreat, the small crowd that had gathered parting as I moved through them. All but the coachman, an old, graying badger who seemed oddly unaffected by the happenings. He stood beside the larger of the two dappled horses that been pulling the coach, calling to me, "He swung first, lad. I'll tell the peace officers that if they come asking around."

"They won't," I said quietly, making my way towards the carriage house door. The coachman was either essentially lying or hadn't gotten a good look; you could claim many things about what had happened, but it would be a stretch to say he'd swung intending to strike me. Either way, the badger was telling me he'd bear false witness. Which didn't comfort me.

It wouldn't matter. The man I'd struck would never bring this up with the town guard. He had sat with me long enough in that box to have something of an idea who and what I was. And no one in his current situation would have the means or wherewithal to bring charges against a holy man.

The knowledge that I would suffer no punishment whatsoever for my moment of anger, coupled with the intense relief I felt at having expressed it and a selfish inner voice that sung, practically jeered, 'retribution!' had my stomach curdling. I was so worn-down by the ordeals of the day that I temporarily forgot my quarry almost entirely, foregoing my usual ritual in each new town of questioning the carriage house staff first. I'd tried to make a habit of it, since discovering whether or not the feline had stayed at one of the few places in town open to non-canine travelers was the most important question to address, first thing. If she'd been through very recently, it meant I was close.

I was in no hurry to get back on the road, so there was probably a part of me that hoped I'd chosen the wrong town again. Her pattern of movement was akin to the veins on a leaf, darting sporadically from place to place, but always inevitably following the central vein—the Eastern Post Road. If not here, I'd catch her trail again soon.

And I was exhausted. I climbed the stairs to my little room on the second story, and shed my vestments and accouterments like they were thrice as heavy as they were. As I folded and stowed them in the room's small footlocker, I briefly considered whether or not it would be worth it to dress in my laundered clothing to go down for dinner... and just as quickly dismissed the thought. I was too tired. My throat was scratchy from what I feared might be a cold coming on—Brother Dolus was quite right there, I was dreadfully prone to them—and the scuffle outside had spoiled whatever remaining appetite I may have had.

I dug my rosary up off the end table where I'd lain it down when I was dressing, unwrapped the coils of it and draped it around my neck, and stiffly settled down on my knees to begin my evening prayers.

I ended up praying for every soul who'd shared that carriage ride with me today. Even the husband. Lord knew what troubles that family had faced. They needed help. God willing, they'd get it.

That night, I found myself not in the crumbling, unfamiliar church that had been the meeting spot for many of my confusing nightly interludes with the Heart Thief... a far-too-frequent denizen in my dreamscapes of late. But instead, a wistful, insubstantial place. I was indoors, that much at least I could tell. There was a window, and through it I caught glimpses of the moon.

Waning, Waxing, Full, all three stood in stark relief in the sky. At the same time. The moonlight painted the contours of the room in violet twilight, white near the edges where the twisting folds of sheets hugged tightly to the bodies entwined beneath them.

My figure, my body, I realized, was outlined beneath. Of course it was. I was in bed… had been in bed. I was sleeping. Wasn't I?

Except this wasn't my tiny room at the carriage house, with the sloping ceiling too short for me that I'd had to duck under earlier that night. Nor was it the single bed too small for my frame, that I'd knelt beside to pray. In fact, the size of the space I lay in seemed to shift to accommodate, going on until it touched the walls. The entire room, the entire space, molded around us, the sheets had no corners, the bed no dips or edges.

And I wasn't alone.

Panic gripped me and sunk its claws in, and despite the inherent lethargy and seeming peace of the scene I found myself in, that panic did not recede with time. It grew, blooming inside me, a rose whose vines were wound tightly around my heart. Half-remembered scenes played out on the walls, fuzzy around the edges like the block-printed ink illustrations inside the fashion magazines I'd studied.

I saw her in those etchings as though they were projected on the walls, wearing the outfit that had led me here, to these counties. The ink lines traced the contours of her cheeks, her muzzle, her ears. They clotted at the tips of long lashes as she turned to regard me in that crumbling church. Some of the memories were real, I vaguely thought, plucked from our time spent near the dovecote. Some of them were probably from other dreams.

Dreams. I was dreaming. This wasn't real. So that meant…

The figure that lay obscured beneath the sheets, curled and clutched around me so tightly. It was probably her. It had to be her.

It was *always* her, these days.

I could not will myself to wake, and lying there staring down the expanse of our sheet-wrapped forms, unable to move and knowing, *feeling* her there, certain it was her… it was agony. A month now, I had spent doggedly tailing her between hamlets and tiny, unfamiliar cities, a month now on the road, a stranger everywhere I went, alone with my obsessive thoughts, pursued by my Father's anxious letters, all to find her *and now she was right here.*

It was wish-fulfillment, I knew. I could always find her in my dreams if not in the waking world, but why, God?

Why, in this way?

Why was she warm in my arms, her fur tufted between my fingertips, her breath on my collarbone, coming out in steady, slumbering puffs? Her muzzle tucked just enough beneath the covers that I would need to pull them back to see her. To confirm what I already knew.

She was nude. We both were. I didn't need to push off the clinging sheets to know it. I could see it in the jut of her hip where one slender leg was wrapped about my thigh. I could tell by the feel of her arm, looped around my chest, petite fingers splayed across my ribs. I could feel the subtle prick of her claws, extending for a moment as she twitched in her sleep.

She smelled like the honeysuckle that always inevitably overgrew in the orchard each year. Like spring. These dreams, her body wrapped around mine now… they were as inexorable as the changing seasons. Bursting through every crack and open window, clinging to every surface like the fragrant pollen that would dust the covers of the books in the library and find its way into your fur and cling there.

She was *right there.* All I needed to do was pull back the sheets. Here, at least, my chase was over. Even if it was all wrong, even if *this* was wrong, could I not experience that moment of exultation? Here, I had caught her.

Here, she was mine.

. . .

I awoke with a sucked-in gasp, and the very first thing I did was fling back the tangled sheets twisted around my lower half and legs. I sat upright, panting and blinking blearily in the dark, the dream's edges at last receding, dissolving into the waking world. The lavender faded into dim orange and black, what little light illuminated the cracking paint and sloping edges of the small room coming from the narrow, clouded window that faced a street lamp outside.

It was still night. I knew not when, but... full dark.

Bracing myself, my eyes traveled down my body, past the steady rise and fall of my furred chest to my legs and the balled-up crumple of sheets and a threadbare comforter. The stove pipe that ran through this room—its only source of heat—had gone cold when the kitchens below went dormant for the night. The room was frigid.

But my body felt hot. Stiflingly warm, in fact, so much so that I could not stop panting.

I groaned out loud in frustration when I glanced at the state of my smallclothes. I had so few opportunities to launder my garments on the road, so I was glad at least that I hadn't soiled them again...

... but the state I found myself in was... obscene. And unfortunately, a common occurrence these days. All but guaranteed when I had these dreams too, which regardless of Brother Dolus's assurances, made me terribly anxious to reflect upon.

It was a maddeningly stubborn condition, and beyond being horribly injurious to my decency should I need to *go* anywhere, it made me feel great physical discomfort the whole of the while I was forced to endure it. At least on the rare occasions I spilled my seed in my sleep, the issue went dormant swiftly afterwards.

When it was like this, I was often... to put it bluntly, *stuck* with it. For some time. And there seemed to be no rhyme or reason to when it would give up the ghost. Nor any remedy for the condition that worked reliably. Cold water splashed in my face might help, and morning exercises could chase it away. Prayer had proved useful once or twice. But nothing worked every time. Not even all three.

I swung my legs over the side of the small bed, scrubbing my palms back and forth up over my muzzle and forehead. I considered and then dismissed several verses I might try, but my mind was still tangled up in the dream, and recitation of anything coherent may have been beyond me. I mumbled the opening verse of Saint Gerard's Prayer for Forgiveness once, twice, the remnant dying on my tongue before I could really get underway.

I didn't deserve forgiveness.

"Oh Lord," I mumbled into my hands, "what is wrong with me? Please deliver your servant some clarity. Guide me, I beg of you."

Something flickered across my eyeline. Rubbing my eyes again and letting my paws fall into my lap, I squinted across the room. It was barely larger than a closet, so there wasn't much to see. My bag, the hook on the wall my harness and weapons were hung from, the footlocker my clothing was stored in, the door, and the strips of dim light coming from underneath it. There was a lantern in the hallway right outside my room, lighting the way downstairs to the privy for all the upstairs guests.

Why was the line broken?

I blinked, trying to be certain I was seeing correctly. But, yes. The thin line of light beneath my door was broken in two places, about evenly-spaced apart. My memory from the night before wasn't entirely clear, but I recalled taking note of the lantern light because it was so bright. I'd worried the illumination coming in under the door might make it difficult to sleep.

Someone was standing outside my door.

Right outside my door. Needlessly close, in fact, unless they were about to knock or were pressed against it for some reason—

I sprung to my feet so fast I forgot how low the sloping ceiling was. My skull collided with one of the wooden beams overhead, a pained bark leaving my muzzle before I could entirely quash it. Sparks danced behind my eyes and I shook my head a few times, getting my bearings.

The shadow behind the door shifted and changed, and then I heard it. Not footsteps beating a hasty retreat, as I imagined I'd hear after making that much noise. No.

Quiet, muffled laughter. Almost whispered, breathy… and brief.

Then footsteps, although hardly in a rush. Soft paws, padding off down the hallway. To the left.

I clicked my jaw shut, shook the daze off one last time, felt my drill training kick in and strode across the room purposefully, eschewing my vestments save the pair of trousers I'd left hanging on one of the coat hooks in the room to dry off the damp. I was shouldering into my harness before I'd so much as finished buttoning up. I could don my harness in less than half a minute when I was focused, and I think I got it done in twenty seconds this time, including affixing my long knife's scabbard. I threw my surcoat on over my shoulders as I unlocked and opened the door, moving out into the hallway while still pulling my arms through the sleeves. But if I was about to go outside for any reason, I needed to have some measure of decency.

There was no time to really consider my state of disarray, not with the reality of someone *spying* on me being all but confirmed. Was it something to do with the altercation in the street earlier? Something benign, like the children of the family who ran the carriage house, sneaking about at night?

Frightfully late for that.

I went left down the hallway, which was not the direction to the staircase, since my room was closest to that. It was the cheapest… being the loudest and so close to the lantern, so of course I'd taken it. The hallway to the left led to nine other rooms, some small like mine, some presumably larger based on the spacing. There was one other lantern down at the distant end of the garishly wallpapered walls—peonies in colors that even I could tell did *not* work well together—and a weathered, faded carpet that only barely masked the squeak of the floorboards beneath it, as I slowly made my way down.

The hallway was dimly-lit, but I still would have seen someone if there were anyone there to see. Had it taken me long enough to arm and dress myself that the person had somehow come back and made their way to the staircase?

No. I would have heard that. I'd had my eyes on the light under the door the whole time, and the stairs were, as aforementioned, loud. Whoever it was, they'd come back this way and gone into their room.

For just a moment, I felt like a fool. Ungodly hour or no, it must have been a child, playing in the hall. Or a peeping adult, I supposed. Why had I been so certain this was dangerous or worrisome enough that I needed a weapon on me? If I ran into someone in this hallway right now, obviously armed and with my surcoat gaping open to my bare chest in the middle of the night, they would justly think I was a madman.

At the very least, my… 'issue' from earlier had receded. The pain from striking my head on the ceiling had seen to that. Solution found, I suppose.

As I drew closer to the end of the hall, I saw that one of the doors, the one to the left at the very end, was ajar. By at least a few inches. Warm light pooled out onto the dusty carpet and a strange scent grew stronger the closer I got.

Some kind of... ink? Dye? I'd smelled something like it before, I was certain of it...

I gasped aloud then clenched my teeth shut and took the last few strides towards the end of the hallway quickly. I moved swiftly, but tried to be as quiet as I could. If I looked like a foolish madman barging into someone's room in the middle of the night, so be it. I was a bloody *Templar* on a mission, I'd make my apologies later if need be. But if I was right, and I turned heel now to fully dress or get my other things, whoever was *in* there would have a chance to escape. And that was a chance I simply was not willing to take.

I stopped only when I reached and boxed in the doorway, pressing my side to the doorframe and leaning slowly to tip my head inside.

It was... a room. More spacious than mine; I'd been right about that. The bed was still made, the linens and furniture looked similar to the ones I had in my own room, so hardly much of an upgrade for what they'd been charging downstairs. An oil lamp was lit on the desk, beside a small stack of books that still seemed to be bound up in a leather strap, likely from however they'd been packed in a travel case. An ink and quill sat beside them, indicating whoever was rooming here, they'd had some intention to write earlier. It didn't look like they'd gotten to it.

There were no bags or coat hung on the hooks near the door, I took note of, scanning my eyes across the nearby wall. But their belongings *could* be in the footlocker. The remains of a crust of bread and... ugh... fish bones from a presumed dinner sat on a plate, neatly covered by a napkin, likely waiting to be picked up by servants in the morning. And beside it, a small bottle of country wine, half-empty and re-corked.

I eyed the footlocker again. It was the only place in this room that anyone, conceivably, could be hiding. There were no closets, and I suppose someone might have been able to wedge themselves under the bed, but that would be tough, by the look of it.

Tentatively, I took a step into the room. And then another. I pulled my blade, shifting it to a backhand position for now, tucked to my side and nowhere near where it could harm someone if I were surprised. It would be far worse to make a deadly mistake here than it would be to be caught unguarded.

The door slammed shut behind me.

The lock audibly clicked into place.

From the outside?!

"Ciraberos lon ecriste!" I swore, turning on my heel and flinging myself against the door, landing with a pound of my fist, while my other hand tried in vain to lift the latch. It wouldn't budge.

A voice, muffled through the thick wooden door, came directly from the other side. *Inches* away from me.

"Is that Ancient Amuraic?" A pause and a soft, husky laugh. The very same laugh I'd heard in the hallway earlier. "They educate you as well as indoctrinate you, do they? How well-rounded."

Her *voice*. God have mercy, I didn't realize how badly I'd wanted, *yearned* to hear it again. The cadence, the breathy depth of it, her affect resting somewhere between confident and careful. When we'd spoken in the garden, it had been so centering, so calming... like a well-orated sermon. I could understand now how she'd lulled so many into a false sense of security.

My quarry, my prey, the Heart Thief, stood on the opposite side of this door. I was utterly certain from the moment the first words left her mouth. I would not forget that voice for the rest of my days.

"You reversed the lock..." I gritted out in realization, noting the blank latch plate on my side. There were scuff marks along the edge of it as well, and uneven paint suggested the mechanism had been carefully tooled off before it was removed and reversed.

"Mnh," she hummed a confirmation, and I felt the door I was pressed against adjust a hairs-breadth, groaning almost imperceptibly. "It took hours, actually... double-acting pin tumbler lock, corroded but high quality for a carriage house... quite the effort. Manor homes could take note, they seem to value their guests' security here."

"'Hours'?" I parroted back. She'd been planning this for hours, somehow?

"Well, that included a few minutes spent picking the lock next door, so I'd have somewhere to wait while you took the bait. And moving my possessions."

She was leaning against the door, I realized suddenly. She was standing in the hallway, inches from me, *leaning against this very door!*

I released my useless grip on the door handle and pressed both of my palms, then the side of my face flat to the solid oak. It was impossible of course, but I swear I could almost feel her body heat, the outline of her, where she had her back to it.

I knocked my fist against the door once, not bothering to pound again, but listening for the sound it made. Thick hardwood, meant to keep out the sound from the hallway to allow the guests here a better chance at sleep. They really *did* care about guest security here.

"Please don't hurt yourself on my account," her voice came again. "You're as likely to break yourself as you are this door, taking it down by force. At least I'd assume so. And in any case, I'll be gone and the whole house will be in uproar by the time you've managed it, if you even can." A pause. "Although now I wonder at the feat of strength that would take. Do you think you could do it, young Knight? You look like a very strong fellow. It would almost be worth seeing."

"Don't toy with me," I growled out, backing away from the

door a pace to give the whole of it another once-over.

"I wouldn't dare," she said so softly I barely made it out. "I'm not so cruel as that."

To be honest, she was probably right about the door. I think I could take it down if my life depended on it, but I'd be as likely to break a bone or dislocate something in the process as succeed. Might still be worth it…

But if I failed to catch her afterwards, I ran the risk of being too injured to travel. Or worse yet, recalled by the Order. And as things stood, if I could find a way out of here, I could still catch up to her. Even with her having a head start.

If the windows in this place weren't so small, I'd consider scaling down to the first story from here, cutting her off at one of the exits. But they were barely big enough for me to put my head through.

Frustration welled up inside me as the reality of my situation truly hit. I'd been right. All these weeks, I'd been *right*. I'd *found* her. I'd been tracking her and some of those sightings had been real, and they'd led me here, right here, to her. In a nondescript carriage house in the middle of unfamiliar countryside, with no local contact with the Order, no Pedigree House to back me like I'd had with the Hudsons, and Ebon Gables a week away by post, at the least.

She was right there. It was really her, not a rumor or a sighting or a dream, this time. I was *this* close to affecting an arrest and…

And she'd locked me in her bloody room.

Images from the most recent dream came unbidden, maddeningly. It was like she'd been made manifest, but I was *still* being kept from her.

I stalked in a circle around the front of the room, my voice coming out in more of a growl than I had intended, but I could hardly help it. "I can help you!" I said insistently. "I'm not looking to *hurt* you, lady, but others may not be so kind—"

"Your name is Isidor, isn't it?" she asked, cutting me off.

My fur prickled at the back of my neck. "You..." Right, the Hudson Estate. "You bothered to learn my name? Why?"

"To be honest, I did not realize you weren't the official House Templar when I first arrived at Hudson Green," she used the name for the Estate itself. Interesting. Showed a knowledge of the area, or at least that Estate in particular. "But it did not take me terribly long after seeing you on the grounds to deduce you were not 'Templar Olvar,' the aged Coon Hound who spends most nights at the town pub. I thought it best I learn the name of the striking young Knight the family had acquired in case it became relevant. I had no idea then *how* relevant it would prove to be."

"I am no Knight," I ground out, moving back towards the door and pressing my palms and forehead to it again, wishing in vain for the wood between us to disappear.

"I do not understand the differences in title within your Order," she confessed. I could hear that she had turned her head, as though to regard me. I could all but picture it. That long neck of hers tipped to the side, whiskers against the wood. Was her fur black right now? Had I imagined the scent of that dye? Did she have one of those big ears pressed to the door to hear me better? As I did?

I closed my eyes. I wanted to be an Inquisitor. I should not have been answering her questions, she should be answering *mine*. She showed no signs of wanting to leave yet. I needed to make the most of this. She seemed to want to talk...

"Knight Templar have served our Nation at War," I explained, keeping my voice measured. I even dropped it in timbre, not wanting to wake anyone else on the floor. That would *certainly* spook her. "I have not. There are other ways to be Knighted, but I am far from worthy of that honor."

"You look young," she said, almost placatingly. "I'm certain you're already an honorable man, it will not take long for the powers that be to realize that."

"You have not caught me in my finest hours," I confessed. "Either time we've met, now. So please, do not embarrass yourself or me by offering false flattery. It does neither of us any credit."

"You can hardly help a weakness of constitution you were born with," she said, then her voice turned honeyed, concerned. "How are you feeling, by the way? Are you quite recovered?"

"I am well," I confirmed, feeling a little mad having such a pleasant 'market street' conversation with the murderous burglar I was attempting to arrest. "Thank you. Those reactions never last very long; I fully recover from them in hours, generally."

A huff, maybe half a laugh. "I meant knocking yourself on the head earlier, actually."

I tipped my ears back. Of course she'd heard that. I *knew* she'd heard that.

"I didn't mean to startle you," she continued before I could respond. "I had intended to knock to get your attention, but then I heard you talking in your sleep, and it was far too intriguing not to listen in."

"That's rather rude of you," I pointed out.

"Oh, I'm aware. Curiosity got the better of me. But to be fair young sir, you've been looking into *my* affairs as well, of late. So, I'd say we're at least even."

I didn't bother to argue the obvious point—namely that she was a *criminal,* and I was trying to bring her to justice. Accusatory language might chase her off, and there was more to be learned here. Keep her talking.

"What..." my mouth went dry, as again, memories of the dream rose unbidden. I'd been talking in my sleep? "What did I say?" I asked, trying to keep my voice from faltering. "In my sleep?"

A pause, and when she spoke again, her tone was very

obviously delighted. Amused. "What are you *worried* you may have said, choir boy?"

"I certainly don't know," I protested weakly.

She laughed again. "Calm, young sir. Prayers, I think. That's what it sounded like."

"Ah." So, either I'd been praying in my sleep or she'd overheard me once I'd woken up. Regardless, we were talking about me again, not her. She had a way of turning the conversation back around, despite my best attempts. "So, you're aware I've been looking into you…" I began.

"Well, you're here, aren't you?" She sighed. "Unless you're touring the lake country for the fall season, I must assume you're chasing me."

"Investigating you," I pressed because it sounded less threatening to me.

"I didn't realize it was *you,* until tonight," she said, "but I knew I was being followed. What would you call that, if not a 'chase'?"

"Fine, but there is no need any longer," I splayed my palms on either side of the door at about the height her shoulders had been when last we'd met. "I've found you. Now let me help you—"

"Why do you think you're not worthy of honor?" she asked suddenly. "You spoke so poorly of yourself before. I'll admit, I learned little about you from our time at the Hudsons." She hummed again, like she was considering a memory. "Except that you train diligently in the morning… for hours… regardless of the weather. You were a polite houseguest, according to every person I spoke to. You are clever at your job because you managed to track *me* here, somehow. How, I have not deduced yet, and that is worrisome."

I gave her no answer to that, obviously. She was trying to prompt information from me, same as I was her. But I was discovering I was learning more by simply letting her talk. So, I did.

"And all of that aside, you put propriety and, I daresay, your own dignity at risk just last night to defend a woman I can only assume was a complete stranger to you," she said. "All very honorable and praise-worthy behavior for a young man. I think most would agree."

My ears burned, my breath hissing past my teeth. I closed my eyes and leaned more heavily against the door. "You saw the altercation in the street." Of course.

"From up here," she confirmed. "You cannot *imagine* how alarming that was. I had an inkling someone might be tailing me, a few times, but to see *you*? So suddenly? This far from where we first met?"

"If I'd asked around about you as soon as I made it in," I

choked out, trying and failing to keep the sunken sensation in my guts out of my voice. "I would have *had* you."

"You'd still have to catch me, church boy. Don't make that sound so simple."

"I found you once," I said, sliding a palm over the weathered wood, my claws clinging at the top of the door frame. "I will again."

"Why did you help her?" she asked. "The canine woman with the pup on her shoulder? No one else even spoke up, let alone involved themselves like you did."

"For all the good it did," I muttered bitterly. "I left those poor souls worse off than they would have been had I not interceded. It was wrong, what I did. Not my place."

"Then why did you do it?" she pressed.

"I was trying to do what I thought was right in the moment," I answered bluntly, even though I knew it was an insufficient answer.

"Violence may not have been the right course of action," she said. "Why didn't you arrest *him*? Turn *that* man over to the law? You can do that, right?"

Her question was simple… yet complex. But there was an easy answer I could give her that was at least impersonal. "He hadn't broken any laws I can think of," I said flatly. "Nor committed any sin worthy of taking him in to the Ministry. It was a breach of propriety and a humiliating spectacle he made of himself and his family, but not punishable under any law of man or God."

"Then why," she took time with her words, "did you *punish* him?"

I clenched my fangs together. "Because it was wrong," I uttered, at length. "What he did… was wrong. And I couldn't bear witness to it and do nothing."

"Hmmm," she affirmed softly and far too slyly for my liking. She'd gotten something there, something she'd *wanted* out of me. And I didn't like that I couldn't discern what exactly it was.

"Darcy," I tried using her name. Maybe it would have some effect. It probably wasn't real, and I wasn't even certain if it was her first or last. But it didn't matter. It was what she'd called herself. "I don't know who you are, were, or what troubles you've had that have led you to this life, but please believe me when I say I am prepared to listen to you, to offer you empathy, and moreover *salvation.* The darkest places in life come before the dawn; there is *never* a fall from grace so far that you cannot climb back up. Canus did not surround himself with perfect men and women, he kept company with the lost and the broken. We are all on a journey of redemption. I am reaching for you, I am *trying* to offer you that hand… it is far too hard to stumble through that black night alone."

"Have you given thought to what I said in the letter I left you?" she asked. "Did you even read it?"

"Of *course* I read it," I said breathlessly. Aghast that she'd think I might have missed it or ignored such a critical piece of information freely given by her. "I used your name, did I not? How else would I have known it?"

"You speak so passionately," she said, the admiration in her voice so palpable, I could hear it even through the door. It sounded real too, but who knew. "You are fervent about what you do, aren't you?"

"You mean my service to the Templar Order? Of course. It is not a commitment I take lightly. It is integral to how I show my love for God," I proclaimed unashamedly. "He is my salvation, and I live to serve His Kingdom in the manner in which I am most suited for. This is my calling."

"That regrettably brings us to cross-purposes," she admitted. "But I won't deny, this does seem to be your calling. No others have gotten so close as you, not for years now. Are *you* alone? Are you hunting me on your own, young Templar?"

Don't give her that.

"Tell me where the Heart of Faith is, and I'll stop hunting you," I said, the deception slipping from my muzzle easily. We were permitted deception in pursuit of our work. God understood. "That is all the interest the Order has in you. Help me return the relic, and there will be no need to arrest you."

"I cannot," she answered simply.

I tried to remain stalwart against the ignition of my anger at her stubborn resistance. "Are you unable to or unwilling to?"

"One or the other, take your pick," she said flippantly. "The answer is 'no' regardless."

"Damn you!" I bit out, my control slipping for a moment, as a wave of hopelessness again crashed over me. My temper was getting the best of me. It had been a *long* day, and I'd gotten little sleep.

"Language, young sir," she tutted.

I bit the inside of my cheek, focusing on the pain to steady myself back to a reasonable tone. I only half-succeeded.

"Whomever you've sold it to or hidden it with," I reasoned, "it *cannot* be worth the pain you are causing to literally millions of faithful innocents who will now be denied their pilgrimage. Whatever your endgame, it is not worth your eternal soul—"

"You are passionate about this particular investigation," she said suddenly. Defiantly. "Yes?"

I snarled, but pressed out a quiet, "Intensely."

"I do not know you as well as I'd like to, young sir," she said, "but 'intense' does seem to suit you."

"Get to the point."

"Do your job," she said, and I felt the weight of her lift away from the door. "Pursue this relic. Investigate its theft. But leave me *out* of it. While I've enjoyed meeting you and talking with you, I would not wish for us to come to blows. And that seems inevitable if we keep running into one another, unfortunately."

"You must know where it is!" I growled. "Don't play coy."

"Do not follow me," she said, and even away from the door, with her voice muted, I could hear it had shifted. Colder, more solid, almost bordering on commanding. There was a hint of a growl in it. "I won't be tortured and locked away by your Church. Next time, if need be... I *will* defend myself."

"I am not afraid of you," I bit out.

"I truly do hope you find what you're looking for," her voice began to fade. I didn't hear her footsteps, but I knew she was leaving. "The books are yours to keep. The young mistress of the Hudson Estate said you liked to read. I think she was rather taken with you, truth be told. But I know you Abbey boys aren't permitted to read much good literature. Those are a few of my favorites. Consider them a parting gift. What little apology I can offer for all the wasted effort you've gone through to find me."

"Darcy!" I called out, slamming myself against the door.

The hallway was silent.

5

INTOXICATED DREAMS

Dear Father,

I know I am sending letters ad nauseam now, but you must forgive me for taking up so much of your time. I need to make Confession and I cannot do so at any Church near to my current location that is approved by the Ministry of Inquisition for disclosing sensitive information. I am thereby relegated, once again, to doing so via post.

My last letter was hastily scrawled the morning I lost her, and I was not able to afford a swift Registered Courier, so I hope it made it to you safely. Despite my humiliating failure to capture her at the carriage house, I had assumed that in a few days' time, I'd be well on her trail again and not delivering you further bad news. But regrettably, that is not the case.

As I write this, I find myself lost, sheltering from the elements with little to no coin to my name in the loft of a dilapidated barn. Additionally and most shamefully, I have allowed myself to fall intoxicated on country wine while reading worldly literature I am certain you would not approve of.

God finds ways to humble us when we grow arrogant. You always said that.

Pray, let me explain.

From the moment she left me there locked in her room, I set about making as much noise banging on the door and the floors to rouse the servant staff as was possible without actually risking injury or destroying my accommodations. As you are well aware, I can be a loud man when I want to be.

Despite that, perhaps because I was in the farthest room from the servants quarters below on the lower floor, and additionally the carriage house was apparently not fully occupied, it took far too long for anyone to show up with a set of keys. My rescuers were one of the sleepy-eyed maids and an aged, large boar who I think I later found out was the cook, playing bodyguard for the lady with the house keys likely because they were concerned I was galloping drunk or otherwise not of sound mind.

Once released and after hurrying to my room so that I could show my Ordination Patents, the nightmare continued. Apparently, in my dazed rush to pursue the Heart Thief at a brisk clip, I had left my own room unlocked. And had the fabled burglar taken advantage of my carelessness and made off with my own meager valuables, you might ask?

Yes. Yes she had.

I haven't much coin to my name as you know, but the remainder of the allowance the Order granted me in pursuit of this investigation, she took. My entire coin purse was gone, as well as my patents, and the few other bits of investigative material I'd gathered. Thankfully, I did not have her letter on me. I'm very glad I passed that off to you and Brother Dolus when I did.

Most of the rest of what she'd made off with were magazines, some from our library back home, others I'd gathered as I'd traveled, trying to discern anything more I could about this area and how it might relate to her. She had also taken my prayer book, and while I'm grateful at least it was not my Tome of Faith... that remained untouched, oddly... my prayer book is where I've been journaling. The loss of it wounds me nearly as much.

None of my scrawlings concerned the case, or the Heart Thief, or anything significant to the Templar Order. Please do not worry yourself there. You impressed upon me from a young age to commit nothing to writing that could be compromising to the Church, unless it be sealed and sent either up the chain from on holy land or mailed with an approved Courier, as this letter has been. Your caution and the edicts of the Order have been prescient—which I'd imagine is precisely why they are so—in preventing what could have been a disastrous turn in this investigation.

My prayer book was more of a personal log of my favorite psalms, prayers, and conversations with God, as well as my musings about my faith and the meanings behind certain passages. Many of the things I've scribbled about in there, I have only shared with you or the other acolytes, if anyone. It isn't that any of them are particularly scandalous or defaming... I just think a few of my inner thoughts are profoundly stupid and not worth sharing.

Still, all of that aside, I cannot work out why she might have taken it. The magazines make sense. She's clever; she'll likely deduce they were how I'd known where to look for her. Without my patents and my coin, I've had trouble traveling or asserting my authority. But why my prayer book? It's so intensely personal and unconnected from the case —from her—and it's valueless. Has she simply taken it to hurt me? To offend me?

I will bear its loss well enough. I'd written it off from the moment I found it missing, and I have more pressing concerns than mourning the lack of it. She'll probably destroy it when she realizes it provides her nothing of value or simply discard it. It is regrettably gone forever. That's that.

It's not that it doesn't matter to me. I've spent countless hours filling its pages, musing on my life, and exploring the nuances of passages from the Tome I seek clarity in understanding. The reality you are burdened with—that I do not avoid Confession, not even through omission or across great distances—is a point of pride for me. But we are permitted some private thoughts on doctrine.

That book has been a place for me to explore my faith and ask myself questions. It was only ever of any value or importance to me. I can't imagine what she wants with it.

I made haste from the carriage house initially, thinking I might be able to use sightings in town to discern which direction she'd fled in. The road there only forked twice and the woodlands in the lake country are treacherous without a guide. Additionally with the weather being as miserable with sleet and cold as it has been moving into winter, it didn't seem likely she'd take off on foot.

But she'd left in the dead of night, and accounts of anyone matching her description leaving town were naught to be found. Only a few night watchmen and a street cleaner were even out at that hour, and not a one had seen anyone traversing the road, other than themselves.

That left me to either take to the roads on foot—a useless gesture, although one I still considered—or speak to the drivers staying in town, to see whom she may have gotten a ride with. I occupied myself in the interim hours stopping by and rousing the local Parish Priest and his two live-in curates. They hardly knew what to make of me, but rallied themselves admirably despite the impossible hour and were willing to hear me out. I met with some expected incredulity considering my story and my lack of papers, but the engraving on my blade and my vestments saw me through. I'm not certain I would be able to assert my identity or station using similar methods outside the realm of holy men, though. I need my patents. Please tell me where I might go to have new papers drawn up.

The Parish Priest, Father Dalton, was very kind to me, providing me with an early morning meal and eventually a mule for my travels. It is all they had to offer and more than I deserve, but pursuing my investigation any other way at this point would have been impossible. Without my coin, I will be depending on the kindness of similar small country Parishes as I travel, at least until I can make it to Redcoven and a Ministry-affiliated Church.

The mule is a tiresome beast and none-too-fond of being ridden, but I've managed to wrestle control of her. I returned to the carriage house once dawn rose to speak to the drivers. One of them, the badger who'd been my driver the day before, was eager to be of service. To put it bluntly, I think the man's life is a bore. He was a world-weary man who did not fluster easily. I suppose you see most everything in his line of work. He took an interest in the dispute the night before, and he was very happy to speak with me over his breakfast.

He at once dispelled any notion I might have had that she'd taken a carriage, at least any that ran the major routes and had reputable drivers. He could name every one of them, and more importantly who had been in town the night before or morning thereafter. He assured me no one had left the carriage house yet. There was an abrupt dead man's turn on the mountain path to the east and a bridge prone to washing out to the west—no one would leave in the dead of night, he assured me. Even extra coin wasn't worth losing a horse, getting lost, or worse.

I dared not hope she was still in town, hiding herself away or sheltering with an ally. I reserved it as a slim possibility in the back of my mind, but set to canvas the town to find out if there were any other means of transport she might have found her way to. And in time, I discovered it.

It took a good portion of the day, but I eventually found myself at the doorstep of a family of polecats, a mother and her three children. I'd been referred there because apparently the husband of the house was known to have a small, single-person buggy he used to ferry goods back and forth between a town not ten miles away. In areas like this, many tradesmen and families are connected, so a short-range courier is probably a lucrative career. His buggy wasn't meant for two, but a polecat and a lean feline may have been able to squeeze into a seat that had doubtless been designed for canines.

And sure enough, when I got there the wife confirmed it. According to her, a wealthy foreign heiress who 'may have been runnin' from a man'—her words—had commissioned her husband for a goodly sum to bring her with him on his trip that morning. Which meant I knew where she was headed.

Unfortunately, my mule has no chance of catching up with a buggy. I set out that very night, determined to make up for the time I'd lost somehow, and in my rush failed to consider two very important things.

One—I have no food. Water, I had made sure I'd brought along. The well in town was free, after all. But as for food, I had only the breakfast in my belly from the Parish. I could—nay, should—have stopped there to get a loaf of bread before I'd gone. But I was impatient and eager to be hot on her heels again.

Two—every hop I've taken before has been with a driver of some sort. I don't know the countryside. Couple that with a chilling fog and washed-out roads, and late into the night, I had to accept the reality that I was lost. I'd most certainly been riding for more than 10 miles, but I hadn't found the hamlet the buggy rider was bound for. I stopped near an old, dry bridge to rest my eyes until dawn light, then set out again.

Daylight did not avail me, and I continued to travel the game trails and rustic roads that criss-cross the rugged countryside out here until it began to sleet. Exhausted, frozen to the bone and hopeless to make any more progress in the poor weather, I sheltered in the first haven I'd seen for miles.

A decaying barn.

And that brings me to the present moment. The loft of the barn turned out to be full of fresh hay, which was a welcome surprise. What's more, the fact that it's still in use means I might not be as far from town as I thought. It's hardly warm, and the hay is stiff with frost and jagged to the touch, but it is a blessed refuge nonetheless. God is looking out for me.

I wish I could serve Him as faithfully as He deserves. But I am constantly grappling with my own poor decisions and failings of character, and I fear I am unworthy of the blessings He grants me. It is a constant trouble.

I am not certain what possessed me—I couldn't sleep, that I remember, and I thought to take out the few things she'd left for me in that room. Ink and a quill, which was odd, but came in handy penning this letter. Three books, all of which were worldly stories, of course. I didn't recognize the titles save one, 'The Admiral's White Claw'. I've seen it in the Library at the Abbey before... and yes, I know it's restricted reading to any of us in the Clergy.

But I felt certain the books she'd left me might hold some kind of meaning to her or to the case. And if there was anything to be gained from investigating them, one worldly work of fiction here or there is hardly going to shake my faith.

The next part, I am far more ashamed of.

At some point into the night, after having consumed a good deal of the shameless and perversely indulgent story therein—a high seas romance between an Amur Admiral and a Kadrush snowcat woman apparently, filthy, just pointless tripe—I became of a mind that the only other possession I had of Darcy's, the half-empty bottle of wine, might alleviate my hunger and warm my body.

I know I am not forbidden alcohol, but I've considered a vow of sobriety just based on the evils I've seen it concoct in others. I've had very little besides beer. And I've never liked it.

I think I might like wine, though. I've had it in cooking before, and I've sipped on the Abbey wine, but this is... different. It's some kind of country wine, and it's thicker, headier, with a sweet aftertaste like honey.

I lost track of myself, just glad to be putting anything in my stomach, and before I knew it, I'd drained what was left in the bottle. That didn't alarm me until a short while ago. I'd thought half a bottle of country wine would be no issue for a man of my size, but apparently I do not handle my drink well, or perhaps because I had no meal with it, I don't know...

I am completely certain at this moment that I am too inebriated to get down from this loft. I lit the lantern on the lower level before I came up, and I had intended to snuff it out before I slept, but it is no good. My few attempts thus far have been near-disasters, and drunkenly falling from a hay loft and crushing my skull would be a truly ignoble death.

My competence with a quill has not failed me yet, thankfully, so I thought to occupy myself penning this letter. I will make proper penance when I am home, but for the time being, know that I prayed for forgiveness for my lack of temperance, and that I am quite beside myself.

I am going to try once more for sleep. I will decide whether or not to send this letter once I've looked it over in the morning.

- *Isidor*

The sounds of the sea. I'd heard them only once in my life. When we'd taken our pilgrimage, all of us at the Abbey. We'd taken a barge from the Crystal Lakes down-river to Leifolk, and I'd gotten to see that big expanse of endless blue. God's wonder, laid out in an impossible vista where heaven and earth meet forever in all directions. The late Admiral Cross once said that only those who've seen the view from far out to sea, so far that the land recedes beyond the curve, can begin to accept their small and insignificant place in God's plan. It is a humbling feeling many could benefit from, in his opinion *and* mine.

That night, I dreamed of the sea. The loft was cold and my mind troubled and addled by drink, so I slept fitfully, waking often and drifting into that faraway place intermittently. The river barge, then the docks we'd walked, Father Helstrom leading the pack of us boys… I saw faces I hadn't seen for years, lads who'd failed to conform and gone stray, some who'd been Ordained before me, and even Nicholas, clutching at my sleeve.

Father Helstrom, younger then but you could hardly tell, and still just as stern and commanding.

The dreamscape—right, I was dreaming—shifted away from memory. Now the blue, the churning waves, the kiss of the heavens upon the horizon, was *all* I could see. And… a ship? I must have been aboard a ship. A warship, I think. There were cannons on the upper deck. No, wait… weren't they on another, lower deck? I couldn't remember. I'd seen very few galleons when I'd been at port, most warships were away at the time, ferrying souls from the crumbling Colonies in the Dark Continent or defending our waters from pirates.

The ship was an amalgam of the pieced-together memories I had of the few warships I'd seen then, all from a distance, illustrations from books, and my own imaginings. I couldn't work out why I was there, but each man I passed milling about doing tasks I literally couldn't fill in with any clarity, seemed to know me. No one stopped me from moving through the ship towards some inevitable destination.

I couldn't remember how I knew where to go, or why I was here, but it was no matter. What mattered was that *she* was waiting for me. That's right…

She was hidden away in my cabin, and no one could discover us. No one could know I was sheltering her. Ferrying her to freedom.

And perhaps myself? I had not decided yet. To give up all of this, to give up this life, this role that had thus far defined me, all for a woman? An enemy of the state?

An enemy… turned lover.

When I slipped inside my cabin, the lantern must have been lit low. The light from outside—once blindingly bright, high noon—was subdued here. Like the night had already fallen.

And there, waiting for me, the slender slope of her back lit along the edge and broken only by ebon spots, was the subject of my indecision and torment.

She did not turn to greet me, the steady rise and fall of her ribs suggesting she slumbered. I approached her, my footsteps soft, and shed my cloak—no, coat—a red coat, trimmed elegantly in gold along… most seams, I imagined. Would I be wearing a cravat, perhaps? A fine vest? I wasn't sure, but I thought that would look right and proper, so… there they were. I shed them as well, stripping down to my long shirt and breeches, and little more. The thick bracelet I'd had since I was a child, my only heirloom, slid down to rest at my wrist as I gingerly reached for her, tracing my clawed fingers through the air over her shoulder.

I yearned to touch her, but not while she slept. Not without her permission.

And just like that, she rolled slowly first to her side, and then her back. And those big, dandelion-colored eyes opened, her muzzle curling into a sleepy smile. Her downy breast rose and fell, covered in soft, indistinct fur that masked her petite, nearly flat chest. I'd seen very few nude women over the course of my life, save when I was *very* young and once when a harlot had intentionally unlaced and flashed me and Brother Dolus while we were visiting a nearby city. That woman had *sizable* breasts, and unrestrained by modesty or laced-up garments, they'd been utterly obscene. But I'd never really thought of that memory with anything other than embarrassment. For myself or for her, I wasn't sure. I was certainly not bewitched by the sight.

The beautiful spotted cat before me had a more elegant and understated figure, and the lack of a voluptuous chest did her no disservice. Her shoulders were strong and defined for one so slender, her arms stretching up behind her head, back arching as she yawned, quite intentionally putting herself on display. Her torso flared down into a trim waistline and thickened up again along her heavily spotted thighs, the black marks trickling down into joined paths. The markings wrapped around the soft expanse of her inner thighs and drew the eye towards the apex of her legs, where...

I did not know what I'd see. I wasn't entirely sure what I *wanted* to see, and I certainly worried about what that meant. But that was beside the point... something about all of this had begun to feel wrong. The wrongness was like an undertow, pulling at my heels, reminding me it was there and would take me in time, but easy enough to ignore for now, now when I was consumed by a blooming want, an all-important *ache*...

She was nuzzling that soft, cool nose of hers into my throat. I could feel her whiskers twitch, her hands gripping at my arms, pulling me to her. I braced my palm into the soft comforter beneath, and moved myself over her on my hands and knees. I tried to keep my hips up, but moments later felt them drawn *down,* in, against her, as if on instinct. I fought the urge valiantly, until with a huff—as if I frustrated her—she wrapped those robust, apparently strong thighs around my waist and *squeezed*.

The sound that left my muzzle was piteously *pained,* moaned out in a stuttering breath, like I'd been punched. I could feel the heat of her there, merging with my own, my body driven without thought by some primordial, deeply-ingrained voice that had no language to offer, only *want, push,* grind *down,* open her *up*—

The strands of guilt clutched at my ankles and tried to drag me back towards reason, but the overwhelming tide of need snapped each of them as soon as they took hold. If any part of me had the wherewithal to stop this, to stop myself, it crumbled when a sound pierced the quiet, freezing my heart mid-beat.

A breathless, husky laugh. I blinked to bring the intoxicating scene beneath me into focus. She was staring up at me, eyes half-lidded, eyelids a dusky gray encased by a frame of gold and black. She was smiling at me like she found my struggles delightful. And the laugh, soft and lyrical and just on the tail end of a sigh, was one I'd heard before. So uniquely her, it was unmistakable.

I'd known it was her, of course. It was always her.

That current of wrongness returned, stronger than before. But then she slipped her fingers through the fur at the scruff of my neck and leaned up to kiss me.

I'd never kissed anyone before. I had no idea how it was meant to feel, but what my mind supplanted was an indescribable warmth and fulfillment of that want that had been hollowing me out, feeding me like no delights of the earth could, seeping into me from her. I was the parched roots of a dying tree and she the rain. Every empty place in me was full, and I wondered if she was as fulfilled by it as I.

My answer came soon enough. Her fingers sunk into my hip, the prick of claws tugging at my flesh, and without hesitance, she pulled our bodies flush. Something *gave* between us, and we were joined, her gasp puffing out into my muzzle.

It seemed impossible that our bodies could fit so perfectly to each other, that she could accommodate my cumbersome weight, let alone our overall difference in size in... all areas... but she was hardly acting as though she were in *pain*. She was not soldiering through this in obligation or carrying out a duty she was bound to by covenant. No one compelled her actions but she. We were at sea, as untethered from our duties and as free to pursue our wants as could possibly be imagined. She was not just tolerating this for my sake, she was as lost to this need as I was.

It was profane. It was heresy. It was rapture unlike any I'd ever known.

She continued to kiss me and clutch me to her as though *I* were the one being claimed, as though *I* were the one fulfilling *her* desires. It was ludicrous—wishful thinking, maybe—but I felt so certain, somehow.

The warmth was burning through my body like a fever,

driving me restlessly to writhe and dig down further into the comforter, to snap my hips down, down, *more,* and somehow deeper, chasing something... becoming fully one with her, maybe... God, I yearned, what was it I was after, again? I felt like I was being pulled apart by need, drawn down to some singular point of sharp, trembling desire, but I could not fathom what more I could possibly need *from* her. From this. How could this moment—which already felt as though it could shake me apart —get any better?

Her tongue lolled out between her lower teeth, her eyes slipping to crescents, and she *purred...* oh, Lord, I had forgotten felines did that when they were in pleasure... God help me... I was *pleasuring* her!

The roaring surge of elation that washed over me struck like a crashing wave. It felt like it had jogged my *soul* loose from my body, the soft-hued image of beauty beneath me slipping away to hazy white, blinding. I rode out the overwhelming and terrifying rush, helpless against the current so succumbing to it instead, until landing heavily back in the restraints of physical form, the waking world cruelly asserting itself.

It was black and dim blue, my breath was coming out in haggard puffs, my face and muzzle crushed to hard, splintered wood. My thin blanket and cloak were tangled up around me like I'd fallen through a tent, bunched up around my feet and between my legs. My body *ached* with the cold I had been unable to feel until just now, an accrued punishment from hours spent ignoring my condition. The barn was nearly as cold as the air outside drifting in through the slats, and I was swaddled poorly for the elements.

Distantly, the mule brayed. And farther off, a rooster called the morning to rise. Slivers of blue light fell in through the decaying roof, the only illumination up here in the loft.

I groaned, long and pathetic-sounding, and dragged a snort wetly through my nose. I couldn't breathe through it, what had been a niggling cold was now settling in for good, so I'd been breathing the frigid air all night with my mouth open. My tongue and teeth felt dry, my throat stung and cried out for water, and my eyes burned. And I felt… strange, otherwise. My heart was thudding too quickly for having been at rest, my nerves stinging, washing me with a suddenly exhausted sensation. I probably hadn't gotten much sleep, but—

Trying to sit up was a mistake. I yelped and bent double, clutching down between my legs where I'd nearly crushed myself while rolling over. I knew immediately I'd spilled my seed in my sleep again. It was easy enough to tell by the wet sensation between my thighs, but I hadn't expected I'd still be so *prominent* down there, now that it was over and all. It had always receded before.

Unable to control myself, I flung my paw down between my legs and gripped the outline of my member. I pulled my palm away a second later as though seared by a hot pan, but I'd gotten enough of a feel to realize…

My knot was out. And the slick pooling at the front of my button-up was still warm. This had *just* happened.

And it was so painfully clear what the cause was.

I'd had these morning issues for many years now, up to and including the rare times I spilled in my sleep, long before I'd ever met her. I had tried not to connect the two in my mind, even though all the signs were there. But to do so at this point would be meaningless. I would know I was lying to myself. What's more, God would know.

Lord forgive me, I had been…

…I had been…

My paw fell, trembling, hesitant, to feel the shape of my manhood, still restrained by my clothing, but absurdly obvious. It was distressingly foreign to me, for a piece of my own body. The contours were unfamiliar, forbidden, a filthy secret kept restrained by my sheath and my self-control. But the one could only hold what it fit, and the other was waning. And now this manifestation of sickening desire, this *thing* was rising from its confines with more and more frequency and forcing me to reckon with it.

I hated it and hated myself. I wanted nothing more than to disown it until the appropriate time, when I was married, and all of this would make more sense. There were rules for marriage. I would know what to do then. All of this would be so much less *confusing*.

I still had it gripped there, beneath my clothing, and what had begun as a growl in my throat yielded to become the whine I truly felt. I was so held captive by my petulant anger that I couldn't even control the noises leaving my muzzle, anymore. Seized by a sudden desire to *make this all stop*, somehow, to reassert some measure of control over this rogue part of my body, I squeezed my palm around the knot. Until it hurt.

Oddly, it was when the pain began to first prickle that I was able to let out a breath. Stuttered, long-winded… slow. But it felt so immensely relieving. I focused on that feeling, closing my eyes and chasing it down a wobbly path towards restoration.

I began to relax and loosened my grip, until I could not easily feel the shape of it any more. I slumped back against the beam I'd slept beside and let my thoughts drift. They inevitably returned to the panicked realizations from earlier, but I was calmer now. I could think on this rationally.

Undeniably…. I had been… sinning with the Heart Thief in my dream. Fornicating. With her.

Darcy.

I tipped my ears back, feeling them brush the wood behind me. I had begun to think of her by name, which was not advisable. Beyond the fact that it was certainly a cover—she would never have given me her real name—I was showing signs of succumbing to one of the most warned-against failures of temperance a Templar could fall prey to: personalizing their relationship with a target.

I was compromised. I knew the moment the words came to mind, instantly, that they were true. The only possible thing to do at this time to protect the integrity of this case, and my own soul, would be to turn in everything I'd found and recuse myself from it. I had given in to the very weakness I'd once scoffed at other men for letting rule them.

I'd been seduced by her.

Every one of the scant few words she'd spoken to me, every brush of her body against mine, every brief interaction, had been fodder for the recesses of my mind to pore over for weeks now. And I could not help but linger on those most damning snippets. The lilt of her voice as she teased me, the whisper of her nimble hands over my body as she'd removed my harness—intentional, certainly—and the warmth of her thigh, purposefully positioned as it was, supporting my head on the bench near the dovecote. Even the way she laughed—it was a lurid display, all of it! She knew precisely what she was doing; every one of her carefully-planned and flawlessly-delivered flirtations tempted me down a road to ruin. And God help me, if not in the waking world, in my dreams I was *allowing* it to take hold.

It made some sense, really. My mind was untethered and more vulnerable when at rest. A perfect opportunity for dark forces to sink their fangs into the weak spots in my soul.

Well, I wouldn't let it happen. So long as I resisted, so long as I held to the clarity of mind God had granted me to see me through the trials of sin, I would not falter. I might stumble. The dreams were a bump in the road. One I would find a way to suppress and make penance for with Confession and... whatever my Priest deemed necessary to quench the fires.

Ciraberos wanted me to fail in this task. The hell hounds would keep nipping at my heels and looking for purchase with their jaws, not just now but for the rest of my life. They would always be there, legion, dragging me towards damnation. This was a test. A trial. How could I even be considering giving up the case? That would mean being complacent in the face of sin, accepting I could *not* overcome it.

It would mean she'd beaten me.

And I was *so* close. The Order may not have believed or may not have taken note of my reports yet, but I knew what I'd seen and heard. She couldn't get lucky forever. Eventually, if I kept up the pursuit, I'd have her cornered.

Felines were all about ambush and surprise. But I had endurance and my pack. She was moving through *our* society, and canines helped canines, first. I just had to run her down and out of options.

My ears twitched. In the damp, quiet air of the morning, carried across the nearby meadow, I caught the first hint of a most welcome sound. Salvation.

Clattering wagon wheels.

It sounded, as I listened more closely, like little more than a hay wagon or a mule cart. Probably a farmer, someone lowly. The clattering tinny noises reminded me of a milk cart, which it may well have been.

Whoever it was, they'd know how to get to town.

I shuffled up to a sitting position quickly and once again regretted it, but for a different reason this time. I palmed my forehead, rubbing my finger pads down the seam of my skull, groaning.

I glanced to my left, where the discarded bottle from the night before lay prone. It seemed to be laughing at me. Squinting, I noticed a haphazardly-strewn small stack of paper weighted down beneath it, scrawled with writing. It was my paper and my handwriting. I couldn't recall exactly what I may have written last night, but it sure seemed to be... a lot.

The wagon was still distant, but certainly coming this way. I had a moment or two to look over the papers while I hazily found my few possessions. It seemed like I'd penned a letter to Father Helstrom, which... made sense. But Lord, what had I written?! I was normally prone to rambling when I sent word to my Father, but he would *never* forgive me for a letter nearly six pages long. I'd need to look the small novel over later and pen something more concise.

Speaking of novels...

I gathered up the three books while I got together my things and took note of just how far my tassel was into the first of the three. I'd read through nearly two thirds of the first book last night? I *was* a voracious reader, but still. Considering how blurry the night was, how much of it would I really remember? Might be worth another look.

A fleeting glimpse of the dream I'd had suddenly asserted itself, and I lurched with a realization. I hadn't just been dreaming about her.

I'd been dreaming about the *novel,* too. I'd transposed us into the story, she and I.

God. I needed Confession.

Cillian Rathborne.

I stared down at the name on the elegantly-printed note in my hand, uncertain what to make of it. It was a Pedigree name, or at least adjacent, a branch family, perhaps. I'd heard of at least one other household with the name, although I couldn't be certain there were any men amongst their number named 'Cillian'. They were a family out of Amurfolk, if memory served, which meant they were prominent enough to have connections in the Capital, but little more than that. Most Pedigree families had a city home there, or at least a tangential connection to family who did. As Templar, we were expected to keep studied on major names and households that played any role in politics, the military, or Church dealings. This family must have skirted the line there because I had a good head for names and theirs was only vaguely ringing a bell.

Probably a family who'd had some kind of scandal in the past, something to take note of in the ledgers, but no important connections otherwise.

The note was envelope-sized, printed on durable rag stock and hand-signed by a banker from Amurfolk and the man in question. He had a fine hand, or at least the seneschal signing *for* him did. It was a custom note, not one of those new fixed denomination bank notes the King had issued to finance the failed war on the Dark Continent. *Paper* money. I couldn't see it catching on.

The subject and recipient lines were blank, or at least had been at one point, and had been filled in recently judging by the fresh ink. And, of course, the account of the man who was showing it to me.

I stared across the counter of the carriage house I'd found myself in, eyeing the nervous mutt, keeping my expression firm, but neutral. Father Helstrom had spent years training me on affect when dealing with every rung of society either high or low. There was a time to throw your authority around and a time to rein it back in. Thus far this man had been tripping over himself trying to be accommodating from the moment I'd come into his place of business. The whiff of fear and the obvious tells in his body language suggested to me he'd had trouble with the law or the Church before. Or knew someone who had.

Or he suspected he'd done something wrong in accepting this note. A guilty conscience was a rank smell you got a nose for after a while. I'd had more than enough experience with my own.

But all of that aside, he'd done the right thing in handing this over to me. So, after scanning it once more, I made an effort to soften my features. "And you're certain the woman who used this... she was feline? Black fur? Large, straight ears? Lean of build, demure and proper in her speech?"

The man was already nodding. "Yes, yes, all those things, Brother. Only, ah..."

I gave him some space to continue, then pressed with an easy, gentle tone. "Go on. Please. You're not in any trouble, I promise."

I was lucky this man had recognized my vestments. He hadn't once asked for my patents. To be fair, I was also armed. That helped.

"Well, ah..." he stammered, "... the description's *uncanny*, only... they weren't no woman."

"Ah," I said with understanding. "Well, she may have been wearing britches. She's a criminal and fond of disguise."

The man's eyes widened, crinkling his spotted brow. "Really?! Aye, well sh'fooled me alright, then. And we don't take notes from women, so believe me when I tell you, she had me sold. Man-like posture, he—I mean she—carried her own bags like it weren't nothin'. Deeper voice'n on most ladies, too, if I remember it right." He leaned an arm over the counter, looking intrigued now. "And you sayin' she's some kinda' criminal, then? Wot'd she do?"

"Well, for one," I held up the note, "she's passing false notes. This is stolen."

The man slumped. "Am I out the whole lot, then? I checked the seal an'everything."

"The Church does not perpetuate theft, sir," I assured him. "You'll just need to wait for us to send along a courier to reimburse you for it."

"I've already paid the coachman," he sighed. "She got one of my best, too, damn it all. Private, swift box."

"The Order appreciates your compliance," I said by rote, not paying much mind to his grousing. My eyes were pinned to the note. Specifically the fact that there were *three* distinct sets of handwriting on it. The signature from the house that had written the note, which could be from the Lord himself, if not a seneschal. The carriage house owner—he'd confirmed that himself.

And hers.

Her hand was distinctive. Elegant, educated for certain, but unusual. The way she accented the flare of the quill along the edges of letters lent the writing an almost foreign appearance. If I had to guess, it suggested someone who'd either written or read a different language before learning Amur. The residual stylization was the sort you'd see when Amuraic had begun transitioning to our modern alphabet. Or Huudari writers who were able to pen in Amur as a second language. I'd read aged texts copied by ancient monks where you could still see the old-world influence. It was subtle, but consistent. I felt certain I was right. And it fit so well into the patchwork tapestry I had of her thus far.

She was fluent and literate in our language and not in the way a commoner would be, who would have best guesses at spelling and bungled structure. She was as schooled as I had been at least, and we received a rigorous education from the monks at Ebon Gables. What's more, she had no trace of accent in her speaking voice that I could detect. She was very well comfortable and at home in our culture and probably had been for some time. But she seemed young, which meant she'd likely grown up here.

Where? Why? And how did a foreign feline *woman* receive the kind of education she'd clearly had?

Oh, she had really given me something to work with, here. Not only was this snippet, this small error she'd made giving me reason for confirmation of many of the guesses I'd already had about her, it was another piece of evidence with her handwriting on it. And another crime, regardless of whether it was stolen or given freely.

Stolen would be less complicated. The alternative was worse. If this man was some accomplice of hers—which would once again make sense, we'd suspected for a long time she might have help or information from within elite society—that would mean breaching Pedigree circles in the investigation, and I was not an Inquisitor *yet*. I was only recently Ordained as a Journeyman Templar in fact; I didn't even have a house assignment. Inquisition within the ranks of the elite was delicate work. That's why the Ministry existed within the Templar order at all.

If it got that far, I'd need Father Helstrom's backing. The idea of going up against a Pedigree House was daunting, somehow more so than the Heart Thief herself. Investigation, I at least felt I had a head for. Bureaucracy was another matter.

I left the carriage house renewed in my conviction, if not my vigor. She was bound for Redcoven. I could have guessed as much. It was the largest city in the area and a good place for a criminal to go to ground. She likely realized if she kept hopping around the small towns off the main trade road, she'd leave an easy-to-follow trail. In a larger city, she could scrub her tracks. Blend in. Lose me.

What I doubted she realized was that Redcoven had a Ministry Office. Ministry Offices were intentionally banal and unadorned to set them apart from the beauty and artful architecture of halls of worship, of Churches and Cathedrals, which were built to honor Him and inspire faith in His followers. The Ministry of Templar served in the shadows of those spires by design. We were the street cleaners, the reapers who did their work in the fields at night, so that when light touched the world, it would be tidied up and protected from sin. We sullied our souls doing the kind of work we did so that those chosen by God by their very birth—the Pedigrees—could live a righteous life, rule our society justly, and die pure.

Our Order did not need to be celebrated or even

appreciated. No pomp, no finery: a modest life, and an equally modest grave. We'd find our rewards in the next life.

The Ministry was headquartered in most major cities, and in fact I'd done some of my missionary work there when I was thirteen. Training with more seasoned Templar, one of them an Inquisitor himself, if memory served. They worked with the young from time to time as part of their own missionary service. I'd do the same someday.

She must have at least considered the chance that I'd follow her here and get my hands on this note. If not, that was a mistake. And she severely underestimated me. But either way, it spoke to her emotional state. She'd paid for the fastest coach she could find here. Doing so was *expensive,* the sum on the note was obscene. Likely why she'd had to use it. She wasn't carrying enough coin to pay for a service so lavish.

Sloppy.

Maybe even... scared.

I got an odd twisting in my gut when I considered the idea that I, personally, was scaring a woman. I didn't like it. But Brother Dolus had assured me many times—these initial twinges of moral strife when we first began doing our jobs in earnest were reflexive, a product of misguided but well-intentioned sympathy that we'd shake off our fur like frost once we became weathered to the work. God gave us a compass in our soul, and if we looked inwards long enough, we'd feel it guide us true. The feelings I was contending with right now were surface-level anxieties based on an immature view of the world. God would relieve me of their burden in time.

Darcy—the Heart Thief—was not just a thief. She was a murderer and the lowliest kind of Heretic. She'd slain our own, two young Templar who'd only been trying to protect our holy relic while it was being transported. I wanted to return the

Heart of Faith obviously, but more importantly, I wanted their souls to be untethered from the shame of their failure. They could not ascend until their bodies were laid to rest in consecrated earth, and the Order would not do that until their task had been completed.

I hadn't known either of them, but I knew the trials of faith and physical hardship they had endured within the Order throughout their adolescence to attain their salvation and ascend. To have all of that denied, to be stymied between death and rebirth, not to mention to be snuffed out so *young*, at all…

Whoever could do that was filth. And they did not deserve my sympathy. They deserved swift and brutal justice. And, if the Order deemed it necessary, death.

I made it back out onto the street and nearly to the mule when that train of thought reduced me to a doubled-over stagger against the nearest wall. My shoulder thudded into the cedar siding of the feed store, startling the shop-keep inside, who I saw gaping at me through the window. I had only barely missed stumbling into the window itself.

My ribs constricted, squeezed tight by a spasm and then the inevitable wheezing cough that followed. It persisted long enough that the ragged end led to an encore, and then another. Damn this cold. I was in the first or second day of it, hard to tell when it had truly taken hold, but it had me in its clutches now. My throat felt burned and parched no matter how much water I drank, my body was aching and sluggish, and the cough would keep me up through the night, I was certain. Especially since I'd have to spend it on the road again. I was hungry, too, and lightheaded. I'd beg a meal at the local Church again, but Redcoven was close and I'd already be losing time on the mule.

All of that aside, what had my chest in its vicelike grip was not the illness *or* the hunger. It was a thought, an image of the future, imagined in detail in my overactive mind.

The Heart Thief, hanging at the gallows. As she inevitably would, once she was tried and convicted.

I swallowed, steadying my breathing. I had *never* imagined myself to be this delicate. Certainly, I had not been tested by the fires of war, as Father Helstrom had. And I had not the maturity and mental fortitude that more aged, experienced men like Brother Dolus possessed. Nor was I foolish enough to believe that rigorous arms training was commensurate to combat experience in the field. I had never had reason to draw steel to defend my life or with any real intention of harming another. Let alone killing someone.

We were prepared to bring the Lord's Justice to bear, if need be. But in my case, the need had not yet arisen.

I had been pursuing this investigation for months now, all while knowing the likely outcome if I were successful. It had been simpler, more straightforward, when there wasn't a face attached to it all. But that shouldn't have mattered. I could not serve as an arbiter of The Word if I was unprepared to handle death. Even something as horrific as public execution, if sanctioned by the powers that be both heavenly and earthly, was part of my duty. I had to be able to sever the knee-jerk emotions, to step back and divorce my passions from the whole of it. This was the danger in empathizing with a target.

I needed to see her as less of a person. I just wasn't sure how. The more and more I learned about her, the harder that was becoming.

I didn't yet know how to restructure my mind to work this way. I was too inexperienced and too led by my passions. But my passions were what had driven me so far in this case, and it was hard to know how to cut them off in one area of life, but not others.

I wished, momentarily, that I'd had more talks with Father Helstrom about this very issue. The only senior in my life who'd ever been particularly instructive on the methodology to retrain your emotional gut reactions was Brother Dolus, and I think he and I were cut from different cloth. To eschew the things he had, the connections he'd never have outside the Order, in pursuit of his *service* to the Order, you had to possess a more reserved countenance. Monks were, figuratively speaking, a different breed.

I ground my teeth together, straightened my posture, and elected for now to bury it down deep. This rumbling thunder of doubt and dread. I had a job to do.

And if I couldn't stomach the thought of being responsible for *this* woman's death—the thief, the *murderer* who had desecrated the holiest of holy, violated the very fabric of our faith, and killed my brethren to do it…

… then I was not fit to be an Inquisitor. I would go so far as to say, I was not fit to be a Templar, in fact.

I could be prone to bouts of melodrama, I knew this. But it was not a stretch to say that this had now become a test of my conviction. The entirety of our Order was tasked with bringing the Heart Thief to justice if we could apprehend her. And perhaps the chain of command above me may not have realized how close I was to doing just that, but *I* knew. And I'd always know.

I wasn't about to let a petty illness, hunger, or my own fainthearted feelings on execution prevent me from doing my duty. God would fill my heart with the comfort of the righteous when all was said and done.

I remembered her words once again, as I readied the mule for travel. I may as well have transcribed them for all the times I'd considered every syllable.

'Do not follow me. I won't be tortured and locked away by your Church. Next time, if need be... I will defend myself.'

God, how I hoped she would. It would make all of this so much easier.

6

THE HUNT IS JOINED

Redcoven was a bustling country city, nestled deep in the bread basket of Amuresca. Redcoven was one of the only other cities I'd visited more than once over the course of my life, because it was relatively close to Ebon Gables, by carriage or on horseback. I'd spent months there in the dormitories as a youth and explored the city with some of the other boys, including Nicholas. I needed no help finding my way through the city, even six years later. Redcoven was hardly as large, densely-populated, or industrious as Auldfuster, but I found it a more pleasant place overall *because* of that.

Even so near to winter, the fields and farmland surrounding the city were a hive of activity, final harvests and shepherds with their flocks, roadside stands selling late-season vegetables and all manner of locally-made goods. I managed to pick up a few baked sweet potatoes being sold by a young cattle dog family who'd set up a roasting fire at one of the crossroads miles outside of the city limits. It was all I could afford with the few copper coins I'd managed to dig out from the pockets of my britches. And it was precisely what I'd needed to lift my spirits and put some strength back in my body.

Cattle dogs were particularly common here, it seemed. Hardly surprising, given the lake country was ideal grazing for goats and sheep. Seeing all the families traveling or selling on the roads here, as well as the cottages and steads nestled out in the rolling hills, it was easy to idealize this kind of place. I knew, of course, that life out here was more complicated and difficult than it appeared. The land only gave what it gave, and country lords country lords desperate to match the wealth of the cities often overburdened their vassals or overcharged as landlords, but it was pleasant at least to imagine a simpler life. If I hadn't been given up as a child, this is the sort of living I'd have made.

I was grateful for the blessing of being raised by the Order, though. While perhaps simpler and more peaceful, a life as a tradesman or laborer would have meant little to no education, and I never would have known all that I was missing. The world was more open to me than it was to these people. And while a greater understanding came with the burden of knowing the depth of mortal folly and suffering, it also meant I could appreciate the beauty of the changing seasons and how they differed all over the world from a learned perspective. Knowing how things were was one thing, knowing *why* was quite another.

A commoner would not have access to the library I'd grown up with, the *books*, or the wisdom of monks on hand. I wouldn't have it any other way.

It was midday when I drew close to the city, and the weather had finally cleared. The skies were spotless blue and the wind had let up. It was still cold, but an ideal late autumn day. I tried to ignore the fact that I couldn't breathe through my nose and enjoyed the sights and scenery as I crossed those last few miles.

There was the occasional watch post quartered by the local militia, but overall, no major military presence in Redcoven. The road was primarily frequented by carriages and tradesmen, all regular, decent folk, so my armaments got more than a few looks. I kept my cloak up over my shoulder to make my vestments more apparent (they were all I had to speak to my station) and did my best to set peoples' minds at ease. I hardly wanted to be mistaken for a mercenary of some sort.

I could see the steeple of the Church of Saint Rhine, easily twice the height of every other building in the city, elegant with its dark black filigree. The steeple was strung with crimson and gold flags, and the moons of the One True God perched at the very top, calling me home. The Templar Ministry was a fortified building adjacent to the lot, understated in comparison to the grandeur that was Saint Rhine's.

I would go so far as to say Saint Rhine's was a cathedral, although they preferred humbler terminology. It was nearly five hundred years old and had long ago been a military outpost turned fort, with a church inside. It had been converted fully into a holy site after the last Huudari war and had the distinction of housing an order of lay monks—rat kin—who had earned their place alongside the canines of the city in that conflict, standing arm-in-arm against the incursion of the lion tribes.

Being as they were rat-kin, the monks here could not ever serve or be ordained as full clergy, of course. But their order was unique, in that the local lords recognized them with nearly the same privileges and honor that would be associated with their canine brethren. It was my understanding that they'd used their status in the city to lift the usual restrictions their people faced in settling in certain districts and to afford them better options in the trades they were admitted to work in.

What it amounted to was simple—there were nearly as many rats in Redcoven as canines, if not more. And the ones that lived here seemed more industrious, more civilized, better clothed, and presentable than I'd been told city rats would be. The only time in my life I'd ever seen so many vermin-kind in one place was when we'd briefly gone to the coast. They tended to live more in port cities, where they could easily find work in their accepted trades at the docks and on ships. Here, they seemed to do just about everything... every manner of shop and craft. They even had their own public houses and buggy services for smaller peoples.

I remembered it from my youth, but seeing it now as an adult was striking. As a child, I hadn't thought of how revolutionary a city like this was. And how *comfortable* the general populace seemed with the species-mixing.

I'm certain there was tension from time to time. But given how hollowed-out many of our other large cities were since the war and the mass immigration of canines to Carvecia over the last century, why wasn't this being done everywhere?

My thoughts were once again lost in one of those mind-tangling questions there were no easy answers to, when I should have been focusing on the task at hand. But I was weary and my mind wandered at the best of times. I found myself nearly passing the grounds surrounding Saint Rhine's and pulled my mule to a stop beside one of the open iron gates, my eyes drawn to the yard. I was coming in behind the Rectory, the narrow, cobbled street here squeezed in against the back of several shops in the market district. It was an entrance not terribly well-known to the public, but how we'd always come in and out as children. The back yard was for ceremonies and morning exertions, and it seemed the latter was taking place now. Although it was the afternoon, the boys running laps around the yard must be getting their exercise in before lunch.

My stomach growled, and I knocked it with my fist, irritated. "Don't you complain, now," I murmured. The potatoes had been awhile ago, and apparently, they hadn't been enough to make up for the last few days.

"Sir?" a thready voice called out across the small field. I looked up in time to see one of the young lads—barely older than I'd been when I'd stayed here—coming to a jogging stop mid-stride. Two others took the opportunity to do the same, hands on their knees behind him, tongues lolling out panting despite the cold air. They'd been at it a while by the look of them.

The young canines all inevitably turned to regard me curiously, the first who'd called out to me hesitantly crossing the field towards the gate, while asking loudly, "Are you here from the Ministry? Father Whitehall was given to expect someone this week, I think. That you?"

I dismounted, stepped through the open gate and tugged off my riding gloves, flexing my stiff, cold fingers. As I approached them, one of the other boys beside the first jabbed him with an elbow in the ribs, and they muttered something to one another quietly.

When I made it up to them, the lad's ears were down and he looked cowed. He straightened his posture and mumbled, "M'sorry for speaking informally, Brother Templar. Won't happen again."

I huffed out a breathless laugh. I'd crossed the threshold, had I? A year ago, I'd have considered myself amongst these boys, a young Brother-in-training. Now they were being deferential to me. I *had* been ordained, I supposed. It felt strange. Most of the other young Brothers and Sisters I knew, I'd grown up with. No such formality there.

"Set yourself at ease, young Brothers," I assured them. "And no, I ah… I doubt I'm the man from the Ministry your Father is expecting. I'm just passing through the area."

"Oh," the lad's ears perked up, "well, then—"

"I don't hear paws on dirt!" an older man's voice called out from the Rectory doorway. Every single boy's fur suddenly stood on end, and I knew that look. I got it every time Father Helstrom had yelled at me growing up.

The old Father who came trudging across the green was a retriever with more gray than gold on his muzzle and one bad eye. He walked with a slight hobble, but not so severe as to need a cane, like my Father did.

He stopped when he saw me and fastidiously tugged at the sleeves of his robe to pull them back down over his wrists from where he'd had them gathered up. Penning something, most likely.

"You must be the young lad the Ministry said we should expect," he said, hurrying a bit more as he crossed the yard towards us.

"I don't think so Father." I shook my head, "I—"

"Yes, yes!" he insisted. "You're the young Templar from Ebon Gables pursuing the Heart Thief investigation. You must be." He surely noticed the surprised expression on my face because he waved an ink-stained hand. "We received word weeks ago that you'd be in the area looking into this case. A Father… Helstrom… informed us you'd spent time in our care in the past and would be likely to take refuge here if you came through the city. You are welcome, Brother!"

Stunned, I opened my mouth to thank the man, but the deluge of good news continued.

"The Ministry sent home one of our local Sons, actually," he said, "just last week, on orders that I believe may coincide with your mission. It was all so sudden—he was on Inquisition with the Eastern Sect for the last three years, with the Border Lords. Nasty work. We're very glad to have him home, and if he can assist you with this investigation of yours, I believe he will be eager to do so."

"An Inquisitor?" My heart leapt into my throat. "The Ministry sent a seasoned Inquisitor?"

The Father only smiled at me, perhaps picking up on the excitement in my voice. "Yes, young lad. They seem to think you're on to something."

. . .

I checked the address I'd been given again to be certain I'd not be surprising a common family in their home. But everything about the building was as described by Father Whitehall, the retriever from Saint Rhine's.

Relatively new construction, dark brick, the apartment itself settled in over a clerk's office. I was glad I'd been able to leave the mule at the Church because there was very little room on the street for her. All Inquisitors were afforded a reliable horse and tack for their work, but I assumed the man probably kept his at the Church in their spacious stables. This residence wasn't far.

I began to ascend the narrow external staircase when the door to the curtained Clerk's office opened and a large man stepped out. Or rather, leaned partially out, far enough that he could lock eyes with me and look me over.

He was canine, a dog for certain, but vaguely wolfish in features like many of the wilder breeds tended to be. He had a thick, long coat of white and light fawn, with a dark brown and black mask around his eyes and down his neck. He looked older than I, but still far younger than most of my other Seniors and had clearly led a dangerous life, judging by the scars crisscrossing his muzzle.

And he possessed two of the most piercing aquamarine eyes I had *ever* seen. Sharp as a blade and just as capable of cutting through you, I'd imagine. I felt like the man could *see* my sins upon my flesh, as clear as day. I knew that look. It was the same calculating, knowing stare my Father would level at me when I deserved it.

I turned on the stoop, fixing my arms at my sides properly. "Inquisitor," I said, guessing but very certain of my assumption.

The man gave no initial response, save to look me up and down once more, then step aside the doorway, gesturing for me to come down.

I made my way to him and hesitated only a moment once I

was on the threshold of the building because the fellow's sheer *presence* nearly knocked me back. He was large and well-built for one, taller than me, his ears nearly touching the top of the door frame. But it was more than just a physical presence. The air around him felt *heavier*, somehow. It was an aura that all but demanded respect and compliance.

He wasn't even wearing his vestments or armor of any kind. Although I *did* note the blade at his hip, with one of his thick palms resting casually on the pommel. He watched me the whole way to him, and his eyes continued to follow me as I entered the 'office'. There was nothing intentionally intimidating about his affect, but then there didn't need to be. His expression was, if anything, calm. Composed. No outward signs of bristling, teeth, or flexing claws. Neutral, but imposing.

The door closed behind me.

I knew immediately this was a Ministry Archive, despite having never seen one before. That explained why he was living above it. The walls were nothing but lockboxes and rows of shelves, stacked with documents and ledgers, containing the secrets of our Kingdom. I tried not to stare like a fool at the trove, only marginally succeeding.

"I shouldn't be permitted in here yet," I uttered quietly, before I could consider my words might cause offense.

"You are Isidor of Ebon Gables," he spoke from behind me and strode up to my side, remarkably light-footed for a man his size.

It hadn't been a question.

"Yes, Inquisitor," I replied, straightening my posture. He must have been a well-regarded, senior member of the Order if they'd entrusted him with an Archive. Even Father Helstrom had to be granted permission to have access to a place like this since he'd retired.

He stepped around to my front, regarding me from barely a foot away. He looked at me for a time, before tilting his head just so. "You don't remember me," he said at length. Again, not a question.

"Have we met, Inquisitor?" I asked, searching my memory.

The first hint of something approaching an expression crossed his features. Maybe fondness, but if so, muted. "You were barely up to my chest, then. And it was the summer, I believe, so… my fur would have been trimmed back. It grows into quite the mane in the winter months."

Oh, Lord. There it was. A flash of memory—

"Small arms training," I said in realization. "You are… Brother Malachi?"

Finally, the quirk of something that was most certainly a smile. Diluted by his overall seriousness, but still unmistakably there. "You do remember."

"I remember," I let out a breath, sensing the air lightening in the room, "being knocked over into the dirt like I'd run into a brick wall every time I got cocky and you shield-checked me."

His chest rumbled in a baritone laugh that he didn't bother opening his muzzle for. "You were small for your age, then. I recall your Brother monk being concerned you would be atrophied due to some affliction of yours and never fill out. I am very glad to see he was wrong." His eyes moved over me again. "You've become quite the strapping young fellow, Brother Isidor. How is your form these days?"

"I'm certain you would still be able to put me in the dirt," I assured him with a quirk of a smile, "Brother Malachi. But better, I hope. Far better. I have taken my training very seriously."

"I can tell," he assured me, gesturing towards the one wooden table and chairs in the corner of the room, stacked in papers and ledgers, as well as what looked like a local map. "And not just because you look well and strong. I've been studying your work since I was recalled to Redcoven. The Ministry is building a file based on *your* investigation."

My chest felt fit to burst. I could hardly get the words out, the relief that was suffusing me was so profound, I genuinely felt I might cry if I were not careful. I swallowed back stone after stone in my throat and finally managed to breathlessly say, "I'm so glad. I was worried… well, that no one was listening."

"I am very sorry," he said, glancing back once over his shoulder as he stepped up to the table, picking up a few letters with broken wax seals on them. "I'm certain it must have been trying, going at this alone. But I assure you, the Ministry has been reviewing everything you've sent. It's just taken time to find its way to the proper channels. And now that it has, we are taking this all very," he looked back up from the letters to me, "*very* seriously."

"Truly?"

"If they were willing to dispatch me from my appointment with the Border Lords," he said, "then you may be certain they consider this important."

"She is here in Redcoven," I said quickly. "Or was, *very* recently. We should begin canvasing—"

"Hold." He put up a hand, his masked brow narrowing. "You think the Heart Thief is in *my* city? Now?"

"I am certain of it," I said, reaching quickly beneath my cloak to my main belt pouch, where I had the payment note tucked away. I produced it and handed it to him still folded.

He opened it carefully and scanned it quickly, not bothering to waste time and asking while he read, "Significance? What am I looking for?"

"I have followed sightings, too particular to be any other feline," I said, "and I must impress upon you—she does change her appearance, but I have met her face-to-face, so I am very sure—"

He cut me off. "You need not argue your case there, Brother Isidor. You have found more information on this scum in the last two months than the entirety of the Inquisition has in two years. You've even obtained physical evidence we can use to convict her and physical descriptors of one of her disguises that has doubtless thwarted our previous attempts to identify her. All without access to Archives or backing of any kind. I have *no* doubt that you can find this woman. I'm here to afford you the support you deserve and to take point in the matters a junior Templar cannot."

He reached out and settled a heavy hand on my shoulder, squeezing hard enough that I felt it even through my weathered, travel-worn, damp clothing and cloak. I exhaled, my whole body going slack. And God bless him, he didn't tell me to correct my posture.

In fact, when I looked up, he was leveling that intense gaze at me. But it didn't feel invasive.

He was *listening* to me.

"Please continue," he pressed.

"I had…" I paused, "… a near-sighting, two towns to the west. It's a bit of a long story, but…"

"A 'near-sighting'?" He quirked his head, then huffed. "Sounds interesting. Alright. I want to hear all of it. Every detail you can possibly relate. But perhaps you should sit. You've been on the chase for some time now, yes? I know how that is. I mean no offense, but you appear run-down."

My stomach chose that exact moment to announce its hunger.

We both looked down. His paw shifted off my shoulder and bumped my chin up to face him. "When was the last time you ate?" he demanded.

"I had some potatoes earlier today," I insisted. "I've been making do on low rations since my coin… well…"

"Mnh," he grunted, tugging out a chair for me. "You need meat. Will mutton do? I've some in the back. Bread, too. Cheese?"

"I," I stammered. *God,* that all sounded incredible. "I probably should eat something," I agreed. "But I won't abuse your hospitality, a little will do." I sighed. "Maybe I'll actually make my next weigh-in."

"Lord, they still have you doing those?" I heard him grumble, almost beneath his breath. "Those will stop once you're accepted by the Ministry. They aren't designed for big fellows like us, anyway. Come on. You can eat and talk."

I followed him, dumbstruck and so overwhelmed with gratitude from what the day had brought me, I could barely find the words.

We did speak over a meal, which he partook of as well. I told him everything. Or, near enough. Certain personal details were better left for Confession with a Priest, but I withheld nothing about the case. He listened intently, only occasionally interjecting to ask questions with a seriousness and fixation that I knew meant he was truly hearing me. He wrote down nearly everything I told him, making personal notes for himself in the margins.

It went on like that for nearly an hour.

I was dizzy by the end of it, relieved down to my bones. So much so that I felt liable to drift off, my body choosing to remind me in my state of rest, the warmth of the hearth uncoiling my muscles, and a full stomach, that I hadn't really gotten a complete night's sleep in days.

And then we got to the part about the payment note, and he stood suddenly.

The motion jarred me back, and I watched him as he strode to the corner of the room, opening one of the lockboxes and sorting through the ledgers there.

"Brother Malachi? What is it?" I asked, watching him.

"Rathborne," he said distractedly. "I know the name."

"As do I," I said. "Although I'm not certain why or how. Some kind of incident. Some kind of scandal with the family, maybe?"

"A mistress, if memory serves," he said, fingering through the ledgers until one caught his eyes. I stood and moved to join him, looking past his shoulder as he opened the file, scanning through it quickly. "I remember because," he skimmed a finger pad across the paper, pausing on one spot and tapping it with a claw, "there is a branch family here in Redcoven. Distant relatives of the late Lord Rathborne. Yes, here."

He held the written account up for me to see. "The investigation was ordered by the Wellford line, an extremely well-connected, wealthy family out of Amurfolk. Their daughter was arranged to marry the only surviving son, the inheritor." He spoke quickly as he read through, "They were concerned about him... mhm... rumors of impropriety with a servant, or more than one. Even after his move to Amurfolk, you see here? There was talk there was a mistress. The Wellfords took it seriously enough to contact the Ministry."

"God, there he is," I said, gasping quietly, the name standing out to me all over the paper. "*He's* the young lord in question."

"Cillian Rathborne," he said, the man's name uttered like a pronouncement in the quiet room. "They never found the mistress. The marriage went through. But the Inquisitor made multiple mentions here of a feline woman. A ghost they could never locate."

"He's still carrying on with her," I whispered, the words sticking in my throat like thorns. Why did the realization shock me so? Why did it make it so hard to breathe, all of a sudden?

"We long suspected she had Pedigree backing," he murmured. "A benefactor, a paramour, someone feeding her information and hiding her. Here. *Here* he bloody is."

He turned his head towards me, the hint of a fang in his subtle grin, his gaze hungry like a dyre. And I suddenly realized what it was I'd been feeling, back in the doorway.

This is how prey felt. Being hunted.

This is probably how she felt being hunted by me.

"Less than one hour with access to the Archives, and just the two of us talking," he said, "and we've *got* something. Something we can use not just to hang *her,* but the bastard who's been aiding her. You're a savant, Brother. You and I are going to bring this little fiend down, and then I'm going to tear the truth out of her. Bone by bone, if I must."

I looked between him and the paper in mute shock. My stomach lurched, threatening to upend the meal I'd just had. I wasn't sure *what* I was feeling, it was all so disjointed and overwhelmed.

His body stiffened beside mine suddenly. Before I could ask why, he had shoved the lockbox closed and was crossing the room, going for the peg rack his gear was hung on, beside my own. I'd only just dressed down before the meal.

"Inquisitor?" I asked, my voice wobbly. "What—"

"Harness up," he said, his authoritative tone brooking no argument. "The Rathborne family has a house in the city."

"What?" I blinked. Shouldn't that have been the first thing he'd told me?

"The branch family," he explained quickly, shouldering into his own harness at a speed and efficiency that put my own to shame. "Go by the name 'Lane'. They have a city home here. They don't spend the winters. It's just servant staff and the elderly couple there now. It's practically an empty house."

"Shite," I said hurriedly, falling back on profanity I should have been ashamed of, but I earnestly could not think what else to say. I understood the rush he was in quite suddenly and moved quickly to gear up beside him.

7

AT BLADE-POINT

The house was one of those finer city apartments people would spend the summers in. Small for an estate, but larger than most common buildings in the city, with its own cozy grounds that wrapped around the left side and back lawn. White-washed brick with a well-kept clay roof and patterned walkways through the front garden, pruned-back rose bushes and evergreen shrubs. A fence and gate to keep out the rabble, but only four foot high. Quaint, comfortable, and moneyed… but not ostentatiously so.

I never would have looked twice at it, searching the city. There were dozens of others just like it, and the family name had no connection to the case I could have ever found on my own. It was amazing what difference the right information could make.

Malachi had a case slung over his shoulder that I'd seen him pull out of a lockbox on his way out the door. I knew what it was because I'd been trained on them extensively. I didn't have one of my own. They were almost exclusively a weapon of death, meant to kill or maim, with precision. They were each finely-tuned, expensive, personalized, and I didn't warrant one being made for me, yet.

He unstrapped the collapsible crossbow from inside its case and released the safety, triggering the mechanism to unfold. He checked the tension once, then loaded a bolt from the clip, staring down the crosshairs a moment as he spoke to me.

"I have no spare, so you'll need to rely on your blade if it comes to it. Tell me you're confident in your skills, and I'll believe you."

"I'm confident I can best her in hand-to-hand combat before I'll need to use steel," I said.

He glanced at me. "If she draws a weapon of her own—"

"I'll do what I must," I promised.

"Good man," he affirmed, collapsing the crossbow again with the bolt safely stowed in the chamber. He hooked it to his harness and slung it over his shoulder. "We'll need to outfit you with a leather gambeson if you're going to do work like this. Cloth won't cut it. Also, I'd meant to ask you. Your hand..."

"I'm a southpaw," I assured him.

"Ah, I think I remember that," he nodded. "That's a nasty surprise if you're any good. Having to reverse your guard is always tricky. Could catch a man unawares in the first few beats, if he's not paying attention."

"Our Senior Monk, Brother Dolus," I swallowed, "seemed to think it would be a benefit to me in the future."

"That's foresight," Malachi nodded. "Most Abbeys would train out a quirk like that. Your Senior Monk's a canny one, bucking tradition." He glanced down at my hand and my missing finger. "Although I suppose in your case, it was advisable regardless."

I only nodded. The pinky I was missing was essential to gripping a slashing weapon, and for stabilization when using it in a thrust, as well. I used my right hand now primarily for deflection and shielding, clad in an arming glove.

"Have you ever effected an arrest?" he asked me, testing the gate first and finding it locked, before putting a paw up between the prongs of the fence and easily vaulting himself up over it.

I tried to stifle my incredulity at the brazen, casual disregard he was showing. The idea of violating the sanctity of an estate's grounds—even a small one like this, couched in between many other buildings rather than on sprawling acreage—when we could just *wait* for the staff to come out to greet us. There was even a bell…

… but then, we'd lose the element of surprise. And if I'd learned one thing from my failures in the past by now, it's that you didn't wait to catch up to Darcy. If we gave her *any* warning, *any* amount of time, and she was truly here? We'd lose her. Again. Or worse, she'd lay a trap for us like she had at the carriage house. Our prey was too clever to let propriety get in our way.

And if we were wrong, Malachi was a dyed-in-the-wool Inquisitor. The real thing. One of the few Templar in the country who was permitted to penetrate, infiltrate, and act with almost total impunity in Pedigree society. The family could bring it up with the Ministry if they took offense, but most wouldn't dare. If word got out that your bloodline was being looked into by the Inquisition, it could mean utter defamation in the court of public opinion and banishment from high society events, lest the stain of rumors rub off on the hosts. Having a House Templar was one thing. An Inquisitor paying you a visit meant something had gone *very* wrong, and no one wanted to be associated with that kind of scandal or earn the ire of the Ministry itself.

"Brother Isidor," he called back to me.

I blinked rapidly, then with a jolt, realized I hadn't yet moved to follow him. I found the same purchase on the meager fence and leapt it as well, landing behind him. "I'm sorry, Inquisitor."

"Malachi, please," he corrected me. "Or 'Brother,' if you must. You didn't answer me."

"Oh," I stammered. "I'm sorry," I said again, wincing at my own repetition. "No, I haven't… I mean. I tried. Not the first time because I didn't realize then who she was, but the second. But you know how that went, so ultimately… no. Not successfully."

"It's just as well," he assured me. "By the letter of the law, you aren't supposed to. If you ended up bringing her in, I don't think anyone would take you to task over it, but better it be done by me. As of two weeks ago, I am officially the main agent assigned with arrest and interrogation privileges for this case. Have no doubt," he promised, "I'll defend our actions any way it happens to go down. You do what you must. If she's even here, that is."

I stepped up beside him on the cobbled walkway before the main entrance, two hardwood doors with heavy brass door knockers.

"Interrogation?" I asked uncertainly. "Why? It's not in doubt that we have the right person. She didn't even deny it when I spoke to her."

"To locate the relic," he explained, and I instantly felt idiotic. "You've got quite the head for hunting down criminals, Brother Isidor, but I excel in information retrieval, often from unwilling subjects. It's why they called me away from the borderlands for this case in particular."

Torture, my mind supplanted. It was an unfortunate necessity of Inquisition that I'd not been trained in, yet. The key was keeping your subject alive, while convincing them through psychological—and often physical—means to part with what they knew. Earnestly, it was work I'd been hoping I'd never have to take part in, but that was probably unrealistic. He'd never talked about it in detail, but even Father Helstrom had told me he'd had to question people… rigorously… on more than one occasion.

"Try not to kill her," he said, checking his stowed blade, his gaze wandering around the edge of the building to the abutting garden. The back of the lot was ringed in a taller brick wall that separated it from the yard on the other side. "If you happen to run her down."

"We'll be together, won't we?" I asked, confused. "You said you wanted to effect the arrest. I have no issue with that, but shouldn't we stick together?"

I preferred the thought, truth be told. I'd failed twice now, and I was tired and still ailing, somewhat. I wanted to catch her obviously, but if my Senior Brother was the one who did the physical catching, I wouldn't feel cheated. It didn't matter to me who did it.

"Actually, I want you out here watching the exits while I talk to the family," he explained. "I have the authority and moreover the necessary patents to smooth things along. And she's probably *in* the house if she's here at all. Best we not reveal our whole hand at once, yes? If she tries to run again, I want her caught unawares. I'd rather they not know there are two of us here."

"Understood," I nodded crisply. Everything he was saying made sense, and while I desperately wanted to see and talk to her again, if we *caught* her this time, I'd have every chance.

And maybe it was better if someone disconnected from our previous interactions was the one to manhandle her. Besides, Malachi had the patents. I didn't. It could be a legal issue.

The Crown- King Carthage and the Pedigree Lords who served in his Council- and the Ministry- the arm of the Faith I was a part of, otherwise known as the Templar- worked as a check on one another, a precarious equilibrium in our Government. I was not a legal scholar and didn't understand it all well, but as far as I was able to ascertain, it was a matter of power balancing power. If we overstepped the bounds that had been established for how we were to conduct ourselves, the Council of Lords and their army of Bailiffs across the country could arrest, imprison, and potentially even execute a Templar the same as they could a citizen. The Ministry could step in and attempt to adjudicate on their behalf, but only if they felt our case warranted riling the Lords. It was a fine line to walk, and Malachi presumably knew the steps far better than I did.

"Go around back before I even knock," he said. "I don't want them seeing you, in case they've some kind of signal or warning worked out."

I nodded, quietly amazed at his thinking. Everything he was recommending was common sense, seemingly. Logical reasoning, that's all it was, but in his case based on what had likely amounted to a decade or more of experience doing this kind of work. He looked to be that much older than me, at least. And I remembered him now, close to my current age or thereabouts, when I was on mission in Redcoven as a child. He'd been one of the quieter Senior Brothers, if memory served. Unbeatable at the foot-list, but not gregarious like some of them had been, not even with his fellows. I think he'd kept to himself a lot. I didn't remember him joining us for any of the gathers around the brazier or on trips into the city's market district.

Wolves could be like that, though. Solitary. Aloof. I wasn't certain if he had wolf ancestry or just looked it, and I was afraid to ask. But despite his unflappable, seemingly cold demeanor, he'd been very kind to me so far.

I turned on my heel to head for the back yard, when something snagged me by the elbow, yanking me back a step. I stumbled and saw Brother Malachi was gripping my sleeve and part of my arm. His eyes were intense, as they often were, but somehow especially so right then.

"Isidor," he said, giving my arm a brief squeeze, "watch your tail, alright? I don't like seeing my Brothers die."

I swallowed and merely nodded. The fact that he'd spoken it thusly meant it was something he *had* experienced.

"She has killed before," he reminded me. "Do not tread softly. If she tries to use lethal force, respond in kind. To hell with questioning her. The Order needs its Sons more than it needs a show trial. We'll find the relic another way."

He slowly uncurled his fingers from my arm and released me. I staggered back, continuing to nod mutely, then dashed off towards the back yard, keeping low to avoid the windows. Reminding myself all the way that it was just precautionary. He'd just seen and done many things in his years of service that had made him wary. I'd encountered Darcy twice now and she'd never tried to kill me. And this time we had the drop on her.

Potentially. If we were right.

The back yard was probably a beautiful garden in spring and summer, partially covered in carefully arranged paving stones, with raised beds of well-manicured rose bushes and small fruit trees. Unlike the Hudson Estate—which I was remembering right now for all the wrong reasons—there were plenty of places to sit. Even a raised patio area with a sunburst pattern of paving stones and a brazier in the center for outdoor gatherings. The Lords who came here must have enjoyed their rural roots more than most city Pedigree would.

I paced the yard, staying under tree cover lest anyone be looking from the windows above. The memory of her spotting me out of the second story window of the carriage house came to mind…

I was essentially just guarding the back exits while Malachi spoke to the servants and the older couple who regularly lived here, likely in the main hall. But just to be safe, I kept a circuit around the left-hand side of the building so that I could see the walkway and gate in the front, just in case she somehow slipped out the front door while he was searching the house.

I'm not certain how long I was out there, waiting. It couldn't have been more than a minute or two.

Movement caught the corner of my eye, a darting shadow far too high up and *far* too large to be any wild animal that would live in a city. It was a cloudless, sunny day, getting on later into the afternoon, so the shadows were long. And this one swept across the whole edge of the yard when it moved.

I tucked myself back against the tree I was near, dragging my cloak in along my arm and peering out from behind a branch of new growth. I waited and watched, and in time the shadow coalesced into a figure, rising to a crouch amongst the shrubbery. They turned and craned their neck upwards to peer in carefully through a window on the ground floor. Judging by where they'd landed, they had come down from the balcony just above on the second story.

My heart hammered against my ribs, and I knew it could be no one but her, but I couldn't jump to conclusions until… I couldn't assume…

They turned, and the silhouette of their ears was suddenly in stark contrast against the white brick.

It felt like providence. A rush of blood thundered through my ears, my veins, my whole body *sung* with elation! But Lord God, she had not seen me yet. I scanned the yard and saw her doing the same, looking for her exit path. Only I had already done that, already positioned myself to cut off her only avenue of escape. She'd have to cross the raised stone area from the right side of the yard to make it either around the left of the building to the front walkway, or less likely, go back into the house via the rear door. If she did that, Malachi would have her. But it looked like she was going to take the obvious way out, which meant…

I waited near the tree, obscured by shadow and foliage, as she crept low and made for the short stone steps down from the patio area. And when I was certain I had the right trajectory to cut her off in two steps or less, I sprung on my heel—

—she heard me in the moment before I began to move, but she only made it down the steps and managed to spin to face me. I had been aiming to catch her at her back and level my blade at her, but I corrected my swing and triple-stepped instead, finding a path for my steel as her hands came up.

Holding… nothing. She had no weapon held in either hand. She did *nothing* to stop my blade-could *do* nothing, in fact—save settle a paw in that last moment of movement over my pommel and the hand I was gripping it with. It was so far from being a grapple, I wouldn't even call it a *grip*.

It was a touch.

She looked up at me, muzzle slightly parted, amber-green eyes wide, her fur brilliant as spun gold in the sun. The ink was gone from it, washed out, and I realized this was the first time I was truly seeing her as God had made her.

Her palm rested over my knuckles where they gripped the blade that was connecting us, the long knife pressed firmly into her cotton shirt and her breast. My aim had been true. The blade was positioned directly over her heart.

"If you must run me through," she said, after a not-insignificant silent stretch had passed between us, "press *hard,* young Templar. Drive your blade in with all the force you have. My heart is tough with scars."

"What?" I uttered breathlessly.

"Do not leave me alive to linger," she clarified. "I've always hoped my death would be quick… sudden. Life is a long torment. Death shouldn't have to be."

"If you want to die so badly, why do you keep running from me?!" I spat out, sounding angrier and more frustrated than I wanted to. And with no reason. This time, I had her.

I *had* her!

"I do not *want* to die," she answered simply. "But I also do not want to suffer."

"I don't intend to make you suffer," I said, the words wasting away on my tongue near the end of the statement. Because they would not prove to be true, and my mind couldn't argue the semantics of it with myself.

It felt wrong to lie to someone about that.

Her eyes fell to my blade and slowly traveled the path up the slim glint of metal to where her hand rested on mine. She hadn't moved it. If anything, she'd worked her fingers into the creases of my own. I don't think she was foolish enough to believe she could pry my hand loose, but I couldn't imagine what other purpose it might serve.

"Take your hand off of me," I said, trying to sound as commanding as Malachi did. What obviously came effortlessly to him was still a work-in-progress for me.

"No," she replied, still looking down at our hands like the sight was a curiosity to her.

"Why not?" I asked ridiculously. Why couldn't I string together a proper sentence when I talked to her? Most of the time, I was as wordy as a bard. Much to the exhaustion of my peers, I might add.

But with her, I just... words... didn't... happen...

"Because you've been lying to me," she said, drumming her fingers against my knuckles and lifting her big eyes back to lock on mine, "and that's rude. I'm entitled to be a little rude in retaliation, I think."

I clenched my teeth. "I... truly am trying to make this as easy on you as possible," I reasoned. Why was I reasoning with her?! Where was my *backbone*?

"It doesn't matter how polite you are while arresting me, young Templar," she said. "Your Ministry is still going to hurt me, and then hang me, and you know it." She lifted her small chin up at me defiantly. "You're delivering me to the slaughter. You can dress it up with talk of redemption and salvation, but the facts remain."

I was faltering. She was working her claws into me with her pleading words, and they were having their desired effect. Keeping my gaze directly on her, and her hands—both the one holding fast to mine, and her free one—I opened my muzzle wide and shouted, *"MALACHI!"*

"Pawning the guilt off on another, are you?" she sighed, like she was disappointed in me.

"MALACHI!" I belted out again, louder.

"Oh, good luck with that, you can't hear anything inside these city homes." She rolled her eyes.

I opened my jaw wider to yell again, when she moved her free hand. I pressed with the blade, threateningly, but she had no weapon in her hand, she was just reaching up, towards me, and did I really want to kill her for that?! I could *do* it, she was so small compared to me, and the blade was right between her ribs, it would only take one decisive drive—

"Madame," I warned, as her palm, close enough now to my muzzle that I could detect a slight quake in it—she really *was* scared, no matter how cool she played it—her palm was inches away, tickling the fur along the ruff of my cheek, and—

And then she was cupping the curve of my jaw, her small fingers splaying out into the border where my shorter muzzle fur began to thicken into my winter coat.

She gave something like a sigh through her nose, although it was hard to tell what she intended by it. Her thumb brushed over my fur once, twice, tucking an errant clump of my neck ruff back, away from my face.

"Madame," I repeated in a harsh whisper this time. "I could

kill you where you stand if you do not heed my words. I am sanctioned to do so."

"I don't think you will," she said softly.

"Mada—"

"I am not a woman," she said suddenly. "Please use my name. That's why I gave it to you."

I fought to keep the suddenly reeling panic I felt from my expression. My eyes roved over them, taking in everything about them that I could in a glance. They were dressed as a man again, wearing a simple, loose cotton shirt and high-waisted, form-fitting trousers, with some kind of jeweled belt or waist wrap that trailed silver chains down their hip. Fanciful, I daresay even pretty, but nothing so dandy that any man at court wouldn't wear something similar. Pedigree men liked their finery, even jewelry.

"Does that change things for you, I wonder?" they... he? Asked me. I brought my gaze back to theirs, my hand twitching where they were still holding it. My muzzle clenched against the softness of their palm.

"Am I about to meet a more brutal side of you, Isidor?" he asked quietly.

He. I could think of no reason the Heart Thief would lie to me about being a man, other than to baffle me. Which was possible. But as a woman they'd garner more compassion, and they must have known that.

It was probably the truth.

"You're abhorrent," I growled out, "dressing and acting as a woman... you're going to confuse people."

God help me, I'd been dreaming about—

"That *is* the point," he said, as though it were obvious. "You think I dye my fur and change up my wardrobe to provide people with *clarity* on who I am?"

"Bloody incubus," I snarled, tossing my head until his palm slipped away from it. My skin *burned* where he'd touched me.

"Prinoch est tolvitrium elono cara," I murmured a warding prayer over myself, trying to stave off the dark thoughts threatening to tear me down right at this moment. I would contend with those conflicting feelings later, when this was all over.

But… then… so she *wasn't* the mistress, after all? Or…

… or was he?

God, this could be more heretical than I'd ever imagined. The well of depravity went *deep*.

His features had fallen, those large, expressive eyes and ears betraying more than his calm, collected demeanor could conceal. "So, you *are* a Templar, after all…" he said.

"I'm not sure why you thought that was ever in doubt."

"How did you find me, this time? How on *earth*? Of all the houses in this city?" he asked, his tone suggesting he didn't expect an answer.

And he wasn't getting one.

"MALACHI!" I called again, trying to keep the desperation from my own voice. I had no means of restraint. My rope was back with the mule; I'd never had a chance to return to Saint Rhine's.

He looked around the little courtyard for some reason, and then said, "I have something of yours. Something I've hidden in a cache. But I think at this point, I should return it to you."

"Nothing you took can be held over me," I proclaimed, shutting that down before it went anywhere.

"No, no, choir boy, you don't understand," he sighed. "I want to *return* it to you. No strings attached. It just seems like it may have been important to you."

My prayer book.

"Then tell me where it is," I said. "I'll collect it later."

Shockingly, he answered. "On the southwestern corner of the city, there's a Smithy near an old oak tree. There's a hollow nook inside; it's there. Covered up with dead leaves, in a potato sack. It's quite dry, don't worry. I had intended to leave a note with the local Church, in case you came by…" he trailed off, looking back up at me. "…but then you found me. Again. Why is it *always* you? Your entire Order is after me, apparently, which seems a dreadful waste of your resources. There *must* be more important things out there for a private religious militia full of assassins and spies to be doing."

"I don't even know where to *begin* addressing all of the defamatory falsehoods in that statement," I snarled, "but I assure you, we take the theft of holy relics and the *murder* of holy men *very* seriously, and there is nothing more pressing I could be doing with my time than what I am doing *right* now."

His ears fell back, something akin to genuine horror falling like a pall over his face. It was such a sudden shift from his forcibly aloof demeanor, it startled me. "M-murder?" he moved his mouth around the word clumsily. "Th… they think I killed someone?"

"Oh, you're good," I chuckled dryly. "What, did you think I wasn't aware? The entire Order knows the extent of your crimes, and those boys' bodies are lying in state still, awaiting the restoration of their salvation before we can lay them to rest. Your continued existence is trapping their souls in torment, between death and rebirth."

"Oh, Lord help me," he gasped softly.

"I am *trying* to bring you back to the Lord!" I reminded him. "You need to repent, or you're bound for the cold fires of the wasteland—"

"No, no, you don't understand," he said, gripping my wrist a little tighter, his words approaching more of a plea than I'd heard thus far. "I did not *do* this, this… I didn't kill those men! I've never *murdered* anyone, God…"

"It's a bit late to plead innocence," I pointed out.

"Oh, shite," he murmured. "You… you really believe all of that, don't you? That these fellows can't… rest peacefully… until I'm hanged for this?"

"It's the truth!" I exclaimed angrily.

"Bloody hell, they'll keep coming, won't they?" He said, pressing his free hand up between his ears and worrying at his fur. "If not you, others. I've really stepped in it this time."

"You are *just* now understanding that?" I scoffed.

"I really don't want to hurt you, Isidor," he said, his voice pained. "Please don't force my hand."

"It is unbelievably arrogant to assume you could," I snuffed.

"Please," he said, clutching still at my hand. His fingers fell so neatly between mine, even clenched around my sword grip. I could feel the heat bleeding through our fur, and I swore I could almost make out his pulse, drumming as fast as mine was. "I… I understand that you're only doing as you were taught, and you seem young, too. Your passion does you credit, but you're wasting it coming after me. I… I feel as though I know you, and I think you know the difference between right and wrong. What they will do to me…"

The words fell off with a tremble. That was real fear. I could even smell it on him.

"I have an oath to fulfill," I said, as solidly as I could manage, "to my Order, my Brothers, and to God. I may not enjoy the thought of you suffering—of anyone suffering, regardless of their crime—but the verdict of the mortal Courts in this case will only echo the verdict of God, and God is clear on what punishments should and must be levied against criminals who've done what you've done. It isn't for me to question."

"You're lying again," he insisted shakily. "You question *everything* in that holy tome of yours. I've read your journal."

My jaw fell open. "You read my prayer book?"

Honestly, of all the things I'd thought the Heart Thief would do with my prayer book, *reading* it had somehow never been one I'd considered.

"Oh, every page," he said. "Why do you think I took it? To spite you?"

I was, of course, horrifically offended…outraged…I hardly knew how to feel! What was one to think of such a breach of one's privacy?! Snarling and grasping for any suitable response, I spat out the first thing that came to mind.

"Your thoughts?!"

No. Why had I asked *that?!* What did their opinion matter?! That wasn't the point!

He blinked up at me, seemingly as stunned by my question as I was.

"Well?!" I gurgled out in a growl, desperately. To hell with it, I was saddled to the horse, now. We rode.

"I…" his expression softened around the edges, fuzzy with discernable thought. His eyes unfocused for just a moment, and I was struck with the realization that this was the first time I'd ever met him that I'd seen him lost for words.

His gaze re-focused on mine after another few seconds, and when he spoke again, the uncertainty had bled away to his usual collected, confident tone.

"It made me sad," he said softly, his first words not at all what I'd expected, but when he continued it grew even more strange, "to think that you and I will never be friends."

"What?!" I coughed on my own saliva, ineloquently.

He gave the slightest inclination of a smile, tempered by that ever-present fear and wariness since the subject of his crimes had come up. "Your writings were thoughtful… intelligent…" He paused a moment, then pressed on, "… lonely. I felt at times unsettlingly familiar with some of the feelings you profess and deeply curious to understand you and your life better than I can from your writings alone. I think talking to you at length would be fascinating." He closed his eyes a moment. "But as I said, we cannot be friends. Or even acquaintances. So, it is for naught."

"I am not *lonely*," I insisted vehemently. "I have a family. A Father. Siblings. God."

"So, you do. But it seems to me," he said carefully, "that you only share your inner thoughts with the page. Or in Confession… and only those which trouble you, or that you feel are wrong. You… wrote as much…"

I swallowed. It was true that I'd used my prayer book primarily as a place to write down the things I didn't feel I could share or bring myself to speak about with the monks or other boys at the Abbey. Darcy wasn't entirely correct, I *had* talked about some of them with Father Helstrom. But I suppose, not very many.

It felt so odd, knowing that someone else—someone mortal, someone other than God, knew them, now. Not… terrible, exactly. I wanted to know what someone might *think* of these things I'd never shared.

He'd told me how he felt about *me*. But I wanted to talk to him—to someone—about all of it! About each subject, each wayward musing. I wanted to know if I was just a fool, or if anything that knocked around in my head had merit.

For some reason, I'd always hesitated at the cusp of each of these questions in asking or speaking with Father Helstrom. There were plenty of other conversations we'd had. But some things, just… it didn't feel right to talk to my Father about them. And there was no one else at home who would be appropriate. That's why I'd started journaling at all. I hadn't known what else to do.

But Darcy would not, *could* not be that person for me. That was impossible. We couldn't really talk about anything at length. Because of who we were.

"It also saddens me," he spoke again, after an uncomfortable —and I'd imagine telling—pause had passed between us, "that you feel you can only share these doubts and thoughts when they make you guilty enough to give Confession. What a terrible association. You should have someone you can talk to candidly without the stain of shame hanging over you."

"Shame is a useful trait for self-improvement," I said,

parroting Brother Dolus's words from many times in the past. "You should try it. You could stand to give Confession, I'm sure."

His shoulders slumped marginally, then he sighed. "There go the walls back up, then." He finally separated our hands. My knuckles felt chilled from the loss of it. He ran a finger along the tip of my blade, eyeline tracing its path towards his heart. "Did you read the books *I* left you, by any chance?"

"I did," I affirmed, lifting my chin. "Trash, all three of them."

"Ugh," he clucked his tongue, "maybe it's best we remain enemies. If you can't respect a classic piece of literature like 'The Admiral's White Claw' then you have terrible taste, and we'd never get along." His muzzle twisted up for a moment petulantly, and he pressed, "Did you even really *read* it? I just don't know how you could call it 'trash' if you did. You probably just skimmed it—you can't imbibe the beauty of the prose that way—"

"I read it cover to cover three times," I asserted firmly.

"You lie yet again!" he exclaimed, his fangs peeking out from beneath his muzzle as he laughed at me.

"Don't make that accusation lightly, where I'm concerned," I fired back. "I have no idea why, but you penned notes for me in the margins, as to which scenes were your favorites and why. I'm assuming that's why the quill and ink was there. And I know they were for *me* because you used my bloody name." I tapped his chest with the tip of my blade, shoving him an inch. "There. Is that proof enough for you?"

"Oh my God," he full-out laughed, now. "You're telling the truth. And the other two books?"

"Only once, but yes."

"How on earth did you have the time?" he scoffed. "And why read 'White Claw' thrice? If you hated it so..."

"I thought there must certainly be something in the texts that would give me a better understanding of who you were," I explained. "A hidden message, an inkling of your methodologies. But it really was all just tripe meant to waste my time, wasn't it?"

"You didn't *need* to read them," he said, concealing his grin only barely by lifting his free hand to his muzzle. "Let alone *three times*."

"It isn't as though there was very much else for me to do, chasing after you for days on the road," I groused. "Let alone at the pace my mule was setting."

"You read the books on horseback?" he asked, eyes wide.

"Not a horse—"

"That is the most lovely, wholesome thing I've ever heard of!" he exclaimed, laughing again. God, his laugh made something twinge in my chest, and I didn't like ruminating on why that was. Not one bit. It should be *different* now that I knew the truth of his identity!

"I mean, to read in a carriage is one thing, but you must be a truly voracious reader to do so in the saddle," he prattled on. "Isidor, I feel… just… deprived, that we must have such acrimony between us. I am only more certain now that we would have been friends in another life."

"You chose to be a criminal," I levied back. "The fault is yours. You could have been a decent, respectable member of society. You could have made better choices."

"Young Sir," he intoned, "becoming a criminal is the only choice I have ever made for myself. You will never make me regret it. Even if you kill me for it."

I was about to question him on the lunacy of his statement, when both of his ears swiveled forward and his eyes went wide as full moons, staring directly above me in alarm. He fell away quickly to his knees in front of me like I were a tower shield. The fact that I let him betrayed all but instantly the lack of conviction in my sword arm because I did not drive the blade home, I merely allowed him to move away from it with a half-hearted chase. But I had very little time to ruminate on that, before a familiar voice swore from above me and something sung past my shoulder, embedding in the ground several feet away from me. It had either been an extremely bad shot, or he'd tipped the weapon at the last moment.

In a state of shock, and forgetting myself, I craned my neck back and looked above me to an open window, where Malachi was leaning out with his crossbow deployed. I began to say something, when he snapped out, "Eyes on her! She's armed!"

I stepped back a foot reflexively, bringing my blade and buckler arm up to guard at the same time as I turned my attention back to Darcy.

Just in time to catch the tail end of his swift motion, as he lifted a slim flintlock pistol from behind his back and leveled it at my head.

For some reason, with what could have been my last breath, I said his name.

His hands were shaking visibly where he held the flintlock, one cupping the other to hold it steady. This wasn't a bluff. He knew how to shoot. He was just scared.

Which wasn't a good thing.

"Isidor," he breathed out in shudder. "I am very… very sorry for this."

There was a clattering overhead, the sound of wood splintering and a muffled grunt of pain from Malachi, as he forced himself out through a too-small window, and then a thud as he presumably landed on the adjacent balcony. I'd seen the man leap and move by now… he'd be here in a moment, but by then I'd—

I tried to reach towards Darcy with my off-hand, knowing at that point I had very little to lose. And I saw his finger flex on the trigger.

At the last second, his wrist… twitched… and the pistol went off. The sound at point-blank range, and the spark, the smoke…

it could have heralded the end, for me. The last thing I'd ever see, smell, hear…

But when I opened my eyes, I was prone on my back on the stone, very much alive. I hardly remembered falling, but being fired at point-blank by a flintlock will do that to a man. My ears were ringing and I may have hit my head when I'd fallen because everything was spinning and hazy. A pair of big, canine paws thundered past me, and then I'm not certain how long later, returned, joined by the man's knees and two strong hands scooping me up by the shoulders.

I blinked, trying to get my bearings, and vaguely heard my name amongst the ringing din. Things were starting to make more sense. I followed the sound of my name to its source, a canine face, masked in dark brown, with two fierce eyes the color of the sky.

"Damn, lad," his words formed up more clearly as he slid one of his palms over the back of my head and brought it up bloody. "You knocked your head good, there. Are you with me?"

"M'I… shot?" I asked blearily.

"Not unless it ricocheted," he growled, settling me back down and beginning to undo my harness, pressing his palms over every part of my body from neck to waist, looking presumably for any more blood. "Damned whore shot right past your head, though. Into the wall over there. I've no bloody clue how she missed a shot that close. God loves you, Isidor of Ebon Gables. God is on your side…"

"Why did you shoot at him?" I asked, my voice sounding odd to me… *everything* sounded odd to me. My hearing was muddy, like I was underwater.

"I had a good line of sight to her shoulder before the two of you moved," he explained. "You moved right into my line of fire when she ducked. I could see the bloody pistol tucked into her trousers from up there. Couldn't take the risk she'd shoot you before I made it downstairs."

"I'm sorry, I..." I mumbled, choking on my words, the whole of it catching up to me at once. I felt my eyes sting. I would *not* cry in front of this man. "I lost him. *Again.*"

"I don't fucking care," he swore. "Are you alright? You need to—come on, sit up if you can—I need to see if you were hit by a ricochet, I need to see your back, come on, lad..."

My body wanted nothing more than to continue lying there, chasing off wave after wave of dizziness and crashing exhaustion, as the reality of what had just nearly happened washed over me. But, fighting back nausea and dark spots in my vision that threatened to black me out entirely, I willed myself to do as he said, groaning gutturally as I bent slowly upwards.

"There... there, now," his voice was still a growl, but it was clear he was trying to imbue it with calm. "You're alright. No blood... except on your head... and we'll get that seen to."

He was holding me by the shoulders. He'd helped me sit up. For the first time in the half a day since we'd met, I realized the man didn't seem to keep to the unspoken barriers that other senior men in the Order had, my entire life. He had no issue with touching me as familiarly as my brothers did, despite being as good as a stranger to me.

Right now, I was exceptionally grateful for that fact.

"I've... failed," I choked around another heavy swallow. "Again."

"No, Brother Isidor," he sighed, looping an arm under my armpit and slowly easing me to my feet, "*we* have failed. And I'm your Senior, so I'm all the more to blame. I made the call to take that shot."

"You had a good reason," I mumbled.

"I also failed to run her down," he said. "She scaled the back wall there. Bloody cats. I couldn't climb it, and by the time I got around, there was no trace of her."

"You should be out there looking," I insisted weakly. "We should—he must be close."

"We will find her again," he said, his voice hard as iron and inviting no argument. "You knocked your head on paving stones. We're taking you to a Physician. Now. I am not losing one of my Brothers over that wench... and did you say 'him'?"

"He's a man," I explained simply.

He seemed to accept it all but immediately. "I knew this profile seemed too clever for a female," he muttered. "I assumed she had help from whatever Pedigree she's seduced, but this is all beginning to make more sense, now."

I sagged and he wrapped his arm lower around my waist, pulling me back upright. "Stay with me, lad."

"God help me. I have had... indecent dreams about her... about him..." I muttered, the words spilling out of me like I was at the gates, admitting my sins to the Chorus.

He stilled, and I was too far gone to know how he looked in that moment, but he felt rigid. We began to move together again, the city a hazy collage to me.

"You don't tell anyone else that, ever," Malachi said. "You hear me? Not ever. Not even a Priest."

"Mnhhhh," I groaned unintelligibly.

"Not ever," he whispered.

8

DOUBT CREEPS IN

I was in the crumbling church again. Everything was less real this time. Nothing made sense any more. Roses grew from between the cracks in the walls, blooming life surrounded me, despite the fact that drifts of snow fell in through the decaying roof. The gales that rattled the broken panes of stained glass chilled me through to my core, but my chest… burned. When I looked down, my heart glowed through my ribs like a kiln.

I tore my shirt up over my head, and it dissolved into ash. Cuneiform lit like embers from amidst my fur, in a familiar pattern. The Heart of Faith, its inscription, burned into my flesh.

I clawed at my chest, desperately, to no avail. I felt like it was blackening my insides with its fire, and soon I began to cough. Smoke, acrid and sooty, and the stench of burning flesh.

"I can relieve you of that."

I looked to the altar, and there he stood. Not in a gown this time, but a loose-flowing shirt and breeches, the top open to reveal his flat, downy-furred chest.

I fell to my hands and knees and crawled towards the altar.

He watched me the whole while, the stained glass behind him shifting between the phases of the moon, and the sun and stars, throwing his figure into stark relief.

When I at last grew near, he slipped down to his knees and reached for me. His palm cupped my cheek and settled against my jaw, his fingers carding through the fur at the ruff of my neck. It felt familiar. Like it belonged.

"This will hurt," he warned me gently, "but I must take that from you. It's killing you."

He reached down, pressing his palm flat against my chest, and began to push. I could not stop coughing, my eyes were full of tears, the ash of my burning body filling my throat.

His fingers pressed past the edge of my skin, sinking into my chest. The burn grew, and intensified, like it would flare out before he ripped it from me.

I couldn't breathe. I was dying, charring from the inside out, my own heart was destroying me. I could still see him there leaning over me, somehow, clearly. His gaze was intense, focused… and then closer. Closer still.

His muzzle crossed the distance between us and slotted in against mine, meeting, somehow… so perfectly. He breathed.

And then I breathed. And it was air, not smoke, filling my lungs. His breath in me. Resuscitating me.

His hand was deeper now, wrist buried past my ribs. He dug for the Heart, closing his grasping fingers 'round it. The fire fought back, burning up the air he had given me. But he only gave me more. I could feel the heat licking between us, drawn through my muzzle into his. His body began to glow…

I dragged in a ragged breath and rolled over to cough grotesquely, deep, wet, and absurdly loud. My head throbbed, my chest ached, my throat clenched around an unscratchable itch.

But I was awake.

I was awake and alive.

It wasn't just the dream that had woken me thinking I was struggling to breathe. I was genuinely struggling to breathe. My cough was back with a vengeance, my head felt fit to roll off my shoulders, and as soon as my memory returned to me, my heart sunk into a depressive pit.

I wasn't sure where I was. The room was dark and unfamiliar, and I was alone. But I recalled the last moments I'd been awake and the whole of the encounter that had come before. I remembered Malachi speaking to me as my consciousness waned… I remembered what I said to him.

God forgive me. I remembered what I said to him.

The door opened, a hulking shadow stepping inside. As if I'd summoned him, the Inquisitor walked into the room, lighting an oil lamp with a candle he was carrying before snuffing the wick on the candle and moving towards me.

I *had* summoned him, I supposed. With my raucous, uncontrollable coughing.

"How long were you traveling through this weather without shelter or all-weather garb?" he asked distractedly, as he poured something from a small flask into a steaming clay mug he'd brought in with him. "Your dedication does you credit Brother, but you'll be of no use to anyone if you're dead. Why didn't you tell me you'd been ill?"

"Just," I wheezed, "a cold. And I was," I coughed, "past… the worst of it."

"It is lingering in your lungs, according to the Physician," he muttered, moving over towards the bed and setting the cup down beside me on an end table. He did not treat me like a child or patronize me. He pulled up a chair and sat beside me, waiting to see if I could do it myself.

I forced myself up to a sitting position, wincing as my head throbbed at the change of angle. I felt… bad… but not like I was dying. Just sick, with a painful bump on my head.

"I get lingering coughs, often," I told him, reaching for the drink he'd set down. I sniffed it but was unable to discern what it was just from the steam. I began to sip from it all the same.

"It's just thin tea, honey, lemon juice, and whiskey," he informed me.

I nearly coughed it up, peering over the rim at him and wiping my muzzle with the back of my hand. "This has alcohol in it?"

He looked concerned. "I'm sorry. It's a country remedy. Have you taken a vow of sobriety? I should have asked."

"No," I answered. "Just… I think my tolerance is bad."

"Oh, Lord," he chuckled. "Nothing to worry about there, I assure you. Barely a capful. Just does wonders for colds with the right mix of ingredients."

"I thought it was medicine," I said.

"Well, it is," he shrugged. "Country medicine. It's all the Physician would offer you in a bottle, I just mixed it myself is all."

"Thank you," I said quietly.

This was intolerable. This man was quite literally everything I wanted to be in life. And thanks to my humiliating failure, he was forced to play nursemaid to me.

"Before you go fretting, set yourself at ease," he said, standing and walking towards the one window in the room and pulling back the curtain for a moment, revealing a dark blue sky illuminated by the faint yellow glow of a lantern somewhere nearby. Heavy white drifts blew in fierce, diagonal lines across the one window square I could see, before he let the curtain drop.

"First blizzard of the year," he said, shaking out his thick fur as he adjusted the robe around his shoulders. "The Heart Thief won't be leaving the city. Not in this. At least not until the roads are cleared. It moved in fast too, so I don't see how he'd have had time to arrange transport. And we found his belongings. At least those he left at the Lane house."

He settled himself back down in the chair heavily. "He's trapped," he assured me. "We'll find him."

I clutched the warm mug in both paws, taking stock of myself and my surroundings fully for the first time. I was in a bedroom. Likely his, judging by the scant few possessions I saw around the room. It was clear this apartment was kept up but didn't see much use. From outside it had looked very small, and the size of the bedroom confirmed that. There was probably a sitting room and a wash room if he was lucky, but possibly not even that. He might have taken his baths at the Church since it was so close.

Certainly, this place was no family home.

"You live alone?" I asked, then immediately realized I should not be probing his personal life.

He didn't seem to mind the query. "Aye," he answered. "I go where I'm needed by the Ministry, I've always been willing to travel for my work, and I've just never seen fit to… settle. Not yet, anyway. Since I move around so much, felt cruel to consider starting a family." He'd been staring off at the window, but he regarded me when he asked casually, "You?"

"I'm nineteen," I said, by way of an answer.

"I knew Abbey kids who got married at thirteen," he said. "Not common, but it happens. Especially the girls." He scratched his claws through his neck fur, idly. "I'm twenty-eight, by the way. Before you ask. So, you can stop addressing me like I'm your Father. We're not so far apart."

"We're several lifetimes apart," I sighed, thumping my head back against the wall behind me, and immediately regretting it. "At least insofar as experience and standing." I clutched at where I was wrapped up, where I'd nearly knocked myself out, falling.

"You've got a good *mind*, though," he said, pointing a claw at me. "That's a gift. Won't take long for you to rise in the ranks, trust me. You'll be my superior in five years or less."

"Heaven forbid," I muttered.

"You need to work on your confidence," he said as he lifted the same flask he'd poured a bit of into my cup to his own muzzle. He let out a breath after he'd swallowed, sounding satisfied with whatever was in there. "As an Inquisitor you need to put forth an unflappable aura of authority, or you'll get walked all over. No one spills their secrets unless they're utterly certain you'll pry them out of their skull one way or another anyway. If you can't rely on intimidation, you at least need to appear certain in your convictions. Preferably both, but one or the other will do. Is your faith in God strong, Isidor?"

The way he asked it… it sounded like an actual question. As if I could feel any other way.

"Of course," I said.

"Well, then trust that He knows what He's doing," he reasoned. "God put you on this path because… well, because you seem to be good at it. He guided you to the very place you are now. Trust in Him, if not yourself. And use that faith to strengthen your own confidence."

I mulled that over in my head. It made a sort of sense. God was infinitely wise, and while I was not so arrogant as to believe He directed my life in all ways—we had the freedom to make our own mistakes and go against His will, after all—the circumstances of my birth, my dietary restrictions, and the poverty that had led my family to give me up, were not decisions any of us had made. And a perfect example of how what can seem to be misfortune is the intentional will of God, leading one to their proper purpose in life. If not for any of that, my family would never have given me up to Ebon Gables, and I would not be serving in my role in the Church now, doing this most important task.

It had to be His will, and if He wanted me here, in this

moment, serving Him thusly, that meant He had faith that I was capable of this. I could do this.

I needed to have less doubt. Of His will and in myself.

I felt my muzzle tick up incrementally. Malachi must have noticed because he gave a slight smile as well. "Did that help?"

"Yes," I said gratefully. I turned towards him, clutching the blankets at my waist and fighting back a tremble of joy. "You have no idea how much. Thank you."

He smiled more broadly. "Always glad to see the fire come back to a Brother's eyes. You're good at this, lad. Trust me. I've looked over your work, and so has the Ministry, otherwise why would they recall me here to help you?"

"Well, that might also have meant they assumed I wasn't up to the task on my own," I sighed, my claws curling at my thighs. "To be fair, that's accurate."

"I have resources, experience, and authority you don't." He waved a paw. "That isn't your fault. You did the research and the legwork. Now's the chase. This bitch is just a slippery one, with a network we haven't penetrated yet. We'll hunt him down, you and I. And then you can help me crack him open. Channel some of that frustration of yours into something useful, eh?"

My throat closed up, and I was seized by another fit of coughing. Each hack made my vision go white and my head throb, but I felt the bed shift as Malachi moved beside me and the heavy slap of his paw on my back. I wasn't sure if it helped any. But he left his rough, calloused palm there after the coughing had subsided, and that *was* a comfort. I wasn't really sure why; I just enjoyed the weight of it. The connection that came from it.

I hadn't realized how very badly I'd wanted something like that, or for how long, until just then.

We sat in companionable silence for a time, until he spoke again. "Do you remember what you told me as we left that courtyard at the summer home, Brother Isidor?"

I froze and subconsciously bent forward, shying away from his touch. I felt the sharp edge of his claws, not digging but pressing against my shoulder, holding me in place.

"Calm," he eased in that level but commanding baritone. Then, "I take it that means you do?"

I swallowed. "I need to make Confession."

He didn't respond immediately. But I felt the bed shift again and he stood, the cutting line of his gaze drawing my own up to it, offering no alternative. He could compel without words.

This is what I wanted to be. An Inquisitor. Right now, I felt a canyon's width apart from him. How did I dare I aspire to this? I didn't have the presence, the nerve, I was a basket case of emotions and melodrama, I was—

"There is that doubt again," he rumbled and opened his palms, offering them to me. "Come, Brother. It is obvious you need this to clear your head. Let me be of service."

I gaped up at him. Was he saying..?

"You want me to give Confession… here? To you?" I stammered.

"In a sense, you already have," he reasoned. "But if you want to clear yourself with God, let me be the vessel for your redemption in His eyes."

"But you're not…" I mumbled.

A Priest.

Even Father Helstrom had taken his vows as a Father of our Parish when he'd retired from the Ministry. Templar were many things, but Priests, they were not. Some wore the honorific of 'Father' because of their age or seniority, but there was a big difference between the vows and the authority bestowed between Priests and Templar. Primarily for reasons of Confession and what remained sacrosanct: held in trust between only the Priest, the Sinner, and God.

"Brother, if I am permitted to tear confession from the mouths of the unwilling," he said without a trace of regret, "I fail to see how God would disapprove of me taking it from those who freely give it. The vows, the titles… they're pomp. You have my word everything you say will remain between the two of us and the Almighty."

He leaned down and plucked my hands from my lap, wrapping them in his own slightly larger ones. Our hand paws were similar colors, mine white, his a light cream, but his claws stood in stark contrast to my own, black, and longer. Inquisitors were not bound by the rules of Court Etiquette to trim back their claws or cover their teeth in public.

He leaned in closer to me. "All that matters, as I see it," he spoke, "is whether or not you trust me."

By doctrine, this was wrong. He was wrong. Every logical part of my mind and my faith told me as much.

But I *did* trust him. And how could I lie about that when I was literally about to give Confession? Lying, especially to an Inquisitor, was a sin.

He stayed standing over me, holding my palms in his. We were supposed to be at eye level, if we really intended to do this, but that would literally mean sitting in bed with me. Which… he'd been doing, a moment ago, and there was also the chair, but—

"Isidor."

I closed my eyes and just nodded.

There was the briefest of pauses and then, his deep voice began the prayer. "God, hear through mine ears the willing testimony of sin from this, your son. Relieve him of the burden of bearing it alone and show him the way to redemption."

I opened my eyes, staring down at our joined hands. For some reason, I couldn't bear to look up at him. But then, given what I was about to say, I could hardly be expected to.

"Tell me about these dreams," he prompted.

My heart pounded against my ribs. My paws were shaking. I had never felt so anxious, so frightened, so utterly unprepared to give Confession. Was it because it was him? Or because of what I was going to say?

He already knew, I reminded myself. I just had to beg forgiveness from God, now. I had to.

"Sometimes," I said around a dry tongue, wetting my mouth as well as I could to get the words out, "sometimes I'm in... a church. A crumbling place, and I-I don't think... I've ever actually been there. It's familiar but unfamiliar. I feel as though I am... meant? To be there? Like coming home, but... it's not home."

"Do you think this dream is a vision of some sort, then?" he asked, his voice steady. Not pushing me, but allowing me to follow the obvious train of thought there, if I wanted to.

"I don't—no," I said solidly. "I might have... perhaps... but not given what happens there. God would send me no such visions. And who am I to receive such direct guidance from Him? No. They are a creation of my mind, I'm certain. A collage of comforting memories meant to self-satisfy, to pave my path towards the things I desire. To justify my sins to myself."

I couldn't see him, but I felt, heard him hum, thoughtfully. "How introspective, Isidor. Not many can peer inwards and untangle our own justifications thusly. I think God would appreciate that you are so willing to question yourself, rather than buy into the notions that would most please you. Good. Continue."

I blinked, momentarily stunned. I couldn't remember ever being complimented while I gave Confession, before. How queer.

"It's not always the church," I said, my ears falling. "Sometimes it's a bed, a room—not necessarily the one I fell asleep in—and many times I even realize I'm dreaming. But I still cannot seem to stop myself."

I formed the words a few times, having trouble, but he gave me the space to continue. "She... he... is there. Almost always. Before I'd met them, when I had dreams like this, they were always... half-formed. It was never a specific person. But now, it's-I—there is no doubt. It's..."

Darcy.

"The Heart Thief," I said bitterly. "I do not know why they have such a *grip* upon my unconscious mind."

"Perhaps you're attracted to them."

"I..." God. He was right, of course. It was the most obvious conclusion. But... "I mean, not consciously," I insisted. "I would never—could never—that is to say, you could not really make a good faith argument against the fact that... they *are* attractive. Beautiful, even. But I don't *want* to be attracted to them."

"I could make that argument," he muttered. "But as you said, it hardly matters. The fact is, it is distressingly common, attraction outside one's own kind. Common, but we must remember, unnatural."

I nodded, "I know," I whispered.

"Contending with unnatural attraction is one of life's many tests," he continued. "As long as we are willing to recognize when we are broken, we can begin to mend. These... flaws in our logical minds, in our sinful bodies, may be life-long afflictions. God does not expect us to be perfect. He expects us to fight our hardest *for* that purity of spirit, even if that means we lose a few battles along the way."

"I don't know how to win this battle," I said, quietly but desperately. "It only seems to be getting worse. I've had dreams like this infrequently since I was fourteen, but they are *so* much more vivid now, and the hold they have over me is strengthening. They have grown more and more..." I stammered, "... obscene, a-and... when I wake..."

"What do you do in these dreams?" he asked, tone

implacable. Not answering the man, even by half, was not an option.

It took me too long to respond. Much too long. But somehow, eventually, I managed. "We touch one another," I said, voice threadbare. "We… put our muzzles on one another, and I put them beneath me, and I-I… we…" I hung my head, shame shrinking my entire body down. "… we fornicate. And when I wake, the evidence of my sin is upon my person. It has gone beyond my unconscious mind, now. I am losing control over my body. It betrays me."

"Your body is no separate person you can blame, Isidor," he said. "It is yours to command."

"It doesn't feel that way sometimes," I whispered.

"Sin is not always within our ability to control," he said, "at least not in its entirety. We falter, we fall to desire inevitably, but we can recognize it. We can repent. Do you know why we sin, Isidor?"

"Because it is mortal to sin," I replied automatically.

"Because," he gripped my palms tighter, "we are broken."

I nodded slowly.

"Admitting it to yourself deprives your ego of its shield. It is important that we have no pride when we stand before God in Judgment. Pride is utilitarian, it exists so that we may be made useful. It is not a defense against sin. That is why we make Confession. Now. It is important to speak the words aloud."

There was silence, and I realized he was waiting for me.

"I am…" I said, finally looking up, "…broken."

He nodded at me, keeping my gaze. "Yes."

"I am ravaged by sin," I said, sniffing. "I am weak before the temptations of the flesh. I want to win this battle, Brother. I want this to—" I dragged in another long breath and let it out with a shudder. "I want it to stop. Please, God. Take this burden from me or help strengthen me in the fight for my soul."

"In these dreams of yours, Brother," he asked, "is the Heart Thief a woman or a man?"

The question stopped me dead.

It had come so suddenly; I had been in the middle of my plea to God. But really, it was the next logical thing to ask, wasn't it? Because it mattered.

It mattered.

The severity of the sin was at issue, here. To have these sorts of feelings, to imagine these types of activities with a woman was bad enough. But with a man...

"I didn't even know they were a man until yesterday," I breathed.

A beat. And then, *knowingly*, he *knew* just by the sound of my voice! He said, "That is not what I asked, Brother."

The answer was undeniable. I couldn't *lie* to him—what would be the point in all of this?!

And I couldn't lie to God. He already knew.

"Both," I uttered, the words leaving my tongue burning like they were bile. I was disgusting. I was unsalvageable. All that talk of having faith in myself, of building up my confidence, and now he'd know, and he'd—

Oh, God. What did the Order do to Heretics? It varied. It could be anything from a public shaming, to corporal punishment, to excommunication. It could be *death*.

Would they really consider any of those for something that had only happened in my head, though?

"What did you do with him?"

I lifted my head again, quickly, only to find him still staring down at me with that cool expression. I wanted to ask, 'why does it matter?' It was all sin.

"We kissed," I said with difficulty.

He waited and then eventually asked, "Is that all?"

"With him, I... yes," I babbled, "she was always a woman in my dreams before then. That's... when I dreamt of her, that's when... the most lascivious things happened. But, Brother, what if it gets worse? What if I keep having these dreams, and he is in them, and—"

"Do you know how two men sin together, Isidor?" he asked, point blank.

Finally, at the very least, my honesty did not condemn me. "I —not really," I admitted. "I've never thought about it much."

He looked me over. It felt like he was staring *through* me, discerning—I suppose—whether I was lying. In that at least, I felt confident. I had no earthly idea what two men would do with their bodies that was meant to be done between a man and a woman. Kissing, I suppose. But I knew the depravity could run deeper than that.

This wasn't a good line of thought to linger on.

"Good," he said finally. "Best you not get an education. There is learning in this world that is useful Brother, and learning that will pave your road to damnation. Better to remain in the dark on some things."

A pounding rap so loud it went off in the apartment like a gunshot snapped both of us to attention. It repeated in quick succession several times, and it took me getting my bearings to realize it was coming from the door into the residence, just outside of this room.

Malachi whipped his head around to stare at the door with a curl of his lip and a flash of fang in the dark, his countenance gone defensive as a dyre guarding their den. His fur stood on end, and he let out a frustrated growl in his throat.

"I apologize for this Brother Isidor, but we must continue later," he said as he released my hands and went over to a hook at the corner of the room, where his blade was stowed.

I had never in my life been interrupted or let go of by someone giving me Confession. I stared down at my palms, not certain what to do.

"Who in the bloody hell demands my time in the middle of a

goddamn snowstorm?" he grumbled aloud, after quickly cinching the sword on his belt. I murmured a brief prayer of forgiveness for him for swearing as he did. Let alone in such a holy moment. But I understood the frustration acutely.

I forced myself out of bed, realized abruptly that I was only wearing my smallclothes, and searched about for my clothing. I found it folded neatly beside me on the end table and went about dressing as fast as I could while Malachi answered the door.

Even from inside the bedroom, I could see how he pressed his ear to the door first, then checked through the peep hole, *then* in the same way he'd answered the door to me, opened it halfway.

"Explain yourself," was how he greeted whoever was there, firm, commanding, as he'd spoken to me when we first met. Just a hint of latent intimidation.

"Are you Inquisitor Malachi?" an unfamiliar voice asked—nay, *demanded*. His accent was refined, he could've been a Pedigree, but it was still astonishing to me that he could speak with such a demanding tone to Malachi. I could only vaguely make out their shadows from the half-open doorway into the bedroom. The man sounded canine, looked to be far shorter than Malachi, and he had something in his hand. That's all I could make out.

"Aye Sir, I am," Malachi responded calmly. "You'd have no reason to be here unless you already knew that."

I craned my neck out the doorway while I tugged up my trousers, and the man's face finally came into focus. Obscured by drifts of snow (because Malachi wasn't allowing him inside), but discernable.

He was a Red Setter, or at least that's what the Pedigree Society called his kind. A head shorter than me and even more than that next to Malachi, his build rather average from what I could tell, with the long rust-colored fur draping off his angular face brushed and styled in handsome, loose waves. He had extremely light brown eyes, like honey, that stood out even more so when in the direct glow of a lantern. He was dressed well, wrapped in a silk scarf, wearing a dark coat and a fine hat, and he had a cane with a metal grip, held in one hand. Likely what he'd used to rap on the door with.

And the man looked... furious. Composed, making an effort to remain even-tempered, but I could feel his outrage from a hall away. When he spoke again, his voice reflected it.

"What Parish are you with? Are you even with the local Ministry?" he snapped. "Who's your handler? What cause was there for an Investigation—what *possible* cause could there be—into my Great Aunt and Uncle Lane?"

Without moving his gaze off the man, Malachi reached aside to the coat hook on the wall near the front door, where a small leather bag hung. I had one just like it that attached to my belt.

"I am Malachi of Redcoven. I am a Son of the Redcoven Parish, Saint Rhine's, and my handler here in the city is one Father Whitehall of Saint Rhine's." He produced something from his pouch then, creased and aged, and folded into quarters. His patents. His had *far* more seals on them than mine had.

"And your business with my extended family?" the man asked after snapping the paper out of Malachi's hand and looking it over, heedless of the snow falling on it.

"Let's not play coy," Malachi drawled, his voice sinking through the floor to barely register as anything more than a growl. He took his patents back, cocked his other arm in the doorway and leaned down and forward. The stranger held firm until he was inches from bumping noses with him, then was forced to move back and away.

"Discomfort them, force them to take a submissive posture."

I heard my Father's words, clear as a bell.

"Cillian Rathborne," Malachi clucked out the man's name slowly.

"Use their name. Use it as an accusation."

The Setter did not refute him. "You cannot," he breathed out through his obvious rage, "just enter one of my homes, unannounced, uninvited, and interrogate my family—"

"Oh, let's not do this," Malachi tutted, still pressing the man back with his very presence. "This dance. I've seen your entire file, son. You know this waltz well. Believe me when I say: you will not bribe or cajole your way out of this one."

He moved suddenly, pressing his advantage against the man until the both of them were outside, and grabbed his cane so hard, he yanked him forward with it.

"Use your body to speak louder than your words can. You can damage resolve far before it becomes necessary to damage flesh."

"Where is he?" Malachi rumbled.

"You are bound by the Crown Ministry Agreement to contact the Patriarch of a line first, by registered courier, before you interrogate other family members," the man—Cillian, he'd all but admitted to it—said. He was gritting his teeth, his breath puffing out his nose in pants, but he was standing his ground, to his credit. He seemed liable to fall off-balance, though. I think he *needed* that cane.

"Mister Lane is the Patriarch of the Lane household," Malachi said. "I asked to speak to him first. He'll tell you as much."

"*I* am the Patriarch of my extended family, since my father and my uncle's demise," he growled out. "Mr. and Mrs. Lane are in my care. You must contact *me* before all investigations into the Lane family."

Malachi only scratched his chin. "Send your complaint to the Ministry."

"If you saw my file," Cillian snarled, "then you already knew the Lanes were my wards. You did this *willfully*!"

"Do you think," Malachi gestured vaguely with a paw, "this impresses anyone, lad? This right here?"

He let go of Cillian's cane quite suddenly at that, and the man stumbled back, catching himself on the railing. Barely. I winced, only glad he hadn't fallen. The stairs here were narrow, precarious, and icy to boot. The man couldn't walk without an aid. A misstep or a fall in his case could have been especially dangerous. I found myself feeling I never would have taken such a risk for sheer intimidation, even if the subject were under Inquisition. Which he wasn't, yet.

I didn't understand the ways of Inquisitors, clearly.

"You don't frighten me," the Setter said in a simmering tone, after he'd steadied himself. "I've dealt with your Ministry before, far worse than you, and I'm not *impressed* by a man who bullies old people."

"The longer you shelter this criminal," Malachi said, "the greater the torment the Ministry will put you through. Where have you got him hidden away, now? Do you really think we won't sniff out his rank stench again? And again? Spare yourself, and him, the terror of an extended hunt. This doesn't end well for you, the path you're choosing—"

"Who is he?!" Cillian demanded, noticing me behind Malachi. The nobleman pointed at me, stabbing his blunt claw in my direction. "Him? That's the young one, isn't it? The whelp who threatened one of my servants outside? You!"

I went still, correcting myself from stepping back, but only barely. He continued to shake his finger in my direction, trying to walk back up to the door before Malachi's arm cut him off. It didn't stop his angry tirade at me, though.

"Who are you? I want to see *his* patents, too. Who do you think you are, drawing steel on my staff?!"

"He's 'staff' now, is he?" Malachi chuckled humorlessly.

"The person you cornered on the patio is my servant," Cillian insisted vehemently. "You frightened them off into a bloody snowstorm, after making wild accusations! Don't think I'm some fool you can run roughshod over. I *know* how these investigations must be conducted by the rule of law. I've got three Solicitors on permanent salary, I will make your life *hell*, you cur!"

He turned his ire back towards me, sticking out his hand again. "You! Patents! NOW!"

Malachi knew I had no patents, but honestly even if I had, they probably wouldn't have been enough for this man. Or enough, period, by the law. I *wasn't* an Inquisitor.

"My Brother here was never in your house—"

"He was on my grounds! Off the public road, past the gate, without *anyone* knowing he was there!" the man cried.

"Which is why he caught the criminal you were sheltering," Malachi stated.

This is why he'd wanted me outside. I didn't understand the law very well, since I hadn't been through my training yet. But I'd felt in my gut we'd been doing things wrongly. And Malachi had known that, and how to avoid the legal implications.

Cillian was trembling, noticeable mostly in his ears. He was staring only at me now, for some reason. And when he spoke again, it was leveled at me.

"You stay away from them," he said, the tips of his fangs glinting white as he spoke the words lowly. Showing fangs as a Pedigree was a *huge* break in decorum. "Do you hear me?"

He'd spoken to Darcy. The look in his eyes said it all. He'd *spoken* to Darcy. He knew *I* was the one who'd been chasing them all this while.

"Sir Rathborne?" Malachi's voice brought his gaze briefly back to him and away from me. "Tell us where he is," Malachi growled, "*now*. Or I will personally request to be your Interrogator when the time comes. And I promise you," his eyes slipped to slim blue crescents. I could see them from his side profile, but imagining them staring me down was properly intimidating. "I will not stop once I've gotten the answers I want. I will not stop when I am satisfied. I will put in enough time taking you apart that even I will grow bored of it. And still, I will not stop."

"You're a bloody lunatic," Cillian rasped through his teeth.

"Don't test me, young lord," Malachi clucked, almost fondly. "I don't honestly like breaking Pedigrees. Too much paperwork afterwards. Make all of our lives a bit easier, would you?"

Cillian's breath steamed out into the air, and he stared up at the towering canine. He gripped his cane a bit tighter, leaned up, and said, "Go to hell."

Malachi slammed the door in his face. I couldn't see him in the moments following, but I watched his shoulders slump back down, saw the wind go out of his sails. He didn't look dismayed, just... relaxing his posture.

When he turned to look at me, his features had schooled themselves back into the more congenial demeanor he'd had with me since yesterday.

"Back to resting for you, Brother. I'll handle this."

We didn't talk about my Confession.

Not for the entire day following. Granted, I spent much of it in bed, save a few trips to tend to my personal needs, wash the road off, and have another two meals down in the Archives with Malachi. We didn't talk about it then, either. Not a word.

And I suppose I'd been expecting to? It was like waiting for the axe to fall. Never in my life had I given Confession—let alone admitted to such a transgression against God—without being instructed on some means for absolution. Even if it was just extra prayers or duties. Something.

Anything.

Malachi asked nothing of me. We didn't even finish the prayer together. I eventually did so on my own, begging forgiveness from God without the aid of a Priest, because I was desperate to tie off the loose end the night had left me with. It felt inadequate. *I* felt inadequate.

But also, humiliatingly, relieved.

Which made the guilt bite all the harder, and I knew I deserved to feel that, as well!

I felt too many things to name. It was all a tangle. My thoughts would wind and unwind throughout my solitary hours in that bed, going over everything I'd said, trying to understand why Malachi wasn't angry with me. Or if he was, when he'd choose to express it. Maybe he was just disappointed. Maybe he was going to turn me in?

He was an Inquisitor. It was literally his duty to do so.

But would he?

Something about the whole of it felt wrong in a way that had nothing to do with the technicality of giving Confession to a man who hadn't taken the right oaths. It was his insistence, his patience with me, how he'd known to ask every right (wrong) question. It had felt... sheltering? Like he'd wanted to give me safe harbor. That's what Confession was *supposed* to be, so why did it set me so ill at ease?

Because it had felt like a secret.

We could keep no secrets from God obviously, and we had in fact called upon Him to listen. But it almost felt like Malachi had offered to take my confession to keep my secrets between the two of *us,* here in the mortal world.

"You don't tell anyone else that, ever. You hear me? Not ever. Not even a Priest."

Why did it feel like he'd said that? Had he said something like that? Why couldn't I remember, exactly?

I wanted it all to come to a head, somehow. I needed to know what came next. But bringing it up was impossible, and Malachi was hardly in the apartment over the course of the next day. He hustled in and out, checking in on me to be certain my needs were being met, and sparing very little conversation save to assure me he was working on the case. 'Applying pressure' to the young lord, in his words. He was calm, certain, professional. He seemed very sure the Heart Thief would not leave the city without us finding out. To be fair, up until now they'd only taken buggies and coaches, at least as far as we knew. There was nothing suggesting they were a seasoned traveler who could orienteer in such rural country, let alone with the weather as dreadful as it had been. And going on foot would have been a death sentence.

I wanted to believe Malachi, and I should have been content to defer to him, at this point. I had done—quite literally—more than I was sanctioned to. But it wasn't just my prayers that left me feeling adrift, unfinished, balanced precariously on the edge of panic...

Up until now, my pursuit of Darcy had been in my own hands. I was given to believe no one in the Ministry thought I was on the right track, or at least that they weren't taking my reports seriously, but apparently that was not the case. They'd sent a seasoned Inquisitor, (as they should have, considering the gravity of this case and this person's crimes) and I was only still a part of all of this because he seemed to think I would be useful to him while he worked on it.

Malachi had been more complimentary and hospitable to me than I deserved, especially given it was my *repeated* failures that had let our quarry slip *again*. He didn't seem to hold that against me. He didn't expect me to be as competent as he was.

A selfish, immature part of me felt it was patronizing, but I knew well enough to check those feelings. They were wrong and I was wrong for feeling them, and ungrateful in the extreme. Malachi was an experienced mentor, a senior member of the Ministry being gracious enough to show me how this sort of work ought to be done, and I'd be a fool to buck the help I'd so desperately been asking for, all this time.

But... the way he did things...

I wasn't completely simple; I knew much of his demeanor, the way he talked to people, was theater. These were the intimidation tactics, the social manipulation we relied upon in our line of work to get most of what we were after from people *without* the need for interrogation or force. In a way, it was a mercy. A kindness.

I just wasn't used to *seeing* it, and it was a shocking awakening. I'd witnessed hints of the cunning, the investigative eye, the watchfulness, in Father Helstrom. The man had been a storied Inquisitor in his day, and you didn't lose that edge just because you went into retirement. But still. I couldn't imagine him doing half the things Malachi had done in his short conversation with Cillian... even going so far as to knock him off-balance on a precarious staircase...

But realistically, he probably had. And worse.

This was the world I had only been given glimpses of through the hardness in my Father's eyes. Or the canny way Brother Dolus always seemed to know everything that happened at Ebon Gables, even when he'd been away for weeks. The Ministry only accepted those who endured years of rigorous training and conditioning for the work they'd be tasked with, and this one day I'd gone through made it clear just how immature I was compared to all of them.

I was in over my head on this case in *so* many ways. Brother Malachi was just trying to protect me, and get the job done. If I found it all overwhelming, it's because it was. This was beyond my abilities and experience. I had to trust him more, and doubt less.

It was just so hard, when every part of me seized up at the thought of what came next. Even physically, sometimes. My body was reacting to my anxieties in ways it never had before. I was fair certain it was part of what was making and keeping me sick.

I wanted—needed this all to be over. But I simultaneously

dreaded what that would necessitate. And I was ringing myself out over the implications of *why* I felt that dread.

For once in my life, giving Confession had not helped alleviate my guilt, nor given me any kind of peace. I could not feel God's grace, nor any clear direction. I felt so... apart from Him. More removed from His guidance than I could ever remember feeling.

I wanted my Father. I needed help. Maybe not Confession, but to talk.

On the second day of snow, lighter now but still falling, Malachi left me after breakfast to make for the Lane house again. He was meeting Cillian this time, to question the family further. He left me with a key so that I could come and go as I pleased. He was literally opening his house to me.

Earnestly, I was glad not to be going along for this round of questioning. It was impossible that Darcy would be foolish enough to still be there, and he was the only person in this case I wanted to speak to again. What's more, the interrogation was certain to be thick with animosity, and I didn't know how to talk to a man like Lord Rathborne without losing my temper and making a fool of myself. The only Pedigree family I'd ever really had any experience with were the Hudsons, and they'd been cordial and hospitable, but very clear on propriety and standing in their home. They'd kept a respectful distance in our working relationship, not involved me overly much in their family affairs, and regarded me on about the same level as a trustworthy servant.

Whatever happened today at the Lane Estate was going to be unpleasant, if the brief interaction Malachi and Cillian Rathborne had already shared was any indication. And it didn't need to involve me. In fact, my presence would be a detriment.

It was cowardly I suppose, but I was happy to leave it to Malachi. He'd informed me the night before that he had some leads on the connections the Lanes and the Rathbornes had in the city, and where they might be sheltering the Heart Thief. I'd spent what time I hadn't been sleeping over the last day in the Archives, pouring over information on Cillian, his family and their history, and while I'd learned a lot, none of it would really help me catch Darcy. I was still firmly at a dead end.

I had to trust Malachi would find information I could not, at this point. Or it would be back to canvasing all over the map in the adjoining towns, until I found another sighting. And that felt like going backwards.

I decided that day to walk to Saint Rhine's. It was barely a few blocks and the snow was only lightly flurrying any more. I'd taken my 'medicinal' tea for the day and while the cough was being stubborn, I was hardly ill enough that I couldn't get a little air and exercise.

I bundled myself up and emerged into the blinding, pristine perfection of a city painted in glittering white. Redcoven had been beautiful before, but the fresh coat of soft, downy snow had settled into every unsightly crevice. It sparkled in the previously bare-limbed trees and tinted every shadow blue-gray. It was ethereal and mostly undisturbed. Like walking through the kingdom of Canus in the heavens.

My borrowed mule was in the stables at the Church and she was being well cared for, I was certain, but I decided I'd go to check on her first. While we hadn't exactly taken to one another, she'd done the hard work of getting me here despite my own failings at land navigation. I'd had an apple with breakfast today and saved half of it for her. She'd earned it, and even the lowliest of God's creatures deserved gratitude for their labors. Besides, she'd likely be returned to her Parish once the snow was cleared, and I wanted to say goodbye.

My breath puffed out around me past the thin barrier of the lilac scarf Mabel had knitted me the year before. Purple was the color of bravery, she'd said. I felt a smile tug at my muzzle as I remembered our Solstice Day celebration together. Nicholas had narrowly bested me in a rope tug contest and indulged too much in the cask of hard cider he'd been awarded by the Brothers. Father Helstrom let him off the hook for the indiscretion, given the holiday. A truly rare grace from our otherwise stern Father. We'd all gathered in the choir as the sun set and sung hymns for hours. Even Nicholas, which had led to many slurred lines and bouts of laughter from our younger brothers and sisters.

I missed my family.

It was natural to miss one's home after being away from it for so long.The last time I'd spent so much time away from the Abbey had been in this city, when I'd come here for training. And now I knew a Senior Brother here, an Inquisitor, who called this place home. Maybe this was all a sign. Maybe Redcoven could become a second home for me, in time. I could make acquaintances with other Brothers at Saint Rhine's, perhaps even friends in the city. I'd never really had friends outside of my brothers and sisters at the Abbey.

But this was part of growing up. Expanding one's circles and knowledge. And if I really wanted to become someone like Malachi, I'd have to be prepared to travel and bring the Word to many corners of the world. Or at least many different Parishes in Amuresca.

These thoughts were pleasantly distracting and briefly eased the tensions I'd been wrestling with the last two days. There was no sin in thinking about one's future, especially as a means to calm a disordered mind. So, I continued thinking on the possibilities, taking in the sights of the city, bedecked in its winter finery, as I walked those few blocks.

I arrived at the stables adjacent to the Ministry Office where I'd left my mule in the care of the stable boy a few days earlier. She was the first to greet me on my left, eagerly rustling inside and tucking her head out the top of her door, ears twisting forward.

"Oh-ho," I snuffed, "happy to see me, are you? Where was that enthusiasm when we were on the road? Might it perhaps be attributed to the apple in my pocket?"

She flicked exactly one ear and looked offended at my accusation.

"No, of course not," I rolled my eyes. "You're just darling, aren't you? How dare I defame your character."

I produced the apple and held it out to her on my palm, patting her cheek as she crunched into it. While she ate, I briefly glanced down the row of stable doors to mentally apologize to our onlookers. I'd only brought the one apple half.

They were in fact all looking at us. Enviously. But one familiar face caught my attention immediately and sent a bolt of shock down my spine.

"Dragonfly?" I blinked, making sure I was seeing correctly. But there was no mistaking the palomino mare, I'd been taking care of her on and off since I was thirteen. She was honey-colored with a forked white stripe down the bridge of her nose and a cream-colored mane. The stripe was distinctive because of its shape.

I patted the mule once more and headed down towards the mare, leaning past her attempt to nuzzle at my pocket, and looked into the stall to make absolutely certain.

"It *is* you," I said quietly. I leaned back out and stroked her nose, while she tried to nibble on my scarf. "Then, someone from home is..."

"Brother Isidor."

I clenched my paws reflexively at the unexpected voice, worrying at the knuckle of my missing finger. I turned towards the silhouette at the other end of the stables, starkly outlined against the glaring white of the sunlit snow outside.

The tall canine made his way towards me unhurriedly, shrugging back the hood of his fur-lined winter robe. He wasn't dressed like he'd been outside for long though. He'd probably just thrown it on recently, judging by the fact that it was still open in the front. He wore civilian dress beneath, weathered and nondescript, which I wasn't used to seeing on him, but I knew he often dressed in secular garb when he was working for the Ministry.

"Brother Dolus," I said, stammering for a moment, still in shock. I just hadn't been expecting, of all people...

"I saw you through the window," he explained, "walking this direction."

I straightened up as he approached and made to stand at attention, but he quickly waved a palm at me. "Please. No need, Brother. In fact, outside of our Abbey, it is better you regard me as no one of importance."

"That would be difficult for me, Brother," I said, trying to settle as he'd asked and appear more casual.

"Try," he said in that dry way he did when what he was saying was a command, but he didn't want to come off that way. Father Helstrom was sterner, more outwardly demanding, but in a way, I preferred it. Brother Dolus could be hard to understand and thus hard to please.

"Why have you come to Redcoven, Brother?" I asked the obvious question.

"Oh, come now Isidor," he said, "you're a sharp lad, I'm certain you can land on the answer there without my help."

"The Heart Thief," I said, because there was no other explanation that made sense. "But... so, the Ministry must have sent you? Because I've sent many letters to Father Helstrom, but he can't have heard we found them here, a few days ago. Not in time for you to have arrived on horseback."

Dragonfly was a sprightly, swift young mare. An Inquisitor's horse, perfect for travel for one fellow with a good seat in just about any weather. But even still, despite the circuitous path I'd taken in my travels to get here, by a straight shot it should have taken him four, five days? If he rode *hard*. And a good carriage would have been swifter.

But more noticeable, more traceable. And more likely to get held up in the poor weather. Brother Dolus always traveled on horseback. Like the Knights and Crusaders of old. All the more impressive because he must have caught the tail end of the snowstorm, and he'd *still* navigated the roads and made the trip safely for himself and Dragonfly.

"I'm here by my own choice," he answered my question about who'd sent him and why, simply but evasively. Answering without really answering. "As this investigation involves my most promising son, you can hardly blame me for worrying, can you?" He approached closer, reaching a hand up and pressing his fingers into the stained, shaved-down spot at the base of my skull where I'd had a stitch or two put in. He made a displeased noise in his muzzle. "Right I was to do so, apparently. This is from the incident at the Lane Estate? Any issues with your vision or dizzy spells since?"

"No, sir," I responded, tipping my head back so he could inspect the minor injury better. "Just a slight fall."

If he knew what had happened at the Lane Estate, it was safe to say he'd been entirely caught up, either by the Ministry or Malachi, or both. Hardly surprising.

"When did you get in?" I asked.

"Late yesterday," he said. "I took my rest at a shrine that night, never you fear. Avoided most of the storm. I knew you were in the city and where you were keeping residence," he anticipated me before I could ask, "but I was assured you were on bedrest for… this… and another of your trifling colds. You really must begin taking better care of yourself, son. Remember, you represent an investment of *countless* hours of schooling and training, as well as other resources that the Ministry can hardly afford to waste. If not concern for your own well-being, think on that the next time you go off half-cocked and behave recklessly." His jowls turned up. "Or think on me and how I shall have to suffer Father Helstrom's agonizing if something should happen to you. That bloodhound can *agonize*, let me tell you."

"Father Helstrom," I said, cautiously optimistic, "is he—"

"One of us needed to tend to the flock, son," he said. "Besides, the man is retired, let his old bones find some rest, will you? No, I have come alone, I'm afraid. But is that not enough already?"

"Of course sir."

"This vexing case," he sighed irritably, "has claimed enough of the Ministry's resources as it is. Now, at least, they seem intent on settling the matter with haste. Better we see to it that it is done, swiftly and with no expenses spared, than languish for a further few years."

"I agree," I nodded.

"Good," he replied curtly. "I'll be assisting the Ministry and the Inquisitor here, going forward. And you, Brother, may focus on your recovery and ready yourself to return home."

"With all due respect, sir," I said, because I'd felt this coming and was as ready for it as I could be, "I am one of those resources that cannot be spared from the case. I know the details of the crime and the criminal themselves, intimately. Even Brother Malachi has said he's found my assistance indispensable."

The Inquisitor's name brought a sudden frown to the monk's features and a darkness to his gaze I had seen very few times throughout my life, but I remembered well. Brother Dolus did not look angry often. But when he did, he was fearsome.

"Are you comfortable, Brother Isidor?" he asked me unexpectedly. "Keeping residence with Brother Malachi?"

"Yes," I said, uncertainty creeping into my voice until the word was almost a question. "He has been very kind, hospitable, and fair with me."

"Mmh," he replied neutrally. There was a pause, long enough that it began to grow uncomfortable between us, and I could feel his eyes *digging* in to me. The boys back home called it 'The Inquisitor's Stare.' Father Helstrom was less subtle about it, more prone to exercise it, and it almost always bore confessions or results. With Brother Dolus it was rarer, but no less effective. All of us knew the penalty of incurring his wrath.

I didn't know what he wanted me to say. I mulled silently over a few things, but only one real indiscretion came to mind and good Lord, I did not want to talk about that with him.

"Take care in how much you… absorb… from Brother Malachi, lad," Brother Dolus at last said, his expression softening. "He has a long and troubled record of disciplinary issues and *serious* infractions of conduct; failings of character I would rather you not emulate or think are normal for us in this kind of work."

"Such as?" I asked, venturing the question quietly so it wouldn't sound too demanding.

"Brother," he chided, "that is between Brother Malachi, the Ministry, and God. You know that."

"Ah." I swallowed.

"… but I will say this much," he murmured. "These were not minor infractions. He is a sinner, Isidor. Washed in the waters of redemption for his transgressions, forgiven by the Ministry and God, but not without much time and blood paid through re-education and penance. That is not something I would want to see one of my sons endure."

"'Re-education'?" I'd never heard of something like that. How was one 're-educated'?

"A work camp, Isidor," he explained quietly. "Malachi made some very grave mistakes in his youth, and he paid dearly for them. He is not a man to aspire to."

My mouth was dry, my hand ached for the empty joint it had lost, but something in me *could* not be still, *could* not be sated, until I'd put to words the voice that was demanding to be heard from the recesses of my mind.

"If he has truly overcome such bone-deep sin," I said, "and endured his penance to prove himself now in the eyes of the Ministry as worthy of his title, despite it all... then I actually think that is *very* aspirational."

Brother Dolus could fool one into believing he was a mild-mannered man, and sometimes emotions could be hard to pick out in his features. But there was a hint of genuine shock following my reply to him.

I waited for it to break. I waited for anger, or disappointment, or worse yet, that coldness he could exude. But instead, he... laughed.

A rasp, breathless enough that I knew it was real. He even closed his eyes a moment, staring down at the straw-littered planks and letting the chuckles shake his shoulders.

"Oh, how I wish Germain were here for that," he said almost to himself, before looking back up at me. "Some time in the world fending for yourself on the roads has finally hardened you up from the sickly little pup you were, Isidor."

"Sir?" I balked.

"You're becoming a man, son," he said. "Standing up to your father or the nearest to it, in any case."

Father Helstrom was *literally* my Father, in the religious sense if not by blood, but I didn't dare say that out loud.

"Alright, I know when I'm beat. You're fixated on this and that's fine. Stay in the city a few weeks longer if you like," he said, waving a hand. "And if you enjoy Brother Malachi's company, so be it. I'm certain at the very least he'll have plenty of busywork for you to do at the Archives, and you're a bit of a bookworm, so you ought to enjoy that. It's hardly as though we're in a rush to get you on another assignment. If you'd like to see this one through to the end, you're safe enough in Redcoven with all of us here."

"I'd like that," I said, letting out a breath. "I was worried you were going to send me back to the Hudsons."

"Oh, no, that opportunity has passed," he said dismissively. "And taken on quite eagerly by another young Templar very happy to find their place in such a fine household. Young Nicholas knew a good posting when he saw one."

"Nick?!" I blurted out. "How… he isn't even ordained…"

"He is training for the position with Templar Olvar, and will succeed him when he retires," he said, cocking his head. "Oh, don't get envious now, Brother Isidor. You had your chance."

"No, no," I insisted, unable to mask my shock. "It's just, he's only fifteen—"

"Our Parish is short on well-trained, unmarried Templar who are available for posting," he said. "We can only bring up so many boys, Isidor. As I said, it takes resources. The Hudsons do not prefer a married Templar on their grounds; their lady objects to the presence of any young, low-bred woman so near to the estate… and her husband. In retrospect, this works out well. It's an ideal, easy post for a young Templar to cut his teeth on for five years or so until he is ready to marry. Nicholas will do well there. And you…"

I hadn't interrupted him. He'd just trailed off, like he was considering how to phrase what he meant to say. Which made me nervous.

"You are a passionate young man, Brother," he settled on. "And those passions need be redirected before they incite you to troublesome behavior."

"Have I done something?" I asked nervously. What did he know? How did he know it?

"No, lad," he chuckled again. "I'm just saying, I believe it is time you marry. You can finish out this case, but afterwards, before you enter your training with the Ministry, would be an ideal time. There is nothing preventing you from being a married man when you apply. It will not hurt your chances. And you'll be sent to the Ministry grounds in Amurfolk for your education; they provide very adequate apartments for keeping a wife."

"I—" I sputtered, "I'm not… I-I'm not even twenty, yet."

"Yes, and if you were one of your sisters, you'd be a spinster already," he said. "Some young men prefer not to marry until they are more seasoned, more experienced with the world. But Isidor, you are not moneyed, you are not weighing many prospects. It isn't as though extended courtships would do you any benefit. And moreover, you are simply not the sort of young man who *should* wait, in my own opinion."

That absolutely begged the question, "Why?"

He gave me a long, even stare. "Very well. Isidor, I am not Father Helstrom. I do not mind being indelicate with you, if I must. You are, as I said before, a *passionate* young man. For some of us, the fires burn a little hotter in our youth."

Oh. I had an idea what he meant, now.

"You struggle with lust," and there, he had just outright stated it. I felt my ears burn and couldn't hold his gaze any longer. "And before you ask, I do not need to take Confession from you to know. Father Helstrom speaks to me in how best to counsel you, because he falls woefully short in knowing how to address these matters." He sighed. "I do not know what he has told you that may have been of any help, but please, allow me to offer my own more educated viewpoint. Father Helstrom means well, but he does not understand your struggles in this sin at least. Trust me." He was very certain-sounding on that point.

"As you say, sir," I mumbled.

"These feelings of yours," he continued. "They are not unnatural, they are not heretical, they are *vigor*. It speaks to your potency, in fact. You'll sire many sons someday, Isidor."

"… really?" I asked after a few moments, tipping my ears up marginally.

"Yes," he said, shaking his head with a smile that seemed genuine. "Desire if directed appropriately is part of God's design for man. It is right and natural that you should feel these things, should want for them, even outside the bounds of marriage. The sin would be acting upon them before you've sealed your union. That is why it is *so* important that young men like you, with health, vigor, and a respectful demeanor that will certainly temper those flames when you are at last consummating your marriage, marry young. Before you have faltered and given way to temptation."

I found myself nodding, murmuring a quiet, "I do understand."

It made sense, everything he was saying. I wasn't sure why it still felt wrong to me. Or at the least, why I was so uncertain.

"Think of a marriage as a hearth," he said, clasping my hands in his. "Properly contained… safe… a fire can warm a home and foster a family. But allowed to burn out of control, without restraint, it can destroy. You need to build your hearth, son. Soon will be the right time to do so. Think of the life you can have, training with the Ministry in Amurfolk, being forged into a sword worthy of the Inquisition. This is what you wanted, yes? Father Helstrom and I will support you. Amurfolk would be an excellent city to break in a wife, too. You'd have all the guidance and support you'd need from Senior Brothers who've navigated their own marriages."

He released my hands and I found myself staring down at them for a time following. I flexed all nine fingers.

He seemed to realize, then glanced back down himself, giving me a fond look. "Ah yes, my 'Southpaw.' You've distinguished yourself so well already, Isidor. I'm very proud, you know, of the man you've become. And you were not blessed well from birth, so it is especially impressive you've come so far."

"Thank you, sir," I said.

"Father Helstrom sent his last letter with me," he said, reaching to his shabby vest pocket to pull the carefully-wrapped and sealed letter out. "No sense wasting a courier. I think this one is replying to one of your letters from over a week ago though, so it may be out of date. All the same."

I took it from him and noted the seal quickly before I stowed it in my own belt pouch. It was unbroken, the stamp bearing the seal of the 'wolf's head' side of our country's gold crown. A perfect, flawless imprint of the design.

Father Helstrom's seal had a scratch in it that crossed over the design on the left corner. A notch. The notch was missing, on this seal.

I said nothing, but forced a smile and thanked him. "Thank you for bringing it all this way," I said. "I'll need to write to him again, soon."

"He wanted for me to sit with you for Confession, as well," he said while gesturing towards the Ministry office. "Shall we? I have a small room that will do."

"Oh, no need," I said, before I'd really thought about it. "I've already…"

He quirked an eyebrow at me. "With Father Whitehall, then? Very well. I suppose I should have known you'd get right to it as soon as you arrived here."

I wanted to correct myself, then. Tell him what had happened. I needed to make proper Confession, and Brother Dolus had taken the oaths, despite not being a Priest. It was helpful to have two elders ordained in one Abbey who could do so, considering how large our flock was. He rarely made the time that Father Helstrom did to take Confession, but he was permitted to. I could have absolved myself properly this time. I could have talked to him about what had happened with Malachi, asked him what to do, or if I'd done anything wrong that night. How to repent, if I had.

But he'd been so disapproving of Brother Malachi, I was

afraid of what he'd say. Afraid of what he might *do*. Not to me, but to him. I didn't want to upset the balance of the case.

Or at least, that's what I told myself.

"We should sit down all the same and discuss everything that's happened," he said, walking with me down the stalls, towards the lane outside. "I want you to tell me everything I haven't heard already from the Ministry."

"Yes, sir," I nodded.

"Something is bothering you, Isidor," he noted, almost idly. But it wasn't a question. "Confession aside, I am your Senior and I like to think, one of your fathers. At least insofar as God has blessed me. You can speak to me of what troubles you outside of the rituals, you know. I'd like that, even."

Despite his unsettling ability to know more than he should, his occasional aloofness and odd way of phrasing some of his counsel, Brother Dolus *was* one of my mentors. As he'd said, even a father, of a sort. I respected him, and trusted he wanted what was best for me.

For the most part.

I took my time, trying to boil down everything that had sent me reeling over the last few days into one question. One thought that I knew I could not ask Father Whitehall or even someone like Father Helstrom. But perhaps Brother Dolus was the right person to talk to about matters like this. Because for all of my misgivings about the man, he could be more grounded, more practical, and more forgiving of mortal folly than most. He had been, and still was, an Inquisitor, and he'd seen the worst the world had to offer in his work, I was certain.

He'd told me repeatedly just now how all of these struggles I'd had with lust were normal, natural. He'd given me advice that had honestly been... sound. Even if I was still trepidatious about the idea of marriage. To see it from that perspective, it felt less dire.

At the worst, he'd have me give Confession. And then, at

least, I could spill it all, and maybe that would fix things somehow.

"Brother," I said hesitantly. "I know this is heresy, but it is also education I may eventually receive in Amurfolk, so please forgive me asking."

"Much of what you will learn as an Inquisitor concerns heresy," he confirmed. "We can hardly investigate that which we do not understand."

"How do two men sin together?"

He stopped walking. I nearly tripped, but stopped in time and turned towards him, worriedly. What I saw on his features was not anger or something worse, but resignation. He sighed out through his nose and stared past me to the street. Towards the direction I'd walked from.

"I'm sorry," I said quietly. "I shouldn't have asked… I'm… I only asked because—"

"I am unfortunately already very aware of why you're asking me this now, Isidor," he cut me off.

I shrunk back. He knew? But then, that's right, he'd said he'd been talking to Father Helstrom about my issues with lust. Which meant my dreams. Which meant he knew or at least suspected the Heart Thief was involved, and he also likely knew that we'd recently learned they were a man, and—

"I think you should move your residence to the Ministry Offices for now," he said. "Or Saint Rhine's. Either is fine."

"Why?" I blinked, confused.

"Because I'm not risking leaving one of my boys in the care of *that* man, that's why," he said, his voice hard. "Absolutely no arguing on this point, Isidor. Understood? Tonight. Get your things together."

He was worried about…

"Malachi?" I asked, shocked. "You're worried about my staying at his residence? No, no. I'm asking for my own clarification—"

"Isidor, I know who put these thoughts in your head," he said tiredly. "Please do not try to protect the man."

He wasn't entirely wrong, but still. "It's not like what you're inferring," I tried to insist.

"If one of my boys was a sodomite, I would know," he said, his tone leaving no room for error. "Especially you, Isidor. I have never raised a boy more prone to vomiting up his feelings and every inner thought at any given chance and time. Females, certainly. But you wear your heart on your sleeve and give Confession more often than most monks." He sighed. "Trust me more than you do yourself, lad. I would know."

"'Sodomite'?" I said after a moment. I knew the word vaguely, in an academic sense, but surely he didn't mean—

"They breed one another in the arse, lad," he stated factually, without preamble. "Or the mouth. Like whores."

I stared at him in dumb silence, aghast.

He patted me on the shoulder, moving past. "Yes, that's the proper response. Horror. You see? You're fine. But I suppose you're right; you had to get an education sooner or later, so there you have it. Now, come. I'd rather be discussing the sodomite Pedigree fellow and his little man-cunt thief, yes? Let's get back to that, so we can be done with this case and done with this city."

On the way back to Malachi's apartment, late into the afternoon, considering how I was going to explain to the big fellow that my Senior Monk didn't think I was safe with him, I remembered my prayer book.

The cache Darcy had told me of. It was one of the few things I'd learned of in speaking with them that, for whatever reason, I hadn't shared with anyone else yet. It wasn't even in my report to the Ministry.

I'd report it eventually, I told myself. But it was my prayer book. It was personal. And I wanted to be certain I got my hands on it first, if Darcy had in fact been telling the truth.

And then I was on a mission, making my way through the city with purpose, towards the spot she… *he* had told me he'd hidden it away. Why I hadn't gone for it earlier, I could hardly justify.

Oh, right. I'd been injured and sick.

I was still sick, the cough stubbornly reminding me of its existence, stuck in my lungs like tar. And rushing through the city streets in the waning hours, the air growing colder by the minute, certainly did it no favors.

But all I could think of was getting my prayer book back.

It isn't even as though there was any particular wisdom in there that would shed light on anything going on in my life right now. The prayers were all those I could read in my Tome of Faith, just selectively-picked for easy reading. And my journalling was, well, all from within. Nothing to be had there I hadn't already ruminated over hundreds of times before.

But I wanted it. I wanted it because… to hell with it, I could admit it to myself. I wanted it because of its connection to him. I wanted it because he'd left it for me, he'd returned it to me, and maybe, just maybe, he'd…

He'd written in the margins of the novels he'd left me. So maybe.

Maybe.

I had to dig through a crust of ice and a foot of collected snow to claw down into the hollow of the tree, then a mass of frozen dirt, leaves, and debris. And then the potato sack was frozen, because of course it was. But it was there, just as he'd said it would be.

I plopped down into the tangled nest of snow outside the hollow after I'd finally plied the small leather-wrapped book free. It was really there. It was solid and cold in my hand; he hadn't lied to me.

The spine cracked when I opened it, and my breath left my lungs on the very first page, because it was exactly as I'd left it. Nothing additional there.

I flipped one page, then another, my shoulders slumping slowly as I went. What had I honestly been hoping for? Was I mad?

And then… and then…

Red ink.

Halfway in, on one of the pages I'd written in long ago, in a few spare pages between the psalms on forgiveness. He'd written in calligraphy, elegant and beautiful, and decorated with a stylized, simple twisting pen pattern that resembled a dove in the top left corner. As if it were a bookmark, begging my attention.

'I like your hand-writing. It's unusual.'

I kept reading. And then I flipped furiously through the rest of it, looking for more. He had only written on the one page. But he'd written a whole paragraph. Not just about my handwriting.

I could have cried.

I gasped, struggling to breathe, coughed, swallowed, and read it again. And again.

God, I needed to find him. God, please.

I needed to find him before they did.

9

GONE ROGUE

It was night by the time I began to make my way back to Malachi's apartment. Dark, but cloudless, the moon nearly full in the sky and throwing the streets into stark relief between patches of pitch and muted blue-gray. The sky was polluted with lantern light here, the stars hardly visible, but I could vaguely pick out the rearing head of the Ciraberos constellation, one of the most prominent in the sky regardless of how clear your vista was. Sailors used it vociferously, swearing by the eye star. Even above their compasses, sometimes. I'd once read that when sailing very far north, compasses could become unreliable. I wasn't sure if that was true, but the Admiral who'd written about it certainly seemed to think so.

That's how I felt right now. Throughout the whole of my life, even before I'd been taken in by the Abbey, God had been my north star. My guiding light, and the assurance of hope for all I had ever wanted to be or could be. But right now, I felt untethered, sailing into unknown waters, drifting farther and farther away with each passing day from His guidance and the clarity of mind that the conviction of my truth gave me. I had never felt so alone... so deep in the bramble that His Word was audibly fading.

It wasn't as though I'd ever have claimed to be in communication with God directly. I was no prophet. But growing up, Father Helstrom had taught me how to hear my 'inner voice': a beacon inside your heart, inherent to all of God's intelligent beings. Feral animals lacked an inner voice, which is why they lived shameless lives of depravity and sin. But it wasn't their fault. They didn't know any better. They were made to be hunted, shepherded, and to carry on the natural processes of the world. They were lesser beasts.

But we had the gift of morality. The inner voice of God, directing us in our lives. We could choose to ignore it of course, and many did. We might suffer the bite of humiliation and guilt for doing so, to various degrees. Some were better at ignoring those punishments. Those people were as shameless as animals, guiltless, and more prone to sin because of it. It wasn't inherent. You couldn't be *born* that way.

But you could wear down your ability to hear your inner voice by ignoring it, by not grappling with your guilt, and *not giving Confession.* And I was worried– nay, scared– that I had done just that.

Throughout my frantic, obsessive pursuit of the Heart Thief, I had on many occasions ignored those quiet warnings. Those hesitations, my uncertainty when I'd engaged in something suspect... my inability to fully grapple with my sin. I'd begun repressing it, pushing it aside until some later date, convincing myself that what I was doing in that present moment was more important.

It was so easy. So easy, I realized, to destroy yourself this way while still *believing* you were on the right path. And still, even though I was coming to realize this, even though I was unable to lie to myself any more about the fact that I was *slipping*, and I *knew* it...

...I couldn't stop myself.

Because I didn't go straight back to Malachi's apartment. Didn't pack up my things and turn right back around, and march directly to the Ministry headquarters. I didn't follow orders that night.

I found myself, instead, prayer book gripped in one paw as I walked, in the moneyed neighborhood the Pedigree estates occupied. This would be considered 'high town' in most cities, but here in Redcoven it was not so very separate from the trade district. Only a few roads over, the paving stones just slightly newer and less cracked. Red, like the clay in the rivers here, as the city's name suggested. Painted with icy swirls of hard-packed snow in between the patterns they'd been laid out in. A marvel of canine engineering. To think how much clay had to have been extracted, how many bricks made, and laid out. The *work* that went into building our cities was mind-boggling when you thought about it.

And it was all done by us common people, in service for our entire lives to those of us who were better bred and thus closer to God. Graced and blessed from birth. If we served well in our lives, we'd be born better in the next. We'd grow just a rung closer to the ideals these people were already living.

And here I was, hunting one of them. Stalking him like a predatory Dyre. Hoping he'd slip up. Hoping he'd give me something... *anything*. Some advantage I could use.

Of course, he had to know he was under watch. Perhaps I wasn't the man he was looking out for, but he knew of my existence, knew the Ministry well from his last investigation. He doubtless knew how to hide his misdeeds.

I don't know why I thought I'd learn anything that night, walking the back alleys behind the Estate Apartments. I just felt I had to try. Because I was desperate.

I'd quickly found the address of the apartment Cillian Rathborne would be taking up residence in while he stayed in

Redcoven, during a brief trip down the Archives the day before. It wasn't hard, Malachi had already pulled all the necessary files. Cillian didn't own property within the city limits under his own name, but his connections were easy enough to trace. Other than the Lane Estate, there was a low-bred Pedigree woman—a spinster—who lived within the city limits in her family's apartment. She had inherited it young and had never moved, living here on a permanent basis with a few servants and little else. Ellen Olman was her name, if memory served. She was a long-time family friend of the Rathbornes apparently, noted in the Archives for having attended most of their events and gathers and keeping up a small cotton milling business with their assistance.

She was probably a personal friend of Cillian's, and it hadn't taken long for Malachi to confirm that he was staying with her here. He'd caught me up on the work he'd been doing while I'd been recovering. We had yet to receive clearance to search the premises, but Malachi had demanded compliance from Cillian at the door once already and been given free reign of the place. It wasn't quite as thorough as a search would be—in that we couldn't damage any of their property to get at areas we couldn't otherwise—but even Malachi seemed to think they weren't harboring him there. The place was too obvious; as I said, they *had* to know we were watching it.

There were Ministry agents at every office in every city that weren't Templar and they blended in better with the population. It was possible one of the servants I saw outside sporadically along these service roads behind the estates was one of them. If they were, I probably wouldn't know. It was also possible one of them might have recognized me, but I was keeping my scarf and my cloak hood up over my face.

Hardly suspicious. It was cold out.

It begged the question *why* I didn't want to be recognized by my own Ministry. Which was another of those misgivings I was currently ignoring.

I found a spot tucked out of sight, behind a frozen mound of wood mulch left over from the gardeners, and between the back stone wall of an abutting yard. I swept my cloak underneath me and sat, tucking myself up as much as possible against the cold, my breath in the air the only giveaway of presence to anyone passing on the street.

I sat and waited for hours. I'm not certain how long. And because it was there, because I had it back, I read through my prayer book. Returning again and again to the paragraph-long letter he had written me in between the psalms of forgiveness and my own journal scribblings.

I dissected every word, every interpretation of what he could possibly mean, over and over again. Trying to find the sarcasm, malice, or some hidden accusation he'd intended. But every attempt to twist the words, to make them mean something other than what they said, felt dishonest. And pointless.

I couldn't square what the Heart Thief had done, his crimes, with… the person, the very real person, I was beginning to know. Something was off, something was *wrong*, and I could not hold on as well to that thread of conviction I had left. Not as strongly as I had when it had been a rope, firmly tethering me to the righteous fury I had felt towards him at the outset.

I felt in my bones that there was a deeper truth, a deeper understanding to be had here. Was that not my inner voice as well? Father Helstrom had always said it could be faint, could be hard to hear above the noise the secular world created, but that when we heard it, we would know. We would know in our heart what was right and wrong.

And this had all begun to feel… wrong. Somehow.

I was more confused than I had ever thought I could be when considering the life of a thief and murderer. And it wasn't even as though I doubted that they'd *done* the crime. That wasn't where my hesitation lay.

I just needed to know why. I needed to understand the Heart Thief or I'd go mad, I was certain. This disorganized state of my mind—where I was beginning to fear I could not tell right from wrong anymore—was entirely due to this case. And more importantly, due to Darcy himself.

I didn't actually think he'd come walking out that back door. But as the early evening wore on, *someone* did. Someone I didn't recognize.

The man was a fox with a black coat, silver tail-tip, and a dash of silver on his face. He looked older, not ancient but a bit gray at the temples. He was *certainly* no servant, dressed as well as he was, but he was using the servant exit and made sure to check the street first with a flick of his ears and a bob of his slender muzzle back and forth.

Then he took the stairs down and began to walk the service road. North. He carried a black, bulging leather bag in one hand, but was otherwise unburdened. No weapons of any sort that were visible, nothing to suggest he was dangerous.

At worst if I was found out, I could feign innocence and claim that crossing paths was a coincidence.

I followed him.

I shadowed him from a distance, easily able to pick out his dark silhouette against the still snow-covered city, even at night. When he turned a corner, I sped up, stopped, and slowed back down a pace once I had him back in sight again. He was walking at a normal pace and not taking unnecessarily abrupt turns, likely just taking the shortest route to wherever he was going. If he realized he was being followed, he didn't let on.

It was a long walk through the city until at last I saw him from the edge of a four-way street, stride up to, unlock, and enter a residence. We were in the trade district in mid-town. Solicitors, legal clerks, and...

Physicians.

I kept my normal walking pace as I moved along the street towards and passed by the house he'd entered, not pausing except to glance at it. Long enough to read the sign.

Ruun Mandrake, Physician and Barber Surgeon.

I made it back to the Archives at last, late into the night. Malachi's lanterns in the apartment upstairs were not lit, save one small bloom of diffused orange that may have been a candle.

I bypassed the stairs and headed for the basement door to the Archives, pulling out a set of keys in shivering hands and wincing at the protesting groan of the lock and the subsequent squawk of wood as I opened the door. I'd rather not have had to explain all of this to Malachi just yet, let alone in the middle of the night.

I shut the door as quietly as I could, shucked off my hood and clenched and unclenched my hands, willing sensation back into them. Usually, my fur and pads were enough to protect me from the cold. I only wore gloves when I rode. But I'd been outside a long time.

I coughed a few times to alleviate the burning in my throat, but did so into my palm to remain as quiet as possible. Lord, I was acting like a criminal now, I really was. But...

I found the first box of archives easily, because although we locked everything down when we weren't here, I'd come for this box innumerable times already. The main key to the Archive ledgers opened it, being as the man in question was currently under investigation. It was an open file.

I sat, skimming the ledgers quickly because of how well I knew them by now, until I found the documents I was looking for. Cillian Rathborne's medical history.

Born with an atrophy of the legs and spine, which had

ultimately afflicted every other heir born to his parents' line. Cillian was the only one to survive childhood, and it was believed for years that he would not walk. He had surpassed expectations there, growing into a passably healthy young man, save the continued weakness in his legs and his reliance on a cane. He saw a Physician in Amurfolk for continuing care for his condition.

But there, there it was. The name I'd hoped, expected even, to find. When he was a child, he'd spend the spring and summers here in Redcoven with the Lanes. And he'd see a Physician here. A Doctor Mandrake.

We'd had no reason to investigate or even take note of the man, at least not yet. We were running down a list we'd compiled of all of Cillian's contacts, but the amount of people who'd crossed paths with him or had connections to his family throughout the files on him was massive. He was a Pedigree: he had associates, servants, tradesmen who'd worked for his family a-plenty. Tracking down and questioning all of those who lived in the city would be an enormous task.

But this man, at least, I knew had visited with him. He'd been acting suspicious. He'd checked to see if he was being spied upon—what possible reason could he have for that, save illicit activity? There was the possibility he'd only been visiting with Cillian for a physical exam or to prescribe something, but—

I *had* to look into him. Seizing onto the first real bolt of certainty I'd felt all day, I stood and crossed the room towards the back stacks, tucked into a closet with no door. It didn't need one; this place was sealed behind multiple locks on the reinforced door, the windows, and every box in the Archive was locked. Different levels of permission to access them. Different keys and different types of lock-boxes.

The black books *we* kept for civilians of Redcoven (the Crown and the local Magistrate kept their own files of course, but ours were probably more thorough since the Ministry cared less about procedure and the restrictions of Man's law when we gathered our information) were right here in this nondescript office, in these lockboxes. Financial documents, deeds, taxes, birth certificates and their histories with the judicial system. They were authorized to be accessed only by Ministry agents from *this* city, or Inquisitors themselves. Malachi had only given me the general key.

I glanced up to the ceiling and twisted my ears, listening for the man. He must have been home, but sleeping. He wouldn't be out at this hour, and he knew I intended to head for the Ministry and Saint Rhine's today. I doubt he was worried enough to be out looking for me. He wasn't my minder, after all.

"I hope you never have a use for this. But in pursuit of the truth, sometimes man's law must come secondary."

When Father Helstrom had said that to me long ago, I doubt he had meant *this*. But, wincing through every motion at this point was becoming a tiresome farce. I was going to do this, and I knew it. Best to just get on with it.

I reached up to the shoulder joint of my harness and worked a claw beneath the strap to find the thin metal implements that were looped into the cloth on the underside. They were meant to be accessible with one hand if need be and were sized perfectly for my somewhat clumsy fingers. They could poke into my chest sometimes when I extended my arm upwards, so I'd removed them and put them in my pack for the last few years, essentially disregarded. A misjudgment on my part, because if I'd had them when Darcy had locked me in that room...

They stayed on me within hand's-reach at all times, now. I would not make that mistake twice.

It had been a while since I'd done this, but I'd actually perfected the method Father Helstrom had taught me *on* these sorts of locks in our own far less protected Archives room. I was certain the locks in a real Archive room were more complex, that the mechanism would be altogether different than the ones I'd managed to trip in the past, or that God himself would strike me down for my hubris here.

But I found the familiar mechanism, fiddled the implement into place after a scant few wrong guesses, and then it just... opened. Like it always had before when I'd practiced.

I stared at the box in dumb shock. For some reason, I'd really thought this would be harder. I suppose they relied on their exterior security and the Inquisitor who took up residence here to keep these records safe.

I opened the box to reveal the black books, sorted alphabetically. It didn't take long for me to find the right one. There, at my fingertips, was this man's entire life. Collected in one small section of one book, stored in one footlocker among hundreds. The Ministry had files like this on hundreds of thousands of citizens of Amuresca, lowly and high-born alike. Anyone of note. Expressly for moments like this, so that men like us could crack open their lives as surely as you might a book and read about their sins and successes.

You're told about this kind of power and privilege, especially being raised as I was knowing I'd be a Templar someday. It's portrayed as aspirational. It's what we train for. I'd never really considered it as anything but inevitable and expected. Experiencing it in the moment was very different to what I'd anticipated. It felt intrusive and made me self-aware in a way I'd not expected.

They had these files on all of us. On Malachi. On me.

Eventually, when I confessed all of this to whomever would hear me, this would be in my file. What I was doing right here, right now. And someone would read it someday and judge me for it. Perhaps rightly.

I leafed through the volume until I reached Ruun Mandrake's file. No pictures, but the history, profession, gender, and species were correct. Had to be him. I tried to avoid the unnecessary sections, looking for the obvious first.

Crime record—none reported.

Incidents with heresy—none reported.

No notations of moral corruption, either. He attended church irregularly. Wife, deceased, children were grown now by the look of their birth dates. Son had gone into practice on his own, daughter had married.

All profoundly average. Not a whiff of anything untoward, and no brushes with even civil law. His taxes were paid, and—

I paused, tracing a claw tip to the small notations made yearly by the Archivist who kept track of property taxes. He had two residences listed, but there was an empty block halfway down one column, back nearly fifteen years. A property he'd stopped paying taxes on, listed on the first year he'd stopped paying not as 'unpaid' but 'condemned'.

I narrowed my gaze at it, reading back a page to where the residence first entered the log. He'd inherited it from his own father, and it was listed as 'The Lodge at Dyre Point'.

A lodge. Probably a hunting lodge, given how rural it was. Dyre Point was so far afield from the roads that it wasn't listed on most maps. I only knew of its existence because its name had stood out in my mind when I was looking over Malachi's local maps. It was ten miles or so from here in the Dyre Wood. Dyre Point was a rocky, mountainous area towards the northernmost end of the woodlands. Other than hunting, it was inhospitable country with little to offer.

Foxes were fond of hunting, and those that could afford the land and permits to do so often kept lodges in their family. This one must have been abandoned for financial reasons or just not kept up well by the man who owned it, because it had been given up to the wilderness fifteen years ago.

I clenched my teeth. If ever there were a safehouse to harbor a criminal... that would be it. Ten miles.

Ten miles was reachable in a snow storm. On horseback, maybe even on foot. Especially if they knew the way.

It was a hunch. A thin one. But I'd followed my instincts in the past and they'd yet to lead me astray.

A thud from over my head startled me so much, I fumbled and dropped the book, wincing as it fell, cockeyed on its side. The spine seemed intact though, so I gingerly picked it back up and set it in the box. Then pushed the box back into place, and re-manipulated the lock.

The noise from the second floor had been singular, not rhythmic like footsteps, and too quiet to have been something falling. It more sounded like something dropping in a controlled motion.

There was a heavy creak and the faintest sound of shuffling. It was a body, I realized. Someone lying or sitting on the floor. They were still doing so.

It had to be Malachi, but why was he on the floor? Oh—knees. Of course. He was *praying.*

... or he'd fallen out of bed. Either way, he was awake. Which meant I needed to hasten up to the apartment, lest I be caught in the act. There was a staircase from his small sitting room right into the Archives, and it would not take him but a moment to leave his bedroom, cross the small space, and open that door.

I made sure to leave the Archives Office first, locking up quietly, before ascending the staircase into the apartment from the outside. I was so far beyond recognizing how guilty I was acting by now, it was becoming second nature.

I switched to the apartment key, working it into the lock, when I heard another more startling sound.

A distant, muffled clap, followed by an unmistakable groan of pain.

Oh God, he was hurt. He must have fallen? Or he'd been hurt during the day in some altercation I didn't know of yet.

I shoved open the door, calling his name out immediately into the quiet darkness of the apartment.

"Malachi?!" I closed the door quickly, turning the lock behind me and hustling down the small hallway towards where I'd heard the noise. "Malachi, are you hur—"

The smell of blood knocked me back a step. But after the brief stagger, I rushed on through the sitting room towards the closed bedroom door, trying the knob immediately and finding it blessedly unlocked.

"Isidor," his voice stopped me when I had the door open an inch. The smell of blood was stronger now, mixed with incense… the cloying, cedar kind we used to cover odors in the Abbey.

His voice sounded reedy, threadbare. Certainly pained. But oddly serene. He didn't sound angry, at least. I tried pushing the door open more slowly, and he spoke again.

"Don't enter if you are squeamish, lad," he murmured. "My penance isn't for the faint of heart."

I nodded as though he could see me and steeled myself for… I knew not what. But the sight that greeted me would not have been in my wildest imaginings.

He was nude, for one. And that might not have alarmed me in and of itself, even though we took an oath of modesty at sixteen. I'd grown up around other boys and shared a dorm with them as they became young men. And Malachi and I shared a somewhat similar build; he was only a bit leaner and taller.

But it was the injuries, the spattered splashes of blood across the wooden floor, and the weapon in his hand that made my throat close up.

He was kneeling in prayer, as I'd guessed. He had his Tome open towards the latter third of the Arynthioch Chapters on Redemption, if my relative estimation at how deep he was into the book was sound.

He had a whip—shorter than a horse whip, but branched into several separate tendrils of wrapped, glistening leather—lying limply-splayed on the floor near the worst of the bloodstains.

Well, no, really the worst of the bloodstains were on his *back*. Broken crimson lines between his dark brown fur, more obvious when they crossed into the lighter variations of his pelt down his inner arms, midsection, and rear.

What's more, there were *so many others there,* aged and healed-over, from what must have been years of overlapping abuse of his flesh. Many had disappeared into his fur, but in some place the scar tissue was so dense, the fur could not grow any more. His back was a map of prolonged, ongoing torture. Some of it crossed over his shoulders, down his clavicle and neck, some on his arms, legs, and buttocks. Even the arch of his tail.

I had no words. When he slowly turned to regard me, he only stared at me evenly across that small room and offered nothing but exhausted serenity. He looked like the monks did when they sang in the choir for hours or fasted for days. Tired. Broken. But ready.

Ready to hear The Word.

I knew it must have been some form of self-flagellation for prayer. The monks would engage in rituals of arduous labor when they fasted sometimes or would sit in ice water baths, or steaming tents to cleanse themselves on holy days. But this was…

"You've come back very late," Malachi said. I only nodded, and for whatever reason, he seemed to accept that and gestured beside him on the floor. "Come. Sit."

I could do nothing else. I removed my cloak and laid it over the chair at his desk, then stepped up beside him and slowly kneeled at his side, crossing my wrists in front of me and clutching one knee. I murmured a quiet prayer of my own, just my evening recitation. He listened, swaying slightly beside me, and joined me by the last few sentences when he presumably recognized the prayer.

It felt surreal, this moment. I noted his Tome just long enough to confirm I'd been right about what prayers he was reading. Redemption and cleansing the sinful soul. The story of Adele, the wife of one of the prophets, who'd flung herself into the sea to appease God's wrath and put an end to the storm that was ravaging their city. In doing so, she had redeemed herself in His eyes for her transgressions against her husband and died cleansed of her sin.

To be honest, it was a passage I avoided. Historians had long since unearthed alternative tellings of the story of Lady Adele, in holy texts written by monks nonetheless, that involved her being tried and sentenced for her crimes against her husband, and that made her less of a willing martyr and more just... a woman who'd been caught and punished for having an affair. The sacrifice was meant to be noble, but the truth of it was muddy, and the account was not written by the Prophet in question himself. It felt like an area of our holy text where man's hand had been at work, more than God's.

Those histories were banned reading, but amongst one of the few banned books Father Helstrom had allowed me to read, because he wanted me to better understand that even the mortal vessels who wrote the Word could be fallible. I recalled vividly that reading those accounts had been the first time I'd begun to realize I could question the Tome of Faith, or at least its Authors.

This close to Malachi, the smell of blood absolutely filled my nostrils. I'm certain he saw my nose twitch, the wince in my eyes, and he was not afraid to point it out. "I know I'm a sight," he said quietly. "Does this frighten you?"

"No," I answered honestly. "I was just startled."

"It is a spiritual discipline," he said. "The ritual of

mortification of the flesh. It is how I make penance for a lifetime of misdeeds, Isidor. It releases me for a time from the burdens I carry. The weight of them."

I simply nodded. I wanted to say more; I just couldn't find the words. I understood this. Deeply. There were many times, including quite recently, when pain or discomfort had helped alleviate the wrongness I felt in my soul. Even something as simple as doing heavy labor or pushing myself to train an additional hour caused pain. And that pain could be cleansing.

"I've never seen this method," I said at a near-whisper.

"It is only," he said, turning to regard me with a snap of his piercing gaze, "for the most severe treatment of a relentlessly sinful mind. Don't you get any ideas; you are *young* yet, and whatever sin is inside you is still malleable. There are many forms of penance and re-education you can pursue before this becomes necessary."

I swallowed thickly, staring into my lap. I could still feel his gaze on me when I asked, "Brother Malachi, what could you possibly think is so sinful in you to warrant such brutal treatment of your own flesh?"

"That is between me and God," he said, his voice weak. "But you must trust in my judgment and the judgment of my handlers, Brother Isidor. It *is* warranted."

I looked across our laps, from my own hands to his. One was fastened to his own knee, the other was hanging limply at his side, still holding the wrapped leather handle of the odd whip, sticky with blood.

"Can I help you to bed, Brother?" I asked at last. "Are your prayers... complete?"

"You will not be joining me tonight, I take it?" he asked. "I spoke to your Brother Dolus. He informed me you'd be moving your residence to the Ministry with him."

I considered how to answer that. I'd shared this apartment for several nights now with Malachi, and he'd been very decent and hospitable, even giving me the one bed to sleep in, while he'd taken the nearby sitting chair. But I was not about to allow him to sleep there again tonight. Not with several fresh wounds on his back. I had been enough of an imposition as it was.

"I'm staying here tonight," I assured him quietly. "It's late, and you need tending to, and you've been so kind as to do so for me for days now. One more night is fine."

He was looking at me, his eyes searching, and there was more than pain there. There was... a vulnerability. An open question, but what it was, I could not say. Maybe it really was just the pain. Maybe I was imagining things.

"I'm sorry, by the way, if Brother Dolus was unkind to you," I said, when the thought occurred to me. I wrapped an arm gingerly, lower on his back along his hips, and began to help him up. He stood under his own power, only wavering a bit, and probably only from pain. He hadn't lost enough blood that he'd be in danger of fainting, or at least I hoped not. I'd have to trust that he knew his own limits.

He certainly seemed to have been doing it for a long time by the look of those scars.

He huffed. "Remarkably affable, actually. He said nothing that was wrong. Only reminded me of what I should have carved onto my heart, long ago."

I had no idea what he'd meant by that, but I focused instead on maneuvering him into bed, then going about getting him some clean smallclothes, and putting a pot of water on the wood-burning stovetop to warm some wash cloths.

"They're shallow," he assured me. "More painful than dangerous. That's the point. I'll be fine, don't worry yourself over much."

"You took care of me," I said around a cough. "Least I can do."

He arched an eyebrow at me from across the room. "Sounds like I ought to be, still. Maybe you shouldn't have been out all day in the cold, young buck. Sounds like you haven't kicked it just yet."

"Lie down on your stomach," I said as I dropped the wash cloths in the pot. "And try not to roll over in your sleep tonight. I'll try to ensure the same."

"Oh, please don't sleep in that chair," he muttered. "Murder on the back. And you're still sick, you need to stay warm."

"We can share the bed. That's the obvious solution."

There was a long pause. And then in a halting voice that was so unlike him it baffled me, he said, "We shouldn't—no. I'm not one of your Brothers, and I'm certain you've taken your vow of modesty by now—"

"We're both men, Malachi," I said, staring down intently at the pot and not at him. "And we're all Brothers. It's fine. I'm not concerned."

Another achingly long pause. And then, after a quiet sigh. "Alright. If it doesn't concern you, it doesn't concern me."

I never really slept. I lay there, my mind spinning, constantly running over the things I'd have to gather, the short preparations I could make before the morning came. And when Malachi's breathing evened out to deep, slow drags, and I knew he'd fallen under fully... I made my move.

I left the warmth of our shared bed and the distinctive faded scents of cedar, blood, and the diluted alcohol I'd used to clean his wounds earlier. Stepping out into the cold apartment and gathering my possessions, I wondered if he was feigning sleep. If he could truly hear me and was allowing me the grace of slipping away. If he did, he did not move or try to stop me. Of course, he thought I was leaving for wholly different reasons. He thought I'd be at the Ministry in the morning.

When I stepped out into the still dark, frigid air of early morning and knew without a doubt that I would not take the lane down towards the church to the Ministry offices, that I would instead turn right and head down the main street, towards the city gates…

I knew I was making a decision here that would fundamentally alter the course of my life. Whether I was right or wrong.

But the indecision was gone. There may have still been guilt—I could hardly tell beneath the power this compulsion had over me—but I was certain I could do nothing else.

The dawn light was muted by incoming clouds, and snow began to fall almost as soon as I made it outside the gates onto the main road. God was either telling me to turn back or closing the door behind me to any others who would follow.

10

THE LODGE

White tufts spun in drifts through the haze of jagged shadows that dominated my vision. The occasional stagger of my burning, failing legs tipped the pale forest floor into my peripheral, but I tried not to look down. Each inch I let my muzzle drop was one I could not recover from, my head drooping steadily towards surrender.

My feet were miles behind me, lost in the numbing cold. Not literally, obviously, I had to believe they were still under me, only because I was somehow still upright. The insulation of the fur wraps might save my toes; I couldn't be sure. I was past worrying about such trivialities, had passed that threshold hours ago. At this point if I lived long enough to make it to the Lodge, or *any* place of respite for that matter, I'd thank God all my days for it. I'd include my gratitude for this mercy in every prayer, morning and night.

Even with two separate maps of the countryside and carefully plotting what should have been a day-long hike at most, I had once again failed to account for the truly devastating effects of the weather and time on neglected roads. I hadn't been walking a mile before everything faded to white, blocking my path both forwards and backwards with an indomitable wall of terrifyingly blank forested countryside.

There was a sun up there somewhere, muted behind the drifts and the gray, and it remained my only means of navigation, but even *it* disappeared beneath the canopy of sunken, swollen branches and the ice throwing fractals of what little light existed in all directions.

My arms were clutched in a cross over my chest, greedily holding what heat somehow blessedly remained in my body to my core. My throat burned all the way down, the frigid air crystallizing like caltrops, lodging somewhere deep below my ribs. As if the cold itself were a personal foe, seeking to exploit the weakness it knew was there.

I had not, in fact, fully recovered from the cold I'd been nursing all month. I had overestimated myself again, it seemed. Brother Dolus would have said I was suffering the trials of my own arrogance, and he would be right to say so.

In my illogical thought maze, I had persistently told myself I must look ahead, and only ahead. Forward. I could still vaguely see the outline of what must have once been a road, even with the stifling coat of fresh snow (now nearly up to the top of my shins). I knew—or at least I thought I knew—that I was still traveling in the right direction, because of my occasional glimpses at where the sun must have been.

But it too was abandoning me. Disappearing below the horizon, which meant I'd been out here trying to walk these ten miles *all day.* Hardly surprising—the snow masked the obstructions of jagged rocks, downed branches and heaven knew what else, and when I wasn't arduously and slowly picking my way around them, I was stumbling into or often losing my footing *to* them, which had resulted in tripping off-trail, catching my feet painfully in a pinch or jab, or just outright falling. I'd even gotten my leg caught up in the spokes of an old, broken wagon wheel once, a metal edge tearing into my calf and drawing blood.

These roads were old. Nearly abandoned, save for hunters, criminals, and those who hunted criminals.

Thus, they weren't particularly well-maintained.

My foot caught on something again; it hardly mattered what but a fallen branch most likely. That was almost always the culprit. I barely had the strength to remain upright and moving in the best of circumstances right now, let alone with one foot tripped out from underneath me and the other finding no purchase on the loose, snow-covered dirt. I pitched forward, sucking in a sharply-cold breath on the way down.

With so much snow on the ground and my body as swaddled as it was, it should have been an easy fall. But every step hurt my aching, weary limbs at this point and I did not tumble with any grace. The pale ground rose up to meet my jaw before my arm could catch beneath it, sending my teeth up in a snap, biting the edge of my own muzzle. My vision went white hot for a moment, and I tasted blood.

Then one of those ice-cold knives in my chest pricked me particularly sharply, sending a wracking cough through my body that seemed likely to shake me apart. Each subsequent hacking gasp hurt all the worse. My lungs begged for air, but each breath I sucked down was colder than the last. I felt as though I would choke on it, drown in the air as surely as I would in frigid waters.

Squeezing my eyes shut, begging between breaths, I rocked to my side and tried vainly to bring my own body under control. But I was faltering. I was losing ground.

No. I was dying. Wasn't I?

That's what this was. It felt too dramatic to think that to yourself, I suppose, until the moment it was true. The dizzying, all-encompassing pain. The primal fear of being unable to draw enough breath, or the right *kind* of breath, to satisfy my body's needs. The odd spikes of energy punctuating the deathly weariness. Which one of these would be my literal last gasp?

It didn't feel like I thought it would. There were no memories, no cascade of longing, unrealized hopes going through my mind. And I certainly had many of those. All I could really think about was the pain and the fear.

And it was dark. So dark. Getting darker, especially around the edges of my vision. Perhaps I *had* fallen from grace of late, perhaps I *had* sinned, but… where was God? If I was about to die, should I not feel His light? His comfort, or at least His condemnation?

Maybe I was further from death than I thought. But I was losing my purchase on consciousness, that much I knew. Maybe first I would sleep, and then I would see Him. Maybe He wanted me to rest. He couldn't possibly wish for me to die this primordially afraid, this desperate.

I was—or at least had been—a faithful servant my entire life. Although I had stumbled in my path sometimes, I had always sought repentance. That's why I was here. I had been absolute in my dedication to this task, no matter the risk.

Had I not?

I would pray. Truth be told, I had been praying for the last hour, inaudibly or in mutters between my teeth. But perhaps God needed to hear me proclaim, as Malachi had said, how *broken* I was. How desperately I needed Him right now. Perhaps that's why I suffered. I had not lowered myself before Him. Not fully. Not as I should have.

I was already prostrate. All that was left was to beg.

I could not drag myself to my knees, but I drew them in against my chest, feeling the brush of my tail tucking between my legs beneath the layers of my tunics and cloak. I had lost sensation in it long ago, at least anything beyond numb pain.

"Progenitor… Father of Canus… He who came before… all of mortal flesh and blood…"

My voice was paper thin and stuttered between breathy gasps, gagging on the urge to cough. Still, I pressed on.

"I beg you, as... all who stood to face the horizon a-and... rose... from the feral crawl of o... our... predecessors... This lowly man..."

A crunch of snow amidst the muffled quiescence of the forest. An animal, perhaps. Come to bear witness.

"... sixth... from the Holiest..." I swallowed thickly, "... six lifetimes apart... from rejoining you in Eden. This Sixth Son, begs of you..."

Shifting shadows over my closed eyes. Perhaps the wind jostling the weighted branches of the spruce that caged this road in. I could hear them now, yes. I could feel the fresh powder hit my cheeks, shaken loose.

"Show mercy," I breathed out, labored and raw. "*Show mercy!* " I repeated as loudly as I could. I could hardly hear myself over the pounding of blood in my ears.

Tentative, careful footsteps. A demon, come to feast on me lest God deny me in this moment, prowled at the edge of the road. The knowledge that they were there tickled the fur along the back of my neck, pulling my ears upright. My instincts were muddled, buried beneath the pounding fog of pain. But I at least knew I was not alone. Not anymore.

Finally.

Even if it was a demon, I was suddenly, profanely glad it was here. I would deny it, I would spit in its face, I would reject any final offer... but I was glad it was here. If God would not answer my call, I was manically, hysterically pleased that *something* had. If not grace, I would at least have defiance in my final moments.

"I throw myself upon the altar of your judgment!" I rasped, voice thin as a taut wire, liable to snap at any moment. "I am your servant... miserably fallible though I am... I am yours. Please..."

What was I asking for? That thought—or the lack of one—

brought my pleas to a sudden, choked-off stop. I felt a noise, a desperate keening, wring itself out from the back of my throat, barely emerging past my teeth. The prayers, the supplications, had come easily enough. But now that it was time to ask for mercy, I… wasn't certain what mercy for a man like me might be.

Perhaps death *was* the escape God was granting me. If I died tonight, I would still die a mostly faithful man. I had yet to cross that horizon into unredeemable heresy. Every moment I was alive brought me closer, and there was no certainty I could contend with the sin inside of me. It clawed its way out even in sleep. It had persisted in the waking world and driven me to…

No. If I could not admit to my sins now, then when? I had made choices. I had made choices that I knew were wrong and convinced myself somehow that all of this would be worth it in the end. That discovering the truth, selfishly, on my own, through lies by omission, ignoring my oaths, orders, and the theft of information, would prove to be just… because I'd *wanted* it to be.

And look at how He had punished me. Gaze, trembling, upon the justice I had sown and reaped.

But the harm on the whole was done only to myself. At least no others would suffer or die because of me. I had held fast to *most* of my tenets thus far. I could be buried clean. If I'd been allowed to continue on this path? Who knew.

Maybe this storm, this failing of my lungs, *was* God's mercy.

More footsteps, soft but drawing closer. A definitive shadow now. Despite the storm, moonlight filtered in through the clouds and my eyes were well-adjusted to the dark, so the shift in light was noticeable. They were near.

"Let come what may," I rasped out, "to this flesh… but you will not… have my soul."

An unmistakable, sharp little noise. A humorless laugh. One I remembered well.

"Templar," their voice, low and soft as velvet, but piteous.

No.

"I assure you I am not interested in your soul."

No.

I must have said the last 'no' aloud, because the figure standing over me gave a quiet tut and fell slowly into a crouch beside me. One slender hand reached out, the tip of a barely-retracted claw hooking under my chin and tipping my head in their direction, despite any weak protestation my body could summon.

"Not whom you'd hoped to find?" He asked me, voice impassive and barely beyond a whisper, sparing my burning ears.

Despite everything, despite the pain and desperation and the encroaching blackness, fury lanced through my body, coupled with a final spike of adrenaline. I felt my teeth gritting, my exhausted muscles coiling. Shaking, I lifted myself onto one elbow, my breath coming out in ragged puffs of smoke in the still, cold air.

"You," I uttered, "are... *exactly*... who I hoped to find."

Warm gold-green eyes stared back at me, ensconced in a beautiful, sad feline face. One long chain earring hung from a cuff on his left side, barely visible under the edge of a fur-lined cloak. Gold with an inlaid rosy pink gemstone. I vaguely remembered it from the Hudson Estate, adorning the Lady of the house more than once.

"You've made it," he said, blinking long lashes slowly. "You've found me.... Again. Impossibly. Well done. What now?"

I had no answer, of course. I couldn't even stand any more, let alone effect an arrest.

I had found my quarry. The Heart Thief stood before me. Again. And *again,* I had no ability to capture him. The Lodge must have been *so* near... I probably just hadn't seen it through the trees yet.

But I'd seen my holy vow through to the end. God would know. He saw me now, even if He chose not to answer my pleas.

"*Why?*" I demanded in a threadbare, fading voice.

He tilted his head at me, ears twitching. "Why?" he repeated uncertainly.

"Why take the Heart of Faith?" I asked desperately.

"Are you asking *me*?" he said nonsensically.

"Yes!" I cried. "What value could it possibly hold for a Heretic like you?"

"None whatsoever."

Ungodly rage, anger so sharp I could *feel* it… or maybe that was just my chest aching from breathing, it was so hard to tell… it threatened to bring the blackness. There was nothing left in me for a physical attack, so the hate just ate at me. Chased away all thoughts of God. Replaced them with white hot, overwhelming frustration. Despicably, coiled within it was the rotten core of what I'd felt so many nights now. Relief that I could lay eyes on him again. Some part of me was just *so* glad that he'd be the last person I ever saw.

"Return it," I slurred, "or you will suffer God's wrath."

"I can't do that," he said, almost placatingly. Like he wanted me to feel appeased.

I grasped at him and got… something. The edge of his sleeve. The hand near to my chin. He let me, and stared down at me, that pitying look in his eyes the whole while.

It made me feel sick.

It made me feel…

I dreamed. In between long bouts of nothingness, peaceful and quiet, the dreams came as they always did. Blessedly most were nonsensical, more like flashes. Nothing I could remember well. The library. The smell of summer in the monastery graveyard where we used to play.

And then, everything sharpened to a point, to one clear, defined memory. Hardly a dream, because it was real. *Had* been real.Brother Dolus's lash on my rear. His hand, his well-filed claws gripping bluntly, but bruising into the loose ruff around my neck. Dragging me, pitching and fighting, down the staircase to the cellar.

The eyes of my brothers, watching me from the kitchen above. Braced, all of us, for what we knew was to come.

I'd bitten him. I could taste the ink on his fur, on his hands, where I'd snapped at him when he'd first tried to haul me down here. He was not half-hearted any more. This would not be like the other times.

He was truly angry at me now.

A pop of fire and a shifting of logs roused me. The sounds of a hearth. My body was yanked back into the present as though I'd been pulled above the waters of the dream, and I sucked in a breath much the same.

It was warm. *I* was warm.

Nonetheless, the breath left me in a wracking cough. My chest, my lungs, felt thawed. But painful still. That sharp tickle clawed at my throat, making each inhale threaten another cough. I tried vainly to stop, to steady my breathing. But the panic came as it had before when I wasn't able to stop. Each cough brought another, fed the itch in my chest, satisfied it yet made it worse.

"Lord, that doesn't sound good. Try to calm your breaths, if you can," a dulcet voice lulled, the bed creaking beside me. "Easy now."

My eyes were still adjusting to the warm candlelit… room? I was in a room. Wooden walls. A bed. A roaring hearth.

A man sitting beside me. Slender. Feline.

My body jumped, as much as it was capable of. I jarred the bed in my sudden motion, trying to lift myself and failing.

Everything still *ached*, my muscles would not respond to me. And something was wrong with my arms.

I tugged at my wrists, laid out comfortably at my sides but something tugged back. I could feel the pressure tighten when I tried to move them up. Bound. I was bound with something. Likely to the frame of the bed below.

Restraints. I was a prisoner.

The warm, gentle comfort of this place, this serene setting I'd woken to, shattered as reality snapped back into place for me. I'd been pursuing the Heart Thief. I'd intended to check this property, this hunting lodge at Dyre Point, because of its connection to Cillian, to his Physician, and I'd decided to do so on my own, without telling a bloody soul where I was going, because…

Because I wanted the Heart Thief to myself. Because I was terrified of what Malachi would do were he to actually capture Darcy this time. Because I knew that once he was arrested, I would never see him again until the day of his execution, and that meant we'd never be able to talk, I'd never have my questions answered, I'd never understand—

"Please…" Darcy spoke again, his voice indeed pleading, or at least affecting something believable as a plea. He genuinely seemed to lose his train of thought for a moment, muzzle parting and then closing, before settling on what he wanted to say. He was really selling the lie. "Please try not to panic. You're not well, and I don't really know how to properly care for someone in your condition, let alone if you fight me."

His gaze moved to mine, imploring, and he repeated more quietly, "Please."

I breathed in staggered, rough pants, turning my head back and forth swiftly, trying to take in whatever I could. Looking around, the room seemed bare. Stripped, dusty, unused. But someone—my captor, obviously—had cleaned it up recently. There was dust in all the corners and on the ancient crown molding, but not in the immediate vicinity of the floor around us. He'd cleared the bedside tables and a writing desk, made use of the hearth. A bowl and decanter of clear water sat at the table, alongside… I smelled cheese. Salami. The wrapped bundle must have been bread.

My stomach growled, betraying me.

"Well, now," the feline slowly smiled, making my insides churn. "I didn't expect that. But if you're feeling well enough, you *should* eat. If you can. Let's start with tea?" He slipped off the edge of the bed, sliding on his hip. I watched his body language, the way he led with his waist in his movements. Like a woman might.

Or a Heretic. Or… and the possibility confounded me but could not be ignored… there were lies upon lies here, and they *were* in fact a woman. Their smell once again didn't give them away. Too foreign. Too clean. The cologne, or perfume was indistinct.

"The tea will help with your throat—"

"Untie me," I said, trying to sound commanding around a suddenly thick tongue.

I hadn't had shellfish or anything like it lately—at least not that I knew of—so this was just my body betraying me. I cursed my inability to talk to this person like the man I knew myself to be. Why did this *always* happen? It didn't seem to matter how many times I prepared myself, went over the things I intended to say, to ask. I always came off sounding like a weak, stuttering fool.

He—I would continue to assume that, seeing as how he'd explicitly said he wasn't a woman and there was no other option that made sense—didn't turn, his slim figure silhouetted against the firelight. He wore a tailored vest that was somehow still loose around the hips and a dark shirt beneath that was certainly too big and billowed at the arms. Unlike him. He'd always been dressed tailored and fitted. These must have been second-hand clothes. Britches, dark as well, hugged his figure yet still, somehow, gave nothing about his anatomy away.

Lord, why was I *looking*? Why did it *matter*?

He was pouring something, the tink of ceramic distinct in the quiet of the room.

"A 'thank you' wouldn't go amiss. You were at death's door when I found you," he said, ignoring my demand of course. He turned with a chipped teacup in hand, holding it gingerly by the handle in one finger, the other gripping it loosely on the bottom. He slowly brought it over towards me, taking measured steps as if gauging my reactions.

He was scared. I got a whiff of the fear, subtle but distinct. He didn't trust his bindings, I realized. I tugged again.

No chance. I was too weak, and however he'd bound me, it tightened the more I pulled.

He stood beside me now, about a foot away, smiling wanly. Teacup held at the ready. But he also had a blade on his person, at the hip. I didn't miss it.

"You were heavy," he said with a light huff of a laugh. It was a genuine laugh, like in the courtyard. I'd heard it many times since in my dreams. Hearing it again, in person, was almost too much. "No offense meant, I just… think I should be commended for my ingenuity is all."

I didn't trust myself to engage in any banter. I was confounded and somewhat offended by his lack of seriousness, given our situation. But this was no dream. He was truly here with me, speaking to me, *one foot away from me*! Real. In *front* of me. Caring for me for some reason, an inverse mirror of when Malachi had done the same. Even with the tea. God, what a twisting, circuitous chapter my life had taken.

It made my mind tangle. Each thought was aborted before it began, each set of words I tried to put together, inadequate. My head was foggy to be certain, but it wasn't just that.

Despite all the obvious questions at the tip of my tongue, I just didn't know how to talk to him. To Darcy. It was no different than the first time we'd met. I didn't know what I wanted to say to him or how I wanted to say it, when it really came down to it.

What I wanted *from* him.

The Heart. Right. Start there.

'Let God guide you'. Father Helstrom's voice.

Then, the image of the bloodhound contorted to become Brother Dolus. I earnestly had no idea what he would tell me to do in this situation. But he was closer to the crime and still an acting Inquisitor, so I tried...

The dream was too fresh. I swore I could still smell the ink, feel his claws in my neck. My thumb worried at the missing digit on my hand.

Back to Father Helstrom, then. His sermons, his steady conviction, could guide me now.

'When your mind is folly and you know it to be so, listen for God. Let God guide you. Do as He would will.'

"Why... do this?" I croaked, reasoning somehow through my tangled thoughts that I needed to start with easy questions. Questions Darcy would actually answer. He'd been evasive about the Heart or anything concerning his crimes in the past for obvious reasons. Best to stick with our surroundings, for now. Assess my situation. Measure my options. "Why bother?" I pressed, voice still thick and humiliatingly weak, but at least now discernibly masculine.

"Why bother bringing you here, you mean?" he clarified, gingerly holding the tea out towards me again. I continued to ignore it. "Rather than, what? Leaving you out there to die?"

"Yes." I said at length. "It would suit you better, would it not?"

"Lord, what kind of question is that?" His features turned displeased. Disbelieving. "Do you really take me for someone so cold? Perhaps at the outset, but at this point, surely—"

"You shot at me!" I barked hoarsely.

"You must realize I missed intentionally," he sighed, glancing down at the tea. "I didn't... know what else to do... I just wanted us both to leave that yard alive."

I didn't bother pointing out the folly of firing a flintlock a few feet away from someone's head and assuming you'd not kill them. There were misfires, ricochets, the fact that it could have deafened me, or the very real outcome that I had in fact *fallen* and could have split my head open on the paving stones.

"I don't believe for a *moment* that you care about my life," I growled out instead, because it encapsulated all of that.

In answer, he simply gestured at me. At all of me, and presumably where I was, and the fact that I was... alive. Wordlessly. And I stumbled over what to say in response to that.

"Lord," the feline cocked his hip—again with that body language, almost languid and lazy. Cats had a natural grace, but still. It had to be intentional, didn't it?

He put the cup back down on the end table and brought his palms up to press over his own face, smoothing back his fur and leaving one palm resting on his forehead as he let the other drop, seemingly bedraggled. "What am I to do with you, Isidor? Please. Illuminate me. Do you think this... *works* for me, somehow? Do you think I want this?"

"I have no idea what you want," I said with a swallow.

"Well, you ought to, by this point," he said, the frustration evident in his voice. He had generally been composed when we'd met in the past, so it meant something. "You bloody well seem to know everything else. You have hunted me across half this country, guessing my every move—accurately, to my dismay—to the ends of the earth in this forgotten wilderness, in a private sanctuary you have *no* right to know of. *How*, by the way? For God's sake, how in the hell—"

"Language," I grumbled.

"Are you serious?" He began to pace near the bed, blinking

rapidly, voice aghast. "You know, if you *must* be my dogged pursuer, you could at least have the common courtesy to take better care of yourself, while you're at it. I despair of having to meet you in such a state…" his ears tucked back, "*…again!* What madness must I suffer under that I find myself *worried* about the well-being of the man hunting me? Honestly. It is too much to be borne."

My mouth ran dry, and I licked my teeth furtively, trying to form words coherently. "How did you even carry me here to the Lodge? Do you have help? Is Lord Rathborne here?"

That had to be it. I was twice his weight, easily. He couldn't have carried me alone.

"If Cillian was here, you'd have been left for dead out there," he said, sitting on the edge of the bed again. "He has more sense than I do. And that's all you'll get me to say about him, so please, kindly don't bring him up again, or I'll fucking gag you."

He'd always favored proper speech in the past, very rarely engaging in swearing. Until tonight. I was touching on a nerve.

"No, I'm afraid you find me all alone here," he admitted, which surprised me. It betrayed his isolation and a potential weakness, if it were true.

He'd left a respectable foot of distance between us, but I still leaned away, curling my muzzle as I tried not to inhale his scent. It wasn't that it was unpleasant. Maddeningly, the reverse. Unfamiliar, subtle, he was always so *clean*. Useful, I suppose, when you were being hunted by canines and fond of using disguises.

"Impossible. You couldn't have—"

"I had a small cart with me on the road. I intended to winter here for some time, so I needed it to supply this place for an extended stay. A horse, as well. Still… getting you *in* the cart was… quite the ordeal." He put a hand on the small of his back, craning and stretching with a wince for a moment.

"Intended," I repeated, hoarsely. "Past-tense."

"Well, you've sniffed me out," he said with a cluck of his tongue and a sigh. "Once you leave here, you'll doubtless report to the big, unpleasant fellow. So, this is no longer a safehouse. I'll need to be elsewhere by the time you return."

"You're going to release me?" I asked incredulously.

"Young Sir, do you think I did all of this," he asked around a chuckle, "dragged you inside, dried and warmed you, tended to you for the last several days, just so I could *gut* you here in this nice warm bed? Really? Or, do you think I intended to," he waved his hands about, dramatically, "interrogate you? Torture you? Something along those lines? That would be *your* plan, young Templar. Not mine."

"Days," I repeated. "I've been asleep for days?"

He nodded. "Nearly two. You were very ill when you showed up on my, well. On this doorstep. The weather was dreadful; I'm not sure what you were thinking coming so far from town without a horse. That being said I must ask, because this is twice now. Do you have a sickness of the lungs, Sir Knight?"

I bit my tongue inside my muzzle. He was getting more information out of me than I him. Again. "M'not a Knight," I reminded him.

"I only ask because..." he trailed off. "Well, they are dreadfully common, alas. But some are more fatal than others. And some... contagious."

"You cannot be afflicted by the illness you first came upon me suffering from," I muttered. "It is a weakness of birth. And this? I don't know, it's just a long cold. They settle in my lungs, sometimes. I'm prone to them."

He nodded. "You've seemed to improve quite a lot since I got you some place warm. I have hope you will recover fully before long."

"Don't toy with me," I growled out, the growl hurting my throat. "You're only worried about having another Templar's life on your list of crimes. That's why you did all of this."

He arched a slim eyebrow. “Earnestly, what difference would it amount to at this point? I have never killed *anyone,* let alone men from your Order, but you still seem intent on blaming me for it, so what difference would one more charge make?”

“None,” I answered solidly. “The penalty for your crimes will not change.”

“You’re making an argument you know is faulty, then.”

“Then you’re just trying to...” I stammered, “... sully... my reputation. So that I cannot continue this investigation.”

He gave me the most confused look. “‘Sully’ your...? How... you know what? Never mind. I’m not certain I want the answer to that.” He waved a paw. “And that also does not make much sense, and I think you know it. If not you, they will send another.”

“I’ve *met* you,” I pointed out. “*Thrice* now. Your anonymity, your disguises, your *deception,* none of it will be as effective on me as another. I *know* you.”

His mouth twitched up for a moment. “Do you?” he asked in a soft, punctuated utterance.

“Not nearly as well as I’d like to,” I said before I could stop to consider the words coming out of my mouth.

His only response to that was to lift both eyebrows and peer into my gaze full-on. It made my chest flutter; it made me both profoundly uncomfortable and excited. Which made me *more* uncomfortable. I wondered if he could see all of that in my eyes.

But I was not about to look away. I would not lose that battle.

“Well,” he leaned back, slapping a palm down on his knee. “Talk me out of it, why don’t you? You make many fine points. You’re right: it *is* too dangerous to release you. The blade then? Or poison? The blade is faster.”

I gawked, stammering. And then he started to laugh. Lyrical, sweet, and surprisingly with a few soft snorts through his nose, which he soon covered with a hand. Not the derisive or ridiculing pitch I'd expect.

"I'm—I'm sorry!" he said, continuing to laugh into his hand for a further moment before shaking his head and sitting back on the edge of the bed, holding out the cup. "I was having a laugh there at your expense. I shouldn't have. You're just very funny, Isidor, and I don't think you mean to be. Which alas, makes you even more entertaining. That was cruel of me. Here."

He held the tea cup close to my muzzle. The warm aroma, herbal and sweetened with honey, wafted into my nostrils and set me to drooling. I wanted it. I wanted it *so* badly.

"It will help with the coughing," he assured me. And then, after a moment spent considering, he brought the cup to his own muzzle and drank one long swallow. His throat bobbed. Then he returned it to my muzzle, nodding. "See? No poison. Just tea. Oh, and there's sugar, and honey, because it's just outright uncivilized to drink tea without sweetening. I hope you agree."

Another cough threatened. I watched the downy fur along his throat bob in another swallow. He'd certainly imbibed it. It was likely safe.

He had a long, slender neck, half-covered under a loosened cravat. The fur looked soft. The cup was still wet where he'd drunk from it, just along the ridge. I came to a sudden decision.

Regardless of what his purpose for me was, whatever hidden motivations he may have had, I could do nothing in service of God or the Ministry if I died of dehydration. Stubbornness here was petulant.

Leaning forward, I mouthed at the edge of the cup and let him tip it back for me. And then I slowly drank, allowing the warm, syrupy tea to coat my throat. I breathed through my nose and steadily drained the whole cup.

"There, then," the feline said. His voice was nearly as

soothing as the tea. A siren's call to damnation. I'd hear that voice taunt me in Hell if I didn't survive this.

"How old are you, Sir?" he asked.

The question caught me off-guard. Leaning back, and with no real reason I could think of to lie, I answered automatically, "Nineteen. Twenty soon."

"So young," he said, breathing out through his nose in a long sigh for some reason. Then, before I could think of a retort, he lifted his gaze back to mine. The smile that bloomed there, hesitant like an early lily, was genuine enough that I saw it in his eyes. "I'd obviously rather you not possess this... ineffable ability you seem to have at tracking me down. Earnestly, it's become exhausting. But in this case, if you were going to throw yourself into the maw of the wilderness with reckless abandon anyway, I'm rather glad you found me. If you'd collapsed just half a mile down the road, I would not have heard you from the Lodge."

"You heard me?" I asked, mortified.

"Oh, Young Sir," he looked on me sadly. "You were screaming."

Waking after what had apparently amounted to nearly a day and a half of sleep meant several things got in the way of much further interrogation. Or... conversation, as it were.

Because to be honest, I wasn't certain who would be interrogating who, at this point.

There were the basic physical needs, of course. I hadn't eaten in days. After drinking the tea, there was really no point in refusing the meal, although I tried to eat modestly. Which had been hard.

I had apparently already made a stumbling visit to the water closet at some point in the middle of my fevered slumbering, which I couldn't remember. And, humiliatingly, it and all subsequent visits required an escort at least to the door. He was rather insistent on keeping my hands bound despite the fact that he'd removed every weapon from my person and put them I knew not where.

And he truly had found *all* of them. Decency be-damned. I couldn't know whether he'd strip-searched me or not, and I hadn't had any weapons stowed *under* my clothes anyway, so there was no way to be sure. I was fully dressed when I woke, unlike under Malachi's care. More decorum despite our circumstances. The only things he'd taken off me other than the weapons were my soaked spats, winter cloak, and outer tunic. He'd lain them all—even my harness—out near the small hearth in the room to dry. Within reach if I wanted them.

It felt like he was making a statement. Perhaps because he'd stolen from me before. My things were my own, and other than those that could be used to hurt him, they would remain with me. My pack was there too, with everything in it taken out and rifled through, but it all appeared to be there laid out on the table, intact. Including my prayer book.

And I'd washed up, which he'd left me alone for. Just a wash basin, so only the essentials. But it felt good nonetheless.

Now, hours later, I sat at one of the chairs beside the table, eyeing it while he checked the latch on the simple manacles he'd been using on me when I needed to move around. He seemed less worried now that I'd lunge at him when he was in the room, so the ropes were abandoned. The manacles were rounded metal, like bracelets, with a simple closure and a delicate, loose chain between the two that would allow me a moderate range of motion. They honestly looked very well-made.

Likely stolen.

"Why do you have these?" I asked, testing the length of the chain between them. I could garrot someone if I really wanted, if I was in any physical condition for a fight, that was. He really should have bound my legs. That's how we did it with prisoners we wanted mobile.

"Ha, oh, that's a story," he chuckled. "I doubt you'd want to hear the whole of it."

I closed my eyes a moment, steadying myself. "... is it... are they for lewd purposes? I've heard some Pedigrees and courtesans engage in that sort of depraved foolishness. It's one of the things we're meant to discourage in our charge families if we catch a whiff of it. Debauchery is a bridge to other sins more injurious to the soul."

He elbowed me for some reason, hard. I made sure not to wince. "My young Lord! What an imagination you have."

"It is not a leap in logic given the other heretical behavior you engage in," I reasoned, stiffening defensively.

"No, they are not, oh, what was it you said?" He smiled at me, far too mischievously for my liking. "For 'lewd purposes'. Honestly never saw the appeal. To make a long story short, you are not the first to track me down. I was briefly in the custody of a bounty hunter, of all people. Caught me at a coaching inn not unlike the one we met at, came upon me while I was sleeping. He roughed me up some, but nothing dire. Wanted the price on my head, I'd wager. Unfortunately, he made the mistake of leaving me alone the very next night in a room I could easily escape from. And he missed my tools."

My ears perked. "Did he?" I asked, trying to sound disinterested. "Where did you hide them?"

"I don't lockpick and tell," he chided. "Come on now."

I sighed and looked down at the manacles after he'd readjusted them. "They're looser now, thank you."

"I've tried to tell you I'm not cruel. Eventually, you're bound to believe me. Anyway. I've had them since then. A souvenir. You're the first person I've used them on, actually." He reached down then and put a finger between the edge of the manacle and the weathered, old bracelet I always wore.

"These clinking together are going to get noisy, but I suppose that means I'll always know where you are. This is beautiful... an heirloom?"

I blinked and toyed with the bracelet with my other hand. It was tarnished silver and only silver-plated at that. It had no valuable stones in it of any kind, only a simple inscription of my name—it had been a family name, my mother once told me—in a foreign version of the Amuraic alphabet from closer to the Kadrush in the northern regions my line had apparently long-ago immigrated from.

Most people would not have considered it 'beautiful'.

"It's, yes, from my family," I said. "Akitas on the whole come from the farthest northeastern regions of the country. Many, many generations ago, anyway."

"I'm glad you have a piece of your people's history," he said. "You've been wearing it every time we've met. It must be important to you."

"It isn't valuable," I said, nearly cutting him off. "To anyone but me. You'll get nothing for it."

He pulled out the chair near me and sat, sighing as he did so. "I don't intend to steal it," he said, sounding resigned.

"You've stolen from me before—"

"Yes, I'm not denying I'm a thief," he muttered. "I'm just saying... not that. It's clearly dear to you, and it *belongs* to you. I wouldn't take something like that. Except for your prayer book I suppose, but that was a mistake. I didn't realize it was so personal, I thought it was just a log of some sort I could use to understand my pursuers. And I did return it to you," he pointed out, patting it where it sat on the table.

"Everything I own 'belongs' to me," I said, befuddled. "As well as everything else you've ever stolen. It all 'belonged' to *someone*."

"Indeed it did," he said quietly and rather seriously. He was staring straight at me. Intently. It was hard to look away. "At some point, it all *belonged* to its rightful owners. To those whom it *mattered* to. Like your heirloom matters to you."

I felt my brow line wrinkle in the dark fur of my mask and fought back a wave of frustration. The mood between us right now, myself and Darcy, was perhaps the calmest it had ever been. I wasn't struggling to breathe, locked on the other side of a door, or holding him at blade-point. We were conversing in a quiet, darkening room, while the coals popped in the hearth and snow fell outside, muffling the world. He was looking at me more openly, I think, than he ever had in the past. Like he *wanted* me to unlock something, here. Untangle the mystery that was… him.

To hell with plotting and planning; I'd always done better trusting my instinct. And my instinct was telling me that my training wouldn't avail me here. I needed to just talk to him like he was a normal person, not a subject to be interrogated. Maybe then, I'd finally make some headway.

"I want to understand you," I said the topmost thing that came to my mind. The blunt statement was apparently effective, because his brows lifted marginally. It was a minor facial twitch I'd caught a few times now when I'd surprised him, which might have gone unnoticed given how subtle it was, but his ears were *far* more expressive, and he either didn't bother to control them or couldn't. "But I can't do that if you keep speaking to me in half-answers. I feel like you want me to fill in the missing pieces, when you say things like what you just said. I fully recognize and appreciate the fact that you're… enigmatic," I said that more than a little exhaustedly, "but I don't want to play games when it comes to understanding one another. Least of all now, given our situation."

He glanced down at his legs, shifting one over the other knee and plucking at a few loose strands of fur that had stuck to the fabric. Mine, from the lighter areas of my body, by the look of the color.

Oh good, I was shedding. At this point I needed to fold my humiliating circumstances into the narrative somehow, because ignoring them was pointless. They were legion.

"Get used to that," I muttered. "I'm blowing my coat again, God knows why. It never seems to correspond to the weather as it should."

"And of course, I prefer dark clothing," he said ruefully.

"Why do you think I wear so much white?" I snorted.

"I'd assumed those were, what do they call them, 'vestments'?"

"They are," I confirmed with a lopsided quirk of a smile. "What can I say? It worked out."

He broke out into another bout of that lyrical laughter that so bewitched me, eventually putting a hand up over his mouth to cover his fangs. He'd done that more than once, I noted. It wouldn't be that strange, except it was an uncommon habit amongst the lower classes or even people in trade. Covering one's fangs was a practice in high society, a matter of etiquette. And it wasn't the only sign of that.

Many things about him spoke to a high-born upbringing, or at least etiquette and society training. His affect, his cadence, even the way he walked, all felt meticulous. Like a well-groomed Pedigree or a tradesman accustomed to elite circles. We received similar training as Templar, and even I didn't have that kind of poise. Everything from his posture to his proper manner of speech supported it.

A courtesan, maybe? That would explain his knowledge of Pedigree society and how he'd drifted in and out of households, knowing more than he ever should have.

It didn't seem right to assume that just because he was a thief, just because he had *some* connection to a Pedigree lord, that he was a prostitute. He certainly employed his *charms*, but...

"I swear I can smell burning when you stare at me like that," he said. "It's distressing I'll admit, but oddly fascinating, how you keep figuring me out. You're doing it right now, aren't you?"

"You're accustomed to not being known," I surmised.

"Most people are never truly 'known'," he countered. "Even you Isidor, I'm sure. There must be facets upon facets of yourself that you'd rather not share."

"You have no idea how wrong you are," I shook my head. "I am infamous at my Abbey for my awkward and sometimes very rude honesty, and for wearing my heart on my sleeve."

He smiled slowly. "You know, I can see that for you. Now that you say it."

"I'm doing it right now," I muttered. "Over-sharing with the enemy."

"I don't want to be your enemy, young Sir," he said softly, his long eyelashes falling over half-lidded eyes. "Especially not when we're trapped together like this. Can we not put all of that animosity aside for a few days, at least? I think you're right that we need to understand one another better. I am willing to make the effort to... open up, as it were... at least insofar as will make this time together more pleasant for both of us. My 'crimes' I would rather not speak on. Can we make that a rule, maybe?"

As he spoke, he'd leaned forward, the leg folded over his knee flexing, his paw brushing over the side of my chair. He hadn't touched me, but his body language and the fact that he was crossing some of the distance between us... altogether, it just made me...

"Will you please," I said through gritted teeth, "stop that?"

A flash of hurt, or maybe surprise, crossed his eyes. His ears went stiff. "I'm just trying to lower the temperature. You said you wanted to understand one another."

"I do," I insisted, keeping a civil tone. "But that is unlikely to happen if I am... distracted or constantly worrying about adjusting my eyeline. You need to have some accountability for your presentation."

He arched an eyebrow, then leaned back, glancing down at his attire. “Is a button out of place? These are a lend, if that’s not obvious. I wouldn’t be caught dead so ill-fitted were I not literally on the run from the law, you know. So maybe *you* should take some accountability.”

“I meant,” I grated out, “that you were a woman when last we met. Or at least I believed you were.” I chose my words carefully, or at least I *think* I did. “The flirtations may seem a necessity to you when you’re in the midst of your crimes, but they are, I assure you, not helping your case with me now.”

“What in the world—” He cut himself off, puffing out his cheeks for a moment and then glaring at me. “When, precisely, have I been ‘flirtatious’ with you, Sir? I would *very* much like to know.”

“You clearly understand etiquette, I should *not* have to explain that your manner of dress, your proximity, the lurid way you speak sometimes, and your physical composure, are inappropriate with a man who isn’t your spouse,” I insisted.

“You think I’m another man,” he said in a dry tone. “Why should any of that matter? Not that I’ve *been* inappropriate, mind you. I know I haven’t.”

“You laid your hands on me during our very first meeting, undid my harness—”

“I was trying to help you *breathe*,” he said around an offended guffaw.

“You’ve used terms of endearment and a dulcet tone unbefitting how a lady—or even a gentleman—should address a stranger, nearly every time we’ve met—”

“I have addressed you *properly*, in the way I might any man on the street,” he insisted. “With ‘Sir’ or ‘Lord’ or your ‘Templar’ title. I admit I’ve called you a Knight once or twice, but you have the bearing, your vestments look like the illustrations of Knights of yore, and in any case it was meant honorably, not as a mockery. And I cannot help my natural speaking voice, *Sir*. It is not meant to be 'distracting,' it is simply how I sound."

"I refuse to believe your manner of address with me on each occasion we've met was as innocent as you're insisting," I snorted.

"Well no," he said, rolling his eyes. "I locked you in a room and shot a flintlock in your face, but our interactions have hardly been 'innocent' on either end, if we're being fair. You nearly drove your blade through my chest, remember."

"I was well in control of myself," I said. "I wouldn't have hurt you."

"What does it matter if your Brothers at the Ministry would have?" he countered, knitting his brow. "You would have delivered me like a lamb to the slaughter."

"You're no lamb," I said and kept it at that. He'd said he didn't want to talk about his crimes, and I was willing to dance along that knife's edge, for now.

"Fair enough, I'll acquiesce to the fact that we are, technically speaking, enemies," he sighed. "I don't like the sound of that, but I suppose there's no denying it."

I didn't like the sound of it either, but I didn't say as much.

"But I'm no slattern," he insisted, tugging at the cuff of one of his sleeves. "I do not debauch myself in order to commit my crimes, I do not seduce, I do not bed my way into the homes I reclaim relics and curios from. And I resent being painted as such. I especially resent any implication that I may have acted untoward with *you* in any of our interactions."

"You seem socially educated," I said. "You must know of the five-paw rule of distance and decorum."

He shut his mouth and glanced away.

"You have crossed that threshold numerous times with me, including laying your hands upon me when it served no *medical* purpose," I said quickly, cutting him off. "In the garden at the Lane home. You touched my cheek."

"You had a blade pointed directly at my breast," he reminded me, biting the words out. "Pressed against me, in fact."

"That accusation brings me to the point where I must remind you of your crimes, and why I am pursuing you, and you don't want me to do that," I reiterated.

"I didn't touch your cheek to *seduce* you," he insisted. "I was trying to, God, I just wanted you to see me as someone mortal. As *someone*, a *person*, not 'The Heart Thief'. That's also why I told you my name. I don't know why I did it in the moment, it just seemed the thing to do."

"It was a breach of propriety," I said. "The way you have carried on with me in general, in even the short spans of time we've spent together, have been laced with indecency."

"Touch shouldn't be 'indecent' on its face," he said stubbornly. "That is an arbitrary and terribly isolating line your society has insisted on."

"So you're *not* Amurescan," I leaned back, knitting my paws together.

"I'm more Amur than I am Huudari at this point if we're going by years. But I remember a world other than the one this society insists upon. Lord… this is why I dress male more often than not. It's not just because it makes travel easier. If you saw me as a man, full-stop, you'd be far less distraught by a casual touch, or how I've manipulated your 'eye-line', or how my clothing is cut, or the tone of my voice—"

"Men aren't supposed to be so casual with physicality with one another either," I said suspiciously. "But what are you on about? You *are* male."

I paused.

"Aren't you?"

He leveled a steady gaze at me, and I felt the floor drop out from beneath my feet. It wasn't even because of any implication; I was too terribly confused at this point to guess at their gender any more. It was because I had an inkling of what they were about to say to me. I'd backed myself into a corner.

"If you think I'm a man," they said, leaning forward and resting their elbows on their knees, head propped up in one palm, "then why are you interpreting our interactions as flirtatious, exactly?"

My mouth ran dry, my tongue sticking to my teeth. I paused for far too long, trying to decide what to say.

"Mmh." Their eyelids fell low, a discerning look cutting through me. "I see."

"Stop that," I whispered roughly. "You're confusing me."

"I cannot help that," they said, each word spoken slowly and deliberately. "No more than I can help what goes through your mind when you hear my voice, or notice that I cut a fetching figure in a tailored pair of trousers, or how my natural markings 'direct the eye unwholesomely' to my 'exotic features'. And yes, I've had that accusation."

They leaned back again, crossing their arms over their chest and adopting a more defensive, and certainly more modest, posture. "It doesn't matter what I do," they muttered. "Ever since I was a child—a *child*—it hasn't mattered what manner of dress I adopt or how modestly I act, how proper, how careful. Simply *existing* invites the lurid gaze of men, the envy and scorn of women, and I am expected to take accountability for that. For *your* lack of restraint."

I swallowed, unprepared for any more, but they continued and it only got worse.

"Well… I refuse, Isidor," they said evenly. "Especially in your case. I shan't be blamed again. You're part of the Order that polices moral purity. The shame is yours. Not mine. If you are 'distracted' by me in any way, those are your imaginings to contend with. I have never done anything to lead you on."

"You're right," I said around the stone in my throat. My voice came out in a croak, ragged and tired. And I'd said it so immediately after they'd finished, it seemed to surprise even them. But…

I shook my head. "You're right."

"Well…" they said haltingly.

"The shame is mine," I continued. I felt it bubble out of me, like I was in Confession. "I'm so sorry. I fell back on blame because…. I am… struggling. With many things right now, but my struggles with sin are not your fault. They cannot possibly be. Sin comes from within."

They blinked at me several times in quick succession and were silent for a while. When they did finally speak, the hard, cold bitterness in their voice was gone, replaced with a more halting, wary tone. "Well. You weren't lying before. You really do put it all out there, don't you?"

"Confession is good for the soul," I said.

"You took that one to heart, didn't you?"

"I take most things to heart."

They huffed, smiling almost despite themself. "You know, if I *had* wanted to steal your heart away, I feel you'd be an easy mark. You're lucky I'm kinder than that."

"Don't doubt my resolve," I cautioned them.

"Never," they promised. "Look. I really do want things between us to… if we cannot find any middle-ground, I'd at least not prefer we be at each other's throats. Would it comfort you— put these thoughts and 'confusions' of yours to rest, if I were to tell you I am in fact male? Or would that not make a difference at this point?"

"I don't honestly know," I answered feebly.

"That's fair," they said softly.

"What I'd like," I said, working up the courage to look them in the eyes again, "is the truth."

They drew in a breath and seemed to mull that over silently, for a time.

"On a great many things," I added. "But, can we start with that?"

"Alright," they agreed with a sigh. "But you won't like my answer, and you may think I'm lying again."

"Do you believe in God?" I asked them, more blurted out.

To their credit, they didn't balk. "Yes," they answered, "but not the God your Tome teaches exists. I prefer not to believe God could be so preferential and cruel."

I bit the inside of my mouth at that but persisted. "Can you swear then, under the eyes of God, that what you'll tell me here in this room is the truth?"

"Sure," they agreed. "I'll swear it. I swear this is my truth, and I'd like to think God knows how they made me and did so intentionally, so perhaps they'll back me up."

"God crafted us all with intention, we are as we were meant to be," I nodded. "Every beauty and imperfection, all part of His plan."

They smiled a little. "I think so, too. Alright, then." They let out a long breath, composing themselves. "I am... neither."

I waited. Then, "What do you mean?"

"I am neither a man nor a woman," they explained. "Neither has ever seemed to suit me fully, I've lived my life as both, and I can't say either's a fit."

"You're..." I stammered, "... are you... neutren?"

"No, I am," they gestured at their person, "intact, as I was born. No modifications save, I suppose, the pierced ears and the occasional dye in my fur." They sighed. "I told you this wouldn't really satisfy you."

"I'm just trying to make sense of..." I looked them over again, the obvious question begging at the edge of my muzzle, but it was *impossible* to put it to words. I had literally just accused them of impropriety, I wasn't about to go questioning what was in their britches.

Out loud.

And even doing so internally felt wrong. I wasn't their intended; I wasn't even courting them. Their body was not my concern, and thinking about—*picturing* it, as I was now, undeniably—was sickening behavior. My ears must have been beet red; I could feel the shame burning in my face.

I must have been silent for a time, because they cocked their head. "How noble," they clucked, sounding earnestly impressed. "You didn't ask. So many do, it's *shocking*. I mean you did ask if I'd been *castrated*, but—"

"It's a holy oath taken by only the most pious in my Order," I insisted. "It's not considered indecent to speak of."

"I'll let you pass on that one," they chuckled. "You know Isidor, you're taking this better than I thought you would. Have you spent your entire life here in this country?"

"Yes," I said. "Why ask?"

"Because where I come from, there is a third group as accepted as men and women. The Ahnantu. In the village I grew up in, there were many of us. We were accepted amongst the men and women and would fill in for duties as needed. I helped take care of my younger siblings, learned to weave, *and* was taught how to set snares and hunt. If I'd grown up there, I eventually would have married and no one would have thought it odd, regardless to whom I was wedded."

"This was chosen for you when you were born?" I asked, fascinated.

They shook their head. "No, if I remember correctly— it has been some time, but— children were not really 'boys' or 'girls' until they were tall enough to reach the branch of a particular tree down by the lake. They were just children. I realized from a young age who I was, that I was meant to be Ahnantu, and I chose for myself. It was only when I came here that I was made to choose otherwise. Your society is rigid. Unyielding."

"God made us to fulfill particular roles," I said carefully. "You cannot deny what is obvious."

"I can and I will," they said, holding their ground. "What is 'obvious' to you is what you were taught to believe. I was taught differently, and what is obvious to me is the truth I live with and know, and I'd wager I know it better than you do. I spent half of my life conforming to your rules, and seeking to please *your* society, and to no avail. There is no real place for me here, no matter how docile, how pleasing, or how faithful I am. It is enough already. I am done living that way. I am, as you said, 'as God made me'."

They spread their arms, then let them drop at their sides slowly. "You wanted me to be honest with you, and I have. Whether you accept it or not is not my problem."

Of all of the—granted, two—answers I had braced for, and each of their unique complications, this hadn't been on the map. I took some time to digest it, considering another retort or some argument from logic, but to what end? The reason I wanted to know wasn't remotely pure, and as it pertained to the case, their gender would not affect what the Ministry would do to them. It only mattered because I personally cared.

And, distressingly, I wasn't sure which answer I'd really wanted. Either brought up questions I wasn't ready to ask myself just yet.

"How..." I trailed off, "... shall I address you, then?"

"How would you speak of, say," they hummed, "a criminal you were hunting, whom you hadn't assigned a gender yet?"

"Well, they..." I stammered, "... we'd call them—"

"There you have it," they said.

"That's rather awkward," I said, mulling over the idea mentally.

"No, it isn't," they said, "Cillian manages just fine, has for years, and I am all but certain you're smarter than he is."

"Well, that's unkind to your patron," I groused.

"I've earned the right," they assured me. "And don't deny it, you're *very* smart, Isidor. Smarter than most people. I'm certain you know it, too."

"If I were, I wouldn't keep finding myself in these situations," I muttered. "Also, why do you keep complimenting me? 'Smart', 'striking', 'thoughtful'—"

"Wow, you've really been holding on to all of those," they said, coughing politely into their fist and presumably hiding a smile. Not well, either.

"And you wondered why I thought you were flirtatious?" I nearly stumbled over my words. "No one *says* those sorts of things about me. I'm not vain, I'm just not used to hearing any of that. Makes it hard to keep my countenance."

"I can't help that I like you," they waved a hand. "And I won't be blamed for it, either. You're very charming, in your own way. But if it comforts you any, if given the choice I'd want to be your *friend,* Isidor. As I said the last time we met. I'm not attracted to you in a courtly sense. Does that ease the awkwardness any?"

It didn't. In fact it stung, and I tried desperately not to show it. It shouldn't have mattered to me—it *shouldn't*. I knew I wasn't physically attractive, and vanity was a weakness we Templar were meant to scrub out at a young age. But it still bothered me.

More than it should have.

"I suppose..." I said, trailing off.

"Night will be falling soon," they said rather suddenly, standing and moving towards the window until they were a slim silhouette against the glare of the midday gray. "Do you mind sandwiches for dinner, again? I'd like to use the bread while it's still any good before we move to preserved food."

"That's fine," I said, staring down at my manacled hands in my lap. Why did I feel like the air had been punched out of my chest?

"I'm going to get a book or two for myself, to pass the time," they said as they headed towards the door. "Would you, um," they paused at the door, glancing back at me. "Would you like something to read? I have some of my favorites with me, and there's an old, little library in the drawing room I could rifle through. Caked in dust, but that's never stopped me from reading."

"Sure," I agreed.

"Any preference?"

I looked up. "Anything that's banned reading in a Monastery."

I swear I caught a sparkle in their eye. "You've got it."

It was the dead of the night when we were intruded upon.

Things had cooled between us after our long talk, and we'd spent most of the rest of the day in relative calm and quiet, save a few exchanges, working through the stack of books Darcy had brought. Judging by the dusty jackets on some and the well-kept but also well-loved covers on the others, (and I could tell, believe you me) they'd pulled from both their own private stash and whatever bookcase had been left here at the abandoned lodge.

We may not have been able to agree on much, but the care and keeping of books seemed to be a similar passion we shared. We'd spent probably half an hour initially just cleaning the covers, with the edge of my tunic in my case, and a pocket square in theirs. We'd both instinctively started doing so before we'd realized the other had, and that had provided a bit of a laugh, at least. But then, there was reading to be had, sandwiches to be nibbled at distractedly, and the room had fallen into companionable silence.

Either the both of us had been absorbed in the books or trying to outlast the other until we nodded off—a little of both in my case, if I'm being honest—but I'd ultimately lost the battle.

I was still contending with the cold, and I hadn't quite beaten back the exhaustion from the last...

... month.

But when I woke, whatever calm we'd managed to find, whatever solace we had, was shattered immediately by the sound of a creaking door and then a somewhat familiar and *very* unexpected voice.

"Oh, my God," the man gasped out loud, "Dar, what have you done?!"

I sat bolt upright and forced my eyes to adjust to the near-darkness, coming to dizzily. All of this was still so bizarre; the last few days felt like a dream. I could hardly get my bearings. Was that really Cillian Rathborne standing in the doorway of the bedroom, clutching at the door handle like it were a lifeline? Staring at me with a look of dawning horror and shock?

Darcy roused less quickly than I had. They were curled up like a pill bug in the oversized, plush sitting chair near the hearth. They blinked blearily and then those beautiful eyes went wide and alarmed, and they scrambled out of the chair. Not in time to stop Cillian, though, who'd dropped his cane and reached under his coat, to pull out—

A pistol. Yes, that's about what I'd expected.

There was nothing I could do. My hands were still manacled, and although I wasn't bound to the bed any more, I would not be able to cross the room in time to stop him if he wanted to shoot me. I stared back at him across the space, trying to decide how best to plead my case, if I even had the time. I had gone my entire life without having a gun pointed at me and now it had happened twice in the span of a week.

"Cillian, *no!*" Darcy bounded the short space towards him, wrapping their arms around his outstretched, shaking one and jerking the firearm down until it was pointed at the floor. "Are you insane?!"

"Are you?!" he demanded in return, eyes wide and glinting in the dim firelight from the hearth. "What were you thinking, bringing one of them here?!"

"I didn't *bring* him here," they insisted, releasing his arm and putting their paws to both of his cheeks, forcing his head down to look at them and not at me. "He found this place on his own—"

"That's impossible, *how*?"

"I don't know, the Ministry has records on everything," they said, shaking their head. "He came alone, and he was freezing to death, I didn't know what else to do—"

"How do you know he came alone?" he insisted, looking again to me. "They never work alone, Dar, *never*. How long ago did he arrive? How long has he been here?"

"I came alone," I spoke up, trying to keep my voice from quivering. "I swear it."

"Your oaths are less than horse shit to me," Cillian snarled. "Dar, whatever he's told you, he's lying—it's *all* lies. They're allowed to lie; they can even swear it on their false God if they need to as long as it suits the Ministry."

I was stunned by his words—the man was a *Pedigree*. He *was* the authority, the Patriarch of his line, the upper echelon our entire Faith held on a pedestal. And he was spouting the kind of Heresy I had literally only read about in books, up until now. To see someone so shamelessly profess it to my face...

Darcy grabbed his cheek ruff, this time more forcefully, and made him look at them again. They dropped their voice, whispering intensely, "I believe him, Cillian. Put. The gun. Away."

The setter slowly stowed his weapon, while keeping his eyes on me. And then he reached for Darcy's shoulder, gave it what looked like a gentle squeeze, and used his grip on them to direct them to the door. "Come on. Not in here."

He watched me the whole while as they walked to the door and made sure to do so until he'd shut it. And then they were gone, their footsteps heading off down the hallway. I didn't know where they'd gone, but I knew this place wasn't large by any means. I waited until I heard a door close—it sounded like just to the room next to this one, which was the drawing room if my guess was correct—then I slipped out of bed.

I went immediately to the table where my harness was stowed and dug my tools out of the hidden pocket on the underside of the one strap.

"Not this time," I whispered to myself, as they fell into my palm. I fidgeted with the manacles, examining the lock—it looked complicated, far more so than the Ministry boxes—when I caught the vaguest hint of voices.

The walls here were thick, and they likely assumed they'd be safe talking in whispers, even just a room away. I think the whole of the Lodge was three or four rooms, so unless they went outside, it wasn't as though they had much of an option. But sound could carry through many parts of a small house.

There. I remembered something from training. There was a hearth in this room, so no need for a potbelly stove, but the stove pipe from the adjoining room vented into the chimney here. I wandered over and kneeled beside the fire, used the coal rake to scratch out the popping embers into nothing so that I could hear better, and got my ear as close to the pipe as possible without burning it.

The first person I heard was Cillian.

"-don't care that he's young, Dar. They're *all* young at some point. They scrape them out of workhouses, orphanages, or off the streets."

"What does that matter?" Darcy, of course. "Don't be an elitist arse with *me*."

"I'm not… that isn't why I said that," he insisted, sounding defensive. "Do you know why they do that, Dar? Why they're all foundlings or unwanted children?"

Silence.

"Because that means they have no allegiance outside the Church," he went on. "No family, no connections, no money, no options. They fill their head with doctrine, train them up to be good little, obedient soldiers. They beat it into them until there's nothing left in their skulls but scripture. The ones that don't make the cut or don't properly buy into the zealotry? They sell them *back* to workhouses, press them into the military, or toss them out on the street with no prospects. The girls get auctioned off as wives as soon as they have their first heat to the highest bidder. Usually to old, lonely men. *That's* where that boy came from, Dar. It's a bloody cult. It is *too* late for them to live a normal life once they get to be that old. He's done for."

"You've never even talked to him."

"What exactly do you want to do with him now? What have you told him?" he pressed. "We can't let him go. He's seen you. He's seen *me*. He knows too much—"

"He'd seen us both before, and the Ministry knows we're involved."

"Dar, it does not matter whether the boy is smitten with you, or whatever it is you think will compel him to keep your confidence—"

"Why are you assuming that?" they bit out, a little louder than the rest of their conversation. I caught the snapping tone, and I'm certain he did, too.

"... holy hell, you *do* think that," Cillian breathed out. "Darcy, my God, even if that's true, it won't matter. They aren't above interrogating their own. If he leaves here alive, they'll get the truth out of him, one way or the other."

There was a long pause, and I worried briefly that they knew they were being listened in on, somehow. But that was unlikely. They might have worried about it though, because when Darcy spoke again, it was so quiet I had trouble hearing it.

"... I don't trust your motives here, Cillian."

"I don't know what you mean."

"I mean, I think you don't like that there's a man here with me, and that is a *stupid* reason to kill someone." Sharper, closer to that whispered snap from before.

Something like a long, angry sigh. "I have supported you through *so* many decisions you've made with your life over the last few years that were far more foolish and reckless and more likely to hurt the both of us than the thought that you might move on, Dar."

"That's your choice. Everything has always been *your* choice," the feline's voice again.

"But this," he spoke again, "goes beyond all of that. This will get you killed. It *will* get you killed, and I... I know I am not the authority in your life, not any longer, but I still want to keep you safe. I want you to live and find some measure of happiness, and I don't know how to help you anymore. I'm just trying to take care of you."

Again, another very long pause.

"You gave up that right, Cillian," Darcy's voice, weak, quiet, and not just because of the distance between us. "You cannot make me happy anymore and I'm not yours to protect. It's not like it was. So just stop thinking that way."

"*You* wrote for help. You were frantic. Bloody hell Dar, what do I need to do here to talk sense into you? This isn't like the last time."

I looked down at the manacles, realizing I'd done nothing to work on the lock. I could have been doing so this entire time, and the conversation was certainly reaching a point where it might end. I fumbled with my tool, trying to find the release inside the tiny lock. Cillian was still here, a room away, with a loaded gun. He certainly still seemed to want me dead.

I was still ill, sans my weapons, and underdressed, but it was now or never. I needed to escape, or there was a very real chance that I'd be dead, very soon.

"I'm not staying the night, I need to be at the Lane's

tomorrow when the older one—the *Inquisitor*, hell's bells Darcy, I think this one's a bloody flagellant, a *maniac*—he comes tomorrow to interrogate them again," Cillian continued, his voice fading somewhat, as they walked farther away from the stove pipe. "The Ministry is riled-up. They are in a *state*, Darcy, and now I suppose I know why. How long has the Akita been missing?"

"His name is Isidor."

"I don't care. How long?"

"Two days, maybe two and a half?"

"Do they know he's here? He must have told someone where he was headed."

"If he had, they'd be here already and you know it."

"They never work alone, that's bizarre..."

The door in the hallway opened, and I didn't catch anything else, save muffled murmurs. I frantically twisted my implements, looking for the angle, using one prong to steady while the other—

It was more complicated than the Ministry box, but apparently, I was better at this than I thought, because I felt and heard them click, and let out a breath I hadn't realized I was holding. The manacle on one hand swayed open, and I let it fall and dangle off the chain. The other, I would have to use my bad hand on, but at least now I knew how—

The door opened, and I froze.

I slowly turned my gaze towards the figure standing silhouetted in the dim lantern-light, and blessedly, realized it was Darcy alone. Cillian was nowhere to be seen, but I heard the door outside open and not close, so he was probably getting something from the stoop.

Darcy's eyes dropped down to my unlocked manacle, the tools in my hand, me, and then back behind them to the empty hallway. Then they hurried inside and closed the door, crossing the room towards me.

They paused only when they were a few feet away, apparently still frightened enough of me not to get close when I was essentially free. Armed, or not.

To be fair, they only had a small blade on them, and they were half my size. If I wanted to, right now, I could probably overpower them. And turn the tables. Take them captive, hold them against Cillian. Escape. Maybe even with *them*.

Something impossible to discern as any particular feeling, unspoken but bone-deep, passed between us. And we both apparently landed on the same idea at the same time.

I closed the manacle back over my wrist, unlocked but on, as Darcy's ears twisted back and the sound of the front door closing echoed down the hallway. Darcy turned their attention back to me a moment later, hunkering down and looking over my work.

"That's fine. He won't check the lock," they said after running their slender fingers over the seam. They looked again to the thin metal tools in my hand and flitted their eyes over to the bed. Nodding, I hid them under the mattress.

"If it seems like he's going to do it, leave," they affirmed quietly. "The windows here can open out. I'll try to keep talking him down. You should get back in bed like you haven't moved. Try playing up the cold, too. He's got a heart in there somewhere."

I did so, even forcing a cough, which soon became three. It wasn't hard to get going again.

"Isidor," Darcy's voice begged my attention. They were standing at the foot of the bed and barely concealing a smile beneath the general fear and weariness. "You can pick locks?"

The answer was obvious, so I didn't bother denying it. I just nodded guiltily.

They made a breathless noise, something between a laugh and a sigh. "Well," they rolled their eyes, "*now* I'm attracted to you."

11

BOOK CLUB

I woke in that ethereal space the Lodge occupied—somewhere between the reality of my life and the otherworldly dreams I'd been sharing with my imagined versions of Darcy—to a warm room diffused by golden morning sunlight, distant birdsong, and the soft tones of a piano playing. For a time, I lay there believing I hadn't in fact woken at all. I drifted in and out, waiting for the dream to shift. Marveling at how real this one felt. These dreamscapes had bled into reality so seamlessly, I could read them with all of my senses, could feel the fading ache in my throat, the hunger churning in my gut, the scent of the feline on the quilt from where they'd sat the night before.

The piano quieted for a few moments, and I drifted. Then, it began again… the initial chords instantly familiar to me. The Hymn of the Wives of Canus.

I sat up slowly, the morning stiffness in my joints confirming I was, in fact, awake. Unless minor aches and pains had begun making it into my dreams, now. I listened for a time, discerning a few things after giving myself enough of a moment to really come-to. It was most certainly the Hymn I thought it was. We sang it—most Churches did—every seventh day. It was one of the Founding Hymns, written by the First Tribe, the followers of Canus. The first songs that had broken through the ancient ways of worship to really be considered something like what we would now call 'music'. It was ancient. It was beautiful.

It was most definitely being played somewhere in the Lodge. On a real piano.

I stood, and something tugged down my wrist, giving a metallic ring. I glanced down at the manacle where it had clunked down against the band of my bracelet. Right. That was still happening. The chain glistened in the warm light, dangling loosely off the edge of the bed, where the other was hanging open, connected by the chain but useless. It must have come undone at some point in my sleep.

I considered re-closing it, but it seemed a pointless gesture now. It was morning. I'd waited inside that room for hours last night, while the two of them—Darcy and Cillian—spoke in hushed whispers in another room. Not the drawing room this time; wherever they were, I couldn't make them out any more.

Despite the fact that I had an assured escape, it had been nerve-wracking. I couldn't know how persuasive Darcy might be to the man (there seemed to be a lot of bad blood there) or when the conversation would take a turn and Cillian would, God-forbid, talk the feline into what he wanted to do.

And even if I could get out in time, I'd be putting myself literally out in the cold, exposed to the elements, with no clear road back to Redcoven. And I'd seen how well that tended to go for me. A master of orienteering, I was not.

Besides, if I did that I'd have to *leave*. Which was bad enough in and of itself, the threat of death aside.

But at some point, relegated to my room like a pup awaiting punishment from their elders, I had fallen asleep again. I had to keep reminding myself that it wasn't a weakness of resolve. I was *ill* and exhausted from all that 'nearly dying' business.

I wasn't sure if Darcy had ever come back in here to look in on me after all of that, but if they had, I hadn't woken. Still, it was morning now. That meant Cillian was probably gone. He'd said he didn't intend to be here in the morning. Did that mean we'd prevailed?

It was odd, I realized, that I was thinking of Darcy and I as 'we'. As a unified force. Ridiculous, really. We were still on opposite sides of the law.

But something had certainly shifted last night. I'd had a chance to capture them. A chance I would have relished not a month ago. Granted, it might not have gone well. Cillian still had a pistol and I had none of my weapons. But he certainly seemed to care for Darcy. Using them as a hostage, I could have…

No. It honestly wasn't even worth hashing it out in my mind. I never would have done it and I knew it. I could lie to myself about my motives being pure when it came to tracking down Darcy. Or at least, I'd certainly been managing until now. But that had been denial, pure and simple. And hardly healthy or virtuous. Or… effective, really. I'd been wracked by guilt all this time. A sign at least that my inner voice was still loud enough to be heard, if not obeyed.

But I wouldn't—couldn't—lie to myself about employing such dishonorable, vicious tactics as taking a hostage. As Templar we *were* permitted to act unscrupulously and to violate our oaths when our task absolutely called for it, and I don't think the Ministry would have condemned me for doing so now. My freedom for theirs. No question. But we were the only ones who could make that call in the moment; we were the ones who'd have to live with our conscience and make our peace with God afterwards. I'd resolved to stick by my instincts, since acting purely doctrinally was something I'd thrown by the wayside already and couldn't exactly be relied upon in this situation. If God had any intent of giving me instruction, none had been forthcoming. My instincts were as close as I'd get.

Real, genuine threats of harm were out, let alone actually attacking Darcy. Not only was that unlikely to work, it felt wrong, given the grace I'd been granted last night. And I simply wasn't willing to overthink it any more than that. It felt *wrong*. Full stop. That's all that mattered.

I could... lie, within whatever parameters were considered reasonable to get the information I needed or to protect myself. I could bluff them, *pretend* to take them hostage even though I knew I would not carry through on any of the threats.

But then that *was* a threat, wasn't it? One could argue it wouldn't hurt them, so it was acceptable. Of course, that was assuming they wouldn't effectively fight back and events wouldn't spiral out of my control. And aside from that, I'd begun to feel, for some reason, that the concept of terrorizing Darcy (more than I doubtless already had, stalking them across the countryside) amounted to actual harm. In a very real way. I didn't need to ask them to confirm it, I remembered the fear in their eyes in the Lanes' garden all too well. I remembered the tremble in their hand when they lifted that pistol. And now, in retrospect, I realized that fear hadn't entirely been for their own well-being. They'd been afraid to point the firearm at me.

I'd seen that very fear on display last night, when Cillian had done the same. Darcy didn't want to watch me die. They'd done everything in their power to avoid that happening, despite Cillian's very accurate point that it would be better for both of them if I were gone. Which—all of this—brought me back around and around to one hammering thought that had bewildered me all night.

Darcy did not act like someone who'd killed two young Templar in cold blood. Or a housekeeper. Or anyone, for that matter. If they couldn't even bear to kill *me*—the man who was trying to arrest them and bring them to justice...

They could be acting. But if so, why let me live? Why stop their protector from... protecting them? Try as I might, I couldn't put the pieces together.

I had lived a literally cloistered existence for more than half my life, and all my adult years. There was much about the world I was still naïve to, much I had yet to experience. But one thing you learned and learned well, growing up as I had, was the concept of fear.

It wasn't just because of harsh discipline from our elders for our youthful transgressions or the shadow of the Ministry looming over everything you did—monitoring, reviewing, archiving—it was the doctrine itself. A truly God-fearing man had a healthy relationship with fear. It was how you showed respect to the Almighty, it was a motivating factor in how you chose to live your life, compelling one to make the righteous choice over the sinful indulgence that would lead us to damnation, and it was the reins the Church used to pull you back to the road when you began to go astray. I was as much in fear of the Templar Ministry as I was proud to be a part of it.

But I didn't want Darcy to feel that way about me. I didn't want them to be afraid of me anymore. It wasn't a logical feeling, I knew that. I was still a loyal soldier of the Ministry that wanted the Heart Thief tried for their crimes. It was natural and correct for them to be afraid of me. And they'd not once claimed to be entirely innocent, so all of that was still in play as far as I knew.

The reality of how much I must have absolutely *terrified* them, hunting them down, guessing their trajectory, and repeatedly landing on their doorstep, given what they knew I represented...

God. Even if I *was* in the right, I didn't like *feeling* this way.

I was beginning to think I'd make a very poor Inquisitor, after all.

The quiet, muffled piano fell off into silence for a moment, mid-hymn. We were only through the first refrain. I listened, wondering if somehow my thoughts had interrupted them. Insane. Ridiculous. But then I *was* losing my mind, apparently.

It began again, haltingly at first as though the pianist was finding their placement in the song. An underconfident hand. But then they'd begun again, and while I'd hardly say their playing was expert-level, they seemed practiced enough to make few major mistakes. The pause must have been to turn a page. They didn't know this song by heart.

I was doing it again. Spying, hypothesizing, and drawing conclusions about someone. I'd always had a knack for solving mysteries in books and short stories and discerning more about people than they may have liked based on surface perceptions and context clues. It's why I'd thought, early on, that this might be the kind of work I was meant for.

Father Helstrom had known, though. He knew what this line of work required all too well. He'd warned me against it for years. He'd even warned me against this very investigation.

But playing Inquisitor right now was especially pointless. I was two rooms away, and for once, there was nothing between us but my own fears and insecurities. Why wonder about them, skulk about and try to guess information on my own, when I could just get up, walk in there, and talk to them?

I stiffly rose from bed, trying my best to smooth down an impossibly sleep-rumpled shirt and my still quite road-worn and dirty breeches. I briefly considered stripping out of them down to my trousers beneath, which were covering enough, and I had smallclothes on under that as well, but the remembrance that they were—by their own declaration—not a man, stopped me flat. Wearing my undergarments, even if it was two layers of them, would be unthinkable in the presence of a woman. Especially given that we were alone.

God, I hoped we were alone.

But they weren't a woman, either. So, what were the rules? I was painfully uncertain.

Ultimately, better to err on the side of caution. Stiff with dried snow and dirt crust or not, my outer breeches were at least properly concealing, and I'd never be able to keep my countenance if I was worried about the outline of my sheath more than I was focused on the moment. Speaking of...

"Behave, I beg of you," I muttered down at the offender in question as I checked the laces at the front closure. I considered putting my other manacle back on, just to be safe, but if Cillian were still here, I probably shouldn't have been wandering around at all, truth be told.

To hell with it. I gave a long, steadying breath out and opened the door to the hallway beyond.

I'd only seen it briefly last night and not well. The Lodge was wood-floored and walled, which was holding up well enough even despite the neglect, but the faded robin's-egg blue paint along the ceiling and molding was cracking and chipping, bleaching near windowsills and slightly more saturated in various rectangles on the walls, suggesting there had once been many frames adorning them. The furniture had been left here for the most part, whenever they'd abandoned the place. It was out-of-style and more practical than you'd see in a Pedigree Estate, but not of poor quality. I slid my fingertips slowly along the dusty top of a shallow shelf on the right side of the hallway, resting between two windows. The curtains were drawn back, allowing the nearly blinding white light of the outside world in.

It took my eyes a few moments to adjust, until the tranquil, effervescent beauty of the wilderness came into focus. It was smothered in a fresh, downy blanket of snow, rounding out all the edges of the unforgiving forest I'd nearly died in. Even the empty, dark, grasping branches of the trees were dipped in glassy ice, throwing sparkles of sunlight through the windows, dancing across the hall. I followed one, thrown strewn across my eyeline by some breeze outside perhaps, until it landed on a door ahead of me.

"God help me," I begged, glancing briefly upwards. "I'm going, I'm going..."

There were two rooms on the left-hand side of the hall, the first of which may have been the drawing room Darcy had disappeared into several times since I'd arrived, the second of which might have been another bedroom. It was the second room the sound of the piano emanated from. The door that was now quite literally glowing with dancing light.

I padded quietly up to the door, remembering all but two steps from being able to grasp the handle that I wasn't *trying* to sneak up on them. But it turned out not to matter—my chain and manacle clinking against my bracelet gave me away. The piano stopped for just a moment.

"Isidor?" Darcy's voice, thankfully. Perhaps timid, but they didn't sound wary or afraid, at least. "You can come in if you want to. Cillian left hours ago. You're safe."

I clenched my fingers in the air a moment before finally gripping the door handle gingerly, turning it, stepping inside.

The room was sparse and bright, the few pieces of furniture that remained in it covered in dusty white sheets. If there'd been a bed in here, it had been taken away. What was left along the walls looked to be cabinets or dressers, judging by their boxy shapes. And not many.

The piano in contrast was dark ashen wood, perhaps once a proper pitch black, but dust had dulled it. It was clear Darcy had wiped it down in the places that mattered, and just like in the bedroom I slept in, swept the floor around it. The space was almost ethereal like many spiritual places felt, with the curtains drawn back fully and the light entering the room directly behind their back at this time of day. The white sheets covering every available surface save the piano, coupled with the relatively empty floor, made the center of the room look almost like a small stage.

And there they sat, fingers resting lightly on the keys, eyes on me as I stepped inside. They wore a light blue floor-length dress today with swirling patterns of white doves along the hem, too loose on them like their other outfit, and a men's coat over it to keep out the chill in this place, no doubt. The coat looked suspiciously like one Cillian might wear.

They gave a tentative, uncertain smile. And then said, "You stayed after all."

"You never checked on me?" I asked disbelievingly.

But then if they had, I probably would have woken up.

"I resolved myself to accept whatever choice you made," they said, staring back down at what I presumed was sheet music in front of them. They licked a finger and carefully turned a page, gently playing a few notes in repetition, like they were figuring them out. I'd heard them play for long enough now to know they were more skilled than that. Their trepidation with me was affecting their ability to focus.

I looked down at the manacle hanging off my hand. "That was quite the gamble for you," I said. "For many reasons."

"Yes," they agreed softly, "it was. But so is keeping you here against your will." They looked up at me again from their music, giving an obviously forced smile. "You put me in quite the predicament, coming here, you know? You're trouble, Isidor of Ebon Gables."

"I..." I paused, "... I *am* sorry my presence meant you were subject to Lord Rathborne's anger last night. I appreciate what you did for me."

They scoffed for some reason, still tapping out the melody of the hymn slowly, while they spoke. "Cillian would never hurt me, don't worry. And we're already veterans in the art of arguing with one another. We're rather efficient at it by now, in fact."

They twisted their ears up towards me, without lifting their eyes from the page. "Why does it matter to you if he's angry at me, anyway? You don't always make a lot of sense to me."

"I just don't like watching that sort of thing unfold," I said, pausing a moment before continuing, "when I'm powerless to do anything to mediate or help. I was the source of his anger, too, so…" I stammered, collecting myself. "I know you're not… a woman," I said after deciding whether or not I wanted to say something different, something that would infer I didn't think they'd been honest with me *or* themselves on that fact. But doing so felt disrespectful and for absolutely no reason. If it didn't matter to the case, it shouldn't matter to me personally, and it didn't matter for how we interacted, why fight them on how they wanted to be addressed?

"But," I continued after they gave me a briefly wary look, like they'd been prepared to defend their identity to me, "he is still your Lord, if not your husband—or paramour—as the case may be—"

"He is not my husband," they said in a rather odd tone. It was hard for me to pinpoint what emotion that was, but it sounded rather snappish. "I suppose 'paramour' or 'lover' would have suited years ago. But not any more… and never again."

The last part was said so quietly as to be nearly inaudible. I swallowed back a sudden burning in my throat that I did not have the wherewithal to make sense of now, but it felt distressingly like envy. "He is your better in society," I said, "and I will assume in resources, since you apparently went to him for help. He has power over you. I do not like watching men with power speak down to or speak angrily to the people in their lives who depend upon them. Not even if those people are criminals. I find it disquieting."

"Like the woman at the carriage house," Darcy surmised softly.

"Has he hurt you?" I demanded. The immediacy and

vehemence of the question shocked even me, despite having come from my mouth. And apparently it surprised Darcy too, because they stopped playing and looked up at me again. This time with an arched eyebrow, like they were trying to make me out.

"No," they answered at length, shaking their head. "Cillian's a good man."

I didn't need to closely examine their body language to know that was a half-truth, at best. The feline may have been guarded with their feelings most of the time, but in this case—

"You're lying," I stated with certainty.

"And you're guessing," they countered. "Look, it's complicated. Cillian would never lay a hand on me. *Not* like the man at the carriage house. But…"

I waited, probably not long enough, but I was feeling impatient. "But…?"

"But," they gave me a half-hearted glare, "it's *complicated*. There are different kinds of pain in this world. I know you understand that, young Sir. I've read your inner thoughts on the matter."

My prayer book. That, somehow more than having looked at it on the table in that room for half a day now, made me remember something incredibly pressing.

Before I could ask though, they spoke again. "I really didn't—don't—want him involved in this anymore. I regret ever writing to him. I just didn't know what else to do, I was getting desperate, and he's dealt with the Ministry before. Please don't ruin his life because of me."

"It's largely out of my hands, at this point," I admitted. "Your Lord Rathborne involved *himself* when he came pounding at Brother Malachi's door that night. He made an enemy, speaking to him the way he did. That wasn't wise."

Darcy visibly winced. "He'd… he'd only just made it into the city and found his way to me less than an hour after I fled from the Lane Estate. I was upset. Frightened. The Lanes were confused—I hadn't really been honest with them about why I was in town, obviously—"

"Obviously," I rolled my eyes. "You mean they don't know you're an infamous antiquities thief?"

The feline gave a slight shrug and a decidedly guilty little grin, "Not exactly."

"The way you act about your crimes baffles me," I shook my head. "I know we aren't supposed to talk about that, but honestly, it isn't a game, you know. The murders aside, you'd hang for the thefts alone. It's nothing to make light of."

"I'm not 'making light' of my accomplishments," they said. "It took a lot of practice and study to get as good at my vocation as I am, and if anything, I'm proud of that."

I made what must have been an aghast noise, and they just kept talking over my affronted, objectionable sounds. "And if you were any investigator worth your salt, you'd have realized why. Especially as a Templar with access to the information you have?" They clucked their tongue. "You should have been able to glean the pattern inherent in my work by now."

"You steal valuable art, relics, and jewelry," I said, mind racing to try to make sense of what they meant. "If you mean the circles you travel in, yes, I am aware you use the Equestrian Dressage Circuit as your primary hunting grounds. That—and some particular regional fashion styles—is how I caught your trail."

"Yes, I saw the fashion leaflets," they muttered. "That was obnoxiously clever of you. But no, Isidor, that is not what I meant. Dig deeper."

"Must we do this?" I asked with a sigh.

"I want you to land on this one on your own," they said, playing again now, while still maintaining eye contact with me. "Why target the particular treasures that I do? It matters to me that you solve this on your own."

"Why?" I pressed.

"You'll understand once you've figured it out. And I believe in you. I believe you can."

I gave a frustrated growl and muttered in Amuraic, a mild curse I knew they would not know.

"Oh, I like that," they chuckled. "You only seem to speak in that tongue when you're frustrated. It sounds ancient and mysterious. Do it more."

"It's old Amuraic," I said. "And I'm hardly fluent in it, I just know a fair bit of it from study and prayer."

"I somewhat doubt that was a prayer you just grumbled."

"No, it was not," I agreed, slowly crossing the room towards them. I approached the feline like coming upon a wounded animal, not wanting to spook them. They—very intentionally, I think—did not look up at me, focusing on their playing. Trying to show they weren't afraid of me. But the wariness showed through in their stiff posture, their flicking ears.

"I'm not going to hurt you," I said softly.

"I know," they said, just as softly. But then, "Or at least, I know you don't intend to. But you can't ever really promise someone that, Isidor."

"Yes, I can," I argued.

"No one can keep a promise like that," they countered. "Even if you truly intend to."

"Yes, I *can*," I pressed. "I'm not going to hurt you, Darcy. If I could have, I would have already. That much is clear to me at this point. I would think it would be clear to you."

"So, you're not going to turn me in, then?"

I brought in a long breath, then slowly let it out. "… no," I said at length. "Honestly, I want to solve this case more than almost anything. But at this point, I must accept it is not meant for me. If I leave this place alive, which—"

"I'm not going to make you promises I can't keep," they said quietly, but determinedly. "But I can tell you I won't *physically* harm you or stop you from leaving, if you think it's safe for you to travel back now."

"Thank you," I said. "I think I'll at least hold off until I'm well. But when I do leave here, I'm going to remove myself from this investigation. I'm firmly settled on that. What will happen between you and the Ministry after that, I cannot say. But I am not fit, not able, to bring you to justice. I'd be a fool to try again, when it's so painfully clear how compromised I am by this case and how disarmed I am by you in particular."

Darcy shivered for some reason, ceasing playing a moment to tug the coat tighter around their shoulders, and glanced up at me from beneath half-closed, long lashes. "That would be quite the romantic statement, given any other circumstance, you know. Are you sure I'm the one acting flirtatious with you, young Sir?"

"I hardly know any more," I admitted, helplessly. "We've been circling one another so long, I'm dizzy. But I didn't intend it that way, and I'm sorry if it discomforted you."

"It didn't," they assured me.

"I cannot arrest you, Darcy," I said. Verbalizing the words, saying them out loud, both to them and myself, was a great relief. It felt settled now. I was giving in, I knew. But that was right. That was, in all ways, the proper course. I wasn't being honest with myself, the Ministry, or God, carrying on like this anymore. "And I cannot hurt you," I continued in a subdued tone. "I swear it. I don't want you to be afraid of me any longer. I want you to believe me... how can I make you believe me?"

"You can't," they said simply. "But don't take that as a personal affront, Isidor. I just don't believe in promises any more. It's not your fault."

I sighed. But acquiesced. "I understand. I will endeavor to change your mind on that subject, then, with patience and time."

"We won't have enough time together," they said flatly. "You may be certain in that. But I appreciate the gesture. And I believe that you mean it."

"Just because I'm not going to turn you into the Ministry doesn't mean I'm done unraveling you," I promised. "I told you —I want to understand you. And you seem to like teasing me with information and waiting for me to figure you out, so if that's how you want it, so be it. I just want it made clear that we're both playing this game willingly; this isn't a chase any more. No getting upset or scared of me if I solve your mysteries. You're literally asking me to."

They smiled a little, gathering the oversized jacket tighter around them, before setting back to the keys. "It was never the chase that scared me."

"You didn't realize how serious the charges against you were. How dedicated the Ministry was to bringing you in and executing you."

"No," they agreed, their voice quivering a bit. "Not until recently."

I nodded, more certain now. "You didn't realize because you see yourself as a thief. Not a murderer."

"'Thief' is just the common parlance," they said, lifting their chin a bit. "I don't even see myself as that."

"I have no idea what that means," I admitted, "but that isn't the point. You didn't kill those men. Did you?"

"We're talking about my crimes again," they pointed out. "We aren't supposed to do that."

"Darcy, it is very important to me to be clear on *this* point," I said. "Did you kill those people or not?"

"*No*," they bit out, not loudly but a bit angrily. "I already told you I didn't. I've never killed *anyone*. No Templar, certainly none of the help in any of the houses I've hit. I swear."

"I believe you," I said, trying to adopt a comforting tone. "I believe you."

Their fur settled a little, and they took a moment to collect themselves visibly. That accusation, more than anything else, seemed to frighten and unnerve them. They didn't get like that whenever we talked of theft. It hurt them, I realized, that anyone would think of them that way.

"Why do you believe me?" they finally asked. "I know I probably shouldn't be questioning here, but I must know."

"Because you didn't kill me," I answered simply. "When doing so would have served your every interest. And you've had two chances now. The two Templar who were killed were murdered in cold blood. Shot in the back. The housekeeper was pushed down a staircase."

The feline blinked rapidly and swallowed in mute shock or horror when I said that. It didn't seem feigned. Too many involuntary reactions at once. That had been genuine.

"I just don't think you have it in you," I finished. "And I suppose I could be wrong about that, but it doesn't feel that way."

"Then who killed them, in your estimation?" they asked, leaning back to look at me.

"Impossible for me to say, obviously," I said. "But if I had to guess? You don't always work alone. Someone else did the killing, and you either don't condone it, didn't know about it, or are somehow sympathetic of the circumstances under which the murders unfolded. You don't want that person brought to justice either, so you're covering for them. Thieves' code? I have no idea. I wish you felt comfortable enough to tell me, but—"

"Cillian is right, you know," Darcy murmured. "You don't need to betray my—or his—confidence willingly. The more you learn here, the more they will squeeze out of you when they get you back. Or beat out of you, if they must. Or worse."

"Do you really think he's right, the things he said about me?" I asked suddenly. "That I'm some unthinking, indoctrinated zealot with no will of my own? That it's 'too late' for me?"

"Oh, my God," Darcy seemed to crumble, "you heard us."

I held firm. "Yes."

They turned on their stool, looking up at me plaintively. "No. I do *not* agree with what he said. Obviously. Didn't you hear me defending you? I know you're more than all of that, Isidor. I read you question the doctrine, again and again—"

"And there's just as much of it I agree with," I said. "I love my faith. I love my God, and I love my Father, Darcy. The man who raised me is a Priest and an Inquisitor, one of these men your Lord Rathborne thinks is essentially a slaver of young children, scraping us off the paving stones of back alleys and selling us into service or using us as unthinking, unquestioning soldiers. He *taught* me to question, to search for the truth in all things; he educated me and saved my life. The education and the life he and the Abbey gave me would *never* have been afforded to me if I'd been able to continue living with my blood family. I was a starving, poor child when he took me in. What would men like Lord Rathborne prefer? That we die on the street?"

"No, but Isidor," Darcy interjected, "why must those be the only two options? I think Cillian only meant that you aren't permitted to choose what kind of life you'll live. They raise you very strictly to suit... certain roles."

"The Church gives us a life denied by the outside world," I said. "Not everyone is born privileged with many options, like your Lord Rathborne. I'm grateful I was blessed with even one. And I *was* given options on how I might serve the Ministry, when I was grown. We don't all make the cut as Templar, you know. Most go into the clergy or take up secular work at the different Parishes."

"What about the women your Order raises?" they asked.

My mind of course went to Mabel, the ache of separation yawning inside of me. This was the longest I had ever been apart from my little sister, since she'd arrived at the Abbey.

"It's good that they've been saved from poverty and death, obviously," Darcy continued, "but what if they don't want to marry the men the Order chooses for them? What if *they* want to be educated as you were?"

"They are all taught to read," I insisted. "Only wealthy women get such an education in the outside world."

"What if they want to study your Faith, as the monks do?" they went on. "Can they do that? What if they want to enter into trade? What if they just do not wish to be married or make children at all?"

"All women want to marry and have children," I said, confused. "It's the natural way. They may not particularly prefer their husband at first, but they will settle over time. They'll be well taken care of and provided for—we don't allow them to marry men of ill means or character. And no, they cannot study as the monks do, but the monks live physically rigorous and deprived lives and that's unhealthy for feminine humours."

"Women's bodies carry kittens and pups to term, they survive in all areas of the world and provide for families doing nearly every form of work a person can do." Darcy sighed. "I think they can handle a bit of manual labor and fasting."

"That's aside the point," I said. "It would be terribly distracting for lay monks to have a grown woman about. How would they keep their minds focused on prayer?"

Darcy tilted their head and gave a bit of a snuff. "Self-control?"

"Some women *do* settle at all-neutren Abbeys," I informed them. "There are a few orders of Sisters, they just pray and study in different ways."

"Let me try asking this a different way," Darcy said, speaking carefully. "Imagine you'd been born... different. Female, or a male who did not wish to train as a Templar. Or someone like me," they said pointedly. "Would you want to live your *entire* life, fulfilling a role and serving God in a way that felt wrong to you? Every day. Until you die. Going through the motions, being someone you aren't?"

"I… would grow accustomed to it," I insisted. "Accept it as God's purpose for me."

"Isidor, I've read pages upon pages of your introspecting on God's purpose for you," Darcy said softly. "Your Order would tell you God's purpose for you here is to arrest me, and you've discarded that because it doesn't suit you."

I narrowed my eyes. "You'd be wise not to question me on that decision."

"But it *was* your decision," they said with a sigh. "Look, you've been fortunate enough in your birth to fall mostly in-line with what your Order expects of you. But they didn't make you; they shouldn't get to determine who you are. Who *defines* you? Who knows your purpose, above all others?"

"God," I answered immediately.

"I don't pretend to know who or what God is," Darcy said, slowly setting their fingers back to the keys, and continuing the hymn. "Where I was born, God was the waters of the lake we lived on. The rain. The sun. In this country, God is more of a creator, including creating all those things. But they are a 'being' here. That isn't the case everywhere. They are also canine and male, because most of the people in power here are canines and male and they choose to see him that way. I don't think the distinction matters, really… a force that powerful is all things and all people."

They were still playing. Slowly, methodically, trying to carry on a conversation while playing. It was barely discernible as the hymn, but still. The melody I'd grown up hearing every seventh day, played quietly in this otherworldly space, passed through my flesh, and touched me within, as it had many times when I'd prayed before. Only differently, like I was hearing it for the first time. Everything about this situation, about this conversation I was having on my faith, was new. Challenging. My chest felt lifted like air was bubbling up through me, my lungs were opening, and my mind with it.

I was excited. I had been looking for this... something like this for so long. I wanted to talk to someone who would question me, untangle these unknowns with me. *Frustrate* me. Ask me the things I sometimes secretly, inwardly, asked myself.

"How are we meant to know our purpose?" Darcy asked. "How are we meant to know who we are?"

"I think God endows us with a sense of who we are," I said. "And I think all people see themselves in God, in return. Rightly or wrongly. It is hard to say."

"What if that sense of who you are is at odds with what your Order demands of you?"

I was unable to form an answer to that immediately.

"Would you let them re-mold you, Isidor?" they asked, and their eyes were on me now. "Re-educate you? Into someone you aren't? Force you to live as an impostor?"

Re-education.

My mind went to Malachi. To the tapestry of scars covering his body. Many self-inflicted. Many probably not. He was the ideal Templar Inquisitor now. But what had it taken? Would I need to be molded thusly after all of this?

Whatever his sin, he had certainly been 're-educated' most brutally for it. Re-shaped into what the Order wanted him to be. Perhaps even what he thought he was supposed to be. But whatever he *was*, at his core, bucked against it. So much so, that his only escape was pain.

Perhaps what he was, inside, was... violent. Angry. I'd seen some of that darkness in him, licking at the seams, seeping out through the cracks he'd made in his own flesh. Turned outward as aggression, on men like Cillian. The subjects of his Inquisition work. And I knew I'd barely seen hints of what he must have done to people he'd hunted in the past.

But maybe... maybe the anger was *because* of what he was forced to do to himself. Maybe the darkness was self-hatred because he couldn't shake his sin.

In that case, what was the sin? What had the Order attempted to "fix" in him?

Some part of me knew. But it was too hard to think about. Because I was beginning to worry the same sin was inside of me. And I didn't want to be that angry. I already had a temper, this I knew. It would be *so* easy to turn it outwards.

I didn't want to be that 'broken', as he'd said. If there was some way to cut it all off at the pass, before I had to suffer through whatever he had.

"What is right for some is not right for everyone," Darcy said. "What about the girls at *your* Abbey? Surely there are some you know. Some you worry for. Do you think they should be forced to marry someone because it's advantageous for them, even if they aren't ready? If they don't like the man?"

"No," I said quickly and firmly. I may have even snapped it. I couldn't help it. I was thinking of Mabel.

"God makes us intentionally as we are, flaws and idiosyncrasies and all," Darcy said, humming softly along with a portion of the hymn. "And I think they endow us with the ability to know ourselves, even if that takes a long time. Even if it takes a lifetime. No one can know that better than we can. Not your Ministry, not the Church itself. Only us. But these holy men, Pedigree, or just moneyed men... these people with power—women even, in the case of Huudari Clan Matriarchs—they all want to tell you who you are. They can justify it with ancient books, laws, or brute force. But they shouldn't be the final authority."

"Then who will be?" I asked. "God doesn't speak directly to most of us. We can't all be prophets."

"You," they said, lifting a paw to poke a finger into my chest, lightly and briefly. "*You* are the authority on who you are, Isidor. You know that already. You're here with me right now because of that, aren't you? That's why they haven't found you. You never told anyone where you were going. Did you?"

I went still and quiet, but that in and of itself was an answer.

They brought both hands back to the piano keys and shook their head. "You're fortunate. You happen to be most of the things they want you to be. At least so far. You're lucky that you haven't run up against that wall, yet. But we all do, eventually. You can only bend the knee so long. Trust me."

"I have been failing in my loyalty to God and Country, repeatedly," I said thickly, "and to an ever-increasing degree, of late. I am not the man I should be. In fact, I am so far from His Grace, I can feel it slipping away."

"Are you slipping away from God, or your Ministry?" they countered. "I think you're a good man Isidor, for all my opinion is worth. Of all the men in your Order who could have hunted me down, I'm glad it was you."

"Well, someone else may have actually captured you and brought you in," I muttered.

"Yes, exactly," they admitted. "But it's more than that. You've always shown me empathy. From the very start, you weren't looking to punish me. You want to *understand*."

"I told you at the coaching inn. I believe in salvation."

"Then believe in it for yourself," they said, turning a page. "You grant yourself so little forgiveness. God—if they even think as we do—would forgive your mistakes. Or at least, I choose to believe that. Why craft us to be fallible, then punish us for being as we are? That's twisted. Cruel. And I cannot bring myself to believe God is that cruel. God, if they do think as we do, should be loving. Forgiving."

I leaned over the piano suddenly, drawing closer to them. Darcy seemed briefly taken aback, but only nervously-so, laughing lightly. "So intense! You're crossing the five-paw distance yourself," they pointed out.

"I'm sorry," I said, leaning back a hairs-breadth. "But I… I need to… finally… I need to ask you about what you wrote in my prayer book."

A bolt of sadness crossed their features, distinct and unmasked. "Do you mind?" they asked, looking slowly towards my hands on the top of the piano. "May I see?"

My claws itched at my palm, but I hesitated only a moment before holding out my right hand. Darcy reached up tentatively and took it in both of theirs. Their slender fingers gripped it and brought it closer to them, and they ran the tip of one thumb down the knuckle bone to the empty space where the smallest finger on my right hand had once been. The skin there was grown over with fur, but scarred at the joint, and cut down full to the knuckle.

They looked it over for a long time, saying nothing. Until at last, they looked up at me and asked, "How? Your father monk really did this to you?"

"He isn't my Father," I said, flexing my other fingers. I could still feel it sometimes, but it was never pleasant. The only sensation I got from it any more was pain. "There are two men who oversee our Abbey. My Father, Father Helstrom, he's stern, but he does not like inflicting physical discipline, save the occasional tap of his cane or a day's hard work. Brother Dolus..."

I had trouble continuing for a little while. Darcy left me space to go on when I was ready.

"Brother Dolus handles physical discipline," I said, my vision blurring for a moment.

"This is a *very* extreme thing to do to a child, Isidor," Darcy said in a long breath. "You must realize that."

"It wasn't entirely intentional," I said. "It was... "

I had to bring my other palm up to my face to clear my eyes for a moment. Darcy was still looking up at me imploringly. "You don't need to continue," they said.

"No," I cleared my throat. "I—I wrote about it in my prayer book between the Psalms of Forgiveness because I've... struggled with this. With forgiving him. So much. And I know I should. I know I *have* to. But it's too hard for me and I don't know why."

I lifted my muzzle a moment to stare out the window. "I can't even talk to Father Helstrom about it because he was there, and he... he harbors guilt about it, and I don't want him to. It wasn't his fault. So, I just... talk to God. And write about it. I've never had anyone else to talk to, anyone else I felt I could, anyway."

Darcy only nodded. While still holding my right hand in theirs, they offered their left. I offered my left hand eventually, so that they could take it, as well.

It was very near to how I'd hold someone's hands during Confession. But there were no rites, there were no promises to God or anyone else being made. And I could stop at any time.

"I just wanted to say," Darcy said suddenly, "again how sorry I am that I read something so personal to you without your permission. I didn't know—but I mean, I had some idea, once I'd gotten a few pages in. I should have stopped then—"

"No," I shook my head, dragging air through my nose. "No, I'm glad. Maybe it wasn't right of you, I don't know. But I'm glad, all the same."

They squeezed my palms in theirs, and it felt like the ice broke in my lungs. Like I could breathe again. I gave a weak cough into my shoulder, then looked down at our hands again. "It probably began when I was eight. I'd been," I began, "misbehaving a lot that week. I hardly remember why. I was a child. At eight, I'd only been at the Abbey for two years then. I wasn't always happy. I missed my mother, my siblings, and I've always been loud about my feelings, so I could be difficult. Emotional. Ungrateful."

"Something tells me you were just being a child, Isidor," Darcy said softly.

I nodded. "I learned discipline eventually, but those first few years... Father Helstrom managed, but Brother Dolus got very frustrated with me. Often. And when he did, I got the strap, or the back of a wooden spoon, or just his palm. One day when he intended to take me off for discipline, I bit him. He dragged me down to the cellar and beat me unmercifully. I may have deserved it, to be honest, but—"

"You didn't," Darcy interrupted me, something like firelight in their eyes. "No child deserves to be beaten by a grown man, Isidor. No matter what."

I didn't bother arguing with them. I just went on. "After that, I never fought him again. He'd broken that rebellious spirit out of me, but it was as if it weren't enough for him. The wound on his hand healed, but his heart never did. I've felt it in him—even to this day—like a pall between us. I have never felt safe in his presence. It's as though there's a debt between us that he feels I can never fully satisfy. And it's all the worse because he can be kind, easygoing, and less rigorous in our teachings, even in comparison to Father Helstrom. Some of the younger children have never even seen this side of him. So, I feel, sometimes, like no one will believe me. Like perhaps, my fear of him is unjustified. Like maybe I made this all out to be worse in my mind than it was? I don't know. It's a strange sensation, thinking your own feelings are illegitimate."

I sighed. Then, finding my footing in the memories, went on, "I felt this way since that last beating, and then when I was nearly nine years old, a year later… if he had been waiting for a chance to punish me again, despite my diligence in obeying him, he found it."

I was a child. It was summer. We'd begun arms training, and I was new to it. I was also still small, smaller than all the other boys, reedy and weak of body. I was trying hard to keep up, but the forms made my arms burn and the exercises we did each morning and night left me gasping and physically ill sometimes.

I was tired and hurting all the time. And my only comfort came when Father would put ointment on my chest at night, or bring me an extra ration of chicken or dried pork.

I was trying to grow up able and strong. I really was. But sometimes it felt like all I was capable of doing was lying back down in bed and sleeping. I prayed for the nights to be longer than they were. But it was summer; the dawn came early. And then training began again. More and more time spent working my hardest, because I needed to catch up.

When the older boys asked me to spar with them after dinner that night, I was proud. I was proud that I'd been invited. They thought I could keep up with them. I'd been getting better.

But it soon became clear they just needed a fourth, and I was not cut out for the aggressive, pounding pace of their matches. And we were using live steel, heavier, so my arms tired faster. They weren't trying to hurt me, but eventually, inevitably, one of them did.

There was so much blood. I'd caught the blade against my fingers rather than the guard, a mistake I would have paid for with some pain, were we using wooden weapons. But we'd been using real steel, even though we weren't supposed to, without our training gauntlets and coifs on.

Father Helstrom was upon us as I lay there screaming on the ground. I was woozy and in too much pain to make sense of my surroundings, save that the boys were shouting, my Father had lifted me into his arms, and then the Abbey was rushing past all around me. The cloisters, the stained-glass saints looking down on me, the concerned faces of the monks and children I knew…

The next thing I remember was lying in the infirmary and hearing Brother Dolus. He and my Father were arguing in hushed tones.

"At least order the Physician here," Father was saying, "it might yet still be saved—"

"It will take nearly an hour to send for and rush the man

here, and so late after supper?" Brother Dolus said. "You're being ridiculous, Germain. It's a *finger*. Men lose their fingers all the time in the military, the navy, in industrial work. It's his smallest, he can afford to lose *one*. Better not to run the risk."

"He isn't a man; he's a *child*," Father Helstrom insisted. "And it will affect his grip on that hand—"

"The boy's a southpaw, no matter how you try to train that out. Having the option will only confuse him."

"It is a mark of Ciraberos's claim on him," Father hissed worriedly. "He can overcome it and be better for it. The stigma—"

"Occultic mysticism from ancient times," Brother Dolus sighed dispassionately. "Honestly, Germain. It isn't true doctrine. Listen to yourself. You're a relic."

"At least wait for the Physician to do it with his instruments," Father pleaded, and then rapid footsteps, as they approached me on the slab. I was frozen in pain, too disoriented to do anything more than raggedly breathe.

"No," Brother Dolus said firmly. "Better to do it now, while he's still in shock. Would you rather he be awake for it, Germain? I've a firmer hand than you, and I don't lack the conviction. I've docked pups' tails before; it can't be much different than that. Give me the damned cleaver. And pin the boy down, lest he move and make this worse."

"No! I absolutely will not allow th—"

"You have two choices here, Germain," Dolus spat out viciously. "Help me do what needs be done for our children as you swore to when you settled here or be dismissed. I tire of fighting with you *every time* we disagree over how to raise these boys. You don't have the final word here or *anywhere* important for that matter. You aren't my bloody better," and on that, his voice became a hiss, "you gave that up with your title and your household. Now get out of the way. I'll have you removed, do not *test me*."

I tried to crane my head up, but all I could manage was to loll it to the side and moan. There was a flash, something metal and shiny, torn from Father Helstrom's hands where he'd been holding it away from the monk and then the distinctive scent and warmth of my bloodhound Father, his robes, the brush of his long ears, as he knelt beside me. His arm settling over my chest, the other coming round to grip my good hand. His green eyes looked down on me.

"If you're there lad, pray with me," he said. "Chapter Eighteen, verses five and six. We lay here in a state of anguish, Lord, but we have the blood of Canus in our veins to see us through these trials, and we shall persevere..."

"... for... we are one as... a pack..." I mumbled weakly.

"...and stronger for it. We are mighty as many. Good, lad." He nodded, gripping my hand tighter, and leaning in closer to me. "A nation of wolves under Thee, we are united against all pain and suffering this world brings to bear—*no,* Isidor, you look at *me,*" he said firmly, commandingly, when I tried to see what Brother Dolus was doing. Even through the pain, I could feel him spreading my damaged finger apart from the others, isolating it. I cried out, and Father Helstrom bumped his nose into my cheek, his voice dragging me back to him.

"While we may suffer now," he said, clutching my hand even tighter, "we know we shall endure, if not alone than as one people. For the love is in the blood... Isidor... our love for our pack..."

"... regardless..." I mouthed dryly, and he nodded at me, "of relation... our blood is a tapestry..."

"... that binds all of we descendants of Canus," my Father's eyes were red-rimmed, "all sons, and daughters, and fathers—"

The clap of the cleaver and blinding-hot pain so shocking it soon overwhelmed me. I may have screamed, but I can't remember. And then another... and another... and then I remembered no more.

. . .

Darcy was still looking up at me, still holding my hands. But their countenance was shattered. They just stared at me in wide-eyed horror. And maybe I shouldn't have recounted the whole of it. Maybe I had been unfair to Brother Dolus in my retelling. I cannot say.

"It took him three tries to remove the injured portion," I said dully. "It was only removed to the second joint, but... infection set in a day later, and the Physician eventually had to remove all of it, anyway. There was concern the infection would get into my blood, but in the end, I endured. And it *did* affect my grip. I cannot say how much, but the phantom pains I've had ever since have made it too uncomfortable for me to use my right hand for very much. I became a southpaw in all ways eventually. It's useful, as Brother Dolus hoped for. Disorienting to my opponents in martial weapon combat. I quickly bested most of the other boys at the Abbey. It's hard to switch your guard when you're accustomed to fighting one way. It takes people a while to get used to it."

"Isidor," Darcy breathed out. "I..."

"You wrote in my prayer book," I said, "in response to my scribblings about this—about how I've had trouble forgiving Brother Dolus, because of my resentment towards him—you wrote that 'The onus should not be on the one who is hurt to make things right. If those who hurt you have done nothing to mend that pain, they do not deserve to be forgiven. But neither can you allow your resentment for them to fester because that gives them space in your heart they have not earned'."

"That was," Darcy blinked, "word for word, I'm fairly certain."

"We train our memory to be as eidetic as possible," I said. "Or at least, I have. It's useful for more than just memorizing scripture. And also, I read it probably hundreds of times now. I wanted so badly to know what you meant by it."

They looked down, considering. "I meant what I wrote," they said at length. "And especially now that I know the specific circumstance. You only wrote in your book that he was somewhat responsible for your hand, I didn't realize… Isidor, honestly," they said passionately, "to *hell* with that man. That sounds very much to me like a grown man who had a grudge against a *child* and took delight in being the one to maim him."

"I try not to feel that way," I said, clenching my hand again reflexively. "But it's hard to fight the sin of anger within me."

"Sometimes anger's warranted. It is alright to accept some things are unforgivable," Darcy said emphatically. "I think forgiveness is important when *earned*. Or maybe when someone has passed, and they have no power over you anymore. But it's fine to protect yourself, and this man is very much still a part of your life, yes?"

"Yes," I said.

"Then you are in the right not to let him close again, to trust him, to *forgive* him, when he might very well hurt you again," they said. "You forgave your Father, yes? Despite his involvement?"

"It took me some time," I admitted, ashamed. "But yes. Father Helstrom could have prevented what happened, perhaps, but he would have been risking his position. And his children. I was only one of many children he cares for at Ebon Gables. Also, he apologized to me. Repeatedly, and confessed that failing to protect me, *he* saw as a failing as a Father. I don't agree, but it meant a lot to hear it, all the same."

Darcy was looking up at me silently and almost trembling. I didn't know what to make of their expression. It was odd, mostly. Like they were on the literal edge of their seat. Or about to run. Oh, Lord, had I frightened them off?

"What's wrong?" I asked worriedly. "Did I—I said too much, didn't I?"

"No, you profoundly anxious lad," they said with a sniff and a slight laugh. "I am fighting the urge to embrace you."

"Oh," I breathed out.

"I don't want to be improper with you again if I can help it," they said. "Least of all now."

"Well," I murmured, "if you want to offer... comfort... of some sort," it still felt insane to say it aloud—all of this, the intimacy of this entire exchange—with my quarry, "I suppose I would not mind hearing the rest of the Hymn of the Wives of Canus."

They smiled and spun around in their chair. "Am I doing alright? I really don't know this one well, I'm stumbling my way through it."

"You're more skilled than you give yourself credit for," I shook my head. "I didn't think you'd know any Faith music."

"Hymns are the first real music you study in any formal music education," they turned back the pages on the worn book of sheet music they read from. "At least that's what our tutor told us."

"'Our'?" I blinked.

"Cillian and I."

"You were educated together?" I looked around the room and pulled up a chair from the writing desk, tugging off the sheet covering it.

"Oh dear, I shouldn't have let that slip," they said, glancing at me. "At least insofar as it concerns Cillian, he wouldn't want me sharing any of that."

"I'm sure," I said ruefully. "Alright, never mind. Are we starting over?"

"Are you going to play it with me?" they asked with a curious smile.

"Well, no," I said, "but it's a hymn. I could… sing. If that's alright. If you don't mind."

"You can sing?!" they all but squeaked.

"We all sing in the choir," I said, putting my palms up. "*Please* do not expect much. I'm hardly talented, I just know the words."

"No, let's begin," they said, eyes bright and excited. "I'm ready when you are."

We spent the whole morning and part of the afternoon in that nearly empty room going through the entire hymnal book. And then Darcy played a few more songs, this time from the only other book of sheet music they were able to find in the drawing room. Secular music that, for the most part, I'd never heard, save perhaps once at a gathering at the Hudson Estate.

We didn't talk any more of Darcy's crimes, or my faith, or the people in our lives who'd hurt us. It was almost normal. Companionable. In different lives, perhaps, we may have met like this at a recital or a social gathering. It was easier not to think of the many, many barricades that would have made that impossible. So, for a time, we didn't. Or at least, I didn't.

I never knew what they were thinking. I'd deduced much about the Heart Thief during the months I'd spent chasing them, but I'd learned more about the feline in the last day than I had in all that time, and there was most certainly an unfathomably deep well of still more I did not know.

I had never wanted so badly in my life. Not any one particular thing, I just… wanted. I savored every second that passed between us, trying to demystify every facial tick, over-examined and re-thought everything I said, everything they said. I cursed myself inwardly if I thought I'd said or done the wrong thing. I wanted to know them, and I wanted to be known.

I was aware somewhere in the back of my mind how very

mad this all was. How deeply I was being drawn in. But they gave as good as they got, hadn't they? Was I imagining that this strange fascination with one another was mutual?

Like a predator that's caught their prey in their muzzle, and now forgets what they intended to do with it. Except... I wasn't certain which of us had caught the other.

The rumbling of our stomachs finally signaled how much of the day we'd whiled away and introduced a new problem.

"I have plenty of potatoes and a few bits of ham left to make a stew," they said, humming. "But we're running low on fresh food, so I'm afraid we'll need to switch to dried vegetables and fish soon."

I instantly made a face, and I knew they saw it. "Oh, picky, are we?" they teased. "Honestly, what kind of Amur man doesn't like fish?"

"I can't eat them," I said. "I'm sorry, it's not entirely a matter of preference. I swear, I'm not particular otherwise, I just can't have fish or shellfish. They make me ill."

A look of realization dawned on their features. "The Hudson Estate. When I saw you there, struggling in the garden, was that because—"

"Yes," I confirmed. "It's a miserable weakness of digestion, honestly. It makes it very costly for me to eat meat, which is why I was struggling with malnutrition when I was young. It's why my mother had to give me up."

"I'm so sorry," Darcy said. They thought for a moment, then put a fist into their palm. "But we'll figure it out. I can eat the fish I have, and we'll find something else for you."

"I can survive on potatoes for a few days," I assured them.

"You're recovering," they shook their head, "and you're a canine, for God's sake. You need meat. Besides, *look* at you. You're a big, strapping, strong fellow; I won't have you wasting away in my care."

"I could stand to waste away some," I muttered.

"Oh, please," they batted at me playfully. "I'll bet most of that's fur. And anyway, slender dandies are a pence a dozen. I like a man with some heft to him. Come on." They offered me their hands to help me up, and when they did, they noticed the manacles. "Those really serve no point now that Cillian's gone."

"You said you'd prefer that you can hear me coming," I said, holding them up, the metal clinking noisily.

"I can always hear you coming," they said with a sly smile, and flicked their tall ears pointedly. "I can hear everything in this Lodge, never you worry. These big, unwieldy things are for more than just show."

They pulled a set of keys out of their pocket and took my wrist, unlocking the last manacle and looping the chain around their hand, at last releasing me fully.

"You're sure about this?" I asked uncertainly.

"It's beginning to feel strange," they confessed. "Don't you think?"

"I suppose so."

"I used to hunt all through these woods," they said. "There's a rifle somewhere here, or so Cillian promised me. I have fresh powder and a horse, and the snow has stopped for now. What say I try to shoot us some dinner?"

We spent an hour or so cleaning up the main room, and I got to see the drawing room and much of what remained of the Lodge, finally. There was only one other room, a Commons area with a small table, hearth, another writing desk, and an enormous Bush-Antlered Elk rug. We threw a potato in the coals while we cleaned, eventually split it, and came upon another issue when we went to stoke the two fireplaces, and Darcy went outside to gather wood… only to discover—

"There's plenty of logs out back in the stable," they grumbled. "But very few split, and I'm not very good with an axe. I wish Cillian had warned me, I'd at least have gathered some kindling on my way here."

"It wouldn't have been dry," I shook my head. "You don't tend fires often, do you?"

"Could you, perhaps..." they began, brushing their hands off on their dress after depositing the small stack of wood they'd brought in.

"Yes," I agreed, smiling. "I'm well enough to be outside for a bit. The fresh air and some light exercise might honestly be good for me, right now."

"Oh, thank God," they sighed. "And 'light exercise'? Chopping wood makes me ache like I'm on my deathbed."

"How very dramatic," I rolled my eyes.

"I get splinters," they complained. "My wrists hurt, my *back* hurts, it takes me forever to get the axe out if it gets stuck..."

"I'll cut us plenty," I promised. "It's no trouble."

And that's how I found myself in the yard that day, enjoying the brief reprieve of sunshine between winter storms, taking in the rugged beauty of this place while splitting logs. What was apparently an insurmountable task for the dainty feline was a mundane, everyday chore for me at Ebon Gables. In fact, sometimes I took other boys' turns at it just to break up my usual physical regimen.

Between the time spent nursing a cold at Malachi's and then the very same cold here at the Lodge, I'd probably been in bed for four days total over the last week. It was finally starting to abate, thanks to my body giving up on me for a few days and forcing me to sleep, but now I felt depleted. Restless. For many reasons I'm sure, but certainly one of them was my lack of movement or exertion for days on end. This was honestly just the thing I needed. Work I was accustomed to that made me feel useful for a bit and didn't tax my body overly.

Darcy had gone off hunting over an hour ago, searching for game fowl. They'd been common out here in these woods years ago apparently and hadn't been hunted in some time thanks to this place being abandoned. So, they were optimistic.

The physical labor was helping keep my mind occupied… for the most part. But it was also making my blood pump, and the lack of the constant companion I'd had all day meant I was left alone with my thoughts, save the axe and the muffled noises of the winter forest.

And my thoughts right now were just Darcy… Darcy… Darcy…

I'd never spent so long in the same room with them. I could smell them on my fur, could hear their laugh like they were still beside me. I could picture the blue of their dress, feel the brush of their long whiskers whenever they'd gotten close, could imagine all too vividly what it might have been like to let them embrace me, despite the impropriety of it—

God, what *was* this?!

I brought the axe down, panting, and looked at the pile I'd amassed. Probably enough, and I'd worked up quite an exertion. I was only wearing what I'd been wearing all day, I hadn't added layers. It was relatively warm for a winter day right now, and my coat was thick enough to keep out most of the cold even without the need for clothing. Provided I wasn't trapped in the middle of a snowstorm, lost in the woods for a day straight, that is.

I was somehow over-heated. Enough so that I felt near-feverish, and that probably wasn't good, either. I let go of the axe handle and unhooked my harness, stripping it off first, then bunched up my shirt in my palms, tearing it up over my head and groaning as the cool air hit my fur. I stood there for a time with my eyes closed, enjoying the light breeze, the distant bird-song, and the creaking of the trees, and tried not to obsessively think about every single time Darcy had smiled at me.

"*Fanis odonimus*," I growled out haggardly.

"What does that one mean?" their voice carried across the clearing, and I spun, startled. With all the snow on the ground, I hadn't heard them approaching, even on horseback. They were riding the chestnut mare full saddle like a man would, despite wearing a dress. They trotted up towards me, an excellent seat despite that. I didn't miss the two dead grouse tied to their saddle bag. My stomach ached at the thought of real meat.

It didn't occur to me for some reason until they were nearly upon me that I was half-dressed.

"Oh," was all Darcy said politely. I felt their eyes on me unavoidably. They tugged their mount to a stop and glanced between me and the pile of wood.

It was a bit late to act modest, but I couldn't help but look down, shyly. It wasn't as though men in cities always covered their chests, especially when working. It would be unheard of for a Pedigree, but I was *not* that. Still…

I might have sucked in my gut a little.

"That's quite a stack you have there," Darcy said after a moment.

"I… oh, the wood," I muttered. "Enough to get us through a week, at least." I scratched my neck idly, feeling the feline's eyes on me, but unable to return the favor. Which was unfortunate, because given they were on horseback, I was more at eye-level with their waist and legs, and…

Their dress was riding up to the knee. It was unavoidable, given how they were seated in their saddle. They still had spats on, but smaller, more modest leathers, not the ones that went fully over their knee like they'd worn in the past. Their slim, golden leg, covered in beautiful arcing patterns of spots, froze my gaze in place. I knew I needed to look away *immediately,* that this was not a display intended for me. They'd been riding through a difficult, snow-covered forest in the mountains. Side-saddle would not have been as safe.

"Isidor?" They'd been speaking. I looked up, ears tucked back in guilt. Caught in the act.

But there was no damnation there, no anger or offense. They looked flushed and breathless, probably from the ride, but not in any way upset. "We should… go inside, yes?" they said, stammering a bit for some reason.

I nodded, and, like I'd done more times before than I could count almost by route, I began strapping my harness back on.

"Why, um, are you wearing that out here?" they asked, their voice oddly hoarse.

"Oh, I—here, I'll show you," I said, finishing tightening the straps before I went to one of the bundles I'd already tied with heavy twine. I hooked it by the closures in my claws, tugged the loose loops of twine up beneath the straps on my shoulders, then pulled them down through and tied them in the front of my chest. Then I hefted the whole bundle up, slowly, and carefully. "The harness is how we carry all of our possessions," I explained, shifting the load a little until it was comfortable. "It makes it easier to carry a lot of weight at once."

"That looks like it weighs as much as I do," they said, something like awe in their features.

"I doubt it, but I'd have to lift you to be certain," I said.

"Hah-oh… hmh… alright," they gave a gasping, nervous chuckle. Again, they were acting strange, and I couldn't help but feel it was my fault, although I wasn't sure *why*. "We should go inside. You've been out in the cold long enough, I'd wager. And I need to… we should… go."

"Alright," I agreed, tucking my discarded shirt into my belt. "I'll meet you inside after you get the horse settled."

I brought the firewood inside, cursing myself silently the whole while. I wasn't sure what I'd done wrong—save the obvious, but that had been a mistake, I hadn't *meant* for them to see me like that—but I was certain I'd made them uncomfortable and I wasn't sure how to fix it.

Dinner had been fine, the roasted meat sitting well with both of us and chasing away any remaining feelings of strangeness from the encounter outside. Whatever that was. We'd settled in to read again, Darcy in their chair, and this time I'd taken the writing desk. It seemed odd to be in bed in the same room with them when I didn't need to be.

"It looks like you finished 'A Craven Man's Duel'," Darcy said, noting that I'd begun sorting through the stack of books they'd deposited on the desk, reading the forwards. "What did you think?"

"I couldn't put it down," I admitted. "I finished it last night actually, while I was waiting up to learn if I was about to be shot or not."

They winced. "I'm sorry. I really should have come and spoken to you once he left. He was only here about an hour after that. It's a long trip back to town and he needed to be there in the morning. He really didn't want to leave you here with me, but I convinced him I had you under control."

"That isn't, strictly speaking, a lie," I muttered.

"No," they agreed with a minute smile. "I really am sorry I didn't give you the all-clear. I suppose I was assuming you'd be gone when I checked on you, and I hated the thought of that for a lot of reasons."

I shook my head, speaking distractedly as I put aside another book into my 'maybe' pile. "Any excuse to stay up late reading. Just promise you won't dock my meals if you catch me doing it again."

I knew it would make them laugh, and it didn't disappoint. They craned their elegant neck towards me, eyeing my pile unsubtly, as their chuckles subsided. "It's one of my favorite novellas, too. Maybe you're not so very hopeless after all. If we can salvage your taste in books, there *is* still a chance for you."

I snorted. "I'll have you know I have excellent taste in books. Although I'll admit a limited roster… speaking of, now that I've finally read his work, I'm not entirely certain why Glaswren is banned outright from our Library. I've never read him before, but I've seen he's a staple in most Pedigree libraries. Lady Hudson had first editions of *all* of his books."

"And I missed them?!" Darcy groaned. "What a shame! Some of their early work is exceptionally hard to find. I only saw those dreadfully-bound second edition novellas from their spiritual mystery years. The ghost stories. Good, but hardly the whole body of their work, let alone *first editions!*"

"I'm happy for Lady Hudson that you overlooked them, then," I muttered.

"Well, to defend my honor somewhat, I was in a bit of a hurry," they said cheekily. "Very distracted by the young, clever Templar that had replaced the old drunk I was prepared to contend with. You have no idea how shocked and irritated I was to see you outside, spryly running laps around the grounds and swinging your sword about for hours like you were training specifically to capture *me*."

I paused, slowly lifting my eyes before saying, "I was."

"Well, you were *supposed* to be an old hound with a bad leg and a drinking problem," they said, resting their cheek in their palm.

"I'm... sorry I got in the way of your crime spree?" I said unconvincingly.

They smiled around a pout. "I'm not."

I looked busily back down at the books, nearly biting my tongue. While I was doing that, Darcy spoke up again. "So do you want to know why the Church might have made Glaswren in particular forbidden reading?"

I looked up. "Yes, actually."

"I am assuming it's not the content," they waved a hand. "Murder never really seems to bother the Church."

I ignored the obvious barb. "So then, what is it?"

"'Glaswren' is an alias," they said mysteriously. "A pen name. They went by 'Glass Wren' in some of the first editions, in fact, until their publishers pushed them to make it sound like a real name."

"Is the Author in trouble with the Church?" I asked.

"The Author," they smirked, "is a woman."

I blinked, staring back at the novella reflexively and considering the story as a whole one last time. I eventually settled on, "I never would have known."

"That's the strange thing about women. They're people like you or I, and if you allow them to be literate, they can write books too."

I opened my mouth for a moment, thinking I'd 'caught' them in a rare slip-up, then realized they weren't lumping themselves in with me and other men. They were simply not putting themselves in either category.

I looked again to the book, digesting the realization that the story I'd been so engaged in had been penned by someone of the fairer sex. If Darcy hadn't told me, would I ever have known? Would it have *mattered*? It mattered to that woman, I suppose—and perhaps any other who wanted to pursue that sort of vocation—in that it must have been very difficult to ever be taken seriously, let alone published. But had it mattered in a literary sense? Had it affected my reading experience or the content of the story?

Considering I hadn't even thought of it until now... I suppose not. Which made me wonder...

"Do you know many other novels written by women this way?" I asked Darcy. "Using an alias?"

They shrugged. "It's one of the few ways they are able to be published or read at all outside of small clubs and parlors. Quite a few publish under their husbands' names or write as a pair. I honestly wonder how many married men crib from their wives for their published works. You may have read more books written by women than you realize."

"Do you have any more here?" I asked.

They smirked and put their jaw in their palm. "I do. But now I wonder if I should tell you. You've got that look in your eye like you plan to investigate something. Looking to prove something to yourself, are you?"

"Nothing like that," I insisted. "I just... feel deprived, I suppose. If there are twice as many people out there writing as I'd been led to believe, there's an enormous breadth of literature I've missed. Now, granted, I'm very particular—"

"Ahhh, a critic. I see."

"Choosy," I corrected them. "But that can be frustrating. It's been hard to find authors I really like, limited to the Abbey stacks. That's why I went through so much of the Hudson's library while I was there... and then the books you left me..."

"And you weren't satisfied with any of them?" they asked disbelievingly.

I know I made a face. "Not to besmirch your taste, but... not entirely, no. I'm especially particular about romantic fiction, and that was *all* you left me. It's one of my least favorite genres, so I am, I suppose, especially critical of it."

"'The Midsummer Joust' is *not* a romance," they scoffed, smiling, but still somehow managing to sound scandalized.

"Yes, it is," I insisted, sighing, "half the bloody book is taken up by the Young Sir Auchland's *pining*."

"Unrequited pining. And anyway, what do you have against romance?" the feline demanded, hardly hiding their grin. "You're a grown man Isidor, not some young whelp. Even if you're not interested in it, you must at least be fascinated by why the rest of the world's so obsessed with it."

"I can't relate to it," I said clumsily. "I can't get in the heads of these characters; it just doesn't speak to me. It all just comes off as profoundly strange and silly. And then I have trouble taking the story seriously, because their behavior and motivations make no sense to me."

"Spoken like someone who's never been in love," they said,

speaking around where their cheek was mushed into their own palm, looking bored.

"I'm sorry to disappoint you," I muttered, "but yes. Just so. I'm an Abbey boy, I've never been to Court, never really spent time around eligible women, I grew up surrounded by my adopted brothers and sisters and that's about it. By the time I *do* start entering society, I'll probably have a permanent posting and already be married. It's likely I'll *never* really understand it, and I can't say that it sounds like I'm missing much. All three of the people in the books you lent me seemed profoundly miserable about their condition."

"You're not wrong," they sighed. "Love and longing *are* a misery, at least for most. And—hang on—did you say you're going to marry soon? Are you promised to someone?"

"No," I said a little too defensively. "But… it's likely my Abbey will match me soon if my elder monk has a say in the matter. He seems to think I should marry young."

"That poor girl," Darcy said, their grin growing puckish when I glared at them. "What? You just said you've no interest in romance. I'm only pointing out that your marriage is then, by default, set to be a loveless one. Not that you're a bad catch. For someone, anyway."

"I think I could be a very dutiful husband," I groused quietly. "Maybe not *romantic*, at least not at first, but I could learn."

"I don't know," Darcy let out a long breath. "'Dutiful' may not sound particularly flowery, but maybe true romance is a man who keeps his word. Who's loyal, and honest, and only makes promises he intends to keep."

I quirked an ear. "What else even is there?"

"Passion," Darcy answered, all but immediately. "But passion is fleeting and disloyal, prone to changing with the winds of fate. What good is it if you can't hold on to it? Love is supposed to last."

"Passion doesn't need to be fleeting," I said quietly. "I'm passionate about my faith. I have been for most of my life."

"Religion is different," they said. "It's self-reinforcing, for one. Most of the world *wants* you to have faith in something, because hopeless people start looking for answers outside the bounds of society, and society doesn't want that. The answer is usually religion or something akin to it. But people don't necessarily *want* you to be in love, or find love, unless it's with *the right people*. Which aren't always—or even often—the people we want to be with. We build cathedrals to worship religion. We build nothing to worship love."

I leaned back in my chair, struck by the simplicity of what they'd said, and how I'd somehow never heard anything like it said before. Maybe because comparing something as mundane as romantic yearning to faith was heretical on its face.

But…

"I would like…" I said quietly, and I felt rather than saw Darcy's eyes on me, "… I would like, I think, to build a home to worship love inside. And a family. I've been rebuilding since my own family cast me aside, and… I'd like to build one that is stronger. More able to endure hardship and time."

They'd said nothing, so I finally turned to look towards the feline. They were still looking at me, their expression wide-eyed and quiet. I was worried I'd said what I'd intended in a strange way, so I broke eye contact and stared down blankly at the book in front of me, fingertips brushing over the binding. "Does that make any sense?"

A long pause, a quiet breath, and then they said simply, "Yes."

I looked up again, almost timidly catching their eye. They were still looking at me—had been this entire time, I was fair certain. Their gold-green eyes fell on mine like a spell, nearly hypnotic. I wasn't sure what was happening, but I felt lit from inside, like God Himself was staring down on us at that very moment. I felt *seen*, as though I were in Confession or singing in the choir. Naught but silence was passing between us, stretching on and on, and it should have felt wrong, felt awkward, but it didn't. It felt…

… like providence.

That was what this was. There could be no other interpretation. Father Helstrom had told me that when God came into my life, when His hand guided me directly, I would *know*. I was a man possessing of terrible uncertainty most days, questioning, always questioning… but this felt *so certain*.

"I think I am meant to help you, Darcy," I said, finally breaking the quiet, but not the gravity of the moment. "I think we were meant to meet. To come together as we have."

They blinked slowly, opening their muzzle slimly for a moment, then closing it. Then trying again, they said in a soft rasp, "How will you help me, Isidor?"

"The way I have been trying to this entire time," I answered, the surety of it feeling like salvation as it settled in place in my heart. "By discovering the truth."

Darcy huffed softly, wrapping their arms around their slim chest. "The world on the whole does not care what is true."

I leaned forward, extending an arm to where Darcy's hands were tightly gripping the book they were holding in their lap. Gingerly, but intently, I eased their fingers off the spine where they were compressing it. When they realized what they were doing, they removed their hand almost horrified, and I wrapped my fingers around theirs, gently. Hopefully, reassuringly.

They looked up from the spine to me, again. I gripped their hand as I might someone at Court or a new acquaintance. And then, a little bit tighter, in a soft squeeze.

"Then I will make them care," I promised.

There was so much in the feline's conscience that they had yet to confess to. Secrets and hidden truths to unravel, many of which concerned the Heart of Faith, I was certain. I was beginning to form my own suspicions over where this was all headed, but I'd learned by now that forcing the issue with them was never the answer. It only shut them down. I had to give them time, if I wanted the full story. And I'd have no more of it that night.

After our last conversation, I had felt better. More certain in my convictions, less afraid I was straying from God's path. But Darcy had gone quiet and pulled inward, gripped by something that seemed, on the surface at least to me, to be turmoil. I couldn't imagine what was going through their mind, but if it was anything like the maelstrom I'd been contending with these past months, I knew it was best to let them be for now. Confession, I was learning, was not *always* good for the soul. And it wasn't always the right time to give it.

Night had come. Darcy had moved to the drawing room to sleep. I was more settled in purpose, but the evenings and slumber presented another, separate issue… one I had not found any way to contend with yet. I put sleep off as long as I could, reading through at least half of another of the books the feline had recommended, but in time exhaustion overtook me. And with my barriers stripped away in dreams, after days spent suffused in their presence, hearing their voice and with their scent still in the room, things had taken the obvious disastrous turn I'd known they eventually, inevitably would.

This time, the dream did not so much appear from the ether as the waking world faded into it. I was aware on some level that the room had changed, that it shouldn't be dusk again, the walls lit in violet and blue, the hearth strangely missing. Everything was cool and diffused, like a haze hung over the small space.

I knew it wasn't real. At this point, I could pick out these dreamscapes from reality, and I knew the state my mind tended to be in when I was here. Lazy and slow, my thoughts meandering and hard to pin down. In a way, it was peaceful here. None of the anxiousness and self-loathing permeated this space.

The shame… the shame always reared its head when I woke.

The door creaked, and I knew before it swung open who would enter. What I didn't expect, even as self-aware as I was of being in a dream, was the state they'd be in.

Darcy's slender silhouette paused in the doorway, one arm reaching up to the frame, fingertips sliding along the edge slowly. I could see the shine of their eyes in the dim light, pointed down at the floor, shyly. They slowly lifted them in my direction, while shifting their legs nervously, the tufted fur along the flare of their hips catching what must have been moonlight from the hall in a halo around their figure. Which only made it more clear…

They weren't dressed. At all.

Their fur was black tonight, the shadows of their spotted patterns catching the light differently, and thus still vaguely visible. When they shifted from foot to foot, the fur between their thighs rubbed together, creating little eddies and curls in the soft down that their free hand was worrying through, trailing from knee to—

Oh. Oh, they were… like me, tonight. Male at least in body. Smaller, of course. They were half my size, so… a modest little sheath and sac with just the vaguest hint of a pink tip protruding. I could have cupped the whole of it in my palm easily.

And I rather wanted to.

My desires were less complicated here. I didn't question nearly as much, didn't reflect on what should have been paralyzing crisis'. Knowing it all wasn't real helped, but…

There was no denying my curiosity. Not here. Not when I was essentially alone with my imaginings, unfettered by reason and self-control. I wanted to touch him… them. I wanted them to touch *me*.

Their palm slid up through the soft fur of their smooth stomach, settling over their breast bone, fingers splayed in the longer, denser tufts of white that largely masked the shape of their chest. I knew from having seen them in various forms of dress that their chest was nearly as flat as their belly, although not formless. It arced elegantly down from their shoulders, soft and puffy with fur. I could see the vaguest hint of the dark spots beneath their pelt that were their nipples—dark like their nose, right? That would make sense, wouldn't it?

I felt my tongue act of its own volition, wetting my mouth and nose. Darcy's eyes were still on me, catching the meager light in the doorway. When I licked my muzzle, they tilted their head and took a tentative step forward. I did what I could to beckon them further, to assure them, nodding minutely with what little nerve I could muster.

It seemed to be enough. They crossed the room towards me, more self-assured as they grew close. I shifted and swung my legs over the edge of the bed so that I was sitting facing them, glancing down my own body as I did.

I was as nude as they were. I wasn't sure when I'd taken off my clothing—but, wait. No. This was a dream.

That's right. This was a dream.

No one would know what happened here but me.

I looked up in time to catch Darcy's eyes as they moved in against me, their thighs brushing between my splayed legs. Their hands slowly slid up my shoulders and settled there, fingers kneading into where my muscles bunched at the clavicle.

I was helpless, trapped in their gaze. They seemed to know it too, slowly smiling as they looked down upon me. Their hands carded through the thick fur of my shoulders and traced their way down my biceps, squeezing.

"I've wanted to feel your arms around me since I saw you chopping wood," they said.

I only nodded again. They'd liked that, hadn't they? That menial chore that would have been so tiring for them, that this big, cumbersome body of mine was competent at. Like how a wife might rely upon her husband to do such chores.

It was good to feel useful. To feel strong and needed.

I reached out for them, my calloused paw-pads finding their middle, fingers wrapping around and nearly touching on the small of their back. I felt their tail flick and their body hitch up a moment in a breathless, obviously accidental laugh as my claws tickled their sides. They bit their lower muzzle and smiled down at me sheepishly.

"I'm sorry," I apologized, tipping my head up and tucking my ears back as their hands moved to stroke my cheeks and then over the back of my ears and neck scruff. They touched me like that for a time, petting me.

"It's alright, darling," they purred, and I'd never really heard someone purr at me before, let alone call me 'darling', but I must have wanted it, because this place was a manifestation of my wants. I knew basically how it would sound. I wanted to hear it again...

My hands were ghosting up their spine and then stroking down the soft bumps, avoiding going against the grain of their fur, I knew at least that much. I spread my fingertips over the supple curve of their rear, the fullness there obvious especially when they wore men's trousers. I'd noticed it more than once.

I wanted to really *feel* the contours of their body, but every sensation was hazy, indistinct. I wanted...

I wanted *so* much. My sheath had grown heavy between my legs, and the release of tension as my manhood eased out from its confines was *not* hazy. That felt all-too-real and solid, a pressing, white-hot need that had become my dogged demon these last few months. I'd known to anticipate it by now, of course, but that didn't make the mounting frustration and restlessness any better.

I whined, I know I did, and Darcy leaned forward, brushing our noses together. They pressed their slight weight on my shoulders by bracing with their hands again and whispered, "It's alright. Let me see."

I brushed my nose along their muzzle and down into the soft fur of their neck, hiding my face in their warmth. They nuzzled the back of my head, purring again. I felt unraveled.

"I don't know what to do," I admitted quietly, nearly in tears.

Their purring was against my ear, and then another breathy whisper. "I do," they promised.

There was pressure on my shoulders, and then the feel of their legs sliding up over mine, their smaller body fitting neatly into my lap, astride me. I gasped, hands clutching at their hips, sinking into soft fur and the meat of their thighs. They purred when I squeezed and pressed their weight into me. I could vaguely feel the outline of their sheath against my own, hardening. My length was full out now, pressing into their belly and the crux of their inner thigh. The brush of their fur against it was blissful torture. Their arms wrapped around my neck, pulling up, and then our breaths were intermingling.

They held my gaze for a long time, stroking my ears and smiling.

"I'm sorry… I'm…" I said, floundering.

"Don't apologize," they said, intentionally rocking against me, pulling a keening sound out from the depths of my throat. "I'm the same way, can you feel it?"

I nodded, wordlessly. I still wanted to touch them, but now we were pushed together. And did they even want me to touch them there? Why would they?

Well, I wanted to touch *myself*, whenever I felt like this. So surely…

As if knowing my mind, their smaller hand wrapped around

where one of mine was still brushing over the fur on their hip and led it to the warm valley between us, where I found my own protruding offender, and then the smaller, less familiar shape of theirs.

I… wasn't sure what to expect. But it was warm, shorter and thinner than my own, and other than that, the details were indistinct. My breath hitched, I braced, mind racing. Was I really doing this?

But, no. No, I wasn't. Because it was a dream. So, I could… I could try and see how it felt…

My paw was able to fit easily around it, the shape of it solid, hot, and a little slick. Darcy's back arched and they gave a cut-off gasp when I took hold of them. I loved the sound they made, the flush of heat and swelling in my palm, the instant gratification of… gratifying them. But then I was holding their sex, I was feeling them, tracing the length of it, and I wasn't sure what more to do.

It didn't seem to matter. They were purring and looking down into my eyes with hazy pleasure. And then their palm was wrapping around my own manhood, fingers splayed wide. What would they—well, I would want them to—

They'd pet it like they'd pet me. Stroke it. Yes, obviously. It was like any other part of my body, only somehow in *more need* of being touched. Their fingers traced molten hot patterns up and down the most overeager, shameful part of me, sending jolts through my nerves, making my muscles jump, and rendering my mind—at least for the moment-blissfully blank. All I could feel was where we were joined by touch. All I could think of was getting closer to them.

What was it Brother Dolus had said? Lord help me, how could I be thinking of that now? But I was.

Men could use their paws obviously, but also their muzzles. And…

Our minds were joined in the dream, and I knew it wasn't

them, I knew it was just my imagined version of them, and how terrible was that? That I'd imagine them this way, that I'd ever think of them like this—

"You want my muzzle on you?" Dream Darcy asked me, breathless against my cheek.

"Nh—" I choked out. What was the point in denying it? They knew. They knew everything I knew. "I'm s-so... sorry..." I said instead, but they were already shushing me.

"I've done this already, you know," they said, again assuring me of their experience. "*I'm* not ashamed of it. Clearly."

Oh, God. They probably had, hadn't they? With... it was clear something had existed between them and Cillian in the past. They'd all but admitted to it. They'd probably done all of this and more.

Their weight had shifted off me. I felt briefly bereft, but then they were sinking to the ground in front of me. On their knees and—and the elk rug was here now. Because the cold, hardwood floor would be so cruel to kneel on. In fact, it was a punishment at the Abbey when you misbehaved. I couldn't imagine finding pleasure while they were being punished. I didn't want them to be hurt doing any of this with me. Even if they *wanted* to be doing it for some reason.

I looked down as their shoulders parted my knees. Their pink tongue came out to lick at their dark muzzle, equally dyed-dark hands rubbing up between the cream-white fur on the inside of my overly-thick thighs. The obscene length of my shame bobbed between my legs, engorged and slick-looking already, the knot threatening in my sheath. I hated it, as ever, but I loved watching Darcy wrap their hand around it. The conflict staggered me in its absurdity.

Darcy seemed to enjoy having me like this, taking in the sight like they were eyeing a meal or something valuable they intended to steal. Their confidence, their sultry gaze, was assuring. I was in good hands.

What would they do with their muzzle? Lick me, most likely, but would it go inside? What about their teeth? Indecision gripped me. Their nose bumped my tip, the first hint of the wet heat of their tongue touched me, and the image began to fall apart.

Desperately, I grabbed for them, trying to touch their cheeks, the ruff of their neck, anything to hold on to the visage. But it all tumbled to blackness as harsh, cold breath hit my lungs, sucked inside—

—and then I was coughing out staggered breaths and blinking in the dark blackness of my room, the all-too-real aches and anxieties of reality crashing back over me, forcing me to contend with the cruelty of being conscious once more.

Without even considering it, I gave a rough, ragged growling bark of frustration, slamming a fist down into the window sill at my side. It was loud—louder than I'd intended, but I waited for a time following, trying to steady my breaths. I dragged the comforter up around my waist in case Darcy had heard and came to check on me. At some point while I'd been sleeping, I'd apparently kicked off my smallclothes and now I had *no* idea where they were.

Nothing. More and more time passed, and I was still alone in the dark, cold room. I could only tell through my nose, my body was still on *fire,* heat pounding through my veins, and my—

Good God, it *hurt* it was so hard. I finally threw off the blankets and curled to my side like a wounded man, groaning gutturally. You'd think I'd been run through from the noise that escaped me. It was weak, pathetic, *humiliating!*

I couldn't help it; it was as if my body were responding to actual aching pain. I was clutching at myself, tears prickling at my eyes, praying for relief. The visage of them—of Darcy—nude and pleasing and *willing* in this very room taunted me with its clarity and realness, while my logical mind screamed at me how depraved it was to cling to those false memories.

The fact is, they *weren't* real. They were filthy, shameful dreams, concocted by my treacherous mind, and Darcy *was* a real person one room away, who—largely speaking—trusted me with their safety. What kind of monster was I turning into?

It wouldn't. Go. Down. In the past, a lot of the time, I'd wake in my own mess, and it would be done. I'd pray for forgiveness, hate myself for half the day, and wait fearfully for the problem to return in a week or two. But this time, I'd woken before I'd spilled, and my knot was nearly out, and no amount of self-loathing or shame was chasing it away.

I whined deep in my throat with my teeth clenched, wrapping my palm around my length and *squeezing* as I had in the past. I did so until my eyes watered, until I could stand it no longer… but it didn't feel *bad!* It *hurt*, there was no denying that, but for some reason it also satisfied, fed the sin inside me, like scratching an itch.

An image, not born of my dreams, but fresh and newly carving itself into my mind, assaulted my squeezed-shut eyes. Darcy's small, delicate muzzle, curled back over their fangs, fully wrapped around the dark pink, obscene girth of my—

I smashed my fist against the mattress, crying out, muffled, into the sheets, nearly a sob. My legs kicked out, throwing me to my stomach, and I clenched my palm around myself again, trying lower down, closer to my knot.

God, please, let this *end!* I know sin was meant to be endured, was, as Malachi had said, a life-long affliction. But at least now in this tormented moment, let these desires end! Every part of my body felt like a bowstring pulled taut to the snapping point, every inch of my skin burned, my fur chafing and pricking my flesh where I had dug my body into the bed. I moved my hand again, my palm rough and overused, the drag against my over-sensitive, aching and—Lord help me—leaking member.

I moved my palm again, squeezing closer to the tip, my breath gusting out at the release of some of the tension. That had worked. That had worked, could I… again…

I bucked into my hand, chasing that feeling, knowing no other option was open to me at this point. Nothing, literally nothing else would make this agony *stop*. And somewhere in the back of my mind, I knew what I was doing, knew the sin I was chasing, committing, but I was so desperate, I wanted so badly to be relieved of everything, to be able to let go of these imaginings, to not be enslaved by them, at least for a while…

I remembered how Darcy had felt when I'd dreamt of them as a woman, of the enveloping warmth of being seated *inside* of them, or how I imagined it would be… but now my mind could also supplant the version of them I'd only just dreamed of. I couldn't imagine how it would work exactly, but to have them down there on that elk rug on their knees, their sex dangling between those soft thighs, exposing the heat beneath their tail for me to push this big, awful thing of mine inside of them, to *mount* them—

I was hardly cognizant of what I was doing. I could feel the build of friction as I rutted into my own palm, simulating something vaguely like what I was imagining—in either version of them, it hardly mattered any more. I knew what I was doing was wrong in every sense of the word, but I didn't care, I didn't *care*—

A feeling unlike any I'd ever experienced in the waking world crashed over me like an internal wave, cutting my breath off and freezing every muscle in rigor, until violently uncoiling them all at once, my hips jumping, my thighs *shaking*. I howled, biting down into my own arm and the comforter as my palm grew hot, wet, and slick. The proof of my shame soon overflowed onto the bedspread, my fur… everywhere.

When I at last began to come down, the burning tension ebbed away. A drowsy, exhausted peace settled over me and brought me down onto my stomach on the sheets. I couldn't bring myself to care what I was lying in. I knew... and I deserved to wear the evidence of what I'd done.

I lay there stricken by the cacophony of my own inner thoughts, the pounding of my heart and the fleeting images from my dream. The peace of my physical release all-too-soon slipped away into cooling revulsion and self-loathing as my logical mind reasserted itself, and I began to reckon with everything I'd just done.

I was losing my battle with sin. *This* was the tipping point. Up until now, I could have begged forgiveness in good conscience. But now...

I was a Heretic.

12

HIEROPHANT

I don't know how I slept after that, but I did. The illness had mostly receded from my lungs by then, but it was apparently clinging enough to leave me exhausted. Or what had happened had drained me. Perhaps both.

The day that followed was the most difficult I'd spent with Darcy at the Lodge yet, and I'm counting the evening Cillian threatened my life.

First off, there was the practical issue of concealing what I'd done, which was both humiliating and disgusting, and I'm not certain I was even capable of doing an adequate job of *that*. Not without any way to fully launder the bedspread. Thankfully (or not) my fur and my own paw had caught much of the mess. That meant a lot of rigorous scrubbing the next day, recoiling at the horrific results of letting it dry in my fur and muttering pleading prayers the whole while. Which felt necessary, given the overwhelming guilt and shame I was seized by, but also, hypocritically, I would have preferred God be turning a blind eye to all of this. So, there was a part of me that yearned for those prayers to go unheard.

I layered the bed in an extra comforter, burnt some of the

incense I used for meditation, and hoped it was enough. Of course, it wasn't. But what more could I do?

I put aside my secular reading that morning, denying myself the indulgence, and focused on my sixth-day prayer schedule, spending extra time and focus on the scriptures that dealt with self-control. I begged of Him in my heart of hearts for the resolve needed to discipline my body, renounce ungodliness and worldly passions, lest I find myself a hypocrite. If I could not rein in my sinful nature, I could not preach the Word to others.

Since I had first met them, I had spoken so self-righteously to the Heart Thief of the evils of their vocation, of their mode of presentation, of their own propriety, and their need for salvation. But it was far more insidious than theft to lust and lose oneself to depraved imaginations as I had. Let alone over an unwilling and unknowing person who was not my spouse, or even my intended. And the more I reflected on it, the less blame I could lay at their feet. I couldn't rightly say I'd been the victim of seduction, other than the seduction of my own mind.

If they had been honest with me about not being involved in the murders, that meant they were nothing but a larcenist, albeit on a grand scale. Still enough to warrant a potential death sentence considering who they had stolen from, *especially* given the heresy angle. But, much of that came down to the power of Pedigree families and the Ministry, not basic morality, or even doctrinal morality. The fact was…

… I was starting to fear I was a worse person than Darcy was ever capable of being. I had very little evidence for this mounting fear, but it persisted. I couldn't prove they were being honest about the murders, couldn't ignore the possibility that they'd had other reasons for sparing my own life in the past, and I couldn't know every other wrong they may have committed. I'm not sure it was worth comparing our sins, but I was, all the same.

Last night was forcing me to reckon with the darkest thoughts I'd ever had about myself. I didn't know what to *do* with those thoughts other than pray. And prayer felt like it wasn't near enough.

Stepping out into the hallway that morning was genuinely one of the hardest things I'd ever done, but the longer I put it off, the more suspicious my actions became. When I began to smell broth boiling, I knew I had no choice. They were readying a meal, and I'd rather join them of my own volition than have them walk into the room to find me fully dressed and sitting on my own tail like a dullard.

I'd managed to scrub and dry my clothing the night before, at least, so I was able to fully dress for once. The vestments felt like a barrier, protecting the world from my sinful body. But they also felt undeserved. A conundrum like many I'd contend with this day. Still, perhaps they'd help conceal any remaining smell...

Darcy—the very subject of my degenerate desires—was waiting for me there, stirring a soup of broth we'd made from boiling down the game fowl carcasses, chopped potatoes, and some kind of absurdly large root vegetable we'd been slowly working our way through that had been with the rest of their provisions from town. A turnip, I think? End-of-season vegetables were always too big, too tough, and ugly inside and out.

Rather like me.

The feline looked up at me from where they were crouched beside the pot, gave a smile that was weak around the edges, and I knew immediately I was found out.

But neither of us said a thing. Darcy's posture and demeanor was as anxious as my own, and that was *not* usual. We'd been discovering an odd comfort with one another of late, or at least a gentler and more polite mode of verbal sparring. While we'd certainly had our moments of awkwardness, sharing the small lodge together, we usually had something to say to one another. But not this morning.

We ate our meal in silence.

At length as we neared completion, Darcy was the one to break it. "We're running low on potatoes and this was all we had of the broth," they said.

"I can live on one meal a day," I insisted.

"No need," they shook their head. "Game is plentiful, and I wouldn't mind going out to hunt. The storm's passed. It's beautiful out there," they said as they stared out the window. "I think I might even go on foot."

I nodded, mumbling an unintelligible affirmative, "Mhmh."

They'd already begun shrugging their borrowed coat on over a slim-fitted men's outfit, today. Oh, God, they'd been male in my dream, and then even afterwards in my imaginings, and I'd still—

"Can I trust you not to steal my horse while I'm out?" they asked passingly—and I think mostly teasingly—as they unslung their rifle from the rack near the doorway, checking it over before shouldering a powder bag as well. It all but bypassed my mind that they'd left the rifle there overnight, freely accessible to me if I'd so chosen.

But when the thought did strike, it stung. They were extending me so much trust…

"Isidor?"

I blinked, looking up. They were paused in the doorway before opening it, gripping the handle. Their expression had morphed to one more concerned. "Are you…" they began to ask carefully, quietly, thinking through their words a lot more than they usually seemed to, "… will you be alright today?"

I saw it, then. Sympathy. Soft, not condemning. Whatever they thought of me, whatever they knew, they were *pitying* me for it, not hating me as they should have.

“Fine,” I said quickly and with finality. “Go on, get some air. Good luck hunting.”

They nodded wordlessly, still looking at me as they opened the door and stepped outside. And then, as it shut behind them, I found myself alone.

I waited at least a minute, until they were well on their way into the woods for sure, before I howled into my own hands.

Prayer was not helping. It felt hollow and dishonest, which in and of itself was a terrifying realization. I *wanted* absolution, I *wanted* to be forgiven, but without access to a Priest or Confession, I was essentially just begging without a witness or consequences. And I didn’t feel I *deserved* to be forgiven. How could I?

I found myself pacing the grounds around the Lodge, intermittently tending to Darcy’s mare, stretching my legs and arms, wishing I had something approximately sword-shaped I could swing around, and eventually settling on chopping wood. The thinking was that the exertion might clear my head and give me some idea as to what I *should* be doing.

I kept my clothing on despite it being even warmer today, suffering through the heat. The snow would probably melt soon, which meant I’d have no excuse not to leave. But how could I leave things like this? How could I *not?* Was I a threat to the feline, now? Brother Dolus had said men lost to lust could take leave of their senses, the sin all-consuming, driving them to terrible acts. The thought of that made my body seize up in fear. What kind of beast might I become? Was I even in control? If I could dream of such things, did that mean that’s what I wanted? How long could I keep these demons barking at the gates at bay?

I’d eyed two massive stumps near the pile, the first go at this, but deduced were rotten at their core and would require more work to hew around than they were probably worth. Now seemed the time. I set to them with a fiery passion, hoping to bake my mind to ash with hard work and reduce myself to charred emptiness, if not solace.

One log in, and I was growing tired, but no better. My arms were only just beginning to ache and it was a more satisfying pain than I would have liked. What was it Malachi had said?

"It is how I make penance for a lifetime of misdeeds." Speaking of the pain he inflicted upon himself, as I was half-heartedly trying to do now. *"It releases me for a time from the burdens I carry. The weight of them."*

I left the axe stuck in the second log, my body crooked over it, bowed at the waist, and panting out puffs of steam into the air. My eyes traveled my surroundings almost desperately, while my body remained prostrate.

I needed… I needed to suffer for my sins. In a strange way, I craved it. The release it might offer. It would be akin to the punishment I might be given by a Priest. By one of my fathers. If I Confessed, right now. But they weren't here, so I just had to… I just had to do it myself.

This pain I was feeling needed to be answered by pain. That's how I'd been taught to soothe this kind of guilt, to answer for my sins and… oh.

It made sense, suddenly.

Malachi understood. He'd taken his salvation into his own hands. Granted, he may have taken it too far; his mortification seemed too severe to me. I couldn't imagine why he felt he needed to suffer as much as he had or why anyone else might have thought that. He didn't seem evil, to me. Just hurting. Warring against his inner demons. As I was now.

It didn't need to be that scarring. A deterrent. A painful reminder etched into my body temporarily and a mental sting that would remain. I wasn't sure how…

My eyes fell on Darcy's tack, stowed in a footlocker and

hanging near the one occupied stall in the small barn here. The door was open, because the mare was in the pen. I knew what was in that footlocker. I'd gone in there for a curry brush earlier.

I stood slowly, stiffly, and made my way over to the box. I stared at it for a long, long time, then eventually kneeled and opened the old, rusty-hinged lid. Most of their tack save the saddle and bridle was stored in there, including a horse crop, which looked lightly used if it had been at all. As it should. Only a truly cruel rider beat on their horse hard enough to wear down their crop, at least one that looked as new as this.

I picked it up, embarrassed to see my own hand shaking. I chastised myself internally. I was a *man*. Fearing pain of this measure was pathetic, especially when it was so richly deserved. I gritted my teeth inside my muzzle, silencing any remaining warnings rattling around inside my mind.

The grip was already short, owing to it being a small crop, not a dressage whip. I'd never tried anything like this, but if I shortened up my grip on the handle even further...

Without putting any strength into it, I tapped it over my shoulder, mimicking what I imagined Malachi must have done with his far more suitable, forked whip. It seemed certain it was made specifically for this type of mortification of the flesh. The riding crop was not, but it'd do.

I was able to reach my shoulders and upper back, but as to whether I could do so with any strength, only time would tell. Bracing myself and looking heavenward, I undid the buckles on my harness and began to shuck off my gambeson.

"I humble myself before you, Oh Lord," I whispered softly. "Look upon your son and know my desire to make penance is sincere. I will rid myself of these wanton thoughts, I swear it. Watch me. I shall conquer this. I *shall*."

. . .

Darcy didn't return for hours. Which was for the best, because after I'd finished in the yard, I was in no shape to do much other than lie down on my stomach in bed and drift off into fitful slumber while I willed the pain to subside.

I'm not certain if the crop had broken my flesh, but I'll be damned if I hadn't put my all into trying. So much so that I'd actually broken *it,* which was common enough on a horse, but I wasn't sure how I'd explain it to Darcy given that beating the mare that hard would be an equally awful explanation for how it had happened. I elected instead to throw the crop in the hearth fire and hope they didn't notice.

I was bruised and by the feel of it, swollen. My entire upper back and shoulders ached, as well as the nape of my neck. It was truly terrible, beyond what I'd been prepared for. The sting of each successive hit had probably numbed me somewhat to the next and the accruing damage I was doing to my flesh. It had felt right—like exultation—in the moment. But, the strange rush of off-kilter euphoria, assaulting me alongside all the pain, had eventually given way to *just* pain. And with it, exhaustion.

I understood better now the state Malachi had been in when I'd found him, and I'd not even damaged myself as severely as he had. I think. There was the vaguest whiff of blood, but nothing like what he'd done to himself. And honestly, some of that may have been from my chewing on my muzzle while gritting through it.

My ability to think was foggy, my whole upper body felt overly warm; I was dizzy and disoriented. I earnestly wasn't certain what my pain tolerance was like compared to other men; it's not like I'd sustained many major injuries over the course of my life other than the one obvious one and the blow to the head recently. Templar training was arduous—even Brother Dolus would say as much—but I'm not certain it was any worse than a man who labored for a living or a rigorously-trained soldier or navy man. Was I just soft? I hadn't known pain could make you feel this odd. Almost drunken.

I suppose in a way, it had worked. Exhausted bewilderment was better than whatever state I'd been in before. I'd take it.

When I heard the front door of the Lodge open, I hardly knew what to do with myself. Darcy had taken their time on this hunt, most certainly intentionally, but the afternoon was wearing on and I'd known they'd eventually be back. I'd shut my bedroom door. I was certain they'd knock before checking in on me. They were remarkably proper, all things considered.

I was right.

A tentative knock, then a demure, "Isidor? I didn't see you in the yard. Are you still here?"

A bolt of panic struck me. Of course, you fool! There was still the obvious possibility that they'd think I'd left. Taking my things and heading back to Redcoven today had been an option. It just hadn't been one I'd ever have considered. But they didn't know what was going on in my head. And if I'd left, that might have been a terrifying or at least worrisome possibility for them, given that I might report on where they were.

"I'm here," I assured them quickly. "Just got tired. I guess I'm not entirely well, yet."

Good, I seemed able to string sentences together well enough. So that was something.

It wasn't entirely a lie, except in every way that mattered. But how could I be honest with them right now? Explaining, confessing to everything, wouldn't just upset the delicate balance the two of us had here in this shared space, it would *frighten* Darcy. And rightly so.

"Oh, well," a pause, "I can blanch and clean the grouse on my own, then. I can just bring you dinner when it's done. I thought we'd make soup again, since I was only able to get the one today. I found the old root cellar though, while I was out in the back yard. There wasn't much salvageable there, save what was preserved."

My ears perked. "What could possibly still be preserved after a decade?" I asked.

"If you'll come out, I'll show you," they said. The words were coaxing. Sweet. I was intrigued, but also... concerned.

It probably should have felt patronizing, but I was the one behaving like a child, shutting myself in here and talking through the door. I couldn't blame them for trying to pry me out of there.

I unlocked the door—a pointless gesture given who I was staying with I knew, but we were playing this game with one another where we pretended we weren't at odds, we'd been respecting each other's space, and it had given me a small feeling of security all the same. I leaned out, staring down at the expectant feline. I'd only taken off my gambeson when I'd come inside, so I was still very much decent. Of course, even the thin undershirt I was wearing felt a misery on my back, but I tried my best not to show my discomfort.

Darcy's big eyes stared up at me for a moment, before they lifted a jar, cupped in both hands, triumphantly.

"Mead?" I blinked, recognizing the style of jar, similar enough to the ones my own abbey made, cast with a honeycomb inlay in the glass. I could also smell it. They'd already uncorked it once apparently, and the scent was distinctive.

"There's a whole honeycomb preserved in there, if we can pry it out," they said, tapping their claws against the weathered jug and staring through it at me, what little I could make out of their delicate features looking absurdly exaggerated.

"That... does sound—" I began, then cut myself off with a slow head shake. I licked back the drool at the corner of my jowls, self-consciously. "No-no, absolutely not—"

"Oh, why not?" Darcy sighed. "It's mead, not potato liquor, and we're sharing. We don't need to finish it either, you know.

I'll practice self-control if you will, and we could use some of it to cook with."

"Is it even any good?" I sighed. "Mead doesn't usually keep for a *decade*."

"It was a cold cellar, and it smells fine," they said, holding it up for me to sniff. Whether I wanted to or not, I couldn't help but smell it, and it smelled *so good*...

Darcy must have seen the way my face went weak, because they chuckled at me. "I wouldn't force drink on a sober man, but it's clear you're just being stubborn. I can tell you want to. You don't have some kind of vow of sobriety do you? Because if so, I'll stop asking—"

"You should stop asking regardless," I muttered. "But, no. I'm permitted to drink, I just... am not very good at it, apparently. Even the half a bottle of country wine you left for me last time did me in. I must not have much of a tolerance for it."

Their ears went back, their cheeks puffed a bit, and they guffawed suddenly. "Wait—what? 'Country wine'? I'll have you know I didn't leave that for *you*, Young Sir. It was just in the room because I'd been writing in there. I left it for the maid staff. And it wasn't wine, it was *grappa*. You drank that?"

I stiffened. "I... thought—"

"The whole of what was left?!"

I stopped talking at that, because it was becoming clear I'd made a fool of myself.

"Oh, you poor sweet, innocent lad!" they covered their mouth with one hand, a Pedigree gesture to cover one's fangs when giving a broad smile. "They let you drink, but they don't instruct you on how to do it, do they?"

"Knowledge on the subject of vice can be a gateway to said vice," I said pointedly.

"It's also how you learn how said vices work," they sighed, "and what effects they'll have on your body. So that you can avoid, say, getting completely sozzled at a party unintentionally or poisoning yourself so badly you *die*. Or thinking table wine and grappa are the same thing."

I twisted up my muzzle. "Maybe alcohol is just a terrible vice in general if it's so very dangerous and difficult to moderate."

"Lord, now you sound like Cillian," they said ruefully. "Look, for some folks, I'd certainly agree, but I'm no sauced old man fondling women at a party. I know how to drink. It helps me take my mind off things," they said vaguely.

I averted my gaze at that.

"If you don't want any, Isidor, that's fine. Do you mind if I have some?"

"How does it 'take your mind off things'?" I asked uncertainly.

"Imbibed in the right amounts, it just helps you to care less," they said quietly. Their voice had lost some of its earlier luster. "Think about the things that make you sad or anxious less. It's medicine... of a sort."

"I don't know who taught you these things," I muttered, "but it sounds like the sort of self-reinforcing vice talk you'd hear in Pedigree parlors."

"You're not entirely off on the mark, there," Darcy smirked a little. "But the talk also isn't entirely wrong. Take it from someone who *has* been sozzled at more than a few parties."

"The more and more I get to know you, the more certain I am of how much time you've spent in High Society," I said. "You know, their lifestyle is not meant for the lowly, like us. They are gifted by blood with more temperance, more innate reason, a more respectable countenance—"

"Oh, good Lord no!" Darcy barely covered a nearly barked-out laugh. "I'm sorry, but I must inform you how wrong you are... the mere idea that Pedigree are more *respectable,"* they snorted softly before clapping their hand over their mouth again. When they removed it, they were still smiling. "I've seen High Society behind closed doors for most of my life, Isidor. I assure you; they are as debauched as the rest of us and rich, which opens all kinds of doorways to the likes of depravity the common folk can only *dream* of."

That one struck a chord, although perhaps not in the way they were intending. They continued talking, but by then my mind was elsewhere. Replaying things I very, *very* much did not want to be thinking on right now.

"I know you're young," they were saying, "but in your line of work, you're going to need to peel away some of that doctrinal teaching or reality is going to be quite a shock to you. Templar—from what little I know—take up positions in Pedigree households to curtail their excesses, monitor the families' behavior and bury their secrets, right? At least anything your Ministry *wants* buried. If you don't know what to expect, you'll either be left in the dark or you'll have a lot of hard realities to contend with very quickly—"

"Will you teach me how to drink, then? Carefully?" I asked suddenly. "'Medicinally'?"

They glanced down at the jug and then back up at me. "Yes, of course. Everyone's tolerance is different, but we'll just have a little with dinner and see how you feel."

"I had trouble sleeping last night," I admitted. "Sometimes the monks did give us a little bit of beer with dinner to help us sleep, growing up. There's something to the medicine angle."

"Well, help me blanch, pluck, and clean the grouse, and we'll make ourselves a nice boil to have with our ancient mead," they said, turning to lead me down the hallway. "You're better at all of that anyway. I always tear the skin."

I followed them, expecting we might go back to companionable silence while we cooked, which wouldn't be so bad. Especially compared to the alternative this morning—*awkward* silence.

But they surprised me, speaking with their back turned as they uncorked the jug and poured out our mead into two freshly-washed brandy glasses likely left here with the rest of the possessions the previous owner had not seen fit to move out.

"I... also had trouble sleeping last night," they said, their voice precarious for some reason, like they were having trouble choosing a tone. "It's normal, you know. Everyone has trouble sleeping, sometimes."

"Sure," I agreed uncertainly. "A lot's happened in a very short time. I'm just... I think I'm very out-of-sorts."

"Yes, precisely," Darcy said as they turned, holding out one of the glasses to me in their thin-boned, elegant hand. My own thick fingers and stained claws looked downright brutish in comparison. "We're two very disparate people in a very emotional situation. Tensions are high, and..." they lifted their glass to their muzzle to sip on a bit of the heady liquid, "... and it would be very normal, very excusable, I dare say, for us to be struggling with similar issues at night. Sleeping."

"I suppose you're right," I said, sniffing the alcohol before taking a sip as they had. I couldn't help but feel they wanted me to say more in my responses to them, but I was lost on what else there was to say, honestly.

"-and it might benefit us, earnestly," they cleared their throat softly, "if we were able to speak with one another on the particular complexities of... getting a full night's sleep... so that we can rest more easily, tonight—"

"No thank you," I said, drinking the rest of my glass.

I swear they rolled their eyes, prying my glass back away from me. "Well, you went through that fast enough. I take it the taste doesn't bother you?"

"It's mead," I reasoned. "Past its prime or not, it's still sweet. The honey in this is good. I've always preferred wildflower honey to orchard honey."

"Let's see if we can't pry that comb out of there in time then,"

Darcy said determinedly. “Come on, let’s get some food in our bellies fast, so we can drink more.”

“Mmhh,” I hummed, moving past them towards where they’d begun dressing the grouse on the table. They were right. They were not in fact very good at this. I’d been dressing fowl since I was young, even before the Abbey, so it was no issue for me. Another confirmation that they’d spent a lot of time not just as a servant in High Society, but as someone enjoying the benefits of it. How? They couldn’t have been a mistress, or whatever the term might be for them, for very long.

When I went to lean over, I was in for a rude surprise. I had briefly, blissfully forgotten about the state of my back. Bending fixed that very quickly though. I stiffened, trying not to whine out in pain. I’m certain I at least winced. And Darcy saw it.

They peered at me from over their glass. “Stiff? I saw you chopped even more wood. We would have been fine with what you did before, you know.”

“You’ll be here longer than I will,” I reasoned. “I wanted you to have enough after I’m gone.”

“That’s honestly very sweet,” they said with a demure blink downwards, briefly averting their eyes. “But it seems like you may have overdone it.”

“I’ll be fine,” I lied.

“You’re lying,” they said all but immediately, “but that’s fine. I’m used to men concealing their feelings from me.”

For some reason that made me feel horrible *immediately*, because I knew they were comparing me to Cillian. And that bothered me more than I cared to admit.

“Isidor?”

I glanced towards the table. Darcy was standing at the edge near where my bag was open, spilled out onto its surface. We’d been rifling through it earlier trying to choose what to read tonight, eventually dismissing the idea of going over one of the books they’d given me earlier to ‘improve my opinion’ of it, as they'd said. We'd opted for something new to both of us, instead: A novella left here in the Lodge that Darcy had somehow overlooked during whatever time they'd spent here before.

Earnestly, it sounded dreadful. A mish-mash of flowery prose clumsily entangled 'round an 'intrigue at court'-style scandal. We were pretty sure the both of us would spend the night laughing at it, which was rather the point.

"Changed your mind about what you want to read?" I asked.

"Did you know you have an unopened letter?" they said, slipping the neatly folded manila papers out and holding them up for me to see. "I don't mean to pry, I just… it's terribly intriguing."

"Oh," I blinked, "that's from my Father. My Priest. One of many I've received during this trip. The most recent. And it's *not* unopened, actually. The seal was tampered with. My Brother Dolus sticking his nose into private communications, as ever."

"You're not curious what he had to say?" Darcy asked, turning it over in their hand. "I thought you liked your Father."

"I got it right before I came here, and it's outdated," I explained. "It's a response from weeks ago to one of the letters I'd sent him at the time. A lot has happened since then. I don't know how relevant it is any more, but you can bring it here."

They did so, plucking at the wax seal as they meandered over and nodding. "You're right about the seal," they observed. "They layer underneath is a slightly different shade of red, if you dig a claw into it."

"Mmh," I nodded, taking it from their offered hand. "Brother Dolus is a consummate Templar. It's disconcerting, but it hardly surprises me anymore."

They folded their legs and sat down beside me, running an elegant clawed finger up and down the edge of the glass they were drinking from tonight. I tried very hard to act interested in the letter, rather than that.

I opened it, skimming the page. It was comforting to see my Father's hand again, at least, but…

"It's about what I thought," I surmised. "Asking me to come home, again. Insisting I'd be ready to take the exam as I am, and that my brothers and sisters are missing me. Oh, here he's…" I blinked, "… he's saying *he* has been missing our conversations in the library. That's unlike him. He isn't usually so sentimental."

Darcy peered over my shoulder. "Is this the longest you've ever been apart?"

"Yes," I nodded. "Even when I traveled to Redcoven for mission training in the past, he came with us boys."

"Honestly, that's rather sweet." They smiled.

"You've never met the man. 'Sweet' is not the word I'd use to describe him."

"What is *that* fascinating gibberish?" Darcy pointed at the bottom of the second page, without touching of course. Manners.

"Oh, that's," I leaned in, squinting at it, "looks like… iron age century cuneiform. He doesn't usually test me as far back as that. Uh. Give me a moment."

"Is it a prayer of some sort?" they wondered aloud.

"Almost always. Sometimes an amusing anecdote," I said. "It's a bit of a puzzle game between us. No one else at Ebon Gables really reads cuneiform, not even the monks. Ancient Amuraic, sure. But cuneiform is a bit more rare, so outside the most well-known scriptures, it's basically a dead alphabet. I've been fascinated by it since I was young, so Father would put together little pieces for me to translate. Write them into the margins of my work books or hide them all over the Abbey during holidays. Me and the others would follow them clue to clue, until we'd discover some kind of cache. Usually sweets."

"This is just getting cuter and cuter," Darcy smiled.

"It's training, too," I said. "I credit him almost entirely with my deduction and investigation abilities. This isn't a prayer though, it's… I think it's part of the letter."

"Isidor."

I narrowed my eyes. "Command characters… cuneiform from this era is distinctive between asking and telling. 'Journey', no it's less formal than that. 'Come… home… and then the next signifies the importance of swiftness, of time. 'Come home immediately?'"

"Isidor," Darcy's voice had begun to sound worried. "Can your Brother Dolus read this kind of writing?"

I looked up at them, blinking through the haze of alcohol and trying to clarify my thoughts for a moment. "No, I don't think so," I said at length. "Dolus is more of a Ministry Agent than a scholarly monk. I've almost never seen him in the library, and his Tome is in common Amuraic, not ancient. I've seen it. I don't even think he speaks his prayers in the ancient tongue like some of the other monks do."

"What does the rest of it say?" they asked, placing a hand on my shoulder to stabilize them as they leaned down to look more closely at the letter.

I looked it over for a long while, pushing through my muddy-headedness to search my memory for the characters. They were even more obscure than many I'd translated in the past, but the characters were similar enough to the later ones I knew far better that I thought I could pick it out.

"Father really ran the risk here of my being unable to do this from memory if it's important," I said, frustrated. "He must have been *very* determined to ensure few others could read it."

"Ohhh, I don't like that," Darcy worried softly.

"Come home immediately," I said with more certainty, "the roots of our… our orchard… are rotten. You… the character subject, it's—it's usually used to refer to whom you're addressing… you are in danger."

Darcy was silent, but their eyes turned to regard me uncertainly.

"It isn't picking season for anything, the... the orchard is slumbering for the winter," I said, confused.

"It's code," the feline whispered. "Did he ever tell you he'd speak to you in code like this?"

"Not in so many words," I said, "but he stressed how important these lessons were. Even when I'd grow frustrated with them, he'd push until I cracked them. Sometimes it took *months*."

"Thieves use code and cants, sometimes," Darcy said. "When we can't speak plainly or speak at all."

"A cryptolect," I said. "We're taught some of the most basic elements the Ministry is aware of, but it evolves too quickly to really pin down meanings for very long."

"That's the idea," Darcy rolled their eyes. "Isidor, I think your Father is telling you the 'rot' is coming from inside your own Ministry. Maybe your own Abbey? Did anyone else have access to this letter other than your brother monk?"

"Unlikely," I said. "He hand-delivered it. I doubt he would have allowed anyone else to tamper with it. Lord. I need to get home."

"Not right now you don't, it's the middle of the night," Darcy tightened their grip on my shoulder.

"I should have read this before. *God*," I gritted my teeth a moment. "I'm worried about him."

"I think he's more worried for *you*," the feline said pointedly. "You're the one that got involved in this."

I stared helplessly down at the letter, my thoughts spiraling. I simultaneously wished I hadn't opened it, but also knew how cowardly and foolish that notion was. It was better that I know this than not, and it would only encourage me to be swifter and more careful on my journey home, when I was ready.

"I'm not certain if I should even stop in Redcoven," I said.

"Maybe I should just head directly back for Ebon Gables. But… no, Malachi, I… he was so kind to me…"

"The bastard who shot at me?" Darcy countered, making a face. "Cillian said he nearly knocked him down an icy staircase, too. Isidor, I don't think he can be reasoned with."

"I just want to check in with him," I said. "Make sure he knows I'm alright. I owe him at least that much."

"That's your choice," they said while crossing their arms over their chest. "But I'd take care who you share this with until you're certain what it means."

There was something in their tone I didn't like. A guarded, intentional aloofness that felt dishonest, or like they were hiding something. I couldn't imagine what they might be hiding this time that the letter may have reminded them of, but I was getting frustrated with all their secrets and constantly needing to unravel them, and I was feeling the effects of the alcohol. So, I just tried to log the odd moment, for now. Add it to the puzzle and make sense of it later.

Work often helped me alleviate frustration, so I set to work on the bird, murmuring a quiet prayer for the animal before I got to dressing it. Darcy put another half-full glass down beside me, saying softly, "For when you're done," with a light touch of my shoulder.

They sat beside me, watching me work, eventually going on. "You say that prayer every time before you dress or prepare meat. It's for the animal?"

I nodded. "A prayer that they know God in their next life. Feral souls cannot understand The Word, but there is a chance they are reborn as a higher being eventually."

"I didn't know your Faith believed feral prey had souls," Darcy admitted.

"You know a good deal about our Faith for a foreigner," I pointed out.

"Well, I was raised with it," they said. "But I'm hardly an

expert like you. And our family's Templar was of little help. I barely knew the man. I only know what I do of your Faith because I read the holy tome."

"You've read the whole of the Tome of the Faith?" I asked, eyebrows lifting.

They crooked their shoulders, smiling a little. "It *is* a book of stories, so... yes."

"I'm no monk," I said, "but I've probably read more than most Templar in-training. Obviously all of the Tome, cover to cover, many times, as well as most of the Abbey Library. What I was given access to, anyway. I've always enjoyed reading, since I first became literate. It felt like a heaven-sent power, like a special talent I was never meant to have. It's a great crime that so many will never know its wonders."

"I felt the same way when I first learned your tongue," they said, watching me from where their cheek was resting in their palm. "It was like the world I found myself in finally made sense. People were less frightening, less mysterious. Reading was the same, except it expanded my horizons beyond just the people I met. I can't say I've ever stopped being amazed by it. Every new story excites me, even if the writer's skill is lacking or I don't like the characters."

"I think I'm more particular," I said, continuing my work, glad we were talking again without any of the anxious fears from earlier getting in the way. Maybe the mead was working. I downed the last of my second glass.

Darcy smiled a little. "That just makes me want to show you more and more of my favorite titles and find out which ones survive your rigorous standards."

"We could be here a lifetime," I shook my head.

"That might not be so terrible."

My fingers twitched around my knife. I set it down, then turned to regard them. I'm not sure what I expected, but they were just smiling warmly and openly at me. It cut me straight down to the marrow.

"You have to admit that putting the cat-and-mouse game aside for a bit and just talking books and doing domestic chores together has been a nice change of pace," they said, expanding on their statement. It didn't feel like a retraction, though.

I looked down at the grouse on the table, the pot boiling that we were readying to blanch it in, the chopped root vegetables. The hearth was crackling low, the main room warmer than the rest of the Lodge, easily the most comfortable space in the house. The light was dimming outside, dark azure blue cascading in through the windows. Anyone looking in upon us would have called this 'domestic'. Darcy was not wrong.

The ludicrous nature of the situation I'd been in for the last few days finally hit me full-force. And with it, enough questions to drive a man mad. How, in a few days' time, had we gone from leveling deadly weapons at one another, my heart intent on bringing the feline to the gallows for a crime of *heresy* of the highest magnitude, a sentence which I would be integral in bringing about and would therefore be expected to attend...

To this.

Sharing this place together—at this point of my own free will, there was no denying that—unbound, with weapons left accessible for me to use if I so chose, with *no* thought to do so.

I was *holding* a chef's knife. I'd been using a woodcutter's axe for days. If literally anyone from the Ministry saw me here, not doing the *one* thing that would be required of me in this position, I'd be excommunicated and sent to an Inquisitor for questioning and possible detention.

But instead, we were discussing books together. We were talking to one another like new friends. Even now, even after I'd spent half the day punishing myself for my transgressions. Here we were, again. Talking like we *weren't* on opposite ends of the world. Like when this strange, surreal truce broke, we wouldn't be enemies again.

What were we doing? How was I letting this continue? I should have left today. Gone back to Redcoven, confessed my sins, or at least begun the process. I could be cast out of the Ministry, excommunicated even, but being dishonest was not an option. I would always know, and so would God. How could I serve Him in good faith? I couldn't, that's how.

"I wish I could read what's going on behind those eyes of yours," Darcy said, barely audibly. I looked over at them to find them still looking at me, resting their chin on their folded arms. "You've been so quiet all day. I'm worried."

Were they worried for me or for themselves? Either would be valid.

"Why do you trust me enough in so short a time to leave your weapons out?" I asked quietly.

Darcy's eyes widened marginally, although they still had a haze to them. The mead had clearly taken more of a toll on them than me. "You mean my rifle? Only I know where the powder is."

That hadn't occurred to me. So, they *had* been taking some precautions after all. Still. "The blades, then," I said.

"We've both had a few chances to hurt one another and neither of us have taken them," they said. "Besides, you promised you wouldn't hurt me."

"I suppose I just don't see why it is you believe me."

"You asked me to," they pointed out.

"You also said you couldn't," I pointed out right back.

"I stopped caring," they finally admitted. "I don't know when or why. I just... decided that if you were going to hurt me or kill me, so be it. It wouldn't be worth it to survive something like that, anyway."

"What?" I nearly gasped.

They shrugged. "You're very kind, Isidor. If someone like

you can honestly be that cold… that duplicitous… I think I just do not like the world very much, any more. That's all."

"You've had too much to drink," I said, concerned.

"I've had three glasses, and they've hardly hit me much yet," they said.

"I am *not* as good a person as you think I am," I rasped quietly. "I meant what I said about not turning you in. Not hurting you. But I'm not… I do not think you should judge the world based on me. I'm a corruptible, sinful… broken man."

"Who told you that?" they asked softly.

"God," I said automatically.

"I don't think God ever said that," Darcy murmured, "about you or anyone else. That sounds more like something people would say about one another." They poured themselves more mead, whispering the next part fiercely. "Hateful people. I hope you don't really believe that."

"I more than believe it," I said. "I can *feel* it. I never used to understand the words before, but I do now. I *feel* broken."

"*Things* can be broken," Darcy said, leaning up and reaching for my paw, gingerly removing the old chef's knife from it, and running one claw along the splintered wood of the handle. "Things can stop serving a utility, to us anyway. I don't think people can be broken. We can be hurt… we can be gone. But we exist, even when we're hurting, so we're not so defective as they make us out to be, are we? We can still *be* someone. We may not serve a utility other people see the value in, but to hell with them. Maybe we find another. Maybe our purpose is just to exist in the world, as we are, to be a part of a larger tapestry or to enjoy something, to rejoice in something, that no one else sees."

"'To see glory in His creation in the corners of the world neglected'," I mumbled.

"That's a prayer, isn't it?" Darcy asked. "I think I recall it."

I nodded. "Chapter fifteen, verse… Lord, I can't remember.

In the writings of Larvistian, on rejoicing in the everyday. He was a monk known for cultivating the wild herbs that grew in the mountains. Some of which he sourced for medicine, some of which he couldn't find a use for then, but still tended, and never revealed the locations of in order to keep them safe. The Royal Order of Herbalists found some of his hidden glens centuries later, havens for flora we'd long thought extinct after the Era of Eastward Expansion. They keep many of them in hot-houses now to preserve them. Some of them *were* eventually used to make new medicines."

"What people misunderstand in these times," Darcy said, reaching forward to settle a hand on my shoulder gently (but they couldn't know about my bruising), "might be more acceptable, or even valued, in the future. Even if it's something that will bring down censure, mockery, or violence now. History books are full of stories of philosophers who were stoned to death for their beliefs or people who studied the natural world and learned truths that were inconvenient for the time."

"And just as many criminals and sinners thought they were just misunderstood," I said, bitterly. "I'm sure."

"*I'm* the only criminal here," Darcy said. "And I think… at least I hope… history may see me differently. But that won't matter to me in this lifetime. It's just the only way I know how to live, anymore. Anything else is unbearable. Believe me, I've tried."

"But if I fool myself into believing these things are somehow allowed, these aspects of myself that I war against, if I give up that fight and give in to them, I could be *wrong*," I said. "These dark thoughts and impulses inside of me that have already compelled me to act so immorally… they could all in fact be as destructive and corrupting as the scriptures say. I can't see how they could be anything *other* than sinful."

"I cannot imagine what terrible thoughts you might have

that warrant such fear of yourself, Isidor," Darcy said dauntlessly. "But I'm not afraid of you. For whatever that's worth."

"Would you really want to spend a lifetime here in this lodge?" I demanded. "With me?"

The question seemed to surprise them for but a moment, as I'd known it would. But that had been the implication, had it not?

"Well," they said, after clearly considering it for a bit, "we'd have to go hunting occasionally, go to town for supplies, more books... but otherwise, why not?"

"You're being ridiculous," I muttered, staring back down at my work. Which was pointless, since I no longer had the knife. "Or drunk. I'm hardly certain which."

They only hummed in response. Their palm was still on my shoulder, fingers kneading in what was meant to be a comforting way, I'm certain. I wasn't resisting the touch—I was much too far gone for that now—but neither was I telling them they were pressing into bruised and tender flesh. And there was, admittedly, a very shameful reason for that.

It felt... good. The reminder of the pain, though minor now, was centering. Calming. God only knows why.

I must have winced at some point though, because they seemed to notice, their hand stilling and slipping away. "I'm sorry. Are you... are you alright? Still stiff? Did you hurt yourself out in the yard, somehow? You seem a bit tender."

"No, I'm," I stammered. "It's good, actually. I'm fine. I don't mind it."

They seemed pleased with that response and stood, bumping their own chair back so they could step aside. I thought they intended to leave me here while I finished dressing the bird, but then I felt their presence behind me—behind my chair. I tried to crane my neck back to see what they were doing, and they poked the bridge of my nose, pointing it back down.

"Head down. And I'm going to lay my filthy feline hands on you, but *over* your clothing, alright? This is also medicinal. Tell me if you don't like it."

I wasn't sure what to expect, probably just more of their hands on my shoulders? The kneading, though... When they put their hands on me once again and pressed their small fingers into the motions, and worked my flesh like dough...

Cats liked to knead. I'd never realized it could be like *this*.

They didn't know what I'd done to my body. They didn't know because I wasn't telling them, and they'd *never* know because I couldn't tell them why. And this should have been agony because of that.

But it wasn't.

My hands were nowhere near my task. They soon slipped off the table entirely, my whole body losing its fight to uphold my dignity like I was dying in the snow, again. Darcy wasn't even putting much strength into the touch, but it was undoing me. It was like the capstone I'd been looking for to finish me off. The missing piece in all of it. I didn't just want to be punished.

I wanted *them* to punish me.

And they didn't even know they were doing it. They were trying to offer me comfort. And they *were*. Just likely not in the way they'd intended. That's the perverse part of all of it. This only further sealed the totality of the mortification ritual. If I *ever* explained all of this to them, and why it was serving to offer me a release from my guilt, they would be aghast, I was certain.

But I couldn't bring myself to care. I was so tired. I wanted to be comforted. I wanted it to be them that did it. I wanted this, and I didn't give a damn why any more.

I was breathing raggedly through my nose, trying to keep my maw shut lest my tongue loll out, and I felt I had sunk in my chair. Darcy did not let my impropriety stop them. They only giggled. "Well, I've found the trick to subduing you, Isidor. Now you are *truly* at my mercy."

"I always have been," I mumbled lazily.

If a man could even come to enjoy the pain inflicted upon himself as punishment, what was left to him? What hope was there for me?

Not in the night, but in the early hours of morning, God sent an answer to me in the form of an avenging angel.

The meal last night had almost been perfunctory. It had taken us far too long to get the grouse prepared, and by the time the soup was boiled and ready to eat, we were both drunk. I don't think that had been the intention, but the food had taken so long, and I suspected the both of us had wanted to be rid of our senses. It was fortunate, really, that Darcy's shoulder-touching was as improper as the evening had gotten.

By the end of the night, we'd even been too tired and too muddle-headed to read together. Darcy had apologized for not 'teaching me to drink more responsibly'—their words—and headed off to the drawing room to sleep, and I to the bed. I'd suspected for some time now that they had no bed in there, but I was hesitant to ask now, lest it sound like an invitation. My own bed was… not fit for anyone else to use, at this point. My sin was not visible, but the scent remained.

Before dawn light had broken, I vaguely recalled Darcy calling to me from outside my room, telling me they were going for a morning hunt.

"The game is wise to me," they'd said something of the like. "I'm going to try my luck at a different hour today."

I must have told them to go, because that was all I remembered before drifting off again. My sleep was deep and dreamless. Blissfully so.

What woke me, I cannot say. Perhaps just the primordial knowledge etched deep into our bones when we are being watched. Perhaps he'd shifted in his chair.

I was facing the door when I slept. A habit I'd gotten into on the road, necessary to keep vigilant. And one I'd certainly doubled-down on since I'd caught Darcy spying on me that night in the carriage house.

But this time, the intruder was not outside my door. He was reclining in Darcy's wooden chair, the very same one they'd sat in during the nights we read together. He'd turned it to face me, barely feet away. Sat down. All of this after unlocking and opening the door, and coming inside. And I'd slept through all of it.

Malachi, or Brother Dolus, or Father Helstrom would never have let their guard down like this. What a pathetic excuse for a Templar I was turning out to be.

The red setter, dressed down but still as elegant as his station required, was staring directly at me when I woke. His body was rigid, one hand paw gripping his cane where it rested over his knee, the other holding fast to the pistol in his lap. His jaw was vaguely trembling. I could not place the turmoil in his eyes. He looked many things at once. But mostly, scared.

I slowly leaned up, blinking tiredly at the Pedigree. I felt as I had the first time I saw him in that hallway, behind Malachi. Staggered by the ferocity and gall the average-looking gentleman somehow exuded, unable to form a coherent picture of the man. He was the possessor of *so* many secrets, only the beginnings of which I had managed to unravel. I was fairly certain I knew more about Darcy at this point than I did about him, and that was saying something.

Why was Cillian Rathborne, of all people, here? What did he want from me?

And… oh, Hell. Where was Darcy?

"They aren't here to get in our way this time," he said, as though peering into my soul. "So."

I leaned up on one elbow and slowly, carefully pushed myself into a sitting position with a knee up to my chest and my other at my side, uncertain if I moved to put my legs off the edge of the bed… if he'd see that as aggressive. I didn't want to test the man. He was armed and I was not.

"Isidor of Ebon Gables," he said, after visibly gathering himself for a moment. "That is your name, yes? You Abbey boys take your Abbey as your surname. Correct?"

I nodded, then tried out my scratchy voice. "Yes."

"You were born in the town of Gladenbury," he went on. "I was given your Patents, eventually. An orphan. Like most of them. But you had a family, they just couldn't care for you, right?"

I cleared my throat. "Yes, that's right."

"Are they still alive?"

"I don't know," I answered honestly. "They gave me up. They never tried to reclaim me."

"No parents, no siblings," he said as though he were mentally checking something off. "No wife that I could find, let alone children."

"I've not married yet."

"You were taken in by the Ministry when you were a child. You've spent more than a decade since in training. This is, in fact, your first assignment. Hunting…" and here he seemed to trip over his own distaste, "… hunting my Darcy down like an animal."

"I was investigating them," I said.

He blinked for a moment in surprise at how I'd addressed them.

"But I honestly was not supposed to apprehend them," I said. "I… went too far. The Ministry didn't send an actual Inquisitor until Redcoven, and by then—"

"By then, you'd already been terrorizing them for months," he filled in for me.

I felt my shoulders sag, my posture and form training kicked in and I tried to correct, but then the truth of his words hit me, my knowledge of my guilt and regret came after, and—and—it was all too much. He was right. Why not just admit it? Even by doctrinal law I'd been in the wrong. I'd overstepped. I'd abused my access to information, the trust of my overseers, and then Malachi, and they were all probably immensely worried about me right now, and I'd done *nothing* to make any of it right.

So, I said, "Yes." Hoarsely, voice laced with the regret I felt, but knowing I deserved no sympathy and would *get* no sympathy from this man.

"Darcy did not steal your bloody holy plate," he said sighing. "This has all been a pointless endeavor. No one should have to *die* over this."

"They've never denied the theft," I said quietly.

"Well I know them better than you ever will," he said, leaning back in his chair. "Sometimes, they lie. Less than I do. Probably less than most people I know, earnestly. But when they do, they usually have a reason. I know very little about this theft, but I know Darcy, and this doesn't fit. Most especially the murders. I'm not certain why they'd let you believe they committed this crime, but I don't want you going to your grave thinking you failed this task of yours so utterly. I'd imagine it must mean quite a lot to you, being tied up in your… 'faith.'"

The way he said the last word with a sneer, almost distracted me from what else he'd said.

I looked up at him slowly, knitting my hands in front of my shin. "That's why you're here now. While they're gone. Isn't it?"

He nodded, but quickly looked down at the floor, swallowing. There was no confidence there. No resolve. His bad leg was shaking, his palm rubbing circles over his knee. "Like I said," he murmured, "no one should have to die over this. But this world is a torment. We find ourselves in these no-win scenarios, where every choice damns us. I don't believe in Heaven or Hell, Isidor," he said, finally lifting his eyes to mine again, "but I believe there is no solace, no peace, to be had here, either. Not ever for very long, anyway. I understand very acutely why so many people need to believe in ascension. Because the thought of living another lifetime on this earth, even with a fresh slate, is intolerable. I wish I could believe in it… an end to it all, and everlasting peace. Truly."

"You're one lifetime away from His grace," I said disbelievingly. "You are *so* close. How can you say such terrible, blasphemous things?"

"Because I know who I am," he said, his voice steadier than it had been so far. "I've been tested, I've had every chance in life to prove I am as blessed and graced by the god our Church teaches us about as they say I am. I should inherently know how to do the right thing, to be good, and kind, and loving… and instead, I've failed. At every turn."

I looked at him. At the pistol. Contemplated the fact that these, once again, might be my last moments alive. Thought about what I'd say to God, to explain myself and the life that I'd squandered. And I felt hopeless for a moment, too.

"You could do the right thing here," I said softly, pleading for my life, I knew. I wasn't ready. Not yet.

"Tell me what that is," he implored, his voice gone thready and as pleading as mine. "Please. Because I have been agonizing over that very question for days. Warring inside over whether I'll break promises I made in the past to others or to myself, whether I'll forever wound and possibly sever my only remaining threads of connection to someone I love… or stand in the square of Redcoven and watch them die."

I tried to speak, but nothing would come. I stared down at the planks of wood lining the floor, heard the distant warble of birdsong as the avians of the wilderness awoke, smelled the mingled scents of myself and Darcy from the days we'd spent here. I listened for God, and the only answer I got was the pounding of my heart, increasing in tempo.

"You see?" Cillian said desperately. "I haven't the wisdom or divine insight to see myself through these trials, to know how to navigate a world with choices this cruel. I *wish* this was even the first time, but it is not. And rest assured, as long as I live, there will be more. What kind of creator crafts us to *feel* so deeply, then tortures us thusly? Good Lord, you're barely twenty. Not even. I don't *want* to kill you."

I felt my teeth shuddering in my mouth, looked up at him plaintively, and found the young Lord with his head in one of his hands, wiping his fingers over his eyes. His other was gripping the pistol tightly. But it wasn't pointed at me. Not yet.

If I wanted to save my own life, this was the moment. This was when I could wrest him to the ground and remove the chance for him to kill me altogether. Darcy would probably even thank me for it. I wouldn't have to badly hurt the man.

Even *he* didn't seem to want to do it.

So why, then... why couldn't I find the nerve to act?

Was I afraid? Certainly not more than I was of death. What could be more frightening than death?

My mind answered me, all but immediately. My inner voice, perhaps. I had been asking God for days now for some kind of guidance. For a path to redemption, for repentance of my sins. Was this it? Was this all that was left to me?

God did not give up on us because we failed in one lifetime. For all my sins, I had yet to cross the lowest of thresholds and forsake Him. My soul was not yet fodder for Ciraberos.

If I died here today, I would be reborn. I would forget who I was... and maybe that was for the best. But I would also be wiped clean of my sins. I would be given another chance.

And they would not find Darcy, because of me.

They would most certainly blame my death on them and be renewed in the vigor of their hunt. But maybe this time, Darcy would evade their pursuers. They had in the past, until I'd taken up the charge.

In a matter of minutes, I had begun to finally understand Cillian. Without having to know whatever it was that had been between them, I understood. He was trying to protect them. And I was in the way of that.

He pressed his hand back over his own head and through the auburn waves of fur between his ears. "Please," he said, "just... just tell me you'll lie to the Ministry. Promise me you won't help them find Darcy. I will make sure they leave the country this time. I will... somehow... I will force them if I must. This thing they've been doing—the thieving—I've *never* understood it. It's a compulsion. It's a balm to their soul, they seem to need it, and I try not to question why because that is the *least* I can do, and because it genuinely seems to help them, somehow. But I'll see to it they never do any of it, ever again, in this country."

"I'm not going to be a part of the investigation anymore," I promised. "And I'm certain they'll leave the Lodge as soon as I do. If I make Confession to my Priest again, I promise it will only involve my own transgressions."

He cracked a pained smile, sniffing and looking up at me. "Oh? 'Transgressions'. What is it between you two, exactly? It hasn't escaped my notice that you're unbound. Playing house here, are you? Something seemed off to me the whole while. They speak of you with such familiarity. Even when they were terrified of you."

"They do?" I asked quietly.

"You're not calling them a man or a woman any more, either," he said, the bitterness palpable in every syllable. It didn't sound angry, though. More sad. "They trust you."

I looked down, shame eating at me in little, sharp-toothed bites. Taunting me for the mild hope I was vacillating around, that this man might not shoot me. Even though I'd already deduced that was what I deserved.

"It would have to be so," he said, fingers clenching around the grip of the pistol. "Of course. I *would* be forced to do something this vile. I've been waiting, hoping, for years that they might move on. Honestly, I'm not certain if there's a part of me that rejoices in the thought of killing the man replacing me in their heart… and that's the truly disgusting part of all of this."

He stood and pointed the loaded gun at me.

"It doesn't matter what promises you make to me," he said, tears boiling at the edge of his eyes. "You could renounce your faith, renounce the Ministry, swear to me you're in love with Dar. None of it would matter. They'll take you apart as soon as they would anyone else to get at your secrets. They'll use something you care for against you. They're looking for you, you know. They are *certain* you're dead, and they're already interrogating people, trying to find you. They'll find this place soon—your Senior Inquisitor in particular is already looking into the Physician, and he has sworn to take me apart bone by bone himself until you're found. He seems *especially* fixated on finding you."

"No…" I said quietly. I didn't want to imagine what Malachi had been doing in Redcoven, thinking I'd been killed. But I should have been. I should have been, all this time.

"You have no idea how difficult it was for me to leave the city without being surveilled," he said, his hand shaking where it was holding up the weapon. "This is the only chance I'll have. The only chance Darcy has. If we leave now, we might—"

"Stop justifying it to yourself," I said exhaustedly. "If you're resolved, then you're talking to a dead man, anyway. Please… just…" I felt my lower jaw trembling, "… allow me the chance to pray. Let me die well."

He shut his mouth, then nodded, mutely.

I lowered myself to my knees, laid my arms out in front of me, palms-up, and closed my eyes. It took me far too long to decide on a prayer, and in the end, I chose the Sinner's Psalm of

Forgiveness for those sentenced to the gallows. It seemed appropriate.

"God, see this wretched soul in his hour of final repentance," I whispered, even though I knew the canine would hear every word, "and show him… show me… grace. Show me the path to forgiveness, to beginning anew, to remaking. For though I have fallen, for though I have broken the covenant in this life—"

"Dar will never forgive me for this," Cillian hissed quietly. "And they'll be right not to. As before."

"-know that I recognize my failing and beg now for your infinite mercy. I am a sinner, oh God. I have stumbled in the shadows of this world, I have lain down in temptation, and here, now, I pay the price for my broken promises to Thee—"

"Stop," Cillian bit out. "Enough."

There was nothing further he could threaten me with. I continued.

"-and to all the world. I am but a child in the bloodline of Canus. I am fallible. I am weak. I may forget myself, but I will never lose hope. Grant me the chance to live again. To be reborn, washed in the fires of redemption. I will not fail thee again. Please. Forgive me."

I bowed my head and kept my eyes closed. I had no desire to see Cillian's face as I died. I thought, instead, of my father. Not my birth father, a blank face I could hardly fill in… but Father Helstrom. The only father who'd ever truly cared for me.

I thought of Mabel. And Nicholas. And the many others I'd grown up with, some gone now, some still at Ebon Gables. I thought of the stained glass I walked past every day, the cloisters, the gardens, the library…

And I thought of Darcy. And all the things I wished I'd said.

I'm not certain when the tears began to fall. But it seemed pointless to worry about my dignity as a man, now. I'd be nothing but a body with a hole in my head soon. I wasn't crying for myself, anyway. I was crying for them. For what I'd done to them through my actions and what pain I would yet cause.

"Please don't hate me," I said, out loud, I know not why.

"What?" Cillian asked sharply.

"My family," I admitted, keeping my head bowed. "That wasn't for you."

What followed was an eternity. Minutes. Nothing but the sounds of the Lodge and our breathing. Cillian's had grown hoarse, stuttering, and eventually… sobbing. He was trying—gritting between teeth, I could tell—to keep himself in check. I was, too.

Those breaths grew closer together, the setter sucking in big gasps of air, and I knew it was coming. I knew he was building up to it.

I looked up. I don't know why.

"Don't take them with you," I somehow managed to say. "Don't try to flee with Darcy."

"What-why?" he asked, sniffing wetly.

"Because they're better at hiding their tracks than you are," I said. "You'll be found. I'm the only one who was ever able to find them. Let them escape the country on their own, if that's what they want to do."

"I'm just trying to keep them alive," he said, snarling. "Do you know how hard that's been?!"

"No," I answered simply. "But I'm sorry it's been so hard for both of you. Don't lose hope."

He gave a howl, long and anguished, and pitched his gun across the room, staggering and bracing himself on the chair. He sobbed again, turning from me, hiding his face. And stood there, steadying himself on the chair for a long while.

"Are *you* going to kill *me*?" he asked, at length.

"No," I answered still shaking. I dared not stand.

He grabbed for his cane, taking it in a hand and grimacing as he slowly straightened up, looking cowed and small in his own coat, somehow. He wore an expression of pure misery, but when he finally looked to me again, his eyes were afire.

"Do you love them?"

I stammered silently, breathlessly, finally answering with, "I don't know."

"Do they listen to you?" he pressed. "Because Darcy stopped listening to me a long time ago. Deservedly so, but it means I cannot convince them to do things that would be for their own good, even when it is *this clear.* You must convince them to find a ship. Even Carvecia may not be far enough, may not be outside the reach of the Ministry."

"It isn't," I agreed quietly.

"Then Mataa. The bloody Kadrush, *I don't care,*" he snapped. "This isn't like the others, we can't just hush this up, and there will be *no* exonerating them. Darcy does not seem to understand—they think this is all just going to blow over or be something they can hide from. They're wrong, and I don't know how to convince them how dire it is. You *must.*"

A sound outside caught both of our attention. The creak of a gate. I knew it to be the gate that led out to what was probably a garden in the summer. It also led up the walkway.

"*Run,*" he pressed softly but desperately. "Please, for the love of God, if you truly believe in him. Do what I didn't. Run away with them. Get Dar somewhere safe. Take care of them. As I failed to."

He was gone before I could manage to say anything.

13

SCAPEGOAT

Cillian must have passed Darcy on his way out of the Lodge; there was only one door in or out. I can't imagine what they might have said to one another, or if I'd ever see either of them again. They could have left me there, still kneeling in that room, and it would have been hours, maybe even days, before I'd think to leave on my own. I was hardly even on earth. My entire being was a fog, drifting between exultation and complete despair.

I'd been so prepared to die. The fact that I was still drawing air through my lungs still in *this* lifetime, had a sense of myself, and would not yet meet my Maker... I kept questioning it. Waves of relief and then gut-clenching fear assaulted me one after another.

Death would have been a release from my troubles, albeit not one I'd been looking for. In a few minutes' time I'd been forced to make peace with it, and now I was returning to my present tribulations. It was jarring.

When I eventually heard the pound of footsteps on hardwood floors, it sounded as though it were through water.

It was Darcy. At some point I looked up dizzily and I could

just barely make them out. The whole world was ringing like I'd gotten too close to a church bell at noon. Their mouth was moving, but I couldn't make out the words. Their hands were on my shoulders, but I couldn't feel them.

Focus. I was alive. Cillian had failed to kill me, either out of compassion or loss of nerve, but it hardly mattered. I was *alive.* That was the miraculous truth.

But also... I was *alive*. And now, I had to contend with the situation I was in. I had to make unbelievably difficult decisions, choices with no good possible outcomes. Just as Cillian had said.

I had to break the promises I'd made to my family, my faith, my God, *myself...* or I had to fulfill those promises and betray Darcy. These had always been the options put before me on the table. It's just that until these past few days, I'd never questioned what was right to be done. I'd begun to think something in this case was missing, long ago. But never that the entirety of what I knew about the Heart Thief might be *wrong*.

And what if it *wasn't* all wrong? What if Cillian was wrong or Darcy was lying to me?

Something fell into its groove in my mind, a certainty—such a rarity for me of late, I clung to it immediately. *Enough*. Enough of wondering when I could ask. Enough of allowing things to go unsaid. I had nearly died for this—more than once now—and so had Darcy. To Hell with playing games.

Cillian was right about many of the things he'd said, I was certain... but on one point in particular. Darcy might need to be *forced* to consider their own well-being. And in this case, it didn't just concern their life, or even mine. There were innocent people in Redcoven getting involved now. My Father at Ebon Gables.

I needed answers.

Hands seized me by the shoulders, not aggressively but firmly, and guided me unsteadily to my feet. I hadn't known the feline could be so strong, but I was moving somewhat under my own power, as well. I just couldn't seem to talk yet. They were asking me questions I couldn't really hear, let alone answer. But I let them walk with me all the same, one arm slung down over my lower back, ushering me forward.

We were in the main sitting room, and they'd placed a cool cup of water in my hand. I stared down at it for a while, before lifting it to my mouth to drink. Only then did I realize how much my body was shaking.

"Isidor, will you look at me?"

I blinked, lifting my gaze to find Darcy standing right in front of me, clearly waiting for me to answer. I blinked again, rapidly, then reminded myself this was real, they'd been sharing this place with me for days, it was borderline normal now for the Heart Thief to be in the same room with me, looking at me imploringly, like I was a friend they were concerned for...

Because I was, wasn't I?

"I'm sorry," I mumbled. "That knocked me for a loop."

"No, no," they said softly, reaching up to my hands again to tighten them around my cup. "It's fine. Drink. Your nose looks dry. Did you just wake up? You're not—"

They stopped speaking suddenly, as their eyes roved over me. I was sipping the water by then, but when I realized where they were looking, I lost my grip on the tin cup and it clattered to the floor, spilling its remaining contents at my feet. I clutched at the fur on my chest, my other hand moving up over the back of my neck, self-consciously.

I'd been sleeping without a shirt on again.

They looked at me, muzzle slightly parted, then shakily reached a hand forward to brush over where the fur creased below my ear connected to my neck. I couldn't help it, when they hit one of the raised lash welts, I winced.

"Oh, my God," they bristled, twisting to stare on the window with a menacing curl of their muzzle that revealed the white tips of their fangs, "did he hurt you? How?! That coward! I'll tear him a new arsehole, I'll run him down on the bloody horse if I have to-!"

I grabbed their wrists and tugged them towards me, shaking my head vigorously. The gesture seemed to shock them—I'd almost never initiated contact between us—but they didn't resist. Only simmered down from angry to confused.

"He didn't do this to me," I corrected them quickly.

Their brows lifted as their paws moved over my neck and shoulders, doubtless catching the edges of the raised, reddened skin even beneath all my fur. I hadn't bothered to look at myself in a mirror yet, despite there being one in the bedroom, but I could *feel* how swollen and tender the flesh was. They'd noticed it even beneath all of my fur.

"Then, how—" they winced as their eyes traced one of the particularly loud and angry marks that wrapped around my collarbone. "You're *covered* in them."

"I did them to myself," I admitted.

The expression of bewilderment, and then hurt that passed in quick succession over their features was more painful to witness than the marks had been to endure. They crinkled their nose up and yanked at my grip, and I let them go, my skin overly warm on every inch of where their body heat had bled into my palms.

"Why?" they demanded. "I worked so hard to get you well, Isidor! I'm no physician, but damn it all, I've been trying!" They turned a few times, making to move away from me but not settling on where, until they finally stomped over towards the small table we'd been sharing, leaning on their palms over it, their thin shoulders quivering. "I wanted you to leave here well, and unharmed… and *not* just because of how it would look. I genuinely just wanted to know you were alright before we parted ways this time!"

I tipped my head down. "I was at death's door when I came

here, and that's twice now you've chased Cillian off. I'm alive because of you. You've no idea how grateful I am."

"This doesn't seem very bloody grateful!" they said, spinning and gesturing helplessly at my state. "What is this, some... some religious rite, I have to assume?"

I eventually nodded, then said, "It's a form of penance. Suffering can cleanse the soul of sin when no other remedy is available."

"I don't think God wants you to suffer, Isidor," Darcy said, voice tired and small. "The world inflicts enough of that on us already. It's one thing to suffer *for* something... but this? What makes you think you deserve something this terrible?" And at that, they looked up at me, knowingly, their jaw set and their eyes glossy. "Is being here with me so awful?"

"No," I said quickly, "but...I..."

"I know you're attracted to me," they said after giving me ample time to say it myself and proving themself to be the more courageous in the end. "I'm attracted to you, too. I'm not... being silly, this time. In fact, I wasn't last time, either."

"You'd said—" I began.

"Just because neither of us is looking to court doesn't mean we can't be drawn to one another against our better judgment," the feline sighed. "Attraction isn't always rational and denying it at this point would be dense. So, let's get that out of the way. We're adults. We can exercise self-control. We *have* been."

I spent the next few seconds too stunned to form a response. The fact is, while I should have been able to admit how enthralled *I* was, I hadn't actually known the feeling was reciprocal. The admission began filtering through my memories like illumination into a dark room, casting so many things in a different light.

I think that's when I began to change how I saw... all of this.

"Is the thought of that so revolting to you?" they asked shakily, wrapping their arms around their midsection. "That you'd have to hurt yourself to feel better about it? Is it because I'm… not a woman? Or not canine? Not 'pure'?"

"I don't think that," I stammered, wanting to cut them off because each guess seemed to be making them shrink even more inwards on themselves. Like they were confirming their own shame.

And why wouldn't they be? According to doctrine, they were right. And I'd spoken about my Faith enough with them by now to deduce they knew our Tome. They knew where they fell in God's echelon.

"Please," they said bitterly, "don't bother to deny it. I've done this dance before. I know the steps. I know who I am and what value I hold in that book of yours."

"I have my own thoughts!" I belted out, more loudly than I'd intended and certainly more forcefully. The statement didn't even make any sense out of context, so I rushed to clarify. "My father taught me to… to question authority when it feels… wrong. Men are fallible. Even the Church. That's why *we* exist to begin with. The Ministry. To question power, to interrogate… to *self*-interrogate, if we must. And I… I do. I have questions. I have *so* many questions!"

The feline's fur settled back along the edges of their cheeks, their ears lifting back up slowly, trepidatious.

"I don't know how to answer them all, yet," I said desperately, "or how I'll settle these… crises… these *contradictions*. There *must* be a pathway towards truth I just haven't found yet. But I know I am not revolted by *you*. I'm revolted by *myself*."

"Because you're attracted to *me*," they insisted. "Because men like you aren't supposed to have designs on people like me."

"Because you haven't *consented* to being a part of my yearnings!" I said vehemently. "Because we are on opposite sides of the law, and I was hunting you not a week ago—because I could not, even if I wished to, *ever* properly court you! God, Darcy, there are *so* many reasons. *Good* reasons."

Their fingers visibly twitched and shifted where they were clutching at their own midsection, arms crossed over their chest still in a defensive posture. "I don't… mind… being yearned after by you."

"I didn't *know* that!"

Their defensive posture stiffened even further. "I tried to talk to you about it. But honestly, I thought it was rather obvious, and you seemed settled on ignoring it. I thought you knew what you wanted."

"Never assume that with me," I said with an exhausted exhale. "I have no courtly experience save what I learned in training. I know how to shadow a man who might be having a dalliance at a party or question servants about their Lord's vice habits. I don't understand any of *this*. And it's mad, you realize that, yes? Even you know that, you must, you rebelled against the idea of there being flirtation between us when I first accused you of it."

Their hands plucked at their waistcoat beneath the oversized winter coat they were still wearing. They were having trouble maintaining eye contact with me, and when they spoke again it was in a murmur, "Well I don't… why does that have to matter? I know nothing—none of whatever this is, this odd warmth and tension between us—none of it will matter when we leave this Lodge. I just thought we'd enjoy it while it lasted. Cross no lines that matter. We don't need to mean any of it, in the end."

"I don't know how to *be* that way, Darcy," I emphasized. "I mean most things I say and feel, and if those feelings persist, they *matter* to me. I can't just play around in the sand with something like this… I-I've never courted before—"

"This isn't courtship," they said with a sigh.

"Flirtation, then? I hardly know," I said, voice thready. "You didn't want me to call it that."

"Because you accused me of seducing you. Which I haven't. Ever. Done."

"I don't think either of us *meant* to do it," I said, raising my voice a little to put some strength into it, "but we *have* been. By God, Darcy, even Cillian sees it. What would you prefer to call it, then?"

Their eyes flitted back over to mine, pupils shrunken to pinpricks. "Cillian? What did he say? Did he accuse you of having designs on me?"

"I wouldn't call it an accusation," I said, slumping. "I suppose… envious? But not angry. It's bloody hard for me to make out what's happening with the two of you because I have no *context*. You both talk around me and talk *about* me like I'm not fully a part of this torrid thing now. I'm left to fill in gaps on my own, and I'm rather good at it, but honestly, it's frustrating."

Darcy had nothing to say to that, only continued to stare at the ground, so I pressed. It was time to buckle in on the point.

"Cillian just tried to kill me for the second time this week."

But that got Darcy angry again, immediately. Their crinkled nose turned into a full-on snarl, and they began to make for the door. "I *am* going to run him down—"

"He's scared for you," I called out, stopping them once they'd rounded the table. "He's worried he's going to have to watch you be executed, and he's not alone."

They turned to eye me from just over the oversized collar of their coat, fingertips resting on the tabletop lightly, like they were still ready to spring away.

"You said it yourself," they said quietly, "the punishment for my crimes will be the same regardless of whether or not they add more on."

"If you *committed* those crimes, Darcy," I pressed, slowly rounding the table to make my way up to them, face to face.

I tried to take their hand and they let me, their fingers loose and a little chilled in my grip, but they persistently refused to look up at me.

"Darcy," I leaned in, "please. I'm begging you. Enough with the games. Did..." I tried to steady my nerves, closing my hand around theirs tightly, "... *did* you steal the Heart of Faith?"

They didn't answer me.

"Darcy, for the love of God," I craned my muzzle down to force them to look me in the eyes, inches away. "People have *died* over this."

"More than you know," they said, barely above a whisper.

"What does that mean? Did you steal our holy relic or not?" I asked, putting power in my voice. "You owe me an answer on this. It's why all of this has happened and it could determine more people's fate than just your own. I'm not asking about accomplices; I just need to know if *you* had anything to do with it or not. Because if the Ministry has the wrong name on that bloody line..."

They finally looked up at me. From so close, the beauty of their eyes was nearly blinding. But when I saw the answer that lay there, lost, small, and confused, my heart sunk down through my chest to the floor.

"Darcy, oh my Lord," I choked. "How could you let me think you did it all this time?!"

"I never said I did," they insisted weakly. "You assumed. I told you I didn't know where it was."

"That's a lie of omission, don't give me that!" I stepped back, putting my head in my hands. "You never contradicted me—you let me believe it! You denied killing those men, why not deny the theft if it really wasn't you?"

"Because I'm not ashamed of being a thief," they said. "But I'm not a *murderer,* Isidor. I don't want anyone to get hurt over objects, no matter their value or importance. It's not worth it."

"It didn't fit the pattern—*God,* it didn't fit—but I kept telling myself you'd not keep something like that from me! You know what this means to me!" I turned my back on them, walking the few feet to the window, staring out the frosted glass. It looked sunny outside, but the melt had stopped. Icicles clung to the trees like ornaments. It must have gotten cold again today.

"You've… you've figured it out, haven't you?" Darcy asked quietly, hope threaded through their voice.

"You issued that challenge to me in bad faith," I growled. "I was factoring in the Heart of Faith. It didn't quite belong; it *never* quite belonged. How was I supposed to make sense of the crimes altogether with bad information?"

"Isidor?"

Their voice beckoned me. They'd moved over towards the fire, slowly sitting down on the elk hide rug. "It's warmer here, and you're hardly dressed. Please sit with me?"

They wanted us somewhere better lit, I realized. I couldn't say why—maybe to read me better—but I didn't put up a fight. I wanted to look them in the eyes while we talked about this.

I moved over to the rug and sat down directly opposite them, crossing my legs, and for once not sparing a care for my state of undress, the way my stomach folded when I sat, or any of my other many, many imperfections. Perhaps because Darcy had admitted their attraction to me, it eased the anxiety briefly. Or more likely, because in the face of what we were discussing, things like vanity and shame seemed unimportant.

We took a moment to sit in the heat and crackling light of the hearth, freshly stoked by Darcy this morning. It was still early, so this room would be sunlit in time. But for the moment, this was the brightest place in the room. Darcy looked radiant… and guilt-stricken.

"Is this my Confession?" they asked, trying to sound cheeky. It didn't quite come off.

"I'm not a Priest," I said. "Or an Inquisitor. And even if I was, I wouldn't take Confession from you. We're too close, and I have my own motives for wanting answers. It wouldn't feel right any more. But if you mean to ask will this… will this stay between us? Yes. Insofar as I can keep it so."

"Even you think they're going to pry this out of you some day," they deduced quietly.

"I don't know," I said, "but I know some of the ways they might try. And I'm not arrogant enough to assume I'm made of stone."

They brought in a deep breath, then let it out slowly. "Alright," they said at length.

"All of the art, curios, cultural relics, even the jewelry you take," I began, "are foreign. Or were, at some point."

They nodded.

"Those earrings you're wearing right now, and that chain belt?" I looked from their ears down to their waist. "Those are Huudari, but not just Huudari, they're from the Chavanasi, specifically. Near the inland sea that stretches up towards the Desert of Glass. There are a lot of lakes closer to the mountains there, if memory serves, and you said you grew up near a lake. Is that where you're from?"

"That's… quite the deduction," they said with the barest hint of a nervous smile. "I didn't think you'd land on that just from a few pieces of jewelry and a story I told you. You're rather brilliant, you know."

"I… no," I flushed in my ears, I was certain, and brushed off the compliment. "It's because you kept it. You chose to keep *that* jewelry and I happen to know its provenance. It was in the ledgers. A set of red gem-inlaid crescent earrings and a trailing chain belt. Once in the collection of Earl Davidson. You took nothing else from his collection and went through considerable trouble for it. There were *much* more valuable pieces in that curio cabinet. I saw the report."

"And…?" they pressed.

"And none of *them* were spoils of war," I continued, "or colonial seizure, or taken during the last Huudari Crusade, or gifts to the Amurescan Crown from rival Clans or Tribes involved in pillaging. *Everything* else you've ever stolen that I had in those ledgers—I've committed them to heart by now—was." I leveled my gaze at them. "You only steal what's already been stolen... or at least what you see as being stolen."

Their smile blossomed slowly to full bloom, and with it a peace settled over their eyes, the like of which I'd never seen on their face before. "I knew you'd figure me out," they whispered.

"Do you even sell what you steal on the black market afterwards?" I asked. "Wouldn't that negate the point? I am genuinely trying to make sense of it."

They shook their head. "I'm commissioned, usually," they said. "Brokers, in-betweeners... when someone wants something reclaimed, there's a network of people like me and more traditional thieves who can potentially get it for them. That's where I started, but I got a reputation quickly for low-bidding jobs that suited me, and now they come to *me*. I only charge what I need to survive and a bit extra for the frivolities and pleasures of life, I'll admit, but I've taken on jobs for less or nothing sometimes, too. Not everyone can afford to reclaim what they've lost... if they're even lucky enough to be alive to do so."

"And you kept that jewelry because it came from where you were born," I said. "No one to return it to?"

"No," they answered simply and curtly.

"Wearing it is foolish," I pointed out. "It's a well-known and unique piece. I identified it immediately."

"I don't care," they said. "I wasn't permitted to keep anything from my homeland when I came here. They can hang me in it."

I sighed. "You know, the families that purchased most of those artifacts, art and so on... most of them weren't involved in what happened to the people they were taken from. Most of those things have been in this country for longer than those people have been alive."

They smiled wanly. "I also do not care about that. It isn't as though the Pedigree, or wealthy Tradesmen, or the collections, or museums they were held by *needed* them. And they'll mean more to the people or the descendants of the people they rightfully belong to."

They leaned in, nearly nose to nose with me. I held my ground, but it was hard when I could literally feel their breath on my whiskers, and their subtle scent filled my nostrils.

"Each of these things I've reclaimed," they said, "was taken originally under duress, or violence, or traded by people who had no right to it in the first place. Sometimes they were taken from *graves*, Isidor. Dug up and pillaged from the resting dead. They wait here, to be reclaimed," their voice faded softly at that, "returned to the people who love them. They aren't just exotic curiosities meant to be *gawked* at. That incense burner that I took from the Hudson Estate? That was from a shrine. A holy relic, like your Heart. It was taken during the last Crusade. The Hudsons were using it in a privy."

I swallowed. "I know. I was alarmed when I first arrived and found it wasn't under lock and key. That's why I moved it into my quarters and put it in a lock box. Why did you warn them, by the way?" I asked, befuddled. "You don't always, and I can't find the pattern for the times you have."

"I send letters sometimes," they shrugged, "to inform them what they 'own' is stolen, in the hopes I'll prompt them to give it up willingly or move the item into storage, where it's usually *easier* to get at. Honestly, you'd be surprised how many times the family will just leave what I'm after in plain sight, away from their other valuables, presumably so that I'll only pilfer the one thing I have my eye on. Most of them know what they have is stolen. Some of them even feel bad about it."

"Right, but the odds are also good they'll lock the item down more securely," I said, "like I did."

"I'm better with locks than I am at scouring an entire manor home without being noticed," they said. "Like, say, having to check *every* single privy in an enormous house like that, rather than singling out the one bedroom it's likely to be in..."

I grumbled, audibly enough that it prompted a chuckle from them. "I'm sorry, but that was predictable," they said. "The Hudsons had no house guards. It was the House Templar's quarters or the main safe, and your door was easier, so I tried it first. Good thing, too, I got my eyes on their ancient behemoth of a safe. Would *not* have had the time, what with how much of my window I spent in the garden with you, instead."

"Why did you stay at my side so long?" I asked. "That part never made sense to me. You could have begged off without looking suspicious if you'd just said you had a task to attend to or something..."

"I, ah," they toyed with their own fingers in their lap, playing with the tassels on their belt. "I liked it... the moment was peaceful, you know? You had no idea who I was, I didn't really know you well, then. But I had this young, strapping fellow beside me in a beautiful garden, the doves were singing—"

"My head was in your lap," I said wryly.

"-that too," they concurred, clearing their throat. "I don't know. It was rather... romantic? Not in the courtly sense, you know. Like poetry. We were enemies, but able to share that moment. There's something very compelling about that."

"I swear, you're in my head sometimes," I murmured. "I had the exact same thought."

They drew their knees up to their chest, their tail flicking behind them, where it protruded from their oversized coat. When they spoke again, it was timid. Demure, even. "I was drawn to you even then, I think. I'm not certain if I'd go so far as to say it was God, or fate, but something..."

"Why not?" I asked softly. "God puts people in our lives for a reason. Our paths were meant to intersect. And I'm starting to understand why."

"Oh?" they blinked at me owlishly.

"If you aren't guilty of this crime, Darcy," I said, "that means someone else is."

They seemed disappointed in my response, for some reason. But I persisted. "I'm hurt that you would keep something like this—something you knew I was passionate about, that meant so much to me—when you care so much about other peoples' relics being returned to them. But more than anything, I'm confused. The Heart of Faith was forged in Amuresca. It's a tablet of our doctrine. It's at the center of a religious pilgrimage —it belongs *here*."

Their muzzle creased in a frown, and I knew what they would say, so I anticipated them.

"I know it was forged from the smelted remains of a foreign spear," I said. "That's an integral part of the story of it."

"Well, the story behind it is..."

I went on, "That spear was lodged in the body of our Holy Patriarch, lost in one of the wars with the Kadrush. I don't know... maybe you don't know this part. They displayed his body, impaled, over one of their port settlements..." I spoke through my teeth, "... next to rotting whale carcasses, and amongst the other remains of his Tribe, before eventually moving the spear to their Kharne's hold, where it remained for centuries, until our Knight Templar and their holy armies took that city and reclaimed the only remnant left of our Patriarch. The act of melting down the spear was meant to symbolize the rebirth of his soul into something more hopeful. Canus died for us, and because he was never properly laid to rest, he was never able to ascend. You can claim the iron itself was stolen, I suppose. But there is a deeper meaning, a meaning integral to our people, to our *faith*, and the Heart is the symbol of that."

Darcy had been listening, and waited until they were certain I was finished to speak again, slowly. Uncertainly. "I'm sorry, I... I knew the story. I'll admit, I didn't really understand it. There are different versions, you know, depending on who you talk to. And where they call home."

"Well, that's the one true tale," I said finitely.

"To you. But thank you for explaining it from your perspective," they said, their tone patient and polite, and very obviously coddling me. I'd be offended, but honestly, I didn't want to fight with them over a history lesson. "Your passion does you credit, Isidor."

"Would you agree," I breathed out, "that the Heart belongs to our people, then?"

"Based on everything you just said," they said, "and the context of the other things I've heard about it… yes. I would agree so. I've never heard of anyone else laying claim to it, anyway. The Kadrushian clans debate your version of the story, you know. But all the same, I don't think they see the plate as particularly valuable, or authentic. I did more than a bit of research and asking about my… circles… on it, when I first learned I was accused of stealing it. Although it bears saying, I am not Kadrushian, so my opinion means very little in the grand scheme of things."

"Then why would you want that as part of your legacy?" I implored. "As things stand, you'll go down in history as the thief who took the very heart of our holy pilgrimage, the soul of our Forefather, from us."

They were staring into my chest, not pointedly but distantly. And their eyes had begun to grow fearful. "I didn't realize the Templar would become involved in this. I just thought it was another spoil of war. Pig iron melted down into a plate with some writing on it."

I tried not to bristle at the description of it. "No," I uttered. "It is *far* more than that to us."

"I'm so sorry, Isidor," they said plaintively, their fingers worrying at the coat bunched in their lap. "When I first heard through one of my contacts that I'd apparently been responsible for this—that they'd pinned a theft on me I hadn't even known of, I—I just thought it would be an impressive mark on my resume. Help me get future work, and maybe go down in history as a famous caper. It's not even the first time it's happened. They've attributed quite a few thefts to me I wasn't responsible for."

"That doesn't explain why you kept it from *me*," I gritted out. "I thought we were trying to trust one another. Even Cillian was only *guessing* that you weren't responsible, when he spoke to me of it. Have you been lying to him, too?"

"Again, I wasn't *lying*, exactly—"

"Horse shit!" I exclaimed, surprising them. "Enough of this, Darcy, I implore you. You're keeping something from me, even now. I can see it. You have a tell."

"What?" they sat bolt upright.

"You stare at your hands when you're being duplicitous. Toy with whatever's closest. Usually parts of your outfit. You'll forgive my saying so, but it's very feline. It's one of the basics they tell us to look for with your kin."

They narrowed their eyes, muzzle tightening. "Don't go Inquisitor on me. That's fucking *rude*."

"I can hardly help my training," I said pointedly. "And remember, you promised me you wouldn't complain once I'd cracked open your mysteries. You're the one who wanted to play this game. No—don't pout—" I reached for their chin, not grabbing, but tapping it back in my direction. "Look at me."

They did, albeit with a glare.

"What else are you hiding?" I pushed. They needed to be pushed, I reminded myself, even though it was making me feel uncomfortable. They could *die* over this, and I was starting to understand that their misdirection and playing games with me during this whole mess was as self-destructive as it was frustrating and dangerous for me and everyone else involved. "I don't think you're a selfish person by nature," I said. "Not based on everything else I've learned about you so far. So, I *have* to believe you have another reason for toying with the truth all this time. This isn't just about bragging rights or your infamy as a thief, is it? There's something more. You said more people had died. What did you mean by that?"

"Damn it all, Isidor," Darcy scrubbed their hands over their face, speaking from between their fingers. "This would be so much easier if you were just a big, simple, *stupid* man."

"Spit it out."

"I can't!" Darcy said, throwing their hands down on their thighs with a clap. "That's the rotting root of it, you fool! The truth doesn't always set you free, Isidor. Sometimes *it kills you*."

"Who else has died?" I demanded.

"A… contact of mine," Darcy said miserably. "A fellow I really liked. One of yours. Excommunicated, I think you call it."

"An ex-clergyman?" I blinked, adjusting to the news slowly. This had to be it. What they'd been keeping from me the other day when we'd found the letter. "Priest, monk, lay-monk—"

"I think he was a Priest in the country somewhere," Darcy said. "He didn't talk about this time in the cloth much, not to me. I went to him soon after I heard about the Heart. He was working in the underground antiquities market, verifying different ancient coinage. He was learned, and I think it was just something he did for extra income for his family. I don't know what reason there was for him for being cast out of the Faith, but I know he'd married a woman, a widower, which wouldn't have been allowed if he still wore the collar. He would talk to me sometimes. He was always nice." They looked to me, swallowing. "He had a lot of questions, too."

"Alright. And he's dead?"

They nodded after a few moments, tucking their muzzle into the crook of their own neck, eyes slipping closed. "It's my fault. I got him involved in all of this, because he was the only person I knew who'd understand much about a holy relic."

"Darcy," I said, "I'm already involved. Whatever you can tell me now can only protect me. Whoever actually did this is still out there, I need to know *everything* I can."

"No!" they bit out, turning their snarl on me. "Because the moment I tell you what he found out, you're going to do the *exact* same bloody thing he did! You said you were going to stop investigating this case!"

"You could hang for this!" I nearly shouted. "Don't you give a damn about that?! If you didn't *do* this—"

"I could hang for the crimes I *did* do!" they shouted right back. And now, suddenly, it was a real argument. And I didn't think I earnestly had the stomach for that. Apparently neither did they, because they tucked their ears back and lowered their tone after a further moment. "What does it matter, Isidor? Honestly? I thought at least this way, when I was eventually caught, I could... write something. A book, if I have time. At least a long letter. Read it from the gallows or pass it off to someone who might care. Maybe you," they said, tentatively reaching out to take my hand again. I was too aghast to stop them. "It's like your monk... the one who hid herbs in the mountains? I might not be appreciated in my time, but maybe in the future, people will look on what I did and at least tell stories about me."

"Is that why you're forging a friendship with me?" I asked, feeling sick. "So that I'll tell your story when you're gone?"

They didn't answer. But that was enough.

"Cillian was right," I said, shaking my head feverishly, "you have *no* thought for your own well-being. No. No, Darcy, I won't... I won't be a part of this. I won't."

I stood, the world swaying slightly as I did. I knew I wasn't sick any more, I was just light-headed from the anguish of the morning. Overwhelmed. I staggered over to the table, and felt Darcy spring up behind me.

"Where are you going?" they cried out.

"Leaving," I declared. "I'm leaving. Where are the rest of my things? My weapons? You promised you'd return them to me—"

"No, please," Darcy begged, "not like this. Isidor, I know I'll never see you again—"

"If you won't give me answers, I will *find* them myself!" I snapped, spinning to face them. "I will not be an onlooker to your drawn-out *suicide*. I will not watch them hang an innocent person, just so you can have a *book* written about you!"

I felt their hands at my sides, and then my chest, and then my shoulders, and soon they were leaning into me, clinging to me. "Please, please don't! God, you'll find your way into it just like he did, and then they'll—"

"Who?!" I snapped.

"I don't know, Isidor, but he's dead, and so are two of your people! I didn't even know until you'd told me, Astolfo and I just thought the Templar who'd moved it were part of the coverup, we didn't know they were *dead*. It's even worse than I thought..."

"Calm down," I breathed out, gently gripping their slim shoulders and giving them an assuring squeeze.

"They were bringing the tablet to the Ashmedrian University Campus when it went missing," Darcy said between halting breaths, their entire body quaking against mine. Guilt assaulted me—*I'd* put them in this state, forcibly. Something had them absolutely *terrified*. But now they were talking.

"I... I thought I could find out who'd actually taken it through my contacts, but it didn't... nothing I was learning made *sense*. No one even seemed to know it had been moved, let alone where or when, there was *no* talk of it amongst antiquary circles, *none*! That just doesn't happen with something that storied, that famous. But, that's also another reason. You can't just offload something like that. Not without a very specific buyer, someone intent on destroying it or keeping it hidden away. You can't steal an artifact of that renown without risking starting a *war*. The whole thing felt so wrong. I wasn't the only one who thought so, either. Astolfo looked into it for me. He thought something smelled off, and... and that's when he found out it had been moved. It was in the same church for centuries, right?"

"Right," I nodded, shakily. I didn't like where this was headed.

"They were moving it," they said, their arms braced against my collarbones, face inches away from my chest, but still hidden by it from my angle, "because of a different relic that was found, nearly a decade ago. A different tablet, stone, it was broken, I think... but they'd managed to piece it together. It had writing on it, from the same age the Heart was forged in. They know because of where they found it, I think. It was buried in the foundation of an ancient temple."

"Solsforge," I breathed out. "It fell in retaliation after the Crusade into the Kadrush that claimed the spear. It was discovered buried in a field by a farmer who kept finding old coins and arrowheads, remnants. They unearthed the whole of it when I was ten years old. I remember Father talking about it. I read about it years later. It had the potential to be a holy relic nearly as important as the Heart."

"Astolfo said the... the writing on both—"

"The cuneiform," I filled in.

"Right. So, it should have matched. Everyone knows how old the Heart is. They were trying to compare the two, to verify the stone tablet's age. But there was some kind of issue with the etchings, or copies that've been made of the Heart. They wanted to compare the two side-by-side to be sure."

"Solsforge was verified through Stratigraphy," I insisted. "Soil layers and other artifacts it was found with, essentially. We *know* how old it is."

"So, then. They should have matched," Darcy said. And it was then I realized they were staring up at me.

I looked down into their eyes, as the pieces and the possibilities they held fell together in my mind. I began to dread what they'd say next.

"Of course, we'll never know, because the Heart never made it to the University," Darcy said. "It went missing. And the Templar escorting it were killed, apparently. We didn't know that, I *swear*. I didn't realize anyone else had died over this, let alone men from your Order. That's why I was surprised when you accused me of it. Astolfo was looking into them… into who *they* were… when…"

"How did he die?" I asked, knowing there was no answer that could be fully believed.

"He jumped… fell," they said, their voice cracking, "off a bridge in Auldfuster. His wife was widowed again. Everyone assumes he took his own life, but Isidor, I knew the man," they insisted, "and I talked to his wife. He was *content*. He was starting his life over in his forty-third year, and he'd just formally adopted his stepson, they had plans to move to the country…"

There was nothing I could say. Nothing. I stood there and listened as they trailed off, my mind spinning like a water wheel. But no matter what dark corners I tried to hide my head in, there was one painfully steady beacon—one obvious conclusion any rationally-minded person could take from all of this—and it was gut-wrenching to consider it. But considering it, I was.

"This excommunicated man," I said, at length. "His name was Astolfo? What was his surname? I'm going to look into him as well as the two slain Templar, to confirm all of this."

Darcy crumbled, slipping away from me, and sinking back down onto the elk skin, hands clutched tightly at their knees.

I didn't know how to console them. I understood now why they'd kept all of this from me. But it wasn't going to change what I was going to do.

I knelt down beside them. "Darcy, if this concerns a bad actor from the Church, or God forbid the Ministry, this is precisely what I trained for. What we're meant to put a stop to before it damages the Faith or the country itself—"

"Just stop," the feline whispered sharply, tucking their head against their knees. "If you're intent on dying over this, there isn't anything I can do to prevent you. Just... leave... if you're going. Your weapons are in the drawing room where I've been sleeping, behind the bookshelf."

I glanced at the fire. "It isn't just that. It could exonerate you. And as for the other crimes, there are paths to repentance, lighter sentences, even a... pardon... maybe, if I could pursue the right channels of power—"

"Stop lying," they muttered. "Listen to yourself. You're terrible at it. Even *you* don't believe what you're saying."

"I have to believe in a path forward for you," I said, leaning down closer to them. I wanted to gather them in my arms. My palms itched from the need withheld. "I told you when I first met you. I believe in redemption. Maybe this is His way of guiding us towards that."

"I don't need *redemption!"* Darcy snapped, shouting into their knees. "I need the past to be unmade. I need my life to have been different. I don't know how to move forward with this one. Everything I am..." their voice trembled, "... everything I have ever been has been rewritten too many times already. I don't want to start over again. It's too late for that. I'm already ruined. I can't trust, I can't love anymore, I can't stay anywhere too long or the sadness and the memories catch up with me. I want what I *had*."

I knew what they meant. I knew *who* they meant. I tried not to let the bite of envy embitter me. This wasn't about me.

I wanted so badly to ask them what it was between them and Cillian. How it is they'd been raised knowing one another. Sharing at least some of the same tutors. How they both knew about this place. How it was Darcy had somehow obtained a Pedigree education and understood the circles Cillian moved through. I thought I could put some of the pieces together, but there was one element of all of it that didn't make any sense, and I feared as I had with the revelations concerning the Heart, the answers would be chilling.

Darcy had let on that they'd come to this country young. Very young. If they'd been some kind of Courtesan in their adult years that might explain their relationship with Cillian. But it seemed like they'd known him when *he* was young, too. Especially if they'd been educated together. They looked to be close to the same age.

I could understand why something like this might be far too hard to speak on to any outsider. For either of them. And it wasn't essential for me to know. Not like the truth behind the Heart Theft.

"Your friend," I said, wrapping an arm loosely around one of their small shoulders. "Astolfo? He started over. Probably twice your age. And you said he was content."

"He died," they reminded me.

"Then we'll have to be cleverer about this than he was," I said. "No offense meant to your friend, obviously. He didn't know what he was getting into. We have a better idea."

"'We'?" they echoed back.

"We're both involved," I said. "Of course, I'll keep you appraised. You obviously can't return with me to the Ministry, but—"

"You mean you're not going to demand I flee the country like Cillian is?" they asked, turning in my grip.

"I'm not going to demand it," I said, "but I am going to *beg*. At least get out to International Waters or beyond the Huudari border. It's not the edge of the world, you know. I can even keep up a correspondence with you if we're careful."

The feline looked down to where my arm was loosely

grazing their back, or rather the back of their coat, and leaned into it a little more. "You'd write to me?"

Were they actually going to listen to me? God, Cillian had been right again.

"Darcy, I will do whatever I must to ensure you get somewhere safe while I look into this," I sighed. "And I know Cillian will, too. But that's as far as we can discuss it. You can't *tell* me what your plans are, alright?"

"You're planning for being tortured," they said, leveling the accusation at me bluntly. "How is this any better than what I was doing? Tell me that."

"There is no solid proof that the Church, or the Ministry is involved in this yet," I said. "Only conjecture. There could be countless academics, Pedigrees, foreigners, or zealots who were worried about what this cuneiform study might produce. It's possible the Ministry is looking into it on their own. Maybe that's why they want you so badly."

"Not that badly," the feline said. "Didn't you say you aren't even an Inquisitor yet? It doesn't seem like they were that determined to crack the case if you were the only one seriously working on it until recently. They announced to the world that I did this over two years ago, put out a bounty on my head, made *sure* everyone knew the Heart had been stolen—"

"They had no choice," I said. "The pilgrimage happens once a year. What would they have done otherwise?"

"Replaced it with a copy?" Darcy offered. "No one touches or inspects it closely, right? If they didn't want your holy rituals disrupted, wouldn't that have been wiser?"

"That would have been heresy," I countered.

"They were worried about the *study*, not your pilgrimage. There are bigger things at stake here, Isidor," they said. "The reputation of your Church, of the Ministry itself, if it was a Templar who falsified anything concerning the relic."

"Knight Templar," I corrected them. "It was a group of

Knight Templar who retrieved the spear, and only Knight Templar are permitted to be the keepers of it."

"Those are members of your Order who are also part of the Military, right?"

"Or the Navy," I said.

"That's even worse," they said. "That means it involves the Aristocracy—the Crown, too. Knight Templar have to be—I assume—Knighted."

"They're a bridge," I agreed, my chest sinking, "between the two. Knight Templar serve the Crown directly sometimes, and even more so historically."

"Isidor, this is enormous in scope," Darcy said, wrapping their own arm back around mine. I felt the tips of their fingers near the farthest edges of my lash wounds, and I tried not to think about how it would feel to have them touch me now with no clothing separating us...

Not the time, rebellious mind. *Not* the time.

"Look, to hell with solving this," they said. "Let's just go. The both of us. If we leave now, everyone lives. They won't be able to question you, they won't have any reason to go after Cillian or his friends and family any more. *You'll* be safe because we'll," they paused a moment, then emphasized softly, "both... be far away."

"We hardly know one another," I stated the obvious. "I don't know what it is between us, but—"

"We could find out," they said hopefully.

God, my *heart*. I could hear it hammering, could feel my body aching from the force of the blood coursing through it, I swore I could hear the angels singing in my *soul*—go with them! Was this what God wanted? Was this what all of this had been leading towards? Was this why we'd found one another, and through our ordeal, the truth?

No. Because I didn't know the truth. Not fully. Not in any meaningful way. Not yet.

And further…

"I have family here," I said. "Brothers and sisters. Serving and living their lives for God, a Father who deeply cares for his Parish, and they all deserve to know what happened to me. I can't abandon them to grieve my loss. I can't cause them that kind of pain. And moreover, I still love my Abbey, Darcy. I want to be loyal to my Parish. My God has been good to me. My family—the ones I can truly call that—have been good to me. If there is a rot at the center of the Church I love, or enemies of my faith bent on destroying us, I *must* uncover it. Before this conspiracy harms anyone else."

Their eyes were slipping slowly closed to near-slits. They didn't look angry or even surprised. Just deeply, heart-wrenchingly disappointed.

"I thought you didn't want to start over," I said.

"I thought I'd be alone," they murmured. "I'm always alone when I have to start over. I don't know why I thought it would be any different this time."

When their hand slipped away from me this time, I felt liable to crumble to ash. Everything inside and outside of me ached. I wanted nothing more than to promise them protection…

… but I apparently still had enough sense in me to know the folly in that. There was work to be done, and I was no mad fool from one of their romance novels. I had responsibilities and love for more of the world than just myself and my own wants. I had a family who was missing me, frightened for me, right now. Even new acquaintances like Malachi who were likely blaming themselves for whatever had happened to me. I had a house to put in order.

But then, maybe. Who could say.

"You'll go somewhere safe?" I asked again. "Somewhere the Ministry can't find you."

"As you say, Young Lord," the feline said in an obedient, quiet tone, as they tugged at the laced edge of their sleeves. "Perhaps

Mataa. I've traveled to the southlands before. It would be easier to send a courier there, at least."

I nodded. "I'll send letters, once I have a destination to send them to. You'll need to reach out first."

"Alright."

"Darcy?" I begged their attention with a tap of my large palm against their shoulder.

They turned to regard me. Their eyes had lost some of their light. "I'm here, now," I said.

"Will you stay one more night?" they asked.

I was too happy to see a fraction of the light return to them to question my motives. And I really should have. The reasonable part of my mind was screaming at me, but it was muted by the incessant tempo of my foolish heart. "I shouldn't," I sighed, staring out the window, "Cillian may have been followed."

"He's nearly as good at going unnoticed as I am when he tries," Darcy insisted. "We've been hiding our interactions from your Ministry for years now."

"They're looking for me… they think I'm dead…"

"You've been gone for nearly five days now," Darcy insisted, "if they think you're dead, one more night isn't going to make much of a difference. Besides, best not to prove them right. It's miserable weather out there for traveling today."

I frowned, "It *has* gotten cold again. The melt is freezing. I should at least wait to see if that means another snow is coming in. I'm dreadful on these roads. And I need to find my way alone again. I don't suppose you have a map of the area with markers I could follow? The roads are untended."

Darcy shook their head. "I don't need one. I could find this place blind if I needed to."

"You spent a lot of time here, once," I deduced quietly. "With Cillian? He seems to have no trouble making the trip here and back either."

"The more I tell you, the more *they* may come to know," the feline reminded me. "The sky was gray again this morning. There may be another storm coming. If that happens—"

"I must leave tomorrow regardless," I said. "I'm sorry. I really should return *now,* but I won't do anyone any good if I get lost in a storm again."

Stupid, my mind continued to rave at me. I could almost hear Father Helstrom's voice. *Foolish boy.*

I ignored it.

"Tonight is all we have," I said.

"Then spend it with me," the feline asked boldly and without shame.

I nearly choked, before I could form a response. And when I did, it was a less than eloquent, "What?"

14

BURNING ALTAR

"Spend the night with me," they repeated. When I began to open my muzzle to stammer out I knew-not-what, they clarified, "Just… at my side. We need not do anything beyond what we've done this whole while, if that's what you want. Prepare a meal, read, talk, sleep. I just… I would rather not sleep in that room alone, again."

"The bedroom I'm in, the bed is not fit for two," I insisted.

"I'm small," they said, then got out in front of whatever it was I would have said in response to that, "but alright. Here, then. Can you sleep well enough on the elk skin? I've slept on many a floor in the past, but I don't want to assume you have."

"That should be fine," I said, trying to sound confident as I took in the size of the large fur rug. Big, but still tight quarters. Better than the bed, though.

And I'd only just… well. Those sorts of bodily reactions that I found so hard to control tended to happen at pretty regular intervals, and rarely in-between when I'd actually completed the act. I was probably safe.

"If I'm staying any longer, though," I said, "we're making good use of our time."

"Whatever time we have left together is good no matter what we do with it," Darcy said, leaning their lower jaw onto their own palm. They looked particularly darling when they did it, and I think they knew it.

"That's a line," I said with a wry smile.

"Did it work?" they teased, sniffing a bit.

"You don't have to charm me," I said, scuffing my claws at the rug. "I am already sufficiently charmed."

"You're leaving," they said pointedly. "That seems insufficient to me."

"We can't discuss what we plan to do," I said, clearing my throat softly, continuing the point. "Where we plan to go, who we're going to talk to... but we *can* share whatever information we have with one another. Whatever else you might have learned when you were looking into the Heart, for instance."

"What point is there to you sharing with me?" they asked. "If I'm just to hide out somewhere while you do all the hard and dangerous work investigating?"

"You already did your share," I insisted. "You evaded capture all this time and discovered the most critical facts."

"And now I wait in the tower while you face down the dragon?" they snuffed out through their nose.

"It's no different than what you were doing living on the run," I explained. "Just safer. Farther from all of it. You were *really* walking on blades, continuing your thieving across the countryside while wanted for all of this, you know."

"I wasn't about to let your Ministry curtail my purloining."

"Yes, well," I muttered, "beyond how foolish that was, it was also illegal, Darcy. I understand your cause better now, but if you want any chance of a pardon in the future, that needs to stop now. There are other ways to return cultural relics."

"Not many that are legal," they countered.

"Lay low and let me do my work," I said, "and I promise I'll help you find some way to pursue your passion in the future that doesn't involve literal cat burglary."

"You're less attractive when you're telling me to step back and let a man handle everything that needs doing, you know," the feline groused.

"They *will* hang you," I reminded them sharply. "This isn't tea parties versus shooting parties. Please… please, please… I will get on my knees if it will help. Let me do what I was trained to do while you do what you're best at."

"Flee?" they guessed.

"Evade the law," I said, narrowing my eyes. "You did it well enough when the man hunting you was me. You do *not* want the next Templar who catches up to you to be Brother Malachi. Or, God forbid… Brother Dolus."

That seemed to set them straight. They gave a long sigh, followed eventually by a slow nod.

"Do you think either of them," they asked quietly, "or anyone you know from the Ministry was involved in…"

"No," I said with certainty. "If that even is the case—which we've no proof of, I'll remind you—Brother Dolus has been tending to Ebon Gables for most of the last two years. He travels from time to time, but rarely as far as Auldfuster or the Capital. And Malachi has been abroad. No one else I know does enforcement work for the Ministry, at least not any more. It would be an unlikely coincidence, regardless. There are thousands of Ministry agents, let alone hired secular agents. But that doesn't mean they won't follow their orders, just as I was. And they won't be as inquisitive about the facts. Malachi wants to see you hanged, and Brother Dolus… to be honest, I've never seen him work, but his focus has always seemed to be… efficiency. He'll probably do whatever ends this fastest and neatest."

"Why does that send chills down my spine?" Darcy said uncomfortably.

"It should," I assured them. "It's about time you started taking the threat here seriously."

"Alright, I will," Darcy said, looking up at me. I'd been standing all this time, while they were back to sitting on the rug. I'd been pacing around the table, I realized. It probably seemed manic, but I think all things considered, I should be commended for how level-headed I'd somehow managed to be through all of this. At least externally.

Internally, I was a typhoon.

"*But*," they said, and I could tell by their tone whatever they were about to say was going to be a problem, "I'm going to take you up on your offer."

I blanked. What had I…? Oh, hang it, best to just ask.

"You'll need to clarify," I sighed. "This has been a hell of a morning."

"You said you'd ask me," they nibbled at their lower lip, smirking slightly, "on your knees."

"Really." I said. It wasn't a question.

"It isn't to embarrass you," they said quickly. "I just… no man's ever done anything for me on their knees before. I want to know what it feels like."

I huffed softly, then gestured at them. "You should stand."

They did so, confused. "Why?"

"Because that's the traditional way," I said as I moved easily into a familiar position for me: supplication. They clearly hadn't expected me to actually kneel, let alone with so little argument, but I had no pride left to speak of where this case was concerned.

Besides, I was used to it.

"This is how it would look if you were a Priest or a woman I was proposing to as my intended," I said. "The point is to be at their feet, to humble yourself before them. If you're sitting it doesn't quite work the same."

They stared down at me, wide-eyed and stunned… and if my

guess was correct, a little giddy. They didn't really seem to know what to do with the moment once they had what they'd asked for, but I didn't mind waiting.

"I'm assuming that's what you meant, of course," I said uncertainly. "I'm… not sure what else a man might kneel before you to do. Beg for your hand or pray for you. I suppose plead for his life, but I think we're finally past that."

They snorted out a laugh, shoulders hitching back, one hand eventually coming up to clap over their muzzle. "You are simply," they said between delighted breaths, "the purest, sweetest young man, Isidor."

"I am, I assure you, neither," I muttered. "My purity is… highly in question of late, and I'm far too brash and blunt to have a kind affect. My brother Nicholas was always the charismatic one. The best I can manage is to have good manners most of the time. *Most* of the time."

"I rather like that what you see is what you get, though," they said. "You are who you present yourself to be. Your inner monologue is your… outer monologue. I hardly ever have to wonder what you're thinking."

"There is plenty I think that I don't say," I assured them.

"What are you thinking right now?" they asked. I'd set myself up for that one, I suppose.

I looked down for a moment, considering. "There's a lot in my head right now," I admitted, then went quieter. "Mostly, I'm worried about you."

They touched the top of my head and then lifted my muzzle, their fingertips tracing around to cup my chin as I did. Their expression was soft and warm. "Worry more about yourself, please."

I hummed, closing my eyes, and wonderfully, their palm began to stroke my cheek. It should have felt demeaning or patronizing, given our positions. But it didn't.

"So, I am not your Priest," Darcy said, "or your intended. What *are* you going to do down there?"

"Beg you to pursue a safer and more righteous life," I said all but immediately. I reached up, wrapping my oversized, calloused paws around their wrist, and on an impulse, brought their hand to my face. I heard them suck in a breath before I pressed my muzzle to their fingers in a chaste kiss.

"Please," I begged. "I don't know you as well as I'd like yet, Darcy… but I'm convinced the world is a better place with you in it. God loves you, and He brought us together for a reason. I know *I* will be in misery if something dreadful happens to you. So, think of me, if not yourself."

Darcy gave another soft, hitched breath, and looked down upon me with no words. Only a warm smile, and eventually a shaky nod. I released their hand gently, and they returned it—as well as their other—to both sides of my cheek ruff. They petted and stroked back my ears and stood there before me a while longer.

I wasn't sure what it was about this moment that fed their soul, but I was happy to give it. I had knelt at many altars throughout my life, but theirs was one that I had come to through great turmoil and hardship, and it felt right, it finally felt deserved, to bask in the peace they were offering me.

"I've almost got it—hang on, I said!" I nudged Darcy's shoulder away from me, making what I'm certain was the most ridiculous face—muzzle twisted up in concentration, eyes crossed, tongue poking out—the very image of divine grace.

"You're going to lose it again!" the feline bemoaned, pushing into my personal space and wriggling their hands in around the jar, trying to pry it away from me.

"Well, I certainly will if you keep… doing… that-!" I gasped out in frustration as the honeycomb once again slid away from my prying claws. "Damn!"

Darcy burst out into a fit of giggling laughter. "*Language*, young Knight! My goodness, what would Canus think?"

"Not a Knight. And Canus was a warrior Lord of the ancient wolf tribes," I grumbled, peering down into the too-narrow mouth of the mead jar, "he would've broken it by now."

"Oh, heavens no, think of all the mead you'll waste!" Darcy snort-laughed. "Here, give it to me..."

"Have we really drunk that much already?" I asked as I licked one of my fingers, eyeing the level of the jar. "I don't remember it being that low before."

"Well, a sizeable amount of it's ended up on *you* at this point," they said, peeling back their sleeves to their elbows and flexing their fingers.

"I still don't see why we can't just pour it out—"

"Wasteful!" they accused, once again.

"-into a *bowl* or something," I finished with a glare.

"We'd never be able to get it back in without spilling most of it," they insisted. "We went over this."

"I think I could," I said, with no evidence whatsoever to back up my claims.

"Maybe an hour ago, but—ha! Isidor," the laughed into their own palm, "I don't know how to break this to you, but I do believe we're a bit jug-bitten again."

"*You're* the one who was supposed to shepherd me," I pointed out, not able to muster much irritation, "in your wily..." I gestured about in the air with a claw for some reason, "... court-savvy, worldly ways. You are a *most* irresponsible tutor."

"Mmhhh, well we probably should have eaten something," Darcy hummed, as they eyed the honeycomb eluding us, floating in the half-empty jug.

"When?" I asked after a long pause.

"I don't know. At *some* point today, surely." They held up the bottle once more, and then plunked it down on the floor in front of them, determinedly. "Alright. Pray for me Isidor, I'm going in."

"I am *not* asking God to watch us. I rather hope He isn't paying attention tonight, honestly," I said, glancing once heavenward.

"God sees everything," Darcy said pluckily, "including how much I'm about to show you up."

"I don't see how that's possible," I muttered stubbornly, "my fingers *and* my claws are longer than yours."

"It isn't all about size, sometimes it's about dexterity," they said, wiggling their fingers, and then clenching them, "and besides… no they aren't."

"Oh, Lord," I blanched, leaning in to look at their claws, now extended. I realized then that I'd never actually seen Darcy's claws fully out. "Do you ever…"

"File? No," the cat said proudly. "Not since I was in society, anyway. How do you think I make entry to all those second and third-story apartments? The chimney?"

I'd gone mute. I was transfixed by the curving, pristine, predatory elegance before me. I could imagine them hooking into the fine edges of a brick wall, climbing fences, stone, trees…

… my shoulders. I'd only felt the very slightest prick of the tips of them when Darcy had kneaded those very same nimble fingers into my aching body. They could have torn me apart. They could have, at the very least, inflicted *far* more punishment upon my flesh than they had.

I was staring with my mouth open—had been for some time—and I probably would have continued to do so, except Darcy gave a thoughtful noise that snapped me back to myself.

"… what?" I asked ineloquently, even though I'd clearly been the one making things odd.

They patted my cheek, the claws brushing past the soft edge

of my muzzle as they slid their hand away a moment later. I shuddered. And Darcy smiled.

"Nothing important," they clucked. "I'm just learning more and more about you every day, Young Sir."

I wasn't sure what they were referring to, and I also wasn't sure I wanted to. I watched quietly instead as they wiggled their fingers into the jar as far as they'd go, and then rolled, tipped, and sloshed the contents around, trying to work the comb up towards the mouth again.

"Such an ordeal," I murmured. "You know most of the honey's probably suffused into the mead by now."

"You're even eloquent when you're drunk," Darcy chuckled. "'Suffused'. Besides, that's not the point. I like chewing on them."

"So do I," I admitted, watching them with bated breath as they hooked the edge of the comb. I'd gotten this far. But unlike me, *their* claw hooked in and got a hold.

"Ah—ahhhh-!" they crooned triumphantly. And with a deft tug, the comb lodged in the mouth of the bottle.

"Don't lose it!" I cried.

I leaned in and helped them extract it through the final breach, and we both shared in a moment of elation and cheer, before Darcy licked their fingers and got up, brushing at the mead stains on their trousers. "Alright, I'll get the knife..."

"Get that novella you wanted to start tonight," I said as I leaned back against the warm stone boxing in the sides of the hearth fire. We were already down to sitting on the elk hide rug, the table long since abandoned. It *had* in fact gotten very cold, and the closer we were to the fire tonight, the better.

Darcy brought the plate with them to sit down beside me. "Come on, eat. You haven't all day and it's better than nothing. Regardless of what your plans are once you're back on the road, you need to rest tonight, or you won't make it very far."

I took the plate and sunk my teeth into the offering, waiting until I was done chewing to speak. "Well now that you've said that, you know I won't be able to sleep."

"A good book and a warm fire have always helped me with that," Darcy eased, sidling a little closer to me. "Nervous about traveling that road again?"

"Worried about what I'll say to my kin," I corrected them.

"Maybe you've an ally in your Father?" they offered.

"I never would have considered him anything but," I said stiffly. "I don't think Ebon Gables is involved directly with *any* of this, if it even *is* a Ministry coverup. My Father is retired and has been for some time. I'm not certain how he may have found out about any of this, but he was famously skilled in his vocation when he was still an agent. I wouldn't put it past him. I think I can be honest with him, at least."

"Just promise me you'll be careful, Isidor," they said, leaning their shoulder and arm against mine. "Be cautious with whom you trust."

"I shall," I swore. "But I think I've a good sense for people on the whole. Even if I'm not as worldly as you."

They folded their legs to the side, clutching around one knee, and didn't answer me. They looked small, pensive, and scared. And I understood some of those feelings because I shared them as well. But oddly, being back on task, focused on something I knew how to do, had the training for, the head for, it had helped boil off some of that indecisive self-loathing I'd been grappling with. I had a purpose again. Something external. Something that didn't involve making sense of my own mind and imaginings.

I was worried for my Father, if he'd already been looking into this. But Darcy was right—he was probably more intent on warning me about what I hadn't known. And he was highly competent, if aged. In one of the safest places I knew of. He was likely waiting for *me*. And together, we'd...

Darcy had opened the novella, snaking an arm around the

back of me and leaning even more against my bicep, getting comfortable. "Let's at least read a few chapters," they said. "It'll help us doze off."

I didn't want to say anything, but I didn't actually want to sleep. I knew that was foolish, but sleep meant I'd wake, and it would be time for us to part. I wanted the night to last. I was worried—and it was a worry grounded in reality—that I'd not see Darcy again. Ever. I didn't know where they'd go and I was willingly giving up the trail for the first time in my pursuit of them. It felt anticlimactic.

But there was no other choice left before me. At least I was no longer searching for a direction.

I leaned in to their touch, keeping my hands fixed in my own lap, but allowing the comfort offered. It was a workaround, I knew, but I wasn't violating any part of my code of conduct or the promises I'd made to God and my Father if I merely allowed the companionable touch. I was being unfaithful in my heart, but I was far past the threshold there, already.

Beyond that though, I just didn't entirely trust myself. Darcy—I was convinced—was not so sinfully minded as I. I wanted to believe in my own self-control, I *did*. But we'd been warned *so* many times, especially as young boys, about the dangers of losing our minds to lust. While the thought of Darcy themselves did not disgust me, what I might do with them if unrestrained did. It was hard to consider myself as so untrustworthy a person, but where sin was concerned, men in particular were weak to that sort of carnal madness. I did not want to be that kind of monster.

So, I focused on my feelings of friendship for them and the story. It became a little more difficult when Darcy's palm began stroking my arm or drifted to toy with the white tuft of my tail. I kept reminding myself that it was idle affection. Nothing more. Feline kin were just more comfortable with that sort of thing. Less hung up on propriety.

We switched back and forth between reading aloud, laughing at the poorly-written dialogue and formulaic story. The writer had been prolific in their time, according to Darcy and more focused on quantity of stories than quality. Entertainment for entertainment's sake. The artistry—what little there was to be had—was only evident in some rather clever plays on words and puns throughout. The book was self-aware of how trite it was.

Honestly, I sort of… enjoyed it. I would have liked to read all of it with Darcy, but we began nodding off by chapter six. I can't remember any of chapter seven. Sleep took us.

If I dreamt, I dreamt of them. My sleep was fitful, anxiety eating at me and causing me to stir, stare into the fire for long stretches, and look down at the feline curled up at my side. I was somewhere between the haze of sleep and consciousness, and found myself wondering more than once if waking to see them there—closer and closer to me each time, it seemed—if that, too, was a dream. My dreams of them and the bizarre reality of our shared cohabitation here in the Lodge had begun to share striking similarities.

We had two blankets, but at some point in the evening, Darcy had rolled up in theirs as *well* as my own, the cold of the night penetrating even here, near the hearth. This Lodge had gone abandoned too long. It was hardly habitable any more.

Eventually, my sleep-addled mind reasoned that it was not worth holding on to propriety at the cost of empathy, and I gingerly reached out for the feline and pulled them in closer under the blanket with me. Darcy stirred in their sleep, eyes flickering with night shine as they blinked once slowly at me in the dark. And then they closed the distance between us, curling their arm against me and mumbling indistinctly, their heat bleeding through into mine as they went lax against my body.

We were still separated by clothing and part of their blanket, but that did nothing to stem the euphoric, desperately-needed relief that settled into my bones at the feel of them against me.

I couldn't remember the last time someone had slept beside me. Not this close. And this wasn't... it wasn't a true embrace. Not really. But I wrapped an arm around them loosely, all the same.

It was answered a moment later by a far smaller limb, slipping around my ribs and settling their hand on the small of my back.

It was like I'd been knocked out. I was able to bask in the sensation for a few moments before I took leave of my consciousness again. I don't think I'd ever fallen asleep so quickly.

"Isidor."

I blinked awake, my body jumping as it was wont to when startled out of sleep. My chest felt heavy. Was I having trouble breathing?

No, no, I... someone was on top of me. Not their full weight, but resting against my chest and stomach with half of their body propped up on one arm. The eyes that stared down at me in the dark were feline and familiar.

Darcy was tangled up in the blankets with me, tousle-headed and hazy-eyed, their ears upright and twitching towards the window. After a few moments, they sniffed and settled their cheek back down on my chest, letting their full weight rest there.

"M'sorry to wake you," they murmured. "I thought I'd heard something. Just a bird."

"Oh," I whuffed a little, glancing down my body at the two of us. At some point I'd rolled onto my back, which was common enough for me. But Darcy had either intentionally or unintentionally followed suit, resting atop me now, at least with their upper body. Our legs were tangled up in the blankets below. I could feel their tail curling and uncurling somewhere near my thigh.

I was warm. *So* warm, but otherwise… in control. I did not feel as though I'd take leave of my senses. And this was *easily* the most compromised I had ever been with someone I…

Lord, what to call it. I hardly knew. Someone I harbored an attraction for.

A reciprocal attraction, apparently.

Darcy rose up over me again with a tilt of one arched shoulder blade, their slender figure outlined by the ambient glow of the hearth behind them. When they did so, our bodies pressed together just a bit more. I could feel the jut of one of their hips, the small swell of their belly as they breathed in and out. Those breaths were coming slightly quicker, just as mine were.

They were staring down at me in the dark again, the handsome outlines of their face framing their feline eyes. They leaned down a little more, an inch at most, shortening some of the distance between us and closed their eyes slowly, pressing their nose into the ruff of fur cutting out from the neckline of my shirt. They inhaled.

Was this a dream? I hardly knew any more.

"Darcy…" I said quietly, questioningly.

Their hands came then, traveling up my arms until they could close their fingers around my shoulders where the flesh was still tender. They used their grip there to push themselves up until their arms were supporting them. And then I felt the careful motion of one of their legs as they swung it over me, and settled back down. They were fully atop me now.

Their eyes never left mine.

If this was real, why wasn't I stopping it? I felt frozen. I didn't know what to say, what to do. I just stared at them in mute shock. Or complacency. I hardly knew what my own face looked like in that moment.

They leaned in again and I felt they were searching me with their eyes, the irises flicking back and forth, following any twitch of my muzzle. They were waiting, I realized. For something… anything… from me. And there was a desperation there, a yearning. One I knew very well.

"Isidor…?"

Their voice, soft, plaintive. And now I knew it was real. In my dreams, they had *never* sounded hesitant.

I was shaking. I could feel it in my feet, in my hands, and see it in front of my face in the shudder of my whiskers. I think they saw it too, because they eased back a few inches, worriedly. We'd nearly been nose to nose.

"Isidor…"

"I don't know what to do," I said, because it was all that came to my mind. It was the same thing I'd said in my dream, I realized.

Their body stiffened like a prey animal gone frightened very suddenly, and I worried it was me. But then I saw how their ears shot up. How their eyes went to the window.

"Did you hear—"

This time, I did. I think I'd vaguely heard it before as well, but attributed it to a bird, like they had. But now, no… no, that was closer, was too loud, it wasn't—

Then an answer from farther away.

"That's a call," I said with certainty, my rigid body falling into practiced, almost mechanical motion at the same time as Darcy bounded off me, throwing the blankets aside. I was on my feet almost as fast as they were, heading for the window.

"Is it…" their eyes scanned the frosted window desperately.

"Yes, it's ours," I said, panic rising in my throat. "Two, at least, calling to one another in the woods. They've found us."

"How far off do you think they are?" the feline asked,

hurrying over to the window and staring out the frosty panes. The light filtering in—what little there was—suggested it was very early dawn. Whoever was out there might have crossed ten miles quickly enough if, like Cillian had the last few times, they'd come on horseback. But that still meant they'd left at night.

Which didn't bode well. It meant they were willing to throw caution to the wayside and that they were certain of their convictions. They *knew* somehow that we were here.

Although perhaps not where. I listened again, trying to gauge the distance between whistles on how faint they were. Both parties were hardly right on top of us, but one was farther than the other.

"I don't know," I confessed. "Maybe a mile? The woods here echo when they're empty like this. But snow absorbs sound. I-I'm not sure." I got stiffly to my feet, stumbling over towards the table in the near-dark. My eyes were still adjusting. "I need to… need to get my things and get far away from you. Now."

We'd gathered all of my possessions in the main room last night. Save a few important pieces.

"My weapons," I said as I gathered my bag up, haphazardly throwing a few last things in before pulling the leather cording taut.

"Would you have them, though?" Darcy questioned, as they shouldered into their oversized coat. "I mean, if we go with the story we discussed?"

"Stars, I don't know," I muttered. "If I was able to get at my bag, then maybe those too? On my way out?"

"We'd have to move the book case," they said, "that could take a while."

"Will you leave them here, then?"

"I could… return them to you," they said, stilling as they pulled their rifle down off the wall, "instead, maybe?" Their tone was hopeful.

I looked at them silently for a few moments, then crossed the room towards them. They needed this, I realized. And my weapons were hardly as sentimental to me as my prayer book, my rosary, my bracelet, or the scant few other possessions I had in my bag.

I reached down and gingerly tipped their lower jaw up towards me with the edge of one of my clumsy, oversized fingers. Their features looked so delicate and refined in comparison to any part of my bulky body. I wasn't sure what they saw in me. But I didn't want them to forget it, whatever it was.

What to say? God, guide me. Let me be profound this once.

"*Sano elnistonacarum*," I whispered the sacred prayer for something treasured. "You've led me to question a great many things this past week. Faith is..." I was talking about God again. Well, it was the one subject I had the most education in and always on my mind, so that made sense. "... faith is," I continued, "not blind obedience, as many see it. To the scholars, it's a search for the Truth. That's what Faith is to me. It's what I hope it can be for all people, some day..."

Darcy was looking at me oddly, but expectantly. They'd obviously not thought this was what I was going to say to them before they left, but they were listening. They were a good listener, I realized, as *well* as clever with their words.

I think I really was fond of them.

"You've made me question a lot of," I briefly stammered, "my... most deeply held truths. Convictions I did not think could be shaken. I am upended, I am... in turmoil. I have never been this frightened of myself, or my Ministry, but I... I am glad."

Darcy's eyes widened marginally.

"Hiding from the truth or having it obscured from you," I continued, "can be a pleasant delusion. But it *is* a delusion. It does no good for me to deny what I've learned. And... I like to learn. Even if what I discover is unpleasant. You've opened my eyes to realities I think God wanted me to uncover. He has certainly led you to me. I've never felt so directed, so destined, in all my life." I let out a long breath. "I was worried, all this time, that these changes inside of me were taking me further from Him. From the Truth. But now I know that is not so. I am still uncertain what he means for us to be—you and me—but I know He intends for us to meet again. And we shall."

I cupped their cheek, smiling a little. "And then you may return my weapons to me."

Darcy gave a soft breath and half-closed their eyes, eventually nodding. "You never say what I expect you to," they murmured. "You're hard to anticipate, Isidor of Ebon Gables. Surprising. You make me anxious, but in a way I think I rather enjoy. I think I have you figured, and then…."

"I'm not one of your protagonists," I said quietly and good-naturedly. I ruffled their cheek fur. "Nor are you."

Another whistle pierced the early morning stillness outside, and we both turned our ears towards it.

"Closer," Darcy said softly. "You need to go."

They picked up my wrist and affixed one end of the manacle to it, locking it in place. The last step before I left. As their hand slipped away from mine, I reflexively grabbed for it and squeezed it tightly.

"It won't be long," I said.

They gave a tremulous smile. "Sooner than you know," they promised me.

The air was cold enough to make my throat ache on each inhale. Winter was truly settling in with a vengeance. If I'd left yesterday and tried to make my way back to town, would I have gotten lost again? Waiting had been wise, after all. Even if it *had* also been a convenient excuse.

My mind was in a daze as I stumbled out into the crackling, iced-over snow, the color of the burgeoning morning a dark, somber blue. I couldn't tell if a storm was on the horizon; the sky looked a uniform shade.

The last week felt like one of my dreams. The farther I got from the Lodge, the less real the memories were. Had that truly all happened? Had I imagined any of it? How much of how I interpreted each interaction, each small gesture or the words that had passed between us, was faulty? Biased by my yearnings, my expectations, or my insecurities?

How had Darcy and I gone from enemies, just last week… to whatever it is we were now? For God's sake, when Cillian had accused me of being in love with them, I'd said 'I don't know'. Ludicrous! Insanity! What had I been thinking?!

But then what was this? Physical attraction was one thing—and we'd both confessed to that towards one another by now, although that was hard to square in and of itself—but there was certainly something else between us. Something complex, powerful, and, crucially, unidentifiable to me. Something I had no previous experience with.

I'd learned how to distance myself from the inner conflicts that came from physical attraction. Darcy was not the first person I'd met outside the Abbey that I'd felt those yearnings for. Many a pretty girl would come to pick up wine or trade with us in the nearby village. I'd felt the pull of attraction towards people with pleasing features and sunny countenances since I was a young boy. It was impossible not to.

But usually, I could school myself and discipline my mind with recitation of scripture or, if it came to it, Confession. And attraction in and of itself—as Brother Dolus had actually been the one to tell me many a time—was not sinful. Father Helstrom could be stricter about propriety, but Brother Dolus despite his other foibles, had always been more paws-on-the-ground about assuring us young boys that these things were a natural part of male vigor and would make us good husbands someday with the potential for large families.

My ongoing struggle with lust was one thing, but the feelings—the fact that they occupied my every other thought—I had for Darcy were not entirely down to physical attraction. They simply couldn't be. Something else compelled me about them, fascinated me, wanted me to talk to them. To ask questions, to speak on scripture, on life, on literature, and on their own feelings of the Divine. And they were willing and *able*, a veritable font of unexpected and different knowledge, insights, and inspiration.

There was no denying it. This is what I'd been looking for every time I tried and failed to speak with Nicholas, or one of the other abbey boys, or even my Father. It's not that the old bloodhound wasn't wise and learned, but he was also my *father*. There were certain things I couldn't get up the nerve to question in his presence, and certainly some personal issues that were awkward to broach. What's more, the few times I'd tried, he'd blanched back from the questions and changed the subject quickly. I think it was awkward for him, too.

Perhaps when all of this was said and done, Darcy and I could quiet our attraction towards one another and go on as friends. Either from a distance through correspondence if they didn't feel safe enough to come back into the country (which I wouldn't blame them for) or in person, and if we could clear their name. I wanted to believe it was possible.

I wanted to, but...

Honestly, the chances that we'd be able to earn a pardon for Darcy were, in my estimation, greater than any chance that the two of us might be able to keep our strange relationship—whatever it was—platonic. We'd been alone together in the Lodge for less than a week, and despite being under constant threat of attack by Cillian or the Ministry, we'd still not managed to keep any respectful distance from one another.

Lord, I still couldn't even wrap my mind around... whatever it was that had happened ten... fifteen minutes ago? When we'd woken together in that room, and by the light of the dusky coals, they'd crawled atop me, and I'd let them, and we'd... we'd...

We'd done nothing, ultimately. Nothing that I'd need to confess. We'd laid hands on one another, but we'd been doing that a lot that last day, and that was a problem, it *really* was, but—

I'd reached the edge of the wood line, passing the last of the fences for the horse paddock. That's when I heard another whistle. I lifted my head, ears tipping towards the east. It was clearer now. Downhill. In the direction of where the 'road' was, or rather had been. They'd probably vaguely found the outlines of it, as I had, and were trying to follow it. They were lower, I could tell that much, and I began to remember that it was a steep ascent, a hill, that had done me in on my march here. They were within a mile or so.

A second whistle, farther off. Whomever that was, they were not as close. Spreading out in a perimeter search. They didn't know where this place was, so they were trying to pinpoint it and converge. The whistle ahead of me, the closer one, was punctuated in threes. A call to converge. He'd found the road, he was certain. He was calling the other to join him.

I headed towards the road with renewed purpose and followed it more assuredly in the dawn light. There had never been any cobbling of any kind here; this was a country road, so when it had gone neglected, the woods had encroached quickly. But one could pick through where the undergrowth struggled to take root in tightly-packed, trod-down earth and where none but the youngest saplings grew.

As I walked, I looked back towards the bare forest, lit with gold as though it had been filigreed, as the first rays of the sun hit the icy branches. There was no trace of smoke from the

Lodge, thankfully. Our fire had become meager in the middle of the night. They'd find the place eventually, inevitably. But hopefully by then, Darcy would be long gone.

"Please run swiftly," I said, voice soft.

Another whistle—but this one cut off abruptly. I squinted and turned my head to stare down the overgrown, forested hill I'd reached the apex of. And there through the wild brush, as clear as a silhouette could be, was one of them. Square-shouldered and canine with triangular ears, atop a sturdy horse. He had seen me as sure as I had seen him.

I hardly needed to act exhausted and worn-down by my ordeal out here—I was. Perhaps not in the way my fellows would assume, but that hardly mattered. I brought my claws to my muzzle and gave a weak whistle of my own.

The man spurred his horse with a crop and shouted something I couldn't make out, pushing the beast into a gallop up-hill, poor thing. I tried meeting him halfway, making my way down the pebbly, overgrown, icy old road precariously but determinedly.

I was only certain it was Malachi when a patch of light hit him and illuminated his features for a moment, mere seconds before he made it to me, his horse frothing and pawing to a stop as he leapt out of his saddle, bounding towards me. I stopped and stood where I was, panting into the cold air, and met him in a collision that nearly knocked my breath out of my lungs.

... but it was an embrace, not a blow.

He wrapped his arms around my shoulders in a bear hug the ferocity of which I had never experienced outside of grappling training. I briefly felt my feet leave the ground and one of his shaking, calloused paws move up to cup the back of my skull, fingers sinking into the thick fur there.

"God loves you, Isidor!" he cried out, his voice just on the edge of a sob. "God is on your side! Oh Lord young buck, you are a sight for sore eyes!" He pulled back just enough to be nearly nose-to-nose with me, entreating me to his big, wolfish smile. His eyes were crinkled, but I could see the red in them, fur jagged with stuck ice and dirt.

He moved his other hand up to cup my face, and began laughing, breathlessly. It was almost manic, yet still somehow endearing. I could feel how much this man, whom I'd only met these past weeks, had been scared for me. The good feelings faded to guilt quickly, but I had to remind myself to express that as little as possible. The fact that I didn't know Malachi very well was relevant, now. In a way it hadn't been before.

I had to be careful. For *so* many reasons.

It was achingly hard to actively remind myself to distrust this man when he was nearly breaking down in front of me, clinging to me like a lost a family member.

"I am alright," I assured him, voice rough for any number of reasons. I reached out to grip his arm with one of my hands, giving it a gentle squeeze and allowing myself a smile that thankfully did not need to be forced. I *was* earnestly glad it was him who'd found me.

His eyes briefly moved over to the wrist of the hand I was gripping him with and the manacle on it. And a shred of the feral anger I'd seen him manifest before flashed through his bright eyes. But he schooled it quickly and looked back at me, giving another trembling smile before pulling me in tightly against him, tucking his head over my shoulder.

I hardly ever even hugged my family like this. But I couldn't imagine what he must have been going through the last week, likely blaming himself for my disappearance, so I allowed it.

"A-are you alright, are you... harmed?" he asked, pulling back and looking me over. "Were you tortured? Sullied?"

I began to answer swiftly before the last comment caught me off-guard. I blinked, considering the question, then shook my head. "No, I'm... I was sick. My illness returned, but I think I'm mostly past it. I haven't been eating or sleeping very well, but... I'll be set right quickly on that front, I think. Just tired..."

"My brother in Canus," he stared heavenward a moment, clapping his paws together, "I told them you'd endure. I told them we'd find you alive. I had faith, brother, I did. Not just in God, but in *you*."

"Malachi, I'm so sorry—"

His ears perked suddenly, and we both heard the whistle, slightly closer this time. "Apologies brother, a moment," he said, then raised his own fingers to his muzzle and issued forth a powerful whistle in return, loud and shrill up-close. My own whistle call was a pale impersonation in comparison.

Another answered, closer this time, and he explained, "Your Brother Dolus. The Ministry actually recalled him two days ago, but he was insistent he stay on until we found either you or..." he looked back to me grimly, "... your corpse."

I looked away at my feet. "I..." I stammered, "... made a *terrible* mistake, causing you all such pain and grief."

"Did you manage to escape with your tools?" he asked, glancing down at the manacle still attached, and the bag I had loosely gripped in my other hand. "Never mind that, I have my own. Let's get that off you. And Lord, you must be freezing."

It was only then that I realized I'd been standing out in the cold in little more than my trousers and undershirt. It sold the lie that I'd been a prisoner all this time, I suppose... but it *was* frigid outside.

Malachi undid the clasp and then wrapped his fur-lined cloak over my shoulders, even going so far as to affix the hood for me, helping my ears through it and grinned a bit. "You're one of the few lads I've met it fits this well. Although you look like you trimmed down a bit since I first met you. We've got to get you fed. Get you healthy again."

While he fussed with the cloak, I swallowed around the

lump in my throat and finally got up the nerve to ask, "How did you find me?"

It was a logical question to ask. Exactly what an escaped prisoner might ask without sounding overly probing. But I did want to know what they knew.

"We knew about the Physician," Malachi said, rubbing my shoulders and glancing past me again, probably keeping an eye out for Dolus. "We knew he was visiting with Rathborne occasionally, but not that there was a connection. We pulled his file, but I didn't catch the detail about the Lodge. It just didn't leap off the page at me. It wasn't until yesterday night when I was poring over everything we had for the fiftieth time that I noted the tool marks on the records box the fox's files were in."

I nearly swallowed my tongue. That was both more than I'd expected they'd have found and also not something I thought I'd get caught for.

He gave me a knowing look, then dropped his voice. "Brother Dolus doesn't know that part, lad. And he doesn't need to. But what the hell were you thinking, going off alone like that? Scratch that, no," he sighed, shutting his muzzle for a moment and licking at one of his own fangs, "no, I... know exactly what you were thinking. They were cutting you out of the investigation and you knew you weren't done. You knew they wouldn't let you work this anymore because of some paltry credentials you haven't gotten yet—and don't bloody need apparently. You're a fucking prodigy, mate, look at what you managed on your own. So, you busted into my records and went off looking for the little cunt alone. I get it. I *really* do. But you could've told *me*."

"I—" the words eluded me, "-I'm s—sorry, Malachi. I don't even know where to begin..."

He looked past me again, clearly still keeping an eye out for Dolus. This time when a whistle came, he didn't answer it. He'd have to explain that one later, but he didn't seem to care right now. He gripped my shoulders a little tighter and looked me dead in the eye. "Your Brother Monk talked to you, didn't he? About my past?"

"Somewhat," I confessed quietly. "He was sparse on the details."

His fur shook in a slight shiver, from the cold or otherwise, I couldn't say. "We all make missteps when we are young," he said, guilt and something deeper… more harmed… bleeding through his words. "The follies of my youth were more egregious than most. More injurious to my church, my Brothers and Sisters, and my Father… bless him, *he's* forgiven me. I cannot forgive myself, but he has somehow found it in his heart. I hope that you can too, Brother. I endeavored only to act kindly with you as a comrade-in-arms. I didn't intend any slight—"

"Malachi, please," I begged, "stop. Please. I don't know about your childhood transgressions, and it isn't my *place* to know. You've paid your penance, I'm sure," I said that part with a wince, "and made right with God. And the Ministry has seen fit to elevate you, so you must have made right with them, as well. You seem to me to be a righteous man. Loving and kind with his Brothers, even those who are but visiting. You've been more supportive of my efforts in this investigation than anyone. I'd like to consider you a friend, if you'll have me." I sighed, slumping slightly. "I didn't do what I did because I was running from *you*. I swear it."

His expression softened slowly. When he spoke again, his voice was small, smaller than I'd ever heard from the big, imposing man. "Friends then, Brother Isidor. You and I. It is sealed."

"The prodigal son lives," a call came from atop the hill. We both looked up, although I didn't need to. I knew Brother Dolus's disarmingly dulcet voice. He was also atop a steed—Dragonfly, the mare I'd first recognized from home—and swaddled in winter clothing, his angular face showing signs of being out in the elements for likely most of the night, just as Malachi looked. I was touched, but also terrified. No matter how I explained this, his anger would be unfathomable. I was in for it.

"Brother," I croaked out. "Yes, I'm… I'm well. Not… not *well,* I suppose, but… alive."

"You are very fortunate Brother Malachi thought to check the deed documents in that Physician's files," the older man said, trotting his horse down the hill towards us. He stopped near us, but didn't dismount yet. His eyes looked me over, searching for I knew not what. His gaze was, as ever, hard to read. He was feigning concern, of that much I was certain. But he was looking for something, too. He sidled his horse up closer to us, and I saw his nostrils flare. I hoped he'd mostly smell Malachi, given I was wrapped in his cloak.

"How were you taken here alive?" he asked at length in a low tone.

"I wasn't," I admitted. "I came here."

Malachi looked briefly alarmed that I'd admitted to it. But there was no way around explaining it. I appreciated that he'd kept my violations in the records room to himself, but how else could I explain how I'd found this place? I'd gone over every option in my head, none made sense save something approximating the truth. "I shadowed Cillian Rathborne," I explained. "I followed the Physician from his visit, back home to his clinic, and then I looked into his records."

Dolus narrowed his eyes, but oddly rather than continuing to dig at me for information, he instead tightened up on his reins and turned, circling us. "Get him back to Redcoven," he said to Malachi. "Make sure he's seen for any ailments or injuries."

"Sir?" Malachi seemed as surprised as I was.

"The Heart Thief is still in the area, fool," he snapped. He didn't bother asking me to confirm it. "Whatever he kept my child for—ransom or hostage, it hardly matters—he clearly abandoned the idea. He's fleeing. Isn't that right, Isidor?"

I held up my cuffed wrist. "He heard your calls and unfortunately identified them. While he was rushing out to gather his possessions and his horse, I took my chance. I'd hidden my kit away earlier, I just needed—"

"Fine," Dolus cut me off. I'd had a whole story worked up, I was honestly rather shocked he didn't want to hear it, or interrogate me about it. "I don't need a bloody novel right now. Brother Malachi, take a detailed report when you get him somewhere warm. I'm going to see if I can't run this fiend down."

"We've been out all night and he's got an enormous head start on us," Malachi reasoned. "You're risking your health, Brother."

"God will sustain me," Dolus said with a sneer of a smile and spurred his horse. "Take him back to the Ministry office and don't let him out of your sight."

He rapped Dragonfly on the rear and she gave a startled whinny, then took off up the hill. We watched him go.

"Good riddance," Malachi growled. He cleared his throat a moment later, then added, "M'sorry. The man's... difficult to work with. And not terribly fond of me, I think."

"I know," I assured him, giving a lopsided smile. "On both accounts. If it's any consolation, he isn't fond of *most* people."

"Any chance he finds the feline?" he asked me, a bit more seriously. "You've had more experience with the fellow now than any of us."

I thought 'I hope not'. But what I said was, "The only Templar who's ever had any luck tracking them down is standing before you. No. No, I don't think he'll have much luck."

"'Them'?" Malachi queried. "He wasn't alone?"

Here, I had to be careful. If I lied and it was obvious, Malachi would sniff me out. The man was more brash than most

Templar I'd known, but he was just as sharp. I'd seen his nose for bullshit on full display in the past.

"'Them' because..." I said, bypassing the question I would prefer not to answer about the guests we'd had at the Lodge. I didn't want to put more of a target on Cillian's back than there already was. "... we still aren't certain of their sex."

Malachi sighed. "Slippery minx. Well, if you still don't know even after all of that, I say it's not worth giving a rat's ass about. What does it matter, in the end?"

I found myself nodding.

"They'll hang him... her... one way or t'other."

I went quiet at that, watching my breath puff out in the air. I found myself listening on the wind for a second set of hoof beats. Paws in the snow nearby. Anything. I had no idea where they were and wouldn't for a very long time. I was only now beginning to realize how anxious and fearful that would make me.

I felt a heavy paw on my shoulder. "Hey, young Brother," Malachi leaned over my shoulder. "I *do* want to hear your story. And we really need to get you warmed up and fed. Can you get up on the horse alright?"

I nodded and he walked back over towards the gelding, offering me a supporting arm as I pulled myself up into the saddle, soon followed by the larger man. He got in behind me, moving his arms in around me to grip the reins, but distinctly seemed to be trying to keep a polite distance between us. Impossible really, given we were riding together, and neither of us was a small man. I could tell he'd have to hold his arms out awkwardly, this way. And it was ten miles.

"Brother," I eased his arms in around me, assuring him I took no issue with the closeness, "please don't discomfort yourself on my account. We're Brothers. Comrades, even. At least, I'd like to be."

"I thought I lost another Brother-in-Arms," he said, his voice husky and laced with regret.

"'Another?"

"You'd be the sixth partner or Brother I've had to bury," he admitted solemnly. "Every time I survive and they don't, I... I wonder why. It doesn't seem right."

I noted that he'd separated the categories of 'partners' and 'Brothers'. So, some of his partners had been secular agents. That suggested there'd been a time when he'd been under Bahdren, a type of shunning just above excommunication. You could serve and act within the Ministry, but only alongside secular people. Your Brothers, Sisters and Fathers could not speak to you, except to pray that you found salvation and repented your sins.

It added another layer to the pain and stigmatization he'd endured over the years, in recompense for... whatever he'd done. And it *must* have been serious, to warrant Bahdren.

"I'm alright, Malachi," I assured him again, because I felt he needed it. "I can tell you what happened on the road home, if you want the full story."

"I'm certain your Brother Dolus will want a full debriefing," he said, "but for now, you can give me the broad strokes. He's probably going to want to go through everything with your Priest present. So, best to save the full story for your Inquisition testimony later. No reason to give it twice."

"My priest?" I turned in the saddle, trying to look up and behind me at him. I caught the hint of a curl upwards in his jowls. "Not yours?"

"Old fellow arrived just yesterday, actually," he said. "Must've taken every swift carriage in the country to get here as fast as he did, through the nights and weather and all. He was going to join us on the hunt up here on Dyre point today. To be honest, we thought there was a good chance we were looking for a body, by now. He'll be so relieved. Old hound was genuinely scared for you, I think. One of those aloof types though. Keeps it close to the chest."

I could hardly believe what he was saying. "Helstrom?" I confirmed. "Father Helstrom? He's here?"

"Sleeping off the road," he said, spurring his horse on down the hill. "Let's go wake him up with the best news of his life."

We broke through the wood line and into tilled-over, snow-covered fields within the first mile, and somehow the road was easier to find on horseback. The lack of a blinding snowstorm helped, too.

I turned to glance past Malachi's shoulder towards the raised mountainous area I'd spent the last week in, guarding its secrets well, behind hundreds of acres of glistening canopy, the tree limbs stretching up like grasping hands into the sky. Perhaps praying to the heavens. I wanted to do the same, and I did, silently.

God, protect them. Both of us would need to survive in order to uncover and prove the truth of the Heart Theft. I was certain of that. It was only when we'd come together that we'd begun to make sense of what we were caught up in.

A smell wafted to my nose, distinct but subtle at first, and a moment later Malachi must have caught it too, because he spoke up without turning around. "Something burning? That's no cottage cooking fire."

I saw the beginnings of the black smoke, distant but obvious when it began to spread like an inky stain across the sky. There was no doubt where it was coming from, either. I knew approximately where we'd been, because I'd been mapping the topography in my mind as we'd ridden away. In case I needed to come here again in the future.

The scent of fire elicited something primordial in most canines, but especially so when the ash on the wind was unnatural. More than just wood. Man-made, acrid, burning roofing tar, paint, treated wood...

... but also, paper. The vaguest hint of sweetness, which I'd caught on some of the old furniture in the place, likely lemon oil liberally applied and rubbed into it over decades. I swear I could almost smell the mead.

The Lodge. The Lodge was on fire.

And I honestly wasn't certain who had set it.

We watched the bellowing plumes of smoke from a stone bridge over a dry gully, the cut through the forest allowing us enough visibility that I could even make out some of the crimson light flickering through the trees. The air was still and quiet, neither Malachi nor I daring to make a sound as we both tipped our ears and noses into what little wind there was.

I listened for hoofbeats. Shouting. Whistling from Brother Dolus. Anything.

I wanted to break away from the malamute and run back into those woods, but I could never have explained why. I wanted to step backwards in time and... I hardly knew. Escape with Darcy? Escape my... life? My Brotherhood?

Leave the Templar? I really was going mad.

Over my time at the Lodge, I had gone from being Darcy's hunter to being their prisoner... to something else altogether more confusing growing between us. Something I dared not put a name to, yet.

But as I stared off at that distant fire, I wanted to know Darcy was safe. I wanted to know they had escaped.

I prayed silently, because I could no longer speak my prayers aloud in the presence of my own kin. They would condemn me if they knew.

God protect us in the days to come.

SPECIAL THANKS TO

Special thanks to all of my Editors, Sensitivity Readers, Beta Readers, and supporters from streams and Patreon. This world and the denizens of it would never see the page if not for all of you.

From the bottom of my heart, thank you.

Kyell Gold - Bryan Ozawa - Cassie - Chris - Alastair - Brandon RavusFur - Randall - Rolf Piercey - Snøw - Glassan - Scandhoovian

Colin Leighton - Marcwolf - BlackDawg - Petrov Neutrino - Commander Wolf - Soulwolven - Trejaan - Lucian Greywolf - Marmalade - AJ Nemeth - Edef - Ferlynx - RaiderWolf - AeroWolfDeer - SILVERWOLF380 - Dyxxander - RF Red Fox - Roarschach - Sylleath - Seth Cherwell - Doug K. - Alteo - Wulfgar Marrock (RGFuzzwolf) - ScionOfSkoll - J. N. Squire from Baguetteland - Flann - Clint Marsh - Madi - Jhey Wolffe - Windwolf55x5 - Lillian Rafter - Y-Fox - Tiderace Jenkins -

SPECIAL THANKS TO

Verager - PhyerPhox - Zachs - Yuuryuu - AiraActual - Mvh. Mads Damgaard Mortensen - Kiska Beaust - Skunkbomb - Andrea Jae - Sunkawaken - Thomas Proffitt

ABOUT THE AUTHOR

Rukis is a freelance illustrator/writer who lives in South Carolina, USA.She has a BFA in Animation from the Rochester Institute of Technology, with a focus in Conceptual Design for Animation and Film. Early in life, she knew she wanted to work in either the animation or comics industry, and struck out on her own after college to do just that. After many years spent working a 9-5 and building her portfolio, she published her first comic *Cruelty* with FurPlanet in 2010. Since then, she has published two other comic titles, various short comics in anthropomorphic anthologies, and written and illustrated ten novels, as well as done a number of illustrations and covers for other writers in the Anthropomorphic community. Her comic *Red Lantern,* novel *Off the Beaten Path* and her cover for Kyell Gold's *Green Fairy* won Ursa Major Awards.

Other than illustration and writing, Rukis spends almost all of her free time hiking, mountain biking, gardening, and working on her small farm in South Carolina.

Her desire for her books is that they entertain, educate, make you feel something, stoke a curiosity for history, and a hope for a more loving and diverse world.

x.com/rukiscroax

patreon.com/rukis

ABOUT THE PUBLISHER

FurPlanet productions is a small press publisher serving the niche market that is furry fiction. They sell furry-themed books and comics published by themselves and most major publishers in the community. If you can't get to a furry convention where they are selling in the dealers room, visit their online stores: FurPlanet.com for print books and BadDogBooks.com for eBooks.

facebook.com/furplanet
x.com/furplanet
animal.business/@furplanet

Milton Keynes UK
Ingram Content Group UK Ltd.
UKHW022006211124
451438UK00009B/234

9 781614 506218